Em

Views of Life in Corporate America from a Middle-Aged, Middle Manager from Middle America.

Author:
David A. Glazer, J.D., CLU, ChFC, CFP, Ph.D.

©2017. David A. Glazer.
All Rights Reserved.
ISBN: 1544184131
ISBN-13: 978-1544184135

Dedication:
To my two sons, Michael and Russell, who – despite my sometimes clumsy and impatient parenting – grew up to become wonderful young men and give me great *naachus*.

Table of Contents

Chapter	Title	Page
1.	*MJ*	1
2.	*From Combat to Unions*	27
3.	*Entering the Business*	57
4.	*Innocence of the Early Years*	79
5.	*Flying Without a Net*	116
6.	*In From the Cold*	154
7.	*Moving on Up; Moving on Out*	200
8.	*Flying Again*	235
9.	*Someone Else's Money*	262
10.	*You Can Go Home Again*	291
11.	*Do the Math*	336
12.	*Merger, Part I*	359
13.	*Merger, Part II*	499
14.	*The Wheels Come Off*	433
15.	*So Now What?*	462

Foreword

This is a fictionalized account based on actual experiences; fictionalized to protect the identities of the personalities depicted within. One should not assume particular individuals in the story, as events and personalities have been altered. This book is part novel, part business management and marketing treatise, and part cautionary tale.

The main character never wins or loses at the game of corporate life, but simply continues to fight on until circumstances force his hand. And in those circumstances he finds a sort of happiness that lies "between the longing for love and the struggle for the legal tender." That is one of the main messages in this story.

When some complain of "waste, fraud, and abuse" in Government, they should compare it to the waste, fraud and abuse in corporate America, particularly in big business, where managing to short term profits have in some cases replaced strategic sacrifices for long-term viability. That is another one of the main messages in this story.

When some see the growth of mergers and acquisitions as a feature of corporate life – as a part of "creative destruction" – they may need to be careful to remember that what happens to some in one merger may happen to you in another. This is still another main message in this story.

Care has been taken to focus on corporate life, and so sacrifices have been made in the details of the character's personal life. Care has been taken as well to explain the inner workings of the product known as life insurance, one of the most mysterious and complicated financial assets anyone can own, and the main product line for the central character of this story.

The "circumstances" that become the climax of the story explain the effects that the Financial Crises of 2008 – leading to The Great Recession – had on those in the industry who had little or nothing to do with creating the crises and, therefore, could not see the trouble coming.

Chapter 1: MJ

With a kiss that meant she wanted him, his blood rushed to meet her desires. She unbuckled his belt – he reached under her blouse and caressed her firm breasts. For a moment of distraction he thought, "a balcony you could do Shakespeare from," borrowing a line he remembered from a 1960s Firesign Theatre routine.

Her tongue was hot. His pants fell to the floor. It took only one button and a zipper to drop her skirt.

"I think that the vast majority of people in this country are sick and tired of being told that ordinary, decent people in this country are fed up with being sick and tired. Well, I'm certainly not, and I'm sick and tired of being told that I am."

The alarm clock Andy Greene used to wake in the morning had gone off, playing a CD: **Matching Tie and Handkerchief**, by Monte Python's Flying Circus, pre-loaded the night before to play the "Another Dead Bishop on the Landing" sketch.

It continued, "Well, I think that the vast majority of wrong thinking people in this country are right." [applause].

"Liberal rubbish," Andy said to himself, remembering the next part of the sketch. And he rose, a bit dazed and disappointed that he'd run out of time to complete the dream.

His next move was not an easy one – into a too-small bathroom that forced him sideways to get into and was placed behind the only bedroom in his apartment. Guests would have to go through the bedroom to use it. Andy had thought it a necessary nuisance at the time he took the 550 square foot rental. "The compensating factor is that I'll make sure the bedroom is presentable at all times, no matter what, if I'm to have anyone over," he rationalized to himself.

A shower with water taking too long to warm up and a quick dressing into a starched and collared dress shirt, with jeans and a standard navy blazer, four brass buttons on each sleeve, and the cordovan wing tip shoes he always wore as an executive in the financial services business, and he was ready for the day's requirements.

Down the elevator that looked old enough to once be operated manually; out the front door – with a wave good morning to the concierge behind the front desk – onto the street, he had but a six-block walk to the job for which he'd left the Northern Virginia suburbs of D.C., and everything he'd known for 30 years, and moved to Manhattan.

"Medium coffee, milk, no sugar, please Muhammad…" went the request from Andy, same as everyday he walked from his Midtown East apartment, through Grand Central Station and then on to the college campus in Midtown.

"How are you, professor?" Muhammad answered, as he poured a cup from a clear glass pot into a glorified paper and plastic cup. "Classes today"?

"Same as it ever was," Andy commented, though he didn't seriously think Muhammad got the reference to the Talking Heads song. "And I'll have that black and white MJ," pointing to a pastry in the glass window below Muhammad, who stood in one of those ubiquitous street vendor trucks seen all over Manhattan, especially during morning rush hour. Muhammad was a cloudy figure to make out behind the vendor cart wall, but Andy could see the scraggly three-day stubble of a gray and black beard and the Fernando Rodney-style cockeyed baseball cap he wore. The beard and the cap made figuring Muhammad's exact age virtually impossible.

Andy always wondered, but never asked, where the term "MJ" came from when street vendors referred to that particular pastry. Andy remembered that it was called a dunking stick in D.C., when he worked there – a long stick doughnut, no hole, perfect for dipping into a cup of coffee. It made a natural sweetener for the coffee, rendering any additional sugar, saccharine, asptertaine, or Stevia unnecessary; moot, to use the vaguely legal expression. Upon further reflection, the shape like a phallic symbol gave rise to the imagination – "are we referring to Michael Jackson, Michael Jordan, or what?" he thought to himself. But he never asked the street vendors for an answer, wishing to pretend he knew what it meant all along.

Andy knew the street vendors liked exact change, to help with the idiots who asked to break a twenty-dollar bill for a $1.50 charge. So, he took off the Jansport backpack he carried each day to campus – as if he, himself, were one of the students – and reached into the side pocket for an amount - $2.25 – he had specifically set aside to pay for the coffee and Danish that morning, placed the single bills under a paperweight Muhammad had put on the counter so bills would not blow away in the wind, and placed a quarter on top of them.

"Thanks, and have a good day," Andy ended the conversation while grabbing the bag into which Muhammad had placed the coffee and Danish. He then placed the bag on a little metal ledge at the waist of the vendor cart, left – he imagined – for just such a purpose. Andy then took out of the backpack the campus ID that he'd wear all day to give him access in the campus buildings - attaching the clip to his belt – suited up the backpack once again over his navy blazer and onto his back, picked up the bag, and proceeded down the street to the front door of the campus building where Andy would be lecturing that morning on all manner of college level business topics.

Andy Greene was a college professor; well, just barely a college professor. East River University (ERU) was one of those "proprietary" institutions, a for-profit business that had sprung up over the past few decades, ostensibly to provide a college education that would otherwise be unavailable to a large segment of high school graduates. Andy had been recruited to work at ERU due in part to his academic credentials, but also because of close to 30 years of practical experience as a business executive.

Andy turned into the turnstile door of the campus building. The security people at the front desk did not need to see his ID badge, which was partly concealed by the front of Andy's blazer, because they recognized him on sight. He had been at ERU on a full time basis for six months now. Slipping past the guards, with a quick "good morning," Andy rang for the elevator to take him to the 7th floor, where a small cubicle in an almost-as-small faculty common room awaited his arrival and a few moments of rummaging through his files to get the materials he would need for this morning's lecture. Many times during a given school-day, the elevator seemed to take forever to arrive; there were four elevator banks, but one was usually out of service, and the faculty took the same mode of transportation as the students to get up to the desired floors. But when Andy arrived at 7:45am – as he did this day – to prepare for an 8am class, there was no wait at all.

Being the first to arrive, Andy inserted the security key that was part of his ID badge into the appropriate slot in the door knob, waited for the two-toned beep that the card worked, took out the card from the slot and opened the common room door. Turning on the lights that had been shut since 10pm the previous night, Andy found the cubicle he usually used and the file drawer (he had but one) where he kept his materials for class.

Andy was very disciplined this way. He rarely took work home with him after classes, preferring to carry as light a backpack through the streets of Manhattan as possible. His strategy was to complete any prep work for classes in the common room, leave his files there, retrieving them before the class in which they were to be used. He had a color and number system, identifying each class by its course number, rather than its curriculum name. There was red for marketing classes, green for finance, blue for management or law classes, yellow for administrative matters. The files were plastic, not paper, so they would endure, term after term, for reuse. A separate set of files, accordion-style, were kept for archiving older materials. Also in the file drawer was a pencil box, for keeping a supply of #2's and erasers for students to borrow during exams, a set of black dry erase markers (the school never seemed to have an adequate supply and so everyone hoarded whatever they could and occasionally had to buy their own), a Webster's pocket English language dictionary, a Roget's pocket Thesaurus, and a German-English translation dictionary that some European students studying at ERU for a semester had given Andy as a parting gift. There was also a financial function calculator, 30-years old, a TI BA II (do they still make those?) and a couple of Zone Bars to snack on if there wasn't enough time for lunch.

At this hour of the day, Andy was alone in the room. Later, the place would be teeming with faculty, all vying for not enough cubicles in the room and trying to get ready for classes. Right now, it was quiet. There was just enough time to step into the men's room on that floor before going upstairs to his classroom on the 8th floor. Relieved no one was in the restroom yet (this was important, as he knew that being first into the men's room in the morning meant the room had just been cleaned the night before; after all, this was a restroom shared with students), he took a moment, after using the sole urinal in the room and washing up, to look into the mirror above the white porcelain sink. He saw this image of himself, a man of 58 years, with an increasing amount of gray on the decreasing amount of remaining hair on his head. They say a man's wrinkles make him look distinguished, but all this reminded Andy of was that he wasn't young anymore. A partial double chin had developed after years of comfort, including a small "balcony of affluence," the pot belly Andy liked to refer to by euphemism. Still, he could run 3 miles a day on the treadmill, if he had enough time to do so (and time was often a challenge), and the green eyes and full lobes of his ears made Andy look like someone who once was attractive. He used starched, oxford button-down shirts, rarely white - today sea-foam green – to mitigate the "balcony," a blazer, today navy blue – sometimes black-and-white herringbone tweed – also helped him look better than he really was. The bottom half was usually jeans, black today / blue other days. He kept to the dress shoes he'd wear most days as an executive; they were comfortable enough to serve as a sensible pair of walking shoes. After all, Manhattan is a walking City, if you don't want to pay cab fares or battle the heat and people on the subways.

This was Thursday morning, and as such, the first class of the day was MKTG205 - the survey class in marketing. At 8am, this was a brutal class to hold. Not only was the time of day too early for many, but the subject was dry, for those who were not going on to be marketing majors in this four-year business administration program. For non-marketing majors, there was always one marketing class that a student would have to take to complete his/her degree program, and this was it. The students, therefore, were not at peak motivation to succeed here. And this was an especially severe problem.

At best, the student body at ERU could be broken into three psychographic groups: there were the great students, who would do well even if you spoke gibberish to them for the 105-minute lecture; they would get the work done and actually read the material. To be honest, they weren't necessarily driven by a pure love of learning; they had figured out that if you could not post a GPA of at least 3.0 on a resume, you had no hope of competing for the "good" jobs. In the meantime, two years of good grades meant an opportunity to transfer as a junior to a "real" college, one with a reputation and traditional organization. At the other extreme was a group who should not have been in school at all; not because of a lack of ability, but because of a lack of motivation to do any work. This group would eventually drop out, flunk out, or – if "lucky" – would be passed on from course to course and receive a degree that would not enhance the brand equity of the school. In other words, they would either be in jail, pregnant, dead, or, if "lucky," flipping burgers in a fast-food joint after graduation. The third group – in-betweeners – was the reason Andy got up in the morning to teach at this school. If he could reach these students, he might make the difference between success and failure for them. Most college faculty at ERU lived for these kids; and Andy was no exception.

Andy entered the room through a solid core, wooden door, and proceeded to the desk at the front, set aside for the instructor. On the desk was the omnipresent Dell desktop computer and screen, a lectern that most faculty rarely used, and two remote controls: one for the DVD/VCR player underneath the desk that rarely worked; the other for the projector located in the ceiling above the class and aimed at the whiteboard behind Andy. When he arrived, Andy could count maybe 8 students of the 35 that were registered for the class. Another 4 or 5 entered straight after the professor, probably waiting to come in until he arrived. Another 6 came in while Andy was logging onto the computer and loading his PowerPoint slide presentation onto the hard drive from the USB drive he carried with him in his backpack to class. Andy had eaten the MJ in the common room before coming upstairs, but the coffee cup still had about half a cup of liquid in it, so he had brought that as well.

Once the slides were loaded and the introductory slide appeared on the projected screen on the whiteboard, Andy turned to face his audience of a half-filled room of 18-23-year-olds, two-thirds female, two-thirds minorities (African-American or Latino for the most part), and opened with, "Good morning… How's everybody doing?"

Andy began passing around a single sheet of 5 ½ X 8-inch paper, with his imprinted name on the top and two columns – one for a printed name and the other for a signature, so that each student could sign in and be marked present for class that morning.

"Does anyone have a current event on marketing to share today?" Andy spoke, expecting the usual lethargic response. He liked to open each class with a current event discussion, perhaps harkening back to his political science days and his news junkie avocation during his many years living in the DC area – known as the political capital of the world (it had been nicknamed by some doomsayers as "ground zero" during the Cold War, in the event of nuclear attack; but lost that moniker after 9/11).

There were one or two non-descript business news items a couple of the "smart" students contributed, although most were about pop culture – the latest scandal involving the latest socialite in Hollywood splashed publicly for all to see on the internet or on "Extra" in the 7pm time slot on broadcast television.

Then, it was time to get into the topic for the day: marketing ethics (a couple of snickers from those who believed the term an oxymoron). There were really two main items that Andy dwelled on for most of this lecture: the Pyramid of Social Responsibility; and the two main theories of the derivation of ethics.

After crafting a rather tortured definitional difference of ethics from morals, Andy launched in, "Who can tell me what the first and most fundamental obligation of a corporation is?" Andy waited for a response; it took a few seconds; Andy knew that people were still half asleep at this hour.

Finally, one female student over to the far right of Andy, meekly said, "To make money."

"Is that the first obligation of the corporation? Really? Are you sure?" Testing the co-ed, who could not have been 20 if she were a day.

No response from her, then another meek, "Well…"

"Why do let me talk you out of a perfectly correct answer? You're right, you know you're right! Stand your ground and tell me what you know. That's right; the first obligation is to be profitable. If the firm is not profitable, the rest doesn't matter. The corporation is owned by shareholders who have a right to expect a return on their investment."

Meek nods from the room…

"So, once the corporation is profitable, what is the next level of responsibility?" Andy pointed to the second tier of a four tier pyramid being projected on the screen from the projector above his head connected to the PC on his desk showing a slide of this idea that Andy had spoken to many times before – he knew the whole thing by heart.

"So? Anyone have an idea." No one responded.

Andy shouted, "I'm dying up here…Someone help me," looking the part of the stand-up comic who is not getting many laughs in a tough room of lethargic customers who'd rather be somewhere else. "The second level of responsibility is to be 'legal.' Legally profitable; otherwise, the firm is in organized crime."

Now Andy moved to the third level on the projected pyramid. "So, what's the next level of responsibility?" Here, someone finally called out, "be ethical."

"Thank you," Andy replied. "Ethics come after legalities. Ethics is not the same as legalities. The law tells you what you 'must' do or cannot do. Ethics is about what you **should** do, the result of being unethical is being disciplined, even denied access to the organization enforcing those ethical rules, but you do not go to jail or suffer Government fines. That's for the law. Does everyone see that?" Some more nods in the audience now.

"And yet," Andy continued, "most authors on ethics will freely go back and forth between ethics and legalities, using laws as case examples of ethics." Andy verbally pulled out Sarbanes-Oxley, an Act of Congress in 2002 known today by the acronym "SOX." The law was enacted to stop the ethical violations that went on at Enron, WorldCom and other firms at the turn of the century.

"The conduct that SOX was intended to stop was already an ethical problem for senior management of the firm, which used the 'reverse Nuremburg defense' to inoculate themselves from responsibility. You know what the Nuremburg defense was, from the Nazi war crime trials after World War II?" No response.

"This was when the Nazis said 'I was only following orders' as a way to push responsibility for atrocities up the org chart. The 'reverse Nuremburg defense' is when the CEO says "No one told me my people were doing this; I didn't know."

At this point, Andy hit his stride. "In Washington, D.C., we call this 'plausible deniability.' And many firms have an unwritten rule that underlings are not to tell the boss too much about what shenanigans they are up to in meeting corporate goals, in order to protect the boss from having to lie later on. Sarbanes-Oxley had among its provisions a requirement that publicly traded firms filing financial statements required by the SEC have the CEO and the CFO (Chief Financial Officer) personally sign off on those financial statements attesting to their accuracy; thus, eliminating any plausible deniability. Once that was put in place, what senior management should have done was now a legal requirement. Congress pulled the standard down to a law so people could be prosecuted for violating it. This is not ethics anymore."

Andy was trying to draw a bright line between the law and ethics, while acknowledging that no bright line really exists.

Then, Andy took in up a notch in enthusiasm and volume. "Now, let's go to the top of the pyramid. This is variably called social responsibility, a/k/a 'morality.' I'm going to suggest something some might find heretical" – as if the students even knew what that term meant – "and say that there is no such thing as corporate morality. First of all, morality is an individual value judgment; everyone is entitled to their own moral judgment and no one has the right to invalidate someone else's moral judgment. A corporation is a collection of individuals, each with their own moral code. So, by definition, there can be no morality of a group. Corporations are 'amoral;' not immoral, but amoral, in that they have no moral compass one way or the other."

One student had the audacity to question Andy on this notion. "But Professor, I see corporations doing charitable work all the time."

Momentum was on Andy's side now… "Correct. It's sometimes called 'philanthropy.' Corporations are always doing good work, giving back to the community, yes. But let me ask you this: how do you know about all this good work?"

The student answered, "Well, I read about it or see it on TV or see commercials where they tell everyone about it."

"Exactly," Andy answered, as if he had just gotten the criminal defendant to confess on the witness stand. He went in for the kill. "And when corporations spend millions telling us all about the millions they spend giving back to the community, we do not call that morality. We call that 'public relations,' a concept in marketing we will be studying as we go along in the course. Morality is what you do when no one is looking, when there is no one to give you credit, or applause. Morality is the richest people in town on Christmas Eve going to the poorest neighborhoods, leaving toys and other goodies for those destitute families at their doorstep, ringing the bell and then running away, lest they be thanked by the recipients. If you stand to take a bow, it is not morality. It may be nice, but it is not morality."

Andy finished this part of the lecture with, "You may not agree with my definition or analysis, but I want to draw a bright line between morality and ethics the same way I did between ethics and legality, so that we can carve out some special ground where ethics lives on its own. Ethics is what we agree to abide by whether we agree with every tenet of the code of conduct or not. It is a group standard applied to individuals. Morality is an individual choice. If someone's morality results in a crime, that's legality; if it gets someone disbarred from law practice, for example, it is an ethical consideration. But it is not morality by itself."

Andy stopped for questions…There were none. Did they absorb the concept? Or were they just bored? Andy could not tell. But that didn't stop him from going on and talking about Rights-Based Ethical theories versus Utilitarian Ethics.

"Rights-Based Ethics says that we are to judge the conduct itself, without regard to outcome. Therefore, the ends cannot justify the means." Andy continued, "Utilitarian Ethics says, 'it depends.' The standard is 'do the most good for the greatest number.' I sometimes call this 'Vulcan' ethics.

The students gave Andy a blank stare. "Vulcan, what's that," they seem to say with their eyes.

"Is anyone a 'Star Trek' fan?" A couple of people recognized the reference from one of the recent movies.

"I mean the classic Star Trek. The whole series was set in outer space, but it wasn't about outer space. A lot of it had to do with the debate between these two theories of ethics, personified by Dr. McCoy, who often took the Rights-Based side of an issue, and Mr. Spock, who applied the Vulcan rule of 'the needs of the many outweigh the needs of the few.'"

At this point many in the class may have started wondering if this were a marketing course or a course in philosophy. Andy concluded with this thought, "You are going to see a lot of unethical behavior once you get out into the business world. You're going to be told 'everybody does it.' It's going to look like 'it's O.K.' This is my one chance to instill in you some sense of ethical responsibility before the corporate suits get to you, so please listen."

At that point Andy could see he was running out of time. "Do you get the sense I have a passion for this topic?" Everyone nodded and murmured agreement. Self-satisfied, Andy dismissed the class.

There was a short break between Andy's classes, so he went back down to the 7th Floor to do some paperwork and see who else from the faculty had arrived. It now being almost 10am, the room was full. Phil Chandler had a running joke with Victor Williams – two full timers in the management department – that Andy walked into in mid-joke and so did not quite get the punchline; something about carriage horses in Central Park. But the lines were delivered with such humorous inflection that they all laughed anyway. Phil was seated in the far left corner from the door; Victor the far right corner. In between were two work stations: one inhabited by Olivia Garcetti, a CPA and accounting prof; the other by the perfectly-dressed Lester Polander, a lecturer in fashion management. Everyone in the room occupied a cubicle with a desktop computer and so faced the wall, away from the center of the room, where a set of file cabinets stood.

This meant that as people worked, and talked, and joked, no one looked at each other. Each was fixed on their computer screens, but chatting with everyone else just the same.

Andy's cubicle was corner to Phil's and it was usual that Andy would simply listen and laugh to the banter going on in the room; more spectator than participant. And this was somewhat strange, not in his personality when in front of the classroom, where he was anything but shy. Nevertheless, Andy had decided it was no use trying to compete with the outgoing personalities elsewhere in the room. Andy had made a conscious decision to be an "under the radar" employee this time around. This could be helpful in the long term as much of the banter was critical of the people and processes at the school, making the school and its management the butt of most of the jokes. At times, the routines were downright cruel and borderline angry. It was not as if Andy had no experience with what happens when employees get together round the "water cooler," or in this case, "Stalag 7." He'd seen this one many times in his 30 years in the corporate world.

"I know," suggested Victor, "let's start a rumor that we're all joining a union. That will get the administration paranoid, won't it?"

Olivia couldn't help herself. "Yes, and get us all fired. Is that the idea?"

"Why not," chimed Phil, "pay us what we're worth or collect a check from the Government."

"Yeah, I don't need this job anyway," added Lester, in his heavy Brooklyn accent. "I built and lost at least three fuckin' fortunes in my lifetime. I do this like it's charity work anyway - keeps me out of the house."

Phil answered, "There's nothing in your house, Lester, except racks of unsold, out of fashion men's suits. Looks like you took one off the rack this morning…" And everyone laughed.

"Well, what union should we join?" asked Victor. "The teamsters? Kind of feel like a truck driver in this job."

Now Andy couldn't resist. "How about the UAW?"

"Who?" questioned Victor. "We don't make cars."

Andy didn't dare get into what he knew about the UAW, which wasn't that much, except for a brief encounter, over 30 years ago.

In walked Leo Finkel. As the most senior member of this group, Leo fancied himself "chief" and Andy's mentor. "Good morning, all… Still can fog a mirror… Guess I'm going to have to work today."

"Hey, Leo," Andy responded. "Any day you can fog a mirror is a good day, right?"

"You learn well, 'grasshopper'." And Leo found his usual spot in the room, around the corner from Victor, who was just rising from his slightly dysfunctional swivel chair – one that he sat too low in because the lever for raising the height of the seat hadn't worked for months.

"Anyway, I'm going in." Victor gave the signal that he was headed to a class. "If I don't return, tell all the women I ever slept with that I was thinking of them at the end; that way, they'll have to upgrade their evaluations of me." The other men all laughed hysterically.

"That's disgusting," said Olivia. "What am I doing in a room with five gross and disgusting men telling awful stories that put women down?"

"Making a living," answered Lester and Phil, in unison.

"Hey, don't count me," Leo called out, "I just got here."

"Got you covered, big guy", was Andy's send off to Victor. Then, he was on his way to get a sandwich for lunch before his afternoon class.

Phil followed close behind, feigning the complaint, "I have things to do, people to see, places to be… See you later, everyone." And everyone gave a weak goodbye in response.

The afternoon class for Andy was a bit of a treat, Leadership, in the Business Management track. Even though Andy had come into ERU ostensibly as a finance and marketing professor, earning a Master's in Financial Services and a Ph.D. in Marketing, it was typical at ERU to swap people around as needed, especially as Andy had background in management in the financial services industry and an MBA in HRM (human resource management).

Andy decided that today would be a good session to introduce his hypothetical organization chart, and talk about how firms actually run versus how the chart says they run.

Starting at the top of the chart, "Here is where we have what is most often called a 'Chairman of the Board,' or I guess 'chairperson' would be more 'PC.' Historically, it was common at many firms for the Chairman, the CEO, and the President to be one in the same person. Today that is rare. Since the days of Enron, and the advent of SOX, it is more common now to separate these into three distinct positions, to avoid conflict of interest.

"The conflict comes from the fact that the Board of Directors should be populated mainly by outside members, people outside the management of the firm. Yet, the Chair – if he or she is also the

CEO – controls the flow of information to the Board and thereby controls the Board. If the Chief Executive Officer is also the Chair, he or she can make sure that embarrassing or negative information never gets to the Board. Today, most firms are advised to populate the Chair position with someone from outside management; perhaps a retired CEO from the firm, but not someone who's currently in active management.

"It is also advisable that the Board not be stacked with 'inside' members, people who also manage the firm, as this will also curtail an independent look at the performance of the firm."

Andy looked for any sign of recognition from the students in the audience; then continued. "The President is often seen as the 'heir apparent' to the CEO position. In large firms, with multiple subsidiaries or divisions, it is typical to have more than one president; perhaps one for each subsidiary."

Andy's chart was invariably a PowerPoint slide, part of a slideshow Andy used in every one of his classes. The lights were down, to make the slides more visible and him less so.

"Now we look at the next level down, sometimes called 'C-level' positions. The letter 'C' stands for 'chief;' chief financial officer (CFO), chief information officer (CIO), chief marketing officer (CMO), etcetera. The one exception might be the chief legal officer, usually known as 'General Counsel.' Well, the cabinet for the President of the United States has a series of 'Secretaries' for each department, but the chief of the Justice Department – the chief legal officer of the country – is known as 'Attorney General.' Oh, lawyers always want to be called something that separates themselves from the masses, you know." And Andy let out a little laugh, to prompt the audience to laugh along, and not take his biting comment about lawyers too seriously.

"Now, below the C-level officers of the firm we have the so-called 'middle managers.' If they carry an organizational title of 'Vice President,' you might see dozens of these 'VP's' depending upon the size of the firm. If you carry a VP title, you are usually an 'elected officer' of the firm, meaning that the Board had to vote to put you in that position. The C-level officers usually have either Senior VP (SVP) or Executive VP titles, are also elected officers, but with a whole different level of access to information about the firm and its strategic plans. Below the VP, there might be room for a 2nd VP, an elected officer title for someone who does not run an entire department. Below that, we get to Assistant VP, Directors, Managers, all usually appointed officers – not elected by the Board but appointed by the top managers on their own. While the SVP and EVP levels have the most access to information – more than the VP – the AVP and others have even less than the VP.

"Below the Manager, you get specialists, administrators, usually non-officers, but nevertheless considered – if possible – to be 'exempt' employees, meaning that they do not qualify for overtime and other protections of the federal Wage and Hour laws – they are considered management, even if they have no one to manage."

At this point, Andy, once again, began to develop a momentum and passion for his subject.

"Why do you think a firm would want to maximize the number of exempt employees?" Andy asked the students in the room.

"To save money on overtime?" answered one male student in the back; one of the few who did not have his laptop or tablet computer opened; one not pretending to take notes when he was really on Facebook talking to his friends.

"O.K., that's one good reason," Andy confirmed. "Any other ideas? Yes?"

A young female student with a fairly robust Hispanic accent said, "Maybe to give the employees a sense of status."

"Good idea. Any others?" Andy waited for any other replies. "How about to put them in the management column so they would not be eligible to form a union?"

A couple of "oohs" and "aaahs" from the assembled crowd.

"But the most immediate reason is to avoid having to pay overtime. When you are a salaried, exempt employee, you're paid based on a set amount regardless of how much time it takes you to do the job. Salaried people in an organization are typically worked well beyond the 40-hour work week we all assume applies in the American workforce. These people work in some cases for little more than minimum wage, if their actual time on the job were divided into their salaries. An administrative assistant makes $60,000 a year, but works an 80-hour week with two weeks' vacation – check my math – I think that comes to about $15 an hour."

Now Andy went back to the top of the chart. "Back to the top guys in the firm…Inevitably, they are playing a merger and acquisition game in many cases. They hope they come out on top in any acquisition, but many times they are from the target firm. Lately, there has been an attempt in business to call an acquisition a 'merger,' to make it look like a partnering of equals when it is almost never so.

"M&A is almost always a standing committee on any Board of Directors. How do you know when a merger is coming? Well, if you are a C-level officer, you'll play a role in examining the merger opportunity. Now, as a SVP or EVP on the org chart, you may get a little nervous about whether this 'merger' is going to put you out of a job. The Boards of both firms know this. So, when it's time to evaluate the merger, and they have to put you in the know because they need your services to study the opportunity, they need to allay your fears of losing your job. They come with a 'non-disclosure' agreement which also has a guarantee of money in the event you don't wind up with a 'box' at the end.

"What's a box? Well, in these situations, you either wind up with a 'box' or a 'package.' The box means you have a box on the new org chart and your job goes on after merger – maybe not the job you want or originally had, but a job. A 'package' is the parachute, the bag of money you get if there's no place for you after the merger. And these packages – handsome severances – can be quite generous; so generous in fact that many signing off on the non-disclosure agreement are incented to push **for** the merger so they can get the money and get out of the firm. Fact is, if the firm is looking to merge, it is possible that they are the prey instead of the predator. And it is probably because there is trouble at the firm and none of the top managers want to be around to clean up the mess later. Also, many C-level managers retain a dream of leaving the paycheck behind and going into business for themselves and this 'package' makes that a viable option."

An example, from Andy's top-of-mind memory: "A typical package for an SVP might look like two year's salary, plus a one-year addition of employer contribution to the exiting manager's retirement plan, plus a 'bridge' benefit of a monthly stipend until the manager reaches normal retirement age for Social Security. This, on the assumption that an over-age-50 executive will have a devil of a time getting a similar job with another company.

"Of course, the executive-manager agrees that to get the package – should it come to that – he or she will have to sign a covenant not to sue, to inoculate the firm from age discrimination or wrongful termination litigation."

Andy is now peaking in passion for this topic. "Below that C-level manager are the VP people. They have no idea what is going on.

They generally do not get a special package. The human resources manual tells than they will get, maybe, 6-month's severance if their 'box' disappears; maybe even less than that (some are one week for every year of service). They hear about it after the deal is done. They also have to sign a covenant not to sue to get their package, and they'll sign, because they have a family to support and can't forego the severance to wait for settlement *in lieu* of litigation." Andy sometimes lapsed into lawyer-speak on these subjects.

"Below the officers, the people at the bottom, also unaware of what is about to happen, may take comfort in that they often do not get cut out in the new org chart. Their salaries are so low, they fit into the new budget. And, after all, we need those people to actually DO the work that needs to be done, rather than just supervise others to do the work.

"If the people at the top are protected with bags of money, and the people at the bottom are within budget, who really gets hurt in this situation." Andy didn't get an enthusiastic answer from everyone, but many pointed at the middle of the chart. "Yeah, the middle manager gets it in the end."

At this point, Andy had taken up most of the class. He asked if there were any questions. The clock on the wall said 3:15 – PM; that is – and so it was time to dismiss the class, with one more comment, "Do you get the idea that I have a passion for this topic?"

Several students muttered, "Oh, yes." A smile grew upon Andy's face as he watched the students slowly file out of the classroom.

Sometimes Andy had evening classes on his schedule. Tuesdays were usual for an evening class. And Tuesdays were brutal because the classes started – not at 6pm as typically occurs – but later, at 6:25, in order to accommodate the students trying to get to class from a full time job. Years before, the students, when asked in a survey what they wanted in improvements to the curriculum at ERU, said they wanted some evening classes that started later so they would have more time to get to class from work. What they did not realize was that this meant that class would go 25 minutes later as well; ending at 9:55 instead of 9:30 (these evening classes would meet only once a week).

But this wasn't Tuesday. It was Thursday, and the week was essentially over for Andy. Leaving the building, he began his 6-block walk to his apartment on the East Side, walking through the Grand Central Terminal, which had become more of a shopping mall than a train station over the years. By now, the only trains that ran out of GCT were Metro North lines that went upstate or into Connecticut. Everything else – New Jersey and Long Island commuters – went in and out of Penn Station, under Madison Square Garden, over on the West Side.

Andy walked a fairly brisk pace at all times, often frustrated at the slow pace of pedestrians in front. The throngs that walked across the main concourse at GCT slowed Andy's pace, but he did finally make it across and decided to stop into the Grand Central Market, a meat and produce market at the Lexington Avenue end of the terminal. He browsed through some tomatoes, picking out one beefsteak that he thought would work well over a burger. He picked out a Kirby cucumber, the small ones that were often made into pickles (but Andy would use them as is). Then he picked out a Vidalia onion (they were in season in the springtime), and a head of romaine lettuce. He had them weighed and priced, paid cash for them, then headed to the butcher down the center aisle and picked out a half pound of grass-fed ground round for the burgers he would grill tonight at home. Last stop was the bakery at the far end of the market. Picking out a package of homemade rolls, his shopping for tonight was complete.

It had taken some time for Andy to break the suburban habit of grocery shopping once a week, for the whole week. Since there was no car to drive, and markets and produce stands abound on the walk home, it became standard to shop only for a day or two, deciding on the spur of the moment what to make for dinner. And let's face it, in Manhattan it was not too often that anyone actually cooked a home-cooked meal in a city apartment – eating out was not only a lifestyle; it was a necessity when you consider the cramped space that qualified as a kitchen in these apartments. Here, you paid for location and security, not for amenities.

The loot Andy bought neatly fit into the Jansport backpack, having divested himself of most of his files and books in the 7th Floor office before leaving school (there was no room for all that at the apartment). It made it possible to get home without having to carry anything.

The apartment itself stood on the 11th floor of a 12 floor building (Andy always wanted to sit up high, after years in garden apartments and two story colonial houses). Before going to the elevator, he crossed the lobby to check his mailbox by inserting the miniature key into the box lock. Finding two items, both bills, and one piece of junk mail Andy immediately threw away in a recycling bin at the end of the mailbox room, Andy stuck the bills into his blazer pocket, right side, outer pocket so it wouldn't interfere with the keys in the other pocket he would put away only to use again to get into his front door. He then made his way across the lobby, past Carlos – the concierge – to whom he gave a "good evening" to as he passed, and made his way to the elevator for his side of a double-winged building. The lobby had recently been remodeled and renovated, as part of a facelift the management company had as part of a plan to upgrade the building from predominantly rent-stabilized into luxury apartments commanding huge increases in rent.

The elevator opened, revealing its pre-war birth. Andy got in as the only passenger. At 11, the elevator stopped, Andy got out and began a short walk past two other apartment doors to Apartment "P," his door, on the opposite wall from the elevator. Inserting the key, he easily opened the door he had become accustomed to opening every day since moving to New York. The door slammed behind him, making a rather hideous bang as it closed. Andy put down the backpack, taking out the bag of groceries and putting the whole bag, for the moment, in the refrigerator. He found himself with an immediate need to visit the bathroom; over the past year or so, he'd discovered the wonderful world of BPH, needing to urinate what appeared to be every 2-3 hours – a sign of age.

After taking care of nature, he opened the water from the faucet next to the toilet; one didn't need more than one step to get from one to the other. And waiting a few seconds for the water to heat a bit, he began throwing water on his face, rubbing his hands into the bar soap made especially for men (so the box said), lathered up and applied some to his face. Rinsing off three times, each time by cupping his hands under the faucet and collecting what water he could, he then shut the faucet and turned around to grab the hand towel on the rack behind him and dried his face and hands.

Once finished drying off, Andy looked straight into the mirror that housed his medicine cabinet, directly above the sink. What he saw had changed over the years – more gray on less hair - and a double chin that revealed the 2-3 pounds he added to his waistline on average each year he was a corporate "suit." After 30 years, it added up. When the pressure of keeping a teaching schedule was finally over for the week, it had become typical for Andy to start thinking – to use the Talking Heads line, "Where? How did I get here…?"

This was not the way it was supposed to end up when Andy – 30 years before – had cashed in his dreams to become a responsible adult member of the middle class. He had plans; lots of plans; plans on plans. And although the plans changed over the years, he never saw himself alone, in a tiny apartment in Manhattan, teaching. He was a captain of industry – O.K., a First Lieutenant. But he was someone that when he walked into a conference room full of "suits," they paid attention to what he had to say. He "knew stuff," one of his mentors would often say.

The payoff for having compromised on his dreams was supposed to be financial comfort and ego gratification from power. But both were gone now. And Andy sometimes felt that he had been "jipped" out of the "deal." He would never be a major league pitcher; he would never be a rock musician and songwriter; he would never be President of the United States, or even a Congressman. So, where was the payoff?

Now, today, he did a good job at something that no one with any power or wealth would notice.

His payoff would remain in his dreams. One night, it would be a dream of making love to a beautiful woman; sometimes one of his loves from years before – he couldn't see the girl clearly but believed it might have been one of the ones "who got away." Another night the dream became a nightmare, filled with warped recollections of actual violence and near-death experiences he or his family had experienced in the past.

Andy's life had been a series of near misses – loves never consummated and violence never fully resolved, certainly not to his satisfaction.

Andy Greene was a broke man – not broken, but broke – both financially and emotionally.

But it wasn't always like this….

Chapter 2: From Combat to Unions

A sudden quiet fell over the hedgerows bordering the driveway and garage on either side. The air was thick with the humidity and heat of August. If one looked closely, peering eyes could be noticed behind the hedgerows; rifles (M1s or M14s), bayonettes, and on one side a camouflaged bazooka. The green of the hedgerows hid the green of the army fatigues worn by those holding the weapons. They waited almost without a sound.

In walked the enemy, about 15 strong, slowly, looking around for a sign of the hidden soldiers. They as well appeared well armed. The enemy wore mainly street clothes, and peered left and right as they came through the driveway from the street and toward the row of garages at the other end.

"Quiet now," whispered Andy, to his comrades in green, as they watched the enemy proceed into their trap. When he was certain that the whole crew of enemy soldiers were in front of them, Andy yelled, "Fire."

With that command, ten of the green clad troops came out of the hedgerow bushes on Andy's side of the driveway, and attacked. Another six came out of the opposite side, and attacked from the opposite direction. Some had water balloons; some came with squirt guns; some with cap guns. These were toy replicas of the real thing, some with nothing in them. The green clad troops collapsed on their enemy; their prey had no chance – surrounded, they suffered relentless pounding of water, until they all ran for the street from which they came. The enemy crossed the street into the next block. Andy's "men" started to pursue, but once it was clear the enemy had left the block, they stopped and all sixteen cheered.

Another victory for Company A – that's what they called themselves. At first, the group of 8-12 year olds in green simply referred to this activity as "playing Army." But after a time, the group realized that the neighborhood in which they lived had perils for those who wandered around without support. The neighborhood had been known for teenage gangs, each of which controlled one or more blocks of the neighborhood. Company A had become a military style gang of its own, consisting mainly of nerds, brainiaks and other misfits from school that were untouchable so long as they stayed together.

It was not that no one in the Company had any physical skills. In this neighborhood, it was helpful if you had either fast hands or fast feet, as many in the Company did. Andy Greene, unfortunately, had neither of those. But he did have a big mouth and a penchant for taking chances, such as leadership of a gang of kids without any specific authority to lead them. Usually, the best fighter or the best athlete leads a gang. In this case, the best fighters and athletes wanted nothing to do with being in charge of a bunch of misfits, so the vacuum became Andy's first opportunity to lead.

In true military style, Andy named himself Captain. He had two lieutenants, two sergeants, six corporals (including his younger brother Harry); the rest were privates. He had the bars and stripes to prove it, having awarded ranks to the troops with army surplus items purchased for just this purpose (years later those captain's bars – two silver bars joined together – still sit in Andy's jewelry box – for safekeeping). Military discipline was a challenge at times; Andy had no real power – other than persuasion and being the loudest voice in the neighborhood – so that if one of the gang didn't want to listen, there was little Andy could do.

The neighborhood was called Lindenwood, a part of the Howard Beach section of Queens, an outer borough of New York City. And this was the summer of 1963. The neighborhood was brand spanking new at that time. Lindenwood had been a swamp on the south shore of Queens, sandwiched between the landfills and sanitation incinerator in Brooklyn to the west, Idlewild Airport (soon to be renamed Kennedy) to the east, the stench of pollution coming from Jamaica Bay to the south, and the waiting street gangs of Ozone Park to the north (yes, real street gangs).

Andy's family had moved to a garden apartment co-op two years earlier from Sheepshead Bay, on Brooklyn's south shore. In those times, Sheepshead Bay was a mix of second generation Italian and Jewish immigrants. Andy fell into the second category, although growing up it was hard to tell the Italians from the Jews. When a family had enough money to leave Brooklyn, Queens – considered "the Island" in those days (for Long Island) – was the next stop.

Howard Beach had three neighborhoods within its original #14 postal code in 1961 (soon to be the 11414 zip code). There was old Howard Beach, solidly Italian and considered upscale working class. There was the emerging Rockwood Park, a mix of Jews and Italians, separated from Old Howard Beach by Cross Bay Boulevard, the main drag in Howard Beach. Rockwood Park was a development of mostly single family homes and duplexes, on the west side of Cross Bay Boulevard. On the north edge of Rockwood Park was the Belt Parkway, as it made its way from Brooklyn to the Airport. On the other side of "the Belt" was Lindenwood, a mixture of garden apartments, duplexes, and 6-story high rise buildings (rumor had it that they were limited to 6 stories in height because of the swampiness of the land beneath).

Lindenwood – like Rockwood Park – was a drained swamp, as the City of New York struggled to make room for families leaving the City for the suburbs. Queens, along with Staten Island, was the Big Apple's answer to moving to Long Island, Westchester, or New Jersey. Lindenwood and Rockwood Park appeared out of nowhere in 1960, rising out of those swamps that emptied into Jamaica Bay. The two neighborhoods were at that time considered an oasis of middle class culture and values, when compared to the lands that surrounded them. Lindenwood, maybe a little more Jewish than Italian; Rockwood Park, maybe a little more Italian than Jewish; they shared a border at the "the Belt" that included the area Catholic Church and Orthodox Synagogue on opposite sides of the same street.

Andy was the third generation of immigrants from an area of the Balkans in Europe known historically by the name of Bessarabia, now known as Moldova, at the mouth of the Danube River as it empties into the Black Sea. Bessarabia had been for generations a fought-for territory between Romania (after its independence from the Ottoman Empire) and Russia. Depending upon when one is speaking about in 19th and 20th century history, the area was considered part of either country. After WWI it became part of Romania; after WWII, it became one of the 15 constituent republics of the U.S.S.R., known as Moldavia SSR.

There is little known about the immigration of Andy's ancestors; in fact, Andy's maternal grandmother never even possessed a birth certificate and did not ever really know her age or birthdate. Andy's paternal grandfather came over around 1910, in the last wave of Jewish immigration to get to the U.S. before the borders closed in WWI, followed by the quota system imposed by the U.S. after that war. If a Jew did not get out of Eastern Europe before the beginning of WWI, it was unlikely he/she would survive to see the end of WWII. Many of Andy's relatives who did not emigrate were killed in the Holocaust that came decades later. Therefore, little is known of the family before 1910. What is known is that the name Greene was an Americanization of a very complicated family name when the family entered Ellis Island – so complicated, no one remembers it. And the "e" on the end of Green was added by Andy's grandfather, because he believed it to add a British touch to the name, and he was such an Anglophile.

What is also known is that the family first settled in New England. Andy's great grandfather had been a cobbler, a shoemaker, in the old country. Therefore, he gravitated to the textile mills which, in the early 20th century, were in New England. Andy's grandfather, Menachem, Americanized to Michael after immigrating, followed in his father's footsteps and worked in those mills as well, sometimes in Maine, sometimes New Hampshire, eventually in Boston itself.

Andy's father Sheldon, "Shel" as he was known, did not follow in his father's business. After having dropped out of college in his freshman year, he took up a chance at a career in the soft drink business and moved to New York, taking some of his Boston upbringing with him nonetheless. Shel met his future wife Estelle, known as "Stella," or "Stel" (as in "Shel and Stel") in Boston, but with better prospects in New York, settled and started a family in Brooklyn. They had three children, all born in Sheepshead Bay. Andy was the oldest, Harry second. A baby girl, Gail, came shortly before they all moved to Howard Beach.

As the summer of 1963 rolled along, a day in the neighborhood often followed a pattern of a pick-up game of baseball in the morning, a dip in the community swimming pool in the afternoon, more baseball in the evening until it became too dark to see the ball. In this way, Company A was a diversion from this routine, not a daily lifestyle. In Howard Beach in 1963, there were no ball fields to play on. So, the kids would improvise. There was a patch of field out back of the row of garden apartments where Andy lived. But as the kids grew older and stronger there were too many incidents of breaking windows when the ball was hit too hard and too far. Eventually, the same gang that played Army together would convert a piece of the cloverleaf interchange for the Belt and Cross Bay Boulevard into a field; that part of the interchange where the northbound Cross Bay traffic exits to go Brooklyn bound on the Belt creates a nice round outfield for playing ball.

As summer turned into fall, the kids would take to street games, like "Skelly," a game of drawn out boxes on a sidewalk using bottlecaps to shoot at the boxes, the caps filled with melted crayon for heft. Once school started, there was less time for such fun. Andy would return to school for 5th grade at P.S.232 and for his third year in Hebrew School at the Rockwood Park Jewish Center, the Orthodox synagogue that was a two block walk from Andy's garden apartment. In late September of that year, at around 4:30 one afternoon, Andy's Hebrew language class was interrupted by the Rabbi, who came in to announce a recess so that all could congregate at the side of the Belt Parkway, next to the temple, to see President Kennedy's motorcade riding down the Parkway from Idlewild, headed for Manhattan and his visit to the United Nations General Assembly. Sure enough, not only could you see the motorcade, but there he was, JFK, in all his glory, standing in the limousine, just a head above the Secret Service agents surrounding him, waving to the unending crowds that lined the Belt that afternoon for a look at the President.

Kennedy was perhaps the first hero that Andy idolized. He used to tell his mother that he was going to grow up to be the ***first Jewish President of the United States***. One month after the U.N. motorcade event, he would trick or treat (for UNICEF) during Halloween as the President, complete with Kennedy mask and a sweatshirt that said "Vim" on one side, "Vigor" on the other, straddling the Presidential Seal. Of course, we all know what happened three weeks after that…

Years later, Andy would say that he never walked around without a song in his head. But he could trace the start of that syndrome to a day in 1964, the first time he heard *I Wanna Hold Your Hand*. Whether The Beatles were Baby Boomer compensation for the loss of Jack Kennedy or something that had no relationship to anything, this was the moment that Andy discovered music; more specifically, rock and roll. From this point forward, the days of Company A and playing baseball in the cloverleaf interchange became less and less and the days of exploring, listening, and ultimately playing the music began to take over.

Andy was at first a Ringo fan. But he soon gravitated to Paul. After all, Paul, like him, was left-handed, and the first time Andy picked up a guitar he held it naturally as a lefty. Unfortunately, left-handed guitars in those days were rare, usually custom made. Even Jimi Hendrix played left handed with a reverse strung right-handed guitar. It wasn't until the time of players like Curt Kobain that left-handed guitars became mass produced. So, when Andy went for his first guitar lesson in 1965, his teacher turned the Framus classical guitar he got from his mother around and said, "kid, you're going to have to play that thing right-handed."

This was very disappointing to Andy. He had counted on being down-stage right, like Paul, singing into the same microphone as George when John sang lead, just like the Beatles stage set up at the time. With only two mics and three singers, the backup vocals had to be managed by a shared mic, which worked for two guitarists when they were singing only if the one on the outside was playing lefty, so that the head of his guitar would not clash into the guitar of his vocal partner.

Besides wanting to be Paul for left-handedness, Andy could see that the "pretty" one was Paul, the favorite of the girls. Andy was just beginning to discover the opposite sex. Ask any guy who took up guitar around this time and they'll tell you that the initial reason was most likely because of the girls. The music itself would become more important, but again, in large measure for the ego gratification as well as for the self-expression and self-actualization of music as a communications vehicle.

So, while in 1963, Andy wanted to be POTUS (President of the United States); by 1965, his lifelong goal was to **play the Cavern Club** in Liverpool, England, the birthplace of Beatlemania.

Andy's growing up in Brooklyn and Queens did not make him a New York baseball fan. Quite the opposite, when as a little boy the Dodgers took off from Brooklyn to Los Angeles, it left many a Brooklyn Dodger fan heartbroken. From 1958 – 1961, there was only the Yankees to root for. And while the Yankees won three pennants in those four years, they were the team from the Bronx, not Brooklyn. Many Brooklyn fans waited for the eventual arrival in 1962 of an expansion team, the Mets, who played at first in the old Polo Grounds in Harlem, one time home of the New York Giants (who also left at the same time for California), until Shea Stadium was opened in 1964. In that little window of time, a small group of Brooklyn Dodger fans who had always rooted against the Yankees looked for an alternative to waiting for the Messianic Mets to show up. They began to follow the Yankee arch rival Boston Red Sox. This made sense to Andy, as he had family history in Boston. His grandfather continued to live in the Mattapan section of that City and always spoke of his love for the Red Sox.

It was not unexpected that Red Sox fans hoped – after suffering with losing teams every year from 1951- 1966 - when it had its "Impossible Dream" year – 1967 – this would be deliverance from "the Curse." The Curse of the Bambino was the myth that the Red Sox trade of Babe Ruth to the Yankees in 1920 turned the relative fortunes of the two clubs around. Every year, from 1963 – 1967, Shel would find a weekend in the season schedule for the Yankees when the Red Sox were in town, and wait until August or

September, to see if a rainout game at the Stadium were going to result in what then was called a twi-night doubleheader, and he would pack his two sons up and head to the stadium for a first game at 5pm with a second game at 8. You don't see twi-nighters on the MLB schedules anymore; now they have day/night doubleheaders with separate seatings – a ticket to one not good for the other. But this was the 1960's. The Yankees, for all their glory, could not fill that cavernous 67,000 seat stadium, and tickets were relatively cheap - $4.00 for a box seat; $.75 for a bleacher seat. This was Andy's introduction to competitive sports, and he was faithful to his Red Sox, much to the derision ("ranking-out" is what it was called then) of his classmates and friends...

Until 1967 – the year of perhaps the greatest pennant race in American League history. Four teams: Detroit Tigers, Chicago White Sox, Minnesota Twins, and the Red Sox, all tied for first going into the last week of the season. Somehow, the Red Sox won the last two games at home against the Twins while Detroit was splitting back-to-back double headers with the California Angels (the White Sox had choked during this last week and wound up 3 games out). This included a rousing finish by Red Sox star outfielder Carl Yastrzemski, who would win the Triple Crown that year. Carl (Yaz, as he was known) was an unlikely star, not born with a lot of natural talent but clearly one who outworked everyone else on the field and a protégé of the great "Splendid Splinter" Ted Williams (a jealous White Sox Manager Eddie Stanky early in that season had referred to Yaz as a "great ballplayer from the ankles down"). Although Boston would eventually lose the World Series in 7 games to Bob Gibson and the St. Louis Cardinals, it was not lost on Andy that the Yankees had come in 9th place that year. Clearly, by 1967, Andy's dream had become being Yaz and ***playing for the Red Sox.*** And he relished the opportunity to rub it in the face of all the Yankee fans that had been on his case for the several years before.

But it was not to be… By his own hand, Andy threw away his chance at revenge. Having completed 8th grade by the beginning of that dream season, Andy was trying to gain admission to the great magnet school in NYC for Academics, Stuyvesant High School. An admission exam had to be taken. Andy was so nervous about the exam that he did not sleep at all the night before. That morning, after a 60-minute commute to the school by bus and two subway trains into Manhattan, Andy was in no condition to take an exam that would have been challenging under the best of circumstances. He had succeeded at getting into a special progress program (now known in many public school districts as G&T, gifted and talented) for 7th and 8th grade, but struggled to keep the required 85% grade average in his classes. Andy kept missing the grade in at least one or two classes every quarter, with an overall average of 84%. This should have gotten him kicked back to regular classes. But he got along so well with his teachers that they kept him in the program all the same. On Stuyvesant exam day, the odds were not in his favor. And when he found out a month later that he was one of only two boys in his class that had applied and failed to get into Stuyvesant, he was crushed.

His disappointment was compounded by the knowledge that this meant going to the community high school for his neighborhood – John Adams HS in South Ozone Park, a school known at that time for its violence and student organized crime: it would usually cost you a quarter just to get into the boys room, taken by a student gang member. Andy's parents realized the situation and before school started in September 1967, before the baseball season had its glorious end, the family moved to Rockland County, a suburb northwest of the City.

Moving to Rockland meant two years of lost social life, until Andy could get his driver's license toward the end of 10th grade. It was a daylight license only; no driving after sunset. But it was a step up from having no mobility unless given a ride by his parents. Unlike Howard Beach, where one could walk most places or at least jump onto mass transit, no such options existed in Rockland. Andy needed wheels, and without them, 9th and 10th grade were a total wash out.

To be fair, all of high school was fairly much a wash out for Andy. His first part time job was selling shoes in a local discount shoe store – Shoe Town – on Route 59 in Nanuet, where he worked during 12th grade. His first purchase with the money he earned was to buy a used violin-shaped, electric bass guitar, a "Beatle" bass as they were nicknamed, a replica of the Hofner bass famously played by Paul McCartney. But this was not a Hofner; Andy could not afford the real thing. Nevertheless, combined with that old Framus classical guitar from his mother, Andy now had entre into a sort of social life – in those days, if you played your social stock rose. And if you could write music (at least some lyrics over some trite chord progression), you were Dylan (Bob, that is) or Paul Simon (Simon and Garfunkel). The bass served a slightly different purpose. Andy worked at the guitar enthusiastically, but was usually the least accomplished guitar player when sitting in with others who played. A jam session might have 5 or 6 guitar players but often had no one with a bass. Andy could then be included by playing bass as there was little competition.

Andy's second purchase with his new found income was to ask a girl out on a date. Andy had done a little dating, if you want to call setups by his parents with the local Jewish co-eds dating. Shel was committed to making sure Andy stayed with his own kind. The Orthodox education in Howard Beach was not observed at home; the Greene's were purely secular. The choice of temple was simply logistical convenience; the Rockwood Park Jewish Center was the only synagogue close by at that time. Nevertheless, the pressure not to be part of an extinction of Jewish heritage through assimilation and inter-marriage was a strong one in 1960's New York.

Andy nevertheless drifted away from dating Jewish and in 12th grade took up with an Irish Catholic, Deirdre Walsh. Dee, as she was known to family and friends, was one of the smart kids in school, 10th in her graduating class. Though a year younger than Andy, she was well ahead of him in the ways of love. She taught Andy everything from French kissing to oral sex. Andy in return taught her how a woman ought to be treated – with respect and consideration (Andy didn't have a whole lot to offer beyond that). The courtship went on for five years, almost all the way through college. But they ended up at different schools; she at Cornell. Although trying three different times to get into that school, Andy was rejected both as a freshman and as a transfer, and so the relationship was long distance after high school, consummated in the back of the station wagon Andy's mother let him use when they were both home from school.

While Andy did reasonably well in high school, he continued to have problems with success on entry exams, and the SAT was no exception. His best scores were 477 verbal and 633 math; good but not Cornell material. So, when Andy finished high school, he was given an opportunity to study in England for freshman year, through a student-abroad program offered by the local community college. Stel, Andy's mother, had somehow manipulated the college to accept Andy for the program, even though it was meant for second year students. Stel argued successfully that Andy was unusually mature and well adapted for an 18-year-old.

So, Andy's first year in college was overseas, in a very small school in a very small village in the Cotswold Hills of England. This was a school set up especially for this particular student-abroad program.

About 75% of the students attending when Andy was there were from this same community college. The others were from other countries; some thrown out of school elsewhere. A couple had been involved in the Paris student riots that broke out in the spring of 1971 and needed a new school to continue studies. Being a year younger than everyone else created a challenge for Andy, insofar as being socially accepted. That bass guitar sure got a workout that year. The school itself was being run on a shoestring budget and eventually closed some years later.

Aside from having travelled to the U.K. as a freshman, the other seminal moment in Andy's college years came after an eventual transfer to the State University of New York, College at Oneonta, in upstate New York. If one drew a line on a map from Albany to Binghamton, and found the mid-point, you'd be in Oneonta. You'd also think you were in the middle of nowhere. The closest site of any note would be the Baseball Hall of Fame in Cooperstown, about a half hour drive northeast from the "Big O."

Oneonta had and continues to have two colleges of note: Hartwick College and Oneonta State. Oneonta State was twice as large and so tended to dominate the town, which had little employment outside of the two schools. In those days, with legal drinking age in New York at only 18, Oneonta boasted one of the highest number of bars *per capita* in the nation.

At Oneonta State, there were two institutions that were growing within it in the mid-1970s: the soccer program, which came one goal away from winning the national collegiate title in 1972 but would go on to develop a highly successful soccer program (Oneonta would eventually host the Soccer Hall of Fame); and the college's nascent radio station, WONY. Nascent it was in 1972 because it ran as mostly a carrier current station, closed-circuit through the campus buildings via small transmitters in the basement of each. On carrier current, it broadcast at 620khz AM; through a very new cable offering, a few downtown listeners could receive it on 106.3mhz FM. When Andy arrived in Oneonta, the station was the hub of counterculture activity. The students running it tried to parallel their love of Pacifica radio, embodied by WBAI in New York City. Although a majority of the students working at the station were fans of rock music, those who ran the station were primarily interested in jazz and other alternative genre. This created a tension within the membership of this student club that would afford Andy his next leadership opportunity.

The station leadership had done one thing that almost everyone there agreed was needed: an FCC license to run a free-wave, non-commercial, FM station that could reach the entire city and beyond. The station management, which consisted of students elected by the station membership itself and a chief engineer that acted as a *de facto* faculty advisor, had started the application process the year before Andy's arrival. And getting approval and setting up the new broadcast infrastructure would be a preoccupation of every station manager for the next several years.

When Andy arrived for his sophomore year, as a transfer, he toured the station. One of his high school friends going to Oneonta State had a roommate who worked at the station. He entered the facility, in the musty and oft-flooded basement of one of the oldest buildings on the campus, and instantly felt at home. This was a place where Andy could find himself, use his booming voice and love of music, and make a contribution to a group effort. Within two months, having gone through training, Andy got a regular time slot on the station's program schedule, and each week, for three hours, Andy was a *bona fide* DJ. For Andy, as well as for the entire station membership, this was not a "club," but an institution, a way of life, something in which many who worked there sacrificed their grades to spend the time necessary to make WONY the best that it could be, even if it was from each sacrificer's point of view.

Andy was a fairly happy rank-and-file member of WONY in the spring of his junior year, when the annual elections for a general manager of the station came up. Running were two of the station's most well known members and leaders – both of whom currently shared the program director's role at the station. Both were jazz DJs on the air, and shared a common philosophy of emulating Pacifica and its alternative format ideas. Both stood for giving alternative music formats, the ones that received little if any airplay at mainstream commercial stations, the best time slots and best exposure on the air. Ralph Benson would go on to an on-air radio career professionally, and was known even at this time as the "best voice we have at WONY." Jeremy Horowitz would go on to work for Bob Dylan and be part of the music publishing business he so hated at the time.

Unfortunately for Ralph and Jeremy, who were good friends at the time, the majority of the station's membership did not follow the Pacifica philosophy. While adhering to the ideal of "free format" radio, meaning the DJ could play anything and everything he/she desired, so long as it did not jeopardize the station's license or FM application, these members followed what could best be called the WNEW-FM philosophy, after the leading album oriented rock station in New York City at that time, home of radio stars like Allison Steele, Jonathan Schwartz, Pete Fornatale, Scott Muni, Carol Miller, and a couple of DJs that you might still find today on Sirius/XM radio's "classic vinyl" or "deep tacks" channels. While the station's programming was a hodge-podge of classical, Broadway show tunes, MOR pop, international, and R&B, over half of the time the station aired rock music emblematic of the 60's and 70's. Andy was part of this larger crowd, which believed that it was being given short shrift by the leadership that gave the prime time slots to their "friends." Andy's preference was playing some of that "British" music he was listening to in England during freshman year:

- Clapton
- The Kinks
- The Who
- Moody Blues
- Procol Harum
- Emerson, Lake and Palmer
- Traffic
- Yes
- David Bowie

Among others, and would slip in a little Monty Python comedy to boot. One of his claims to fame was that he watched the original *Monty Python's Flying Circus* television show in England before it was syndicated for airing in the U.S. Another was that he'd seen the original *Steptoe & Son* television show, featuring Wilfred Brambell as the grumpy father before it became *Sanford & Son* (Red Foxx in that role) in the U.S. (Brambell is also best known for playing "Paul's grandfather" in The Beatle movie, *A Hard Day's Night*).

The WNEW crowd also considered itself somewhat counterculture, but only moderately so. These members fancied themselves as professional on-air personalities in the future, though most would never appear on air again after graduation. They were preparing themselves for that career in commercial radio. So, as the election race began, many in the membership were looking for an alternative to the Pacifica model. Having no experience in leadership of this institution, having never served on its executive board, where most candidates usually come from, Andy threw his "hat into the ring," so to speak.

When the station's music director saw Andy's candidacy statement posted on the office door of the station, where it was required to be posted for notice to the membership, he remarked to Andy, "Wanting to bring some variety to the race, Andy?" This implied that the candidacy was not serious. How could a rank-and-file member, virtually unknown to most of the membership, seriously think he could become station manager?

During the ensuing three weeks, however, support for Andy's candidacy grew. This was less because of anything Andy did or did not do as it was that his position on the issue of programming philosophy and treating members fairly, without favoritism, seemed to connect with the members. One thing that did occur was that for the first time the station membership voted to allow absentee voting by the members. This would obviate the need for a member to attend a station meeting to vote, usually held every other Sunday evening in the student union building. The other candidates did not oppose absentee voting for fear of looking like they were anti-democratic. This proved to be the deciding factor in the election.

Jeremy had decided to drop out of the race a week before the election meeting, and threw his support behind Ralph. This now meant that Andy would need a clear majority against the other candidates.

Andy made one attempt to consider dropping out of the race himself and also getting behind Ralph, whom he regarded with great respect for his voice and his musical knowledge. One night, a few before the election, Andy was downtown, cruising the local pubs in Oneonta, and happened upon Ralph sitting at the bar, alone, at one hangout Andy knew Ralph usually frequented. He came up behind Ralph, sat down next to him, and started a conversation…

"Hey," Andy began, "How're you doing?"

"Good," Ralph replied.

"You getting ready for this election thing?"

"Yeah, what an ordeal."

"I'm sure you've got a good handle on what the station needs."

"I've got some ideas of where to take the station from here."

At this point, Andy inquired, "Tell me about them. What do you want to do for the station?"

Ralph took this statement in a way Andy did not intend. "I'm not telling you," he scornfully answered, as if to say he thought Andy was picking his brain for ideas he himself could use. The election meeting would allow each candidate to make a brief statement before the election ballots were cast. Ralph appeared to think that this event would turn the tide, as he was sure Andy was nothing but an empty suit, with no real ideas, someone who looked the part but added nothing, that there was "no there, there." In fact, Andy, in his clumsy way, was looking for something he could hang his hat on when he decided to drop out of the race and throw unanimous support to Ralph. But Ralph miscalculated, both the motivation of Andy's question and whether the pre-ballot statements would have a decisive effect on the outcome of the election.

The election night was electric. In the room set aside in the Student Union for the meeting, first Andy spoke. "What I want more than anything is an end to the fraternity style management we have here at WONY. I want to know that all members are treated equally and fairly." There was some talk of completing the FM license approval and getting the station on the broader airwaves. But it didn't matter; the membership, at least a lot of it, heard what it wanted to here. With Andy, there was a feeling of equal treatment and opportunity, regardless of what music was played.

Ralph opened his statement with a slew of paper that ran to the floor, and proceeded to go through a litany of ideas, all of which were valid and eventually Andy would incorporate.

After a half hour of listening to the candidates and taking questions, the candidates left the room for discussion by the membership. Ralph and Andy sat in armchairs about ten yards down the hall from the closed meeting door. They could hear some shouting though no words could be discerned. The two factions of the station were hollering at each other.

Then, the door burst open and banged against the outer wall, ricocheting back from the impact. The first people out of the door were Ralph's supporters, disgusted and grumbling, giving Andy dirty looks as they filed out. Cheering could be heard in the room and Andy looked in to see a crowd of people congratulating him. He had been elected; 27-24 in the voting total, including 6 of 7 absentee votes. This meant his victory was based on the absentee ballots. And why not? Absentee members were usually those who felt the least committed to the station and therefore rarely came to a meeting. Giving them a vote meant giving those most upset with the current administration a chance to upend the election. The insurgent, Andy, would now be WONY general manager.

Governing did prove to be more difficult than the election itself. There were squabbles along the way. However, Ralph did eventually end up being Andy's program director and so stayed on the executive board. The station did achieve FM free wave status the following April, on Andy's watch. Clearly, Andy got more credit for this achievement than he deserved; five years of work went into this FM application. Considering Andy took a lot of blame for things that went wrong during the year that were not his doing, Andy felt it came out roughly even, at least that's what he told himself.

Graduation from Oneonta State was an anti-climax that May; the real achievement in Andy's mind was getting to lead the station for a year. It did cost him his Dee, who that winter had decided to get engaged and eventually marry a fellow Cornell student. But although the loss hurt, there was little time for mourning and anger –

Andy had managed to get into law school and was headed to American University in D.C.

Law was always assumed to be the path for Andy, orchestrated by his parents, who believed that a career in the professions was the surest and safest way to success, both financially and socially. At age 13, Stel took the young Andy into Manhattan to take an aptitude test to determine the likely best career paths and strengths of this young man. Andy did score high in items related to the law, although he also scored high in two other areas: teaching and the performing arts. Stel discounted both; teaching meant to her public school teaching which in New York City at that time meant a dangerous occupation for little pay. The performing arts, acting and music specifically, were simply a pipe dream with little chance of success, as far as she was concerned.

So, law was the path that the family could financially support. And when Andy had an unusually good day taking the LSAT (scoring 663), his admission to law school was assured… Well, not to Cornell, but to several others. Andy decided after Dee was out of the picture, that it was time to get out of New York entirely, and opted to go to Washington, D.C., for school. He also opted to live in Virginia, as opposed to the District or Maryland, as Maryland was seen as too much "New York South" and living in D.C. at that time was seen as either too expensive or too dangerous.

Law school was mainly a painful blur for Andy. He had decided to go to school at night and work during the day, in order to limit the amount of financial support he needed from Shel, his father. But that option seemed to vanish after the first semester, when he nearly flunked out of school, wound up on probationary status with a 1.8 GPA, and thereupon decided to give up work for awhile in order to raise his grades. Where college seemed a breeze, Andy was not entirely prepared for law school, the rigor and drudge of all the case briefs and minutia of the law.

But Andy excelled at a couple of things. The first was his ability to find alternative coursework that he could do for grade and credit to raise his GPA. This included a second-year stint as a paralegal intern in the County Attorney's office in Fairfax, VA. The second was a little known Rule 45 of the D.C. Court of Appeals that allowed third-year law students to represent indigent clients in its courts and administrative offices without compensation but with academic credit. This second item gave rise to students-in-court clinics at the area law schools, and Andy's alma mater, American University, ran such a clinic. One represented inmates at Lorton Prison, called LAWCOR. A new legal clinic was also started, representing civil clients in small claims, landlord-tenant disputes, human rights violations, veteran's benefits claims, and other civil matters. This civil clinic is what Andy joined for third year and represented 6 different clients, never losing a case while earning 6 credits of A for his work. This included a couple of rent strikes, a couple of small claims cases, and an odd human rights case in which Andy somehow got hold of the private number for the Mayor's office and was able to negotiate a settlement for a client that would not have been possible without that phone call.

Truth be told, while Andy was applauded by faculty advisors at the clinic for his trial skills as a litigator, there is a lot more to the story than that. As Andy's advisor said many times, "The law is not written for the rich, it is written for the poor, but only the rich have access to the system to enforce the law." Once a non-paid law student walked into the system, it turned the system upside down. Suddenly, tenants were no longer being herded into court to be evicted unless they paid up. The law student now gave those tenants options to oppose the landlord, slumlords most of the lot. The law gave tenants the right to withhold rent if their apartments were considered "uninhabitable," which many times they were – no hot water, no heat, rat infestations, etc. Oh yes, tenants knew that they had rights like this; they just didn't know how to make sure they could preserve those rights; such as the need to escrow the rent in a separate account until needed repairs were made. They also didn't know the proper procedure for resisting a rent increase on rent controlled property. But Andy knew, and it drove the slumlord attorneys crazy, so much so there was one attempt at getting Andy thrown out of court for the "unauthorized practice of law." But to no avail; the District Government knew what it was doing with Rule 45 – "we can't guarantee the poor will win, but we can guarantee a process that is fair by levelizing the playing field."

Litigation gave Andy the opportunity to make the courtroom a stage and to use his voice and stage presence – his performing arts side – come out. But it also took its toll. Litigation was a high pressure business and Andy soon found no pleasure in managing multiple cases with miniscule procedural requirements. Law school ended with Andy achieving an overall 3.03 GPA, but with little prospects for entry into a law firm as an associate attorney. Having passed the Virginia Bar Exam first time out, there were no jobs for a B student from the third best law school in D.C. And this being the late 70's, many firms were beginning to search for female lawyers to create diversity in their ranks, or for minority candidates. Andy always thought that a bit weird, "I thought Jews were a minority," he surmised, "only 3% of the country's population, and next to Black folks the most hated and persecuted bunch in the land, but apparently we don't count."

Andy eventually accepted a position downstate, in Charlottesville, with The American Legal Group, or ALG as it was known. ALG was the brainchild of three lawyers from the University of Virginia, one of whom became the major shareholder, Bill Morris. With his two henchmen by his side, Bill built what could best be described as a "rent-a-lawyer" firm. An attorney needing a memorandum of law, legal brief, jury instructions, a draft of pleadings, or other legal documents drawn up, but who had no staff to do the job could call an 800 number and hire one of ALG's lawyers to do the work. This was financially very lucrative for attorneys and for ALG. The client-attorney calling in would be charged anywhere from $28-38 per hour for the work, which work would be a ghost writing effort – in other words, the identity of ALG's authorship was never revealed; it was as if the client-attorney had done the work him/herself. So, he/she would bill the end client at the usual rate: $100-300 an hour. Had the attorney hired an associate or law clerk to do the work, the client would have been billed at that rate, $40-50 an hour. This allowed a huge gross margin for the attorney and made a lot of business for ALG.

ALG did equally well. A staff lawyer (associate) at the firm in 1978 was usually offered no more than $13,000 a year salary to start, but was expected to generate at least 35 hour per week of billable work. Given a 50-week year, that was 1750 hours, divided into that salary came to less than $7.50 an hour. Add in benefits and the result was still less than $10 an hour for the staff associate. This meant a minimum gross margin of $18 per billable hour. ALG had as many as 40 associates working full time, out of the law library at the UVA (University of Virginia) law school across town. This meant that if all 40 were billing out 35 hours per week to client-attorneys the firm would gross over $25,000 a week or over $1.3 million a year. After paying clerical staff and servicing the mortgage on the building headquarters, there was still plenty to fuel the two Mercedes that Bill and his wife owned and showed off rather cavalierly to all who came in contact with them.

This put an ALG staff lawyer near the bottom in professional prestige. But Andy had had economics courses in school and understood the capitalist ways of an open marketplace.

"ALG is making unusual profits and the marketplace should be narrowing that margin down," he would say in conversations with other staffers.

"There's only one way to improve our situation," one answered, "and that is a union."

A union sounded ridiculous to a lot of the staff lawyers at ALG. Attorneys do not organize into a union; it was beneath most of them. And Andy agreed. Nevertheless, the arbitrage that ALG was taking advantage of needed to be closed somehow.

This gave Andy his third leadership opportunity. And he urged management to form a "Personnel Committee" consisting of equal parts the three major owners and three members of the staff lawyers, to explore personnel issues as they came up. Management did not argue against this Committee as they saw it as a vehicle to defuse any discontent among the staff without the staff resorting to things like collective bargaining. Oh yes, if the staff were talking about unionizing it meant that management would soon learn of the talk – after all, they had their moles among the staff.

Andy joined this Committee and immediately began to argue for a lower number of required billable hours. 35 hours a week sounded manageable, until you realized that it was billable hours, not working hours. There was also non-billed administrative work that went on, and often it was up to the staff lawyer to approach the client-attorney for an extension of time to complete a negotiated project, and these staff attorneys were shy about trying to get additional billable hours out of the client – they did not know how to "sell" their labor to other lawyers.

So, they simply sucked up the time as non-billable rather than negotiate more time and ended up coming up short each week. Coming up short created a deficit of time which, each quarter, had to be subject to a true-up, an adjustment to pay. Of course, the opposite was also true. If a staffer billed more than 35 hours a week, he/she built up a surplus which became an eventual bonus at true-up time. Andy found it easier than most staffers at the firm to negotiate larger amounts of time for projects. He had the gift of selling that allowed him to present the need for extra time to the client-attorney and get the extra billable time in. He generally ran a surplus, for which he received bonuses each quarter. So, for Andy, getting a lowering of the required billable hours each week was simply going to make his own surplus each quarter even bigger.

The other staffers didn't know of Andy's surplus. But management did, and were a little skeptical of Andy's proposals at Committee meetings. "Why can't the other associates do as you do?" they asked.

"It's not about me," Andy answered, "it's about the average associate you have here and their inability to bill 35 hours week in and week out. Ask any associate in a law firm how many hours they bill on average each week, and you won't get 35 as the number; you'll get something much less."

"But this is not a law firm… as such," they would answer.

"Since our clients are law firms, perhaps we should adopt more of a law firm atmosphere."

"Perhaps. But are you now calling for a change in work environment instead of a change in work quota?" They would always try and re-route the argument to something other than money.

Andy essentially was the staff spokesperson on this Committee; seen as the staff's leader in such talks. Meanwhile, talk of union continued at the water cooler, the library, and out at the local pubs in town. Andy liked organizing what he called the "Thursday Night Caucus," a meeting at a local bar or restaurant of the staff lawyers to hang out and wind down from the pressures of legal research and writing, and to keep a high morale among the "troops." He also selfishly saw it once again as social entre to the group. "The leader and organizer would always have to be accepted by the group or there would be no group," was his thinking.

After about 6 months on the job, Andy learned that organizers from the UAW, United Auto Workers, had approached a couple of the disenchanted staffers about organizing a collective bargaining unit and joining the UAW. At this point, many of the staffers looked to Andy for leadership. He had, after all, been their spokesperson on the Committee. Could he not see that the Committee was a co-opting mechanism by management to defer any action on staff demands?

For the first time, Andy declined a leadership opportunity. While relishing the leadership position, he saw himself as working "within the system." And what was an auto workers union doing trying to help a law firm organize a union? By 1979, the union movement had stalled in the United States. Organizing blue collar workers was not seen by organized labor as the most target-rich environment. Outsourcing of manufacturing jobs had begun and the labor base among their core constituency was dwindling (a lot of commentators believe the decline of manufacturing in the U.S. began with the Reagan Years; to be sure, the 1980s may have accelerated the pace, but the trend started as early as with the recession of 1973-74). Organized labor saw what most economists saw; the U.S. was becoming a services oriented economy and one way to exploit that change was to go after more upscale workers, professionals, such as teachers, and maybe even lawyers.

Andy stood aside, creating a leadership vacuum. This allowed a more militant and angry group to take control of the organizing movement. Led by a first-year attorney, Rupert Fields (RF to his friends), a formal application went into the NLRB for an election to determine if a collective bargaining unit of staff lawyers at ALG would be formed.

The movement was doomed from the start. For one thing, RF talked too from-the-hip and created fear among the staff. In one newspaper interview, he talked of the "excesses of management" at ALG and got personal about the "opulent living of the Morrises" rather than confining remarks to the movement itself. The newspapers ate it all up, seeing this as a real human interest story, rather than just another union organizing project. When published, the staff – not wanting to alienate the very people they would have to negotiate with later – got nervous, not so much as to vote against the union but enough to silence their support somewhat. And Morris himself saw an opportunity to drive a wedge between the militant organizers among the staff and the ones who might be persuaded to a more reasonable course.

So, one night a party was organized at which a few top line client-attorneys attended and at which a group of staffers were invited. These staffers, some of whom secretly favored the union, were seen as people who might still be persuaded to vote no. In fairness, all staffers were invited, but the militant organizers declined to attend, much to their loss. The party consisted of lobbying attempts by management and the client-attorneys toward the staffers in attendance.

One client-attorney, Bernard "Bernie" Feldman, a highly visible personal injury lawyer and leading member of the American Trial Lawyers Association (ATLA) came up to Andy and introduced himself. But Andy already knew him. Andy had done some work for ATLA as an editor of their monthly newsletter in the role of paralegal intern during his third year of law school. ATLA was based in the Georgetown section of D.C. and was the bar association for litigators, personal injury and criminal defense attorneys in predominance. Since Andy was a nobody, and Bernie was a somebody, it was not unexpected that Bernie would not remember Andy.

"So, you worked at ATLA? I'm very well known in that organization," Bernie boasted. At 5' 9", but as wide as tall, Bernie was well advanced in braggadocio.

"Yes, I worked on its monthly newsletter," Andy reminded him.

They then embarked on a who-do-you-know-there exchange. After a couple of names were mentioned back-and-forth, Bernie mentioned one Kathy Calloway, another long-time, full-time associate at ATLA. Kathy and Andy had had a very brief romance while they both worked there, although it never came to much.

"Yes, I know Kathy, she's a good friend of mine," Andy commented. Andy did like to stay friends with former girlfriends, even the ones who dumped him, better not to burn bridges.

"Not as good a friend as she is of mine," Bernie pompously boasted again.

And this reminded Andy of a story Kathy once told him, of the so-called casting couches and dating lists that were prepared by the executive office at ATLA to entertain the high muckety-mucks among the membership whenever they came into town. And it all started to make sense.

The second reason the union movement was doomed was that the lawyers there were never going to stay at the firm long term. As soon as a better job came along they were gone. ALG was a placeholder to afford some employment while recent graduates from law school continued to try and land something with more money and a lot more prestige. With no long term commitment to the movement, there was little hope of maintaining a cohesive group even if the union had won the election. In fact, during the election campaign, two of the staff lawyers who were for the union had left for better jobs.

Which leads to the third and ultimate reason for the failure of the union: Management, through its moles, had learned of the plans to apply with the NLRB and before the application was sent in had gone out and hired six new associates with no ties to the union. In fact, they were hired specifically because they had stated their dislike for unions and organized labor. Had the NLRB gotten the application before these hires, they would not have been part of the collective bargaining group. But because they were already on board, they had the vote as well as everyone else.

On a hot July day in Charlottesville, in 1979, the vote took place. The initial vote was 17-16 in favor of the union. But this did not include the votes of the new associates. RF had challenged the 6 votes, surmising that they were probably "no" votes, and arguing that they should not be part of the collective bargaining group. That evening, the union leadership met, including Andy, and came to the conclusion that they did not have a legal leg to stand on. Part of the thinking was that the organizers were probably not going to be around long enough to see through what they had done. Partly it was a fear that winning would lead to a strike, which no one wanted. For Andy it was that he could see that they could win by losing – management was sufficiently scared of what had happened that even in winning they would accede to many of the requests being made through the Personnel Committee. That Committee had been disbanded during the election campaign but surely would be restored as a sign of goodwill by management.

So, the next day, the union organizers released the 6 votes being challenged. The 6 were in fact all against the union. The election was lost. Andy then saw an opportunity to restore the Committee and continue with his work within the system. But in a last poke at Andy for not having led the union movement himself, the staff – when given the opportunity to elect representatives for the restored Committee – decided to put someone else in charge of representing them. Andy was out. But his prescience was spot on; management immediately lowered the quota of billable hours from 35 to 31 per week. And the Committee approved an across-the-board raise in salaries of 9% for all associates with at least one year on the job (9% sounds like more than it actually was in that inflation in 1979 was running at 12%).

Within a year after the election, virtually all who had supported the union movement had left for better jobs. Andy likewise left ALG for an editor position with a law book publisher, with offices based in D.C., which meant he would now move back to Northern Virginia.

Chapter 3: Entering the Business

Being an editor of a law book publisher proved even more boring to Andy than being a staff research attorney. The job most often involved reading new rulings and decisions by the U.S. Supreme Court. Then the editor would digest each principle of law being espoused in the majority opinion into a one sentence statement of what the legal principle was. This digest was called a "headnote." It would have a filing code attached to it to identify what kind of principle it related to so it could be found in legal research later. Then, the headnote was dictated into a Dictaphone by the editor. The microcassette with the dictated headnote would be given to a transcriber, euphemism for secretary, who would generate a slip of paper, 5 ½" by 8 ½" with six lines of copy on it, for the editor to proof. The editor would then make changes and corrections, and hand it to a more senior editor for checking before it went into an early version of a computer for inclusion in the next edition of the publisher's encyclopedia-style reports of the Supreme Court's decisions. The publisher, Attorney's Cooperative Publishing (ACP), was actually based in upstate New York, but managed an office in D.C. specifically for this publication.

To be sure, the process of "headnoting" Supreme Court decisions has become over the years more streamlined. In 1980, with the age of the personal computer in its infancy, this process was agonizing and stifling, with little interaction with colleagues or the public. Still, Andy was able, over a two-year period, to achieve a modicum of success at this job.

During this period, Andy had become involved with an attorney in private practice in Northern Virginia. Sarah (Sallie, as she was known) Anderson, had been introduced to Andy during his time interning in the Fairfax County Attorney's office by the librarian for the Fairfax Bar Association, the library contained within the County Courthouse (the Courthouse was an historical relic; it having been the headquarters for the Confederate Army in the early days of the Civil War). Sallie was a few years older than Andy and so was already in practice when Andy was still in law school. They maintained an acquaintance during Andy's time in Charlottesville, seeing each other every other weekend in what developed over time as a monogamous romance. When Andy returned to Northern Virginia to work for ACP, they decided to live together. Then, in somewhat of a legal contract negotiation, they decided to get engaged. Legal contract is the best description as it was more about Sallie feeling her "biological clock" was ticking, and it was either put up or shut up for Andy. So, he put up by shutting up, and in 1981, the two were wed.

Where Andy felt confident in business and leadership situations, he was much less so in the areas of love, and Sallie took charge of the early relationship decisions in their marriage; well, most of them anyway. In 1981-82, Sallie continued to build a sole practice in law while Andy struggled to keep up by providing a smaller but more stable paycheck from ACP.

In March of 1982, ACP invited into D.C. its salespeople from around the country for a motivational sales meeting. This happened annually but never had taken place in D.C. The editorial staff at ACP were invited to attend and observe, though they had no formal part of the meeting.

In the ballroom of the famous Omni-Shoreham Hotel, ACP pulled out all the stops to charge up the sales force. A multimedia display and motivational speakers were on hand throughout the two-day meeting. Andy watched with rapt attention to every detail of the meeting: how the speakers addressed the audience of salespeople; how the multimedia effects (including music) were used to lift the energy level in the room; how the salespeople engaged in friendly competition with each other to determine who would lead the pack. This last item often went on outside the formal meeting, in the lobby and corridors of the hotel. During breaks, Andy could hear them talking, with each other and their regional supervisors. Andy managed to meet a few of them, although it was not encouraged for the editorial staff to get too engaged with the marketing team of the company. But through all of this, Andy felt strangely at home.

Sheldon Greene fell into sales after failing at journalism school in Boston. A shy young man, the necessities of supporting a wife and eventually a family forced him into the only occupation that always has jobs open: sales.

Shel started as a route salesman for Canada Dry, out of its plant in Masbeth, Queens, around the time of Andy's birth. He soon rose to be a supervisor for a group of salespeople, who sold and took orders from grocery stores (called retail accounts) and bars and restaurants (called institutional accounts) to vending machines (the iron bandits). In the late 50s and through the 60s, soda was distributed mostly by tie-and-jacket salesmen who went into businesses and cultivated relationships. The soda was delivered by a different set of people, truck drivers. By the late 60s this distribution model had integrated sales and order fulfillment into one job, done by the truck drivers, at least at the two big competitors: Coca Cola and Pepsi. But the smaller brands continued to stress service and relationship by keeping the roles separate. By the same measure, while Coke and Pepsi had gone entirely to using independent bottlers to wholesale the product, the smaller brands continued to have some O&O (owned-and-operated) factories, called "plants," to manufacture and bottle the product.

By today's standards, Shel might never have gotten very far in business due to his lack of a college education. But in the 1950s it was still possible to get ahead through hard work and relationship alone. And Shel learned quickly how to do that; so well, that by the

70s, Shel was running one of Canada Dry's O&O warehouses, in Orange, NJ.

Shel had learned never to take staff for granted. He was considered by almost all he worked with as a "mensch," a good human being. His long time secretary, Gladys, a feisty Irish-Catholic-American if there ever was one, became so loyal to Shel that when she became terminally ill with cancer in the early 80s, Shel gave her a *chai* necklace, meaning "life," in Hebrew, a good luck charm if you want to think of it that way. She wore it constantly, and was buried with it when she died.

When Sheldon ran the warehouse he would arrive at work early, but not too early. There were two doors one could go through to get to the sales offices on the top floor, which was also where Shel's office was located. The easy way, the shortest route, was to go through the front door of the building, where a staircase awaited for climbing up to the second floor, avoiding the entire warehouse back end, where the truck drivers and maintenance people worked. All of the salesmen went through that front door every day. Not Sheldon Greene… He always made sure he parked in the back and walked through the warehouse itself, saying hello to each employee as he went. He knew each worker by name, some 30-40 of them, and something about each one's family. Everyone knew he was about business, but appreciated the time he took each morning to greet the "union guys," the blue collar workers who made the warehouse run properly every day.

This wasn't just because Shel was a nice guy. To be sure, he could be short of patience with people if he felt they were not getting the job done. You could say he "didn't suffer fools gladly," and could be heard balling out a recalcitrant salesman from the sales office above from time to time. The young Andy saw how his father handled himself with "the help." Shel used to say, "Be kind to the people on your way up, because you're going to see them again on your way down."

Andy witnessed this self-taught form of management close by. He travelled with his father sometimes during the summers when he was in high school. While in college he actually worked a couple of summers at the Orange warehouse, driving a van around New Jersey's supermarkets, packing out the Canada Dry soda deliveries onto the grocery store shelves.

When Andy travelled with Shel in the summer, Shel was a district manager working with all the bottlers in upstate New York. In each city upstate, Syracuse, Utica, Albany, Rochester, even Messina, the soft drink bottling and distribution was usually owned as an independent family business. These bottlers were predominantly of Italian descent in those days. It was a well known rumor that in some cases, the owners had associations with organized crime, although never definitively proven. Shel had to work with these people regardless of background and associations. Whether these businesses were truly legit or a legit side to a more nefarious string of businesses for which the bottling business allowed the laundering of money, this has never been established either way.

What is true is that the bottlers and their families treated Shel and Andy as family. There wasn't enough they could do for the teenage son of their Canada Dry rep when they both came to town. If some of them had ties to organized crime, Shel never knew, so Andy never knew. Shel knew enough not to ask questions. In return, Canada Dry had a huge following at the consumer end of the soft drink business in the 60s and 70s. You might say Shel was a "connected guy." What you could definitely say was that the company's distribution channel in upstate New York was deeper and more effective than the company had anywhere else in the country.

In the late 70s Shel had progressed in his career so much that he had come into the home office on Park Avenue in Manhattan and was *de facto* the chief marketing officer of the whole company. No, they didn't call the position CMO (for Chief Marketing Officer) but it was the equivalent in reputation and influence. Shel reported to a COO (Chief Operating Officer), one Herman Hagler (Double-H as he was known). Hagler had become somewhat of a rival of this upstart Jew from nowhere. Hagler saw Shel as a rival to the President's position. Hagler was somewhat old school, which included a streak of anti-Semitism as well. He had little regard for someone without a full college education. Hagler was only a year or two older than Shel; he was always dressed in the best suits, French-cuff shirts, lots of bling on the hands and wrists. He always drove a Cadillac; he belonged to the best country club that his Westchester community could offer. He was also very fit; never smoked; looked very trim.

Shel, on the other hand, was always struggling with his weight. One way he kept it from getting out of control was the one pack-a-day cigarettes he smoked, usually Marlboro filters. He favored short sleeved shirts so he wouldn't have to struggle with fitting long sleeves into his suit jacket that otherwise was already a little on the small side given his "balcony of affluence." Shel was a good looking young man, but age had taken some toll, some hair as one piece of evidence. So, Shel did not necessarily look the part.

One day Double-H called Shel into his office at headquarters. Unlike how it is done in the corporate world today, the boss confronts the employee head on if there's a problem. Double-H at least knew enough to have this talk on a Monday morning, not Friday afternoon, but the fact that it happened at the beginning of the week might yet have led to its own unraveling.

"Shel," Hagler started, "I've decided to make a change in marketing. We need to bring people in with new ideas and a fresh perspective.

You've been with the company a long time, but I have become concerned that you don't have that new idea or fresh perspective. I'm letting you go. HR has a package of exit benefits for you and they are waiting for you now to go over it with you. Thanks for all your service here."

And Double-H offered his hand. Shel, in shock, could not speak. The mensch in him met his hand and shook it, but he was seething in anger. "I don't get it," was all he could say.

"It really is nothing personal, Sheldon." Hagler could feel the anger emanating from Shel's handshake, and became a bit defensive, causing him to get even more blunt and curt in his remarks. "I'm afraid you're simply out."

Shel knew that it *was* totally personal. He understood that Double-H saw him as a rival. He felt Hagler was protecting himself from someone who had more energy and could outwork him. Surely, Hagler knew that eventually the company President, Norm Simms, would move him out of the way for someone who could change the company's direction. Shel considered Double-H to be an "empty suit," someone who looked the part but brought nothing to the table. He tried not to project that attitude in his dealings with Hagler, but now surely felt that some of that feeling had come out along the way.

Shel drove home, still in shock, and came in the door of their two-story contemporary that they had bought, highly leveraged, when they moved out of Queens for Rockland. He looked around, realizing that he had huge financial obligations; not just the house, but he was still financing Andy's law school education, Harry was in college, and Gail was soon to follow. Stel, who had just begun a florist business in town, met him at the door. And for the first time in memory, Stel saw Shel break down and cry.

"What's the matter, honey, what happened?"

"I was fired today." Shel could barely get the words out.

"How? How could that happen? After all these years?"

"It was Hagler…He's had it in for me from the start."

Nothing much more was said. Stel knew that tonight was for commiserating; tomorrow would be for planning ahead. She always knew what Shel needed.

The next morning at headquarters the phone lines began lighting up, much earlier than usual and much more volume than usual. Through work buddies of Shel, the news got out, even before a formal announcement had been made by the company that he had been fired. On the phone lines were bottlers, salespeople, and even the union guys he knew from the warehouse, calling in to complain about the firing. The calls came from all over the country, from virtually everyone Shel had worked with over the over 25 years he'd been with the company. The calls kept on coming.

"Who the hell is behind this firing?" was a typical call.

"This can't stand. Shel was our guy," was another common refrain.

"Sheldon Greene is the face of this company from where I stand," came from several.

The union of truck drivers Shel had worked with in Orange threatened to strike, although it was unlikely that would ever happen.

For three days, the calls kept coming. Sometimes you are better known for what you don't do than what you **do** do, and because no formal announcement of the termination had gone out through company channels, the firing was unofficial, at least from the field personnel's point of view.

Norm Simms stepped in. He went into Hagler's office on the third day.

"You've really created a mess here. I haven't stopped hearing from the field all week."

"It will die down after a time," Double-H defended. "Nobody is going to sacrifice their jobs over this."

"I had concerns about this move from the start, Herm, but I let you make the call as it was your issue. Did you ever consider how popular Greene was with the field?"

"The field is beside the point." Hagler answered, but Norm cut him off.

"The field is everything." He began raising his voice in anger. "We're nothing without the distributors. Haven't you learned anything here?"

"The field is looking for leadership, and from someone who can look the part. There are plenty of guys with the same idea power as Greene. We'll be able to replace him. I already have two candidates waiting in the wings; college education for both, one from Cornell. We'll weather this storm, Norm, I'm sure of it."

"I don't know what bug you've got up your ass Herm, but we're not going in that direction. We haven't sent any formal announcement out on this to the field, and we're not going to. I'm going back to my office and calling Greene and rehiring him." At this point Hagler went pale, but Simms was on a roll. "As for you, it might be wise to look for other opportunities elsewhere. If this is your idea of leadership, you've badly miscalculated," and slammed Double-H's door behind him.

Shel was back at work by the next week. Hagler was allowed to resign. After only 5 years at the company – having come into the position after being recruited away from a competitor, Double-H nevertheless received a severance which included two years salary. But only he, Simms and the head of HR knew about the payment at the time because they wanted to stage the exit as voluntary. The Board of Directors learned of the situation not until its semi-annual meeting three months later. In a final slap in the face to Shel, because his position was one step below the COO, his severance package that he would have gotten was one month severance for each year of completed service, which amounted to the same duration as Hagler got even though he had been with the company 5 times as long. As his salary was not as high as Double-H's, the exit package would not have come out as good.

In April 1982, Andy received both good news and bad news: The good news was that ACP was promoting him to full Editor, from Associate Editor, the only one of four editorial attorneys in the D.C. office hired at the same time that got the promotion; the bad news was that the D.C. office was closing and relocating back to upstate New York - Rochester, to be exact.

The closure of the D.C. office should not have been a huge surprise to anyone there. Expenses in maintaining an office in Washington were extremely high compared to upstate New York. The technology was developing that obviated the need to have an onsite presence in the Nation's Capital. And the culture clash between those in D.C. and those in Rochester had become an issue for the company – the D.C. office ran more loosely and more culturally diverse than what it had at headquarters.

And the recent disaster – the crash of Air Florida's flight #90 into the 14th Street Bridge over the Potomac River, scared headquarters from a distance. On the day it happened, January 13, 1982, the D.C. editorial staff had been sent home early due to the ice storm that was raging that day. But the Federal Government had also sent everyone home early as well, and the result was a huge traffic jam on all the bridges from D.C. to Virginia that afternoon. Andy, for one, was stuck in the 9th Street tunnel approach to the bridge, unable to move forward, He tuned the car radio to WTOP to get a traffic report when Lem Tucker from CBS came on the radio to report the crash. Almost instantly, everyone tried to back out of the tunnel. Once out, Andy had decided he would return his car to the parking lot he had a monthly space in and take the Metro out to Virginia. But as he moved back to the lot, another announcement came on the radio to tell of a fatal derailment of a subway train on the blue line at McPherson Square and the line to Virginia was closed. Andy had to go totally around D.C. via the Beltway to go over the Woodrow Wilson Bridge, several miles downstream the Potomac. It took all afternoon and most of the evening for Andy to get home.

Andy was offered the opportunity to relocate to Rochester. Newly married, Andy had to consider Sallie in this decision. Sallie Anderson was Virginia blueblood, a descendant of a member of the Daughters of the Confederacy. She was a study in contradictions. A hard-nosed feminist who had worked toward the failed attempt at getting Virginia to ratify the Equal Rights Amendment in the late 70s, she was oh so proud of her Virginia roots, and never missed an opportunity to remind people about them. She was born and raised on the Peninsula of Tidewater Virginia – Hampton, Newport News – and schooled in Richmond and Williamsburg. There was never any doubt what her opinion was of relocating north.

For his part, Andy was ambivalent about the idea of returning to upstate New York, after three years in Oneonta. It was cold, to be sure, and an area that had seen its better days as an industrial hub of the northeast. Surely, the cost of living was much lower, including property values, but was it worth leaving the "Center of the Free World," as D.C. was often called in those days?

Andy declined the offer of relocation, almost at the last minute, and took a small severance that was offered as an alternative. In the summer of 1982, Andy began looking for a new job. Going into private practice was always an option, but with one spouse already working on "variable comp" as a sole practitioner, anything less than an associate's position with a law firm would be unacceptable. Andy's prospects of that were as slim as they were four years earlier coming out of law school. Looking at the competing law book publishers was an option. But the idea of launching into another agonizingly boring job seemed a dead end to him.

One has to remember what 1982 was like in Washington, D.C., and the whole country for that matter. The United States was in its deepest recession it had experienced since the 1930s. In order to tame inflation – that in 1980 was approaching 18% - the Reagan Administration had set in motion an intentional recession, by cutting the federal budget. As an example, these cuts were made famous by the firing, in 1981, of the PATCO air traffic controllers at Washington National Airport and elsewhere, for staging what the Administration called an illegal strike. The budget cutbacks in the Government of course hit D.C. the worst. No longer could Washington be thought of as a "company town" for bureaucrats. The Government was getting smaller. So, the opportunities there were hard to find.

Nevertheless, through a neighbor friend of Andy and Sallie – a patent attorney with the U.S. Patent and Trademark Office – Andy learned of an opening for a trademark attorney there. And he worked that relationship into an offer to join the Office as a GS11 Trademark Attorney in early October.

At the same time, Andy was working on a job opening for an "Advanced Underwriting Attorney" at Atlantic Mutual Life Insurance Company (AMLIC), the only life insurer of any substantial size based in D.C.

What is an "Advanced Underwriting Attorney" you ask? It is a generic name for a position traditionally located in a life insurer's marketing department where advice and training is applied to use life insurance as the funding vehicle to solve tax, estate, and business planning issues for affluent clients. The Advanced Underwriting Attorney would operate a phone line open to field sales people who were looking for advice and counsel in their live cases involving live clients. The attorney, while being careful not to be cast in the role of practicing law, would dispense generic advice, framing the cases presented to him/her as hypothetical, and perform research to hone the specifics of the strategies being offered to the agent, who in turn offered those strategies to the client and the client's advisor (lawyer or accountant in most cases). While it was not required that everyone in Advanced Underwriting have a law degree – there were some who held advanced designations from the industry who could hold their own with any tax lawyer – it was seen as more credible if the advice were coming from a lawyer.

What were Andy's qualifications for such a position? Well, about as good as they were for being a trademark lawyer – which is to say, none, other than a basic law degree. Andy's background in the law was mainly in litigation, especially personal injury cases. While in Charlottesville with ALG, for example, Andy had gotten to work on some high profile cases, such as the Beverly Hills Supper Club fire in Kentucky, in which over 100 people died, but mainly from inhalation of toxic vapor coming from the aluminum wiring in the Club than from the fire itself. And he got to work on the case of the fatal car bombing in D.C. of Chilean Ambassador Orlando Letelier and his assistant, Ronnie Moffitt – no, not the criminal case, but the wrongful death lawsuit against the Chilean Government who, it was alleged, had the bomb planted to rid itself of one of the remnants of the Socialist regime it had just overthrown.

Neither of these cases, while making great cocktail party gossip in Georgetown, would help Andy's resume for either job. The trademark lawyer position was a layup, given the inside track he got from his neighbor. The advanced underwriting position, on the other hand, would require some outstanding persuasion in interviews (there were no benefactors clearing the way).

On the other hand, this position at AMLIC was in the marketing department, not the legal department. Thus, legal background was not necessarily the clinching qualification. Marketing knowhow combined with a steady legal mind was what the company was looking for. And Andy exploited this opportunity. In interviews with his would-be boss, the boss' boss, and the CMO, the ability to project a business and marketing attitude showed through. Lawyers can talk your ear off, but mostly about the law. As one went up the ladder of leadership in this marketing department, talking like a lawyer became a liability, not an asset.

In Andy's final interview, this one with George Forson, the CMO, George saw in Andy someone he could mentor, almost like a father figure. George was more of the hard-knocks type, long on life insurance sales experience but short on formal education. When George began inquiring into Andy's non-legal background, Andy offered up stories about his own father and the soft drink business, about his days on the air in radio, about watching the sales people trying to sell law books, and George ate it all up.

"It's important that you understand, Andrew, that while you may be a lawyer by education, this is not a law firm. Is that a problem for you?"

"On the contrary," Andy answered, and with just a little false bravado, "if I'd wanted to be in a law firm, I would be there."

"Why is it that you would choose a non-practicing position like this one, rather than practicing law, a very prestigious profession."

"My background in marketing is what makes me who I am, George. Marketing was required knowledge at the dinner table when I was growing up, listening to my father's stories and the characters he dealt with every day. If you didn't understand marketing, you had little to talk about with my Dad."

"I'm impressed with the respect you have not only of marketing, but of your father."

And with that, Andy received an offer within a few days after that interview. On the same day, Andy got a call from the head of the trademark unit at the U.S. Trademark Office, offering him that GS11 position. GS11 in those days started at approximately $25,000 a year salary, with federal government level benefits (the best), a defined benefit pension still in existence at that time, and a guarantee of work that started at 8:30am every day that would have Andy home by 5:30pm each evening, very predictable, very steady, very reliable, the ticket to a career in which the idea of losing your job was almost unheard of at the time.

On the other hand, the offer from AMLIC was for $24,000 a year, a 401(k) plan that took one year before he could participate, decent but not outstanding benefits – with one exception. The department head, Tim Pershing, when making the offer to Andy face-to-face, made it clear that some fast track education would be needed to fill in Andy's knowledge gaps. Tim offered a blank check for Andy to pursue any and all education he desired – on his own time – although encouraging him to matriculate into The American College, the institution of higher learning in the life insurance business, where he could take courses by self-study and exams when he felt he was ready. To clinch the deal, it also included re-entry into an MBA program Andy had started while at ACP but had to take a leave of absence from when he left the publisher. Andy came from the kind of family, typical in the Jewish tradition, stressing education as the ticket to success. Andy was to become the poster child for that tradition. And Andy accepted the AMLIC offer.

The Trademark Office was aghast when Andy told them he was turning them down. "No one turns down such a great Government position," was the refrain from the Department head who called Andy after he gave the Office notice of his decision.

"Well, call me crazy, but I feel more comfortable in another arena." He did not specify but he was referring to marketing. He had no idea what marketing life insurance products would be like, but he knew where he did not want to be: getting his fingernails dirty searching trademarks at the U.S. Patent and Trademark Office, for the rest of his life. To be fair, had the Department head come back with a higher GS level for the position, say, 13, that would have raised the salary to over $30,000, Andy might have changed his mind. He could be bought, but he was expensive.

That evening Andy called Shel and Stel to tell his parents of his decision to go into life insurance marketing. Shel had not come home from work yet when Andy called. But later that night, Andy got a return call from Shel.

"I can't believe it. I was sure you were going to take the Government job. That would have been the safe bet."

"But not the way I wanted to live my work life."

"Well, Andy, I am very proud and happy for you. I wasn't sure you had the *chutzpah* to make that decision, but I'm glad you did."

"Dad, now we'll have something to talk about." This meant that finally there was some common ground for the two of them.

"You bet we will," Shel spoke with pride. And then he said something else that stuck with Andy. "You give me *nacchus*, my son," a Yiddish word roughly meaning a pride a father feels for a son who has done well in life.

The passing of pride from father to son was a big deal for Shel, who never mastered the art of showing his children how he felt about them. He was always compensating for that by work, and providing for the family. But now he had something he could share with his child – marketing. This passing of wisdom from father-to-son was a hallmark of the Greene family. And so, on the first Monday in October, rather than paying attention to the opening of the U.S. Supreme Court's new term, Andy entered a building just walking distance from that Court and began a career in the life insurance business.

Michael Greene, called Mikey by friends and family, had built a career in the shoemaking business during the 1940s, 50s, and 60s. His love of Boston was rewarded when he became a foreman on the assembly line at Stetson Shoes, their plant located at that time in Braintree, just south of the City. As a foreman, he was a first line floor manager, and supervised dozens of workers, most of whom were Italian-American, living in Quincy, Braintree, Randolph, and surrounding towns on the "South Shore."

Mikey had come up the hard way. As a young immigrant who could only speak Yiddish in 1910, he was already 9 years old but was put into first grade in school in order to learn English. He became a voracious reader. He had one other talent as well: he played the violin, and was an accomplished classical musician, although mostly self-taught. In his teenage years in Boston he was part of a string quartet that played small performances (they didn't call them "gigs" in those days) for smaller pay, but it was a supplement at a time when everyone in the immigrant community was poor.

By the time World War II ended, Michael was firmly entrenched as a Stetson foreman. He did not take the job lightly. However, at a time when unions in these factories were still relatively weak, a worker was lucky to have a foreman who bothered to care about the workers; it was rare to find someone who took interest in the lives of their reports. Michael was one of those exceptional people who knew everyone on the line, something about their lives and families, and took the time to express that interest so that the workers on the line became very loyal to "Mikey" over the years.

The majority of the workers being of Italian descent, it was not uncommon to find Jewish managers in such foreman positions at that time. Both groups immigrated to the U.S. during the same time period. So there was a sort of simpatico between the groups. This helped Michael despite his being from a different background.

One such Italian family from Quincy, Rossilini, had several second generation immigrants working on Michael's line at Stetson. At least two of the brothers and two of the sisters from the family worked full time for Mikey. This went on for many years and the friendship between Greene and the Rossilinis blossomed.

Michael always felt his Jewish heritage, although he was not religious himself. In fact, he worked hard to lose any European accent. He wanted full assimilation into mainstream America, as he wanted it for his only child, Sheldon. Less interested in assimilation was his wife, Rachel, whom he married when he was very young. The couple settled down in Mattapan, a section of the southernmost end of Boston proper, south of "Southie," beyond Savin Hill and Roxbury and Dorchester, the part of Boston that tourists do not know about. In the 1940s and 50s, Mattapan was the hub of Jewish-American culture in Boston. The main boulevards that bordered Mattapan were Blue Hill Avenue and Morton Street. The local synagogue could be found near that intersection, as was the G & G, the local kosher deli, a favorite hangout for the young people in the neighborhood. Morton Street in those days was lined with the shingles of aspiring doctors, dentists and lawyers, who served the community there. On Blue Hill Avenue was the famous Simka's Hot Dogs, the foot longs that competed in size and taste to what New Yorkers experienced at Nathan's of Coney Island. There was the locally famous Oriental movie theatre, with wonderful ornamentation in the viewing hall that became a popular Saturday night date for young Jews in the neighborhood. Also on Blue Hill Avenue were small shops, including the barber shop where Michael got his hair cut. His barber happened to be the father of the soon-to-be-famous actor Leonard Nimoy, of Star Trek fame. The Nimoys also resided in Mattapan.

By the 1960s, Mattapan began to change, and rapidly. The Jews began moving out. Having made what money and careers they were able, they headed for suburbs, like Sharon, Stoughton, Canton, and other south shore communities about 10 miles south of Mattapan and just beyond Braintree. Others went west, toward Newton, Natick and Framingham. All of these communities today still have large pockets of descendants of Jewish immigrants, today third and fourth generation. The people who then moved into Mattapan were predominantly Black. This was near the place where Martin Luther King, Jr. went to Seminary school. This was near where the Rev. Louis Farrakhan, known then as Louis Walcott, grew up as an immigrant from the Carribean.

But Michael did not want to move. He had become comfortable in his top floor railroad flat in one of those omnipresent triple-decker clapboard buildings that were the most common form of apartment building in Mattapan. By 1966, when Michael finally retired from Stetson, he was the only white person left on his block. Rachel had died from cancer several years before, so Mikey was alone. Sheldon had moved and settled in New York by this time. But Michael still loved his neighborhood and never wanted to leave. The grandchildren came to visit when they could, and Michael came to New York when he could. He'd say to Andy, "When are you going to come down to Boston to visit." Andy didn't have the heart to say that on a map, he'd be going "up" to Boston from New York.

Andy did make several visits up to Boston on his own, by bus, as he considered his grandfather to be his favorite relative. They were very close, and Grandpa-Mikey instilled and reinforced in the young Andy his love of Boston. They would take long walks from the T station (MBTA, or subway) at Park Street and go across the Boston Common to the swan boats in the Public Garden, then onto the shoe store on Mass Avenue that Michael's brother, Malcolm, owned and operated (Boylston Shoe). Sometimes they would go into Roxbury, to visit his other brother Daniel, who owned Greene's Hardware, on the north end of Blue Hill Avenue, beyond Franklin Field.

Michael had no issues with his new neighbors who swiftly took the place of the Jewish immigrants on his block. But then came April 4, 1968, and the murder of Dr. King in Memphis, and all bets were off. That night, riots broke out all over Mattapan, Roxbury, and Dorchester. The pandemonium all over the City was so loud, that it almost ended a Rolling Stones concert going on in Boston Garden. Michael drove home from visiting his friends, the Rossilinis, in Quincy. He had a parking space in a covered garage, but in that neighborhood, the garages were separate from the apartment buildings and Michael had a two-block walk to his apartment from where he parked his car. He was attacked on his way from car to house by three youths, shouting "Get Whitey! Get Whitey!!" Michael was knocked nearly unconscious. After the youths left, Michael managed to sit up, then stand up, bleeding from the head, his wallet gone, but his car keys still in his pocket. As the riots continued, Michael, in a semi-conscious stupor that he said later he could not remember, managed to go back to his car, rather than home, and drove back to the Rossilini home in Quincy, where he assumed he would be safe.

That was the last time Michael saw his neighborhood in Mattapan. The next day, Shel and Andy both drove up from New York to arrange for a place for Michael to live. That had already been arranged by the Rossilini brothers, who knew some of the local bureaucrats in Quincy and pulled some strings to get the retired Michael Greene moved to the top of a list for subsidized senior housing about a mile away from the Rossilini home. Shel then arranged for the movers to come into Mattapan and within days Michael was settled in a new apartment, up on the 10th floor of a recently opened high rise building off of Hancock Street in the middle of Quincy.

Rossilini had taken their former boss in and cared for him until he was settled. It was never a question; it was what needed to be done.

Shel found out later that during the riots Boylston Shoe had been vandalized and Greene's Hardware had been burned to the ground. Malcolm eventually put the store back in shape and reopened. But it was not to be for the hardware store; Daniel decided at that point to retire.

The loyalty that the Rossilini family felt for Michael, and the entire Greene family for that matter, was not only unusual in those days between boss and underlings, it was a salute to the kindness that Michael showed to the family through the years they worked for him. Michael, alone and injured in the middle of a riot, could in his semi-consciousness only think of one place to go, and that is where he went, and it perhaps saved his life. A good deed returned.

Michael would go on to marry one of the Rossilini sisters and she cared for him in his last years as if a mother-to-child, until Michael died in 1994.

Chapter 4: Innocence of the Early Years

Andy hit the ground running when he entered his new job at AMLIC, at least from a training point of view. On his first day on the job, after the usual HR introductions about procedures and benefits choices, he was given a small cubicle in the middle of the marketing area, on the third floor of the building just a stone's throw from Capitol Hill. In the cubicle, Andy received his first office computer, an IBM PC-XT, with all of 10mb of hard disk storage accompanied by two 5 ¼" floppy disk drives (today they no longer exist, but were for a time known the "B" drive on a computer, which is why you don't hear of B drives today). This computer put him on a par with what Sallie had in her law office, and he was impressed as he remembered she had spent nearly $10,000 on that computer when she bought it earlier that year.

On the second day on the job, Andy was put into a field training seminar that was being held at National Headquarters (a/k/a Home Office). This was a meeting for top sales people, to learn of the newest wave of life insurance products that the company was offering.

The trainer at the front of the room was a huge man, all of 6' 6" and a voice to match. He was affectionately called "Boomer," but his formal name was John Parker. Andy had walked into the middle of his presentation.

"It's important to understand the revolution going on in these products. Today, we live in an environment where people can buy CDs with 15% interest rates on them, money market funds with similar interest. You can't offer conventional whole life insurance to your clients anymore, with 4% guarantees on them. These new products we've put out there this year will make it possible for you to offer competitive rates of accumulation in the cash value with these other cash equivalent investments."

"Investments"? Andy thought to himself. The only thing Andy knew about life insurance coming in is that there was whole life and term. Whole life was more expensive, and had a savings element to it that you could borrow on, called "cash value." Term was much less expensive, but it had no cash value accumulation element in it.

"We're talking about Flexible Premium Adjustable Life (FPAL), affectionately known in the marketplace as 'Universal Life.' We've been offering these products for a year now. We were the first mutual company to come out with them. And they have become the hottest thing in the marketplace. While some of you have started selling these products to your clients, some are still hesitating."

Boomer went on to explain that Universal Life (UL) "allows the client to pay anything he wants, or nothing at all, as premium. So long as there is enough money in the cash value to pay the next month's cost of insurance and other charges, the company goes in and deducts that from the cash value and the policy continues."

"Sounds like a loaded gun to me," shouted one agent in the audience, sitting right next to Andy.

"It can be, "answered Boomer, "unless you are counseling the client on a regular basis. The key is to fund the policy early on with plenty of premium, use the compounding interest at high rates to do its job, and soon the interest earned on the premium may be enough to carry the policy's charges indefinitely."

"Yes. Except we have to force the client to start funding the policy heavily in the first few years. He won't want to do that."

"There is no free lunch," Boomer explained. "You can pay me now or pay me later." Andy would come to learn in time that trite expressions and clichés were a hallmark of marketing life insurance.

"Here's an example." And Boomer put a transparent piece of plastic on top of the base of an overhead projector to show the numbers on the plastic to the whole room. "You see here how this client, a male, age 45, non-smoker, buys a $100,000 UL policy and puts $2,000 dollars annually into it. That's more than twice what our annual renewable term would cost him in year 1." Taking a pencil to mark where he wanted the audience to pay attention, he continued. "The cash value in this policy in year 10 is now more than $20,000, more than the sum total of all the premiums he has paid. The interest he is earning is causing the cash value to increase faster than the charges against the policy. If we stop paying premiums in year 11, look at what happens! The policy continues to grow and by the time he's 95, if still alive" (some chuckles from the audience) "he will have more than the death benefit in the cash value."

"This isn't insurance anymore," commented another agent in the audience, sitting to Andy's left and one row ahead. "It's an investment."

"Precisely!" Boomer boomed, "and with a self-completing feature if he doesn't live that long. The death benefit is paid to his family income tax free. And the cash value is tax sheltered."

Here, Andy perked up, because Boomer was now talking tax law. "Under IRS rules, he gets to pull money out as the return of his basis (premiums) first – call it FIFO – and those withdrawals are not taxable. You don't have to take policy loans on that money."

Now Boomer had to put his compliance hat on. "Of course, although we're paying 14% interest on the cash value, compounded monthly, we do not advise illustrating the policy just at the current rate. We don't know how long these rates will last; they're historically high. So, we advise illustrating the policy at an 'assumed' rate of 8% or 9%. You can see that with our software, you can show current, assumed, and guaranteed columns for this product."

The agent sitting next to Andy piped up. "And it's that guaranteed column that bugs me. What are the guarantees on this product?"

"4% and 1980-CSO mortality assumptions. But we've never experienced either of those. Even our old whole life products managed to pay a dividend every year, even during the Depression, because we always earned more than the minimum interest and our mortality was always better than the standard tables."

Believing he's answered the agent's question, Boomer continued. "Now there is a new law coming into force beginning next year. It's called TEFRA, (Tax Equity and Fiscal Responsibility Act) – doesn't the Government love acronyms?" [Some laughter] "What it does – for the first time – is create in the tax code a limit on the amount of premium you can pour into these policies, a limit on the amount of cash you can accumulate at a given death benefit and still call it life insurance, with all its tax benefits. The software had built into it these limitations so you won't have to worry about exceeding them. Use the current software until the end of this year. Tell your clients to get in on this great opportunity now, before the new law takes effect. The new software will take over in 1983."

Boomer was also a lawyer, although he specialized in pension law. He was covering for Andy's predecessor, Dick Samuelson, also known as "Snake," who had left the advanced underwriting area of marketing for the legal department, seen by lawyers as a more prestigious position. Boomer was also giving Andy some time to get up to speed in his new position before he – not Boomer – would be doing these kinds of presentations.

The Advanced Underwriting Unit in marketing at AMLIC would now simply be Andy and Andy's boss – Jerry Ciccolo. Jerry came to AMLIC from a small company in Connecticut, and was also a lawyer. But, like Andy, he preferred marketing over law practice, and would teach Andy several practical techniques in handling calls from the field. Jerry in turn reported to the head of the Marketing Services Department, Tim Pershing, who also headed up the pension area and Boomer as well. Tim in turn reported to George Forson, the CMO. George in turn reported to the Chief Operating Officer of the company, one Elliott Kelleher. And the buck went from there up to the Chairman and CEO, Wayne Madison. While George was from Florida originally, and Elliott from Wisconsin, Wayne was a transplanted Texan. Nevertheless, all settled in Northern Virginia, mainly in communities such as Vienna, Great Falls, and Burke, all affluent and upscale reasons why Fairfax County, Virginia had become known as the first or second richest county *per capita* in America, depending upon when you were measuring wealth.

As the meeting ended, Andy got to talk with the agent sitting next to him, his first acquaintance with anyone from the field. "Art Presser, from Philadelphia," the agent introduced himself, "I hear you're the new meat – I mean, guy – in advanced marketing." And he moved toward Andy to shake his hand.

"Andy Greene," Andy recited as he met Art's hand.

"You're a Landsman?"

"How do you know that?" Andy inquired.

"I can usually figure out another Jew inside of a minute."

"Is it in the handshake? Is it in my name? Is it my New York accent?" The last of which Andy had worked hard to lose due to his on-air days in college radio.

"No. It's in the look and in the facial features."

"Oh, you're not going to tell me it's the size of my nose, are you?" Andy was only half- joking, but let out a weak chuckle which would be equivalent to a "lol" on a text message today.

"No. And no offense. It's just we need to band together as best we can in the face of all these Southerners in this company."

Andy, not wanting Art to learn of his Southern Presbyterian wife, tried changing the subject. "What did you think of the presentation? Do you sell UL now?"

"I do, sometimes. I'm a little shy about it because I see some dangers down the road for this product if we're not careful. But the clients want it and the saying goes, 'the customer is NOT always right, but the customer is still the customer.'"

With that Andy looked behind Art to the picture on the wall showing Art as the 1982 Agent-of-the-Year at Atlantic Mutual. Art Presser was a veteran in the business, already 50 years of age. He was shorter than Andy, no more than 5' 9" but nevertheless dressed in his daily sales clothes – starched white shirt, bow tie, braces buttoned into his dress slacks to hold them up, and cordovan wing tip shoes, Bostonians, Andy surmised. Art noticed Andy looking behind him and turned.

"Yeah, that's me, but it really doesn't mean much. It doesn't put any extra money in my pocket. It's just that they now have to listen to me at these meetings. They don't have to agree with me, or do anything I suggest. But it's nice that they have to listen to me now."

Sometimes first impressions are not only of an individual, but of an entire group of people, or of an entire occupation. Art and Andy began to strike up a friendship and alliance that would last through most of their days in the business, and this meeting made a positive impression on Andy about the personality of a successful life insurance agent and businessman – not plaid suited and shifty, but a *mensch*; like Andy's father; like Andy's grandfather.

Because of that, Andy began to notice that many of the executives and sales people in the company were similarly dressed as Art Presser. So, Andy began to follow suit – he gave up the three piece that lawyers wear (too stodgy) – he began wearing the cordovan wing tip shoes and using braces instead of belts for his pants. The suit jacket was usually double vented – cooler-looking that way – and he took on wearing bow ties some of the time. In fact, the bow tie would become Andy's signature whenever he made presentations to the field sales force.

As October became November and November became December, Andy began taking consultation calls from the field. The first thing Jerry Ciccolo taught him was "don't pretend to know the answer if you are not sure you know. Tell them you'll need to research the issue and get back to them. Then, make sure you give them a day and time when you'll get back to them that is longer than you think you'll need and make them happy when you get back to them earlier than that."

"Yes," Andy concurred, "similar to what we used to do at this firm I worked at in Charlottesville."

"It's O.K. to say you don't know offhand. The agent wants you to give them accurate information in a time frame that is prompt, but it doesn't have to be immediate. And, by the way, most of the field has been told about you coming on board and know that you're new, so their expectation about being quick with the answer is not that high. Keeping a helpful and friendly tone is more important at this stage."

"I need time to learn the ropes, so each case will be a learning experience for me."

"Yeah, but you'll find that issues repeat themselves over and over. I guess it won't be long before you're able to have the answer in your head to a lot of what comes up."

This was easy work for Andy. It was like ALG without having to write briefs!

Tim Pershing, Jerry's boss, had enrolled Andy in master's level courses at The American College, intended to eventually earn Andy a Master of Science in Financial Services (MSFS). At the same time, Andy matriculated into the school's more basic program for their Certified Life Underwriter (CLU) and Chartered Financial Consultant (ChFC) designations. In addition, Andy was taking classes again at George Washington University for his MBA, majoring in human resources management; then simply called "personnel management."

How could he do all this? Jerry and Tim had an agreement with Andy that when work was slow, Andy could study material from these courses on work time. After all, it was part of Andy's training that he learn this and it was for the company's benefit that he earn these degrees and designations. All costs for these courses, even the MBA, were paid through a budget Tim had control over. All but the MBA courses were self-study; schedule to take the exam when you're ready. Andy would try and line up similar courses to take at the same time. For example, he'd worked out that he needed to take macroeconomics at GW; he'd also sign up for the economics course in the CLU program at the same time. He was studying for two courses in one sitting. The ChFC designation only required three different courses from the CLU, so there was lots of overlap there.

Nevertheless, it was rigorous and time consuming. This was a first strain upon Andy and Sallie at home. But since Sallie was working long hours in her law practice, it wasn't a major issue for now. By the middle of 1985, Andy had earned the CLU and ChFC designations, an MSFS degree, the MBA, and had become a "certificant" Certified Financial Planner (CFP) to boot.

In December 1982, Tim decided the Department needed some more depth in sales skills training, rather than in product training, for the sales force. So, he hired a master's in psychology from Georgetown, Vivian Yellin, into the Department. Vivian had no background in life insurance or in financial services. Her job was to transcend that straitjacket and teach the field, and the marketing home office people for that matter, better human sensitivity skills in order to be more effective in sales and marketing. Tim was very high on Vivian. The rest of the Department was far less so. Vivian turned out to be somewhat preachy in approach and did not spend the time using the very skills she was trying to teach others to use in her transactions with the Department, or the field.

Vivian was a big woman, at 5' 10" or more, and maybe close to 200 lbs. Although still young (30ish) and single, she was nothing to look at, which in the 1980s and a male dominated department could mean a problem. In fact, one of Tim's goals in hiring Vivian was to break up the "old boys club" in the Department. Tim was trying desperately to change the culture; instead, what developed was an intra-department war.

One of Vivian's tasks was to teach the Department how to de-genderize their writing and oral presentations; use his/her instead of assuming everyone is male, that sort of thing. Another associated task was that Vivian was given the editor's role over all written material going out of the Department to the field, including an advanced sales manual called FPC (Financial Planning Concepts) that was Andy's job to write, from scratch. This meant Vivian would in a way be Andy's boss on this project.

If the editing were limited to a second opinion on English language grammar, usage, tense, number, and the like, it was no problem for

Andy. When Vivian began to question the content itself, this became an issue. Jerry was supposed to supervise the content of what was being written. He resented what he saw as an intrusion into his territory and the supervision of his people by an outsider – someone who knew nothing of the business or of tax law. Andy tended to agree with his mentor and boss, Jerry, but was also confused about who was really driving this project.

The first chapter Andy composed for the FPC Manual would be one of the most complex concepts in all of advanced underwriting: Split-Dollar. The concept of Split-Dollar is the shared funding between employer and employee of a life insurance policy insuring the employee and mostly payable to the employee's family. There are as many variations to this concept as there are cases in which this concept is used. But Andy spent a considerable amount of time mastering the fundamentals of the concept and had written a fairly exhaustive chapter on this technique. As Split-Dollar was one of the more glamorous and highly profitable techniques to sell lots of life insurance in business situations, everyone seemed to want some ownership over every word in that chapter, including Jerry, Tim, and Vivian. And this is where the split in the Department began. Tim was defensive in wanting to protect the wisdom of his most recent hiring decision, and he began to distance himself from Jerry, and by proxy from Andy. Boomer and others in the Department also eventually lined up against Vivian and Tim. The two of them circled the wagons around themselves. They felt estranged from the rest of the staff. Tim felt outnumbered, and in January decided to even the score a bit. He went out and hired a second advanced underwriting attorney, this one with an LLM in tax law – but with no insurance industry experience. Sue Belcher was all of 27, just out of law school in St. Louis, and recently married to a civilian manager in the Pentagon, ex-military. Sue was short, sort of mousey looking, drab dressed. Some of "the guys" in locker room talk in the men's room would speculate as to a lesbian relationship between Vivian and Sue

– they became fast friends, inspired by Tim. As for the rumors about Tim, they included hideous references to threesomes with the two female hires.

To be sure, whether true or not, none of this was appropriate, and by today's standards would surely be considered harassment in the workplace. In early 1983, it was what it was. Andy cared little about the alleged sexual shenanigans of the lot of them. In Andy's mind, he wanted complete control over his own work. Jerry had only occasionally suggested changes to Andy's writing, and Andy could respect that; besides being Andy's boss, he was more learned in these complex tax planning concepts. Beyond that, Andy wanted no interference from people who did not understand the content itself.

But now Sue was put in charge of policing Andy's content. She was, after all, a master's in tax law – that's what an LLM is, after all. But concepts like Split-Dollar escaped the curriculum in law school. When Andy had to explain to Sue what the concept was all about, he became resentful of having to train the person who would be editing his work. For her part, Sue took an instant dislike to Andy, who talked more like a sales person than a lawyer. Sue's image of Andy was also tainted by Tim, who drew lines of allegiance around himself and his two loyal female employees, to the almost total exclusion of the rest of the Department.

As January became February, and February became March, little progress had been made on this first chapter of FPC (ultimately, it would have 16 chapters to it). In early April, George Forson started asking questions about the progress of the Manual.

"We're getting there, George," was Tim's report.

"I could use a little more detail than that, Tim."

"Well, we're getting some resistance from the writer. He is not taking well to the editing from our new attorney in the department."

"Who's the writer?" George asked.

"Andy Greene. He's not acting professionally. He's acting more like an agent than an attorney and his writing needs some seasoning."

"Seasoning??? This former law book editor needs seasoning? Tell me more, Tim."

"Andy is simply not coachable. He won't take to advice and counsel from me, Vivian, or Sue."

"Let me ask you something, Tim: How does Andy get along with the rest of the Department?" George was surmising the problem, based on Tim putting himself, Vivian and Sue in the same boat. George didn't know much about Sue, she was new. But he had heard complaints about Vivian, and he did not like what he'd heard.

"I guess he does reasonably well."

"How does the field think of him?"

"I'm not sure I have any data on that, George."

"Well, why don't you get some data then, Tim. That is what we really want to know. I can tell you Timmy, my boy, that I have heard a few nasty comments about Vivian's rapport with the field, and with your Department. It's not good."

Tim got defensive, but didn't dare show it to his boss. "I think some in the Department are 'poisoning the well' for Viv. I think she needs a clean slate."

"That may be, but the field seems to have made up its mind about *Viv*, as you call her. What we want now is for this not to be the same road that your new attorney hire goes down." A pause, and then an idea. "Do we have a training seminar coming up here for field people?"

"I think so," Tim spoke meekly. "We have a mini-one-day seminar on executive bonus plans for agents working in the small business market coming up next week."

"Put your Sue on the schedule to make a 30-minute presentation. Also put Andy on the program as well. Give Sue a topic to speak on that she is comfortable with and will be interesting for the audience; same with Andy. I want to sit in and see them in action. Then I want to hear what the field in the room thinks."

So, just after Tax Day (April 15), the meeting was held, expanded to go beyond Executive Bonus Plans. After a brief introduction by Jerry, Sue got up to present. She had no visuals. She just spoke... About the pitfalls of filling in false information on an IRS Form 706, the estate tax return - lot's of numbers; lots of concept; hard for the audience to follow all the detail without even a handout. For sure, Sue knew her stuff. What she didn't know was communication skills. What she also failed to realize was the attention span of her audience.

Andy got up. This was the first time he would present to a field audience. Jerry did not know if he was ready.

"Here's the deal folks: Executive Bonus is the simplest advanced sales technique you can use in business planning. It's so simple I'm not sure I can even call it an advanced sales technique." A few in the audience chuckled; most had known something of the concept, but rarely used it.

Andy continued…

"You already know that this is just having the employer bonus the premium dollars for a life insurance policy owned by the employee. Then the employer includes that money in the employee's W-2 at the end of the year. I'll bet you already know that, right?" And a few of the 21 men in the room nodded. "Then why do you not use this simple technique more often?"

"The employer's accountant says it's too costly," came from one in the audience.

"What do you think he means, 'too costly'?"

Another agent jumped in, "Well some of our clients own Sub-S corporations and the corporation doesn't pay taxes."

"Very good," Andy complimented. "Then you don't use it there. But with your C corporations, they pay taxes. In fact, the reason why the client has a C corp is often because it makes a lot of money and the owners don't want that on their personal income tax returns. The problem?"

"How do they get the money out of their corporation? It's trapped," said a third member of the audience.

"How they get it out is to take bonuses, such as this Plan. Yes, they'll pay taxes on that money, but at a lower tax bracket than the corporation would pay."

"Sure. But then the client complains, 'but I don't want the tax added to me, personally.'"

"So," Andy knew where he was going with this long before the last comment from the audience, "We *gross up* the bonus to cover the tax. Not gross-out, ***gross up***." And the audience broke out in laughter at the gross-out comment. "This means we simply add to the premium an extra amount to cover the tax on the bonus.

"Now, if you're from Schlockmeister Mutual, you'll think, O.K., so we'll figure the tax on the premium bonus and that will be the extra bonus, right?"

"No," came the answer from several in the room.

"Right, because there's also a tax on the extra bonus, too. But only because you are here at an Atlantic meeting will you go home with a competitive advantage over Schlockmeister… You bonus an amount that covers all of the taxes, premium and extra. The formula for that," and up came an overhead slide, "is **$B = P/1\text{-}t$**, where B is the total bonus, P is the premium, and t is the employee's marginal tax bracket. Now, repeat after me: '$B=P/1\text{-}t$;'"

And they all repeated, some halfhearted, "$B=P/1\text{-}t$."

"Say it again…"

"$B=P/1\text{-}t$…"more loudly.

"Again, louder…"

And they repeated as directed, "$B=P/1\text{-}t$!"

"One more time…"

Even louder and with more enthusiasm, "**$B=P/1\text{-}t$!!**"

"That's right, where B is the total bonus, P is the premium on the policy, and t is the client's marginal tax bracket. Thank you for your time."

And with that, Andy walked back from the front of the room, leaving his one slide on the projector, and was roundly applauded by all in the room, even George, sitting in the back with a cat-that-ate-the-canary smile on his round face.

After that, Andy began getting requests to travel into the field and be a speaker on various advanced underwriting topics in agency meetings. Eventually, these grew into all-day affairs, with a sales meeting in the morning, a lunch to handle questions, and in the afternoon a "doctor is in" session in an agency conference room in which agents would bring their live cases in and have a one-on-one consultation with Andy. In this way, Andy got the opportunity to have a direct impact on sales, much to the joy of George, much to the dismay of Tim.

Tim would be bounced out of marketing, and got temporary salvation in a staff position in the legal department, following "Snake" Samuelson up to the 6th floor. Samuelson had reported to Tim when he was in the Marketing Services Department; now it was his turn to return the favor by putting Tim up for an open position in Legal. Ironically, he was given the task of overseeing the accuracy of the content of advanced sales training materials, such as the FPC Manual, and so the material continued to be caught in a territorial battle. Marketing had the subject matter expertise over the material, but Legal had the job of making sure the material was accurate and did not generate lawsuits or compliance infractions.

The last time Andy talked to Tim, it was to bring the Split-Dollar material up there one more time to get approval. A shouting match ensued between Andy and Tim, during which Tim ended with, "If you want to fight it out with me, asshole, I'll be waiting for you."

Andy did not respond. He didn't need to. Snake heard him and Tim was fired two weeks later. Well, OK, not fired *per se*. He was a victim of a "Reduction in Force," or RIF, as the Federal Government calls it in Washington. His position on the organizational chart was simply eliminated, making it unnecessary to fire Tim for cause. This was the typical way a company got rid of an employee it didn't want but did not want to generate a wrongful termination lawsuit.

Vivian was soon forced out after Tim left the Department. She wasn't fired, but she saw the handwriting on the wall and left for another job in another town by the end of April.

Sue stayed on, but while an LLM may trump a JD in law practice, it didn't work that way in marketing, and Andy was given free reign to write without her interference.

Jerry didn't do so well. George fired him in May, saying to Andy after the firing, "Jerry's contribution to this organization was" and he held up his hand with his thumb meeting his index finger to make a zero. Why Jerry "got the sack" and Tim a RIF was never revealed to Andy or anyone else in the Department.

By June of that year, Andy was essentially leaderless. But in July, a new head of the Marketing Services Department entered the arena. Francis Xavier Meaney. Frank, or FX, as he became known over time, was an ex-Marine, retired, with at least a dozen years experience in life insurance marketing and sales. His most recent position was with Commonwealth Mutual, based in Center City Philadelphia, in charge of training, sales support, and advanced underwriting. Commonwealth was a smaller company than Atlantic and it had its own purge via RIF. Timing is everything in the corporate world, and the RIF came just as the opening at Atlantic was posted in the trade press and with an executive search firm, known as DAZ International, which Atlantic used on a contingent – not retainer – basis.

FX was a very down-to-earth, no nonsense manager. With a challenge in the patience department, being a former USMC officer, FX nonetheless had mastered the art of human relations and it showed in his ability to lead more than manage, the difference being his ability to get his reports to do what needed to be done without being ordered to do so. Frank understood the limitations of "authority," the paper job description that outlines who you can coerce and what your "territory" of responsibility is. True power, FX would eventually teach the young Andy Greene, is the ability to get done what needs to be done from other people without having to coerce them. Andy would not only learn this lesson, but analogize it to his own experience of leading groups of people – even Company A – by strength of persuasion, charisma, or whatever – when little or no authority had been given him.

Often when someone loses the boss that hired him/her, there is always a problem with the allegiance of that employee to the new boss. It is why many incoming executives like to purge the old staff and bring in their own people. FX faced a situation where that was not going to be possible, and he knew it. But with time, he got both the opportunity to hire into his team and win the respect and admiration of the existing staff, especially Andy.

But the relationship started immediately with a disappointment for Andy. Everyone knew that the Advanced Underwriting Unit would need a leader. That leader would either be Andy, based on marketing knowledge and relations with the field; Sue, because of higher legal credentials at that point; or by bringing in someone from the outside. Andy felt he should be the leader of the Unit, a chance to lead and move up. Sue felt she should be tapped because of her master's degree. FX would want to hire his own Unit leader from the outside, but George dismissed that request, wanting Frank to promote from within, to bolster Department morale by proving that advancement within the company was, in fact, possible.

But George would not put his own opinion of Andy and Sue out there for Frank or anyone else's viewing. He wanted to see what Frank would do on his own, as a test of his executive perceptiveness.

So, FX had bad news for Andy: There would be no leader of the Unit for now. Sue and Andy would work side-by-side, and have to cooperate with each other to get Unit goals accomplished.

Andy was flabbergasted… "How would the boss know who was getting what done; who was making the best contribution?"

"Oh, I'll know, trust me," was Frank's reply each time the subject came up.

In compensation, FX implemented a change in the name of the Unit and in the position title for Andy and Sue. They would each now be called "Marketing Counsel," and the Unit would be known as the Marketing Counsel Unit. This at first irked the legal department, including the General Counsel, Charlie Slavin, who had a pre-disposed dislike for advanced underwriting and its placement in marketing instead of in the legal department. And he was not alone in that thinking. Slavin assumed that any lawyer worth his salt who was stationed in the marketing department of an insurance company would much rather be placed in the legal department, where they would work as if in a law firm, with other attorneys, doing corporate law. And from a control perspective, Slavin believed that anything involving the slightest in legal advice and counsel, even if not given to customers but only to agents, should report to the legal department.

Slavin's recent scorecard on this attitude was one-for-two. Snake Samuelson had worked out well as a move from advanced underwriting to legal. Snake had excelled in corporate law, partly due to his own good personal relationship skills in working with the other departments in the company. But Tim Pershing's move from marketing to legal did not work out so well, and precisely because of the attempted use of position power to coerce a result resisted by marketing, the writing of the FPC Manual. Since the time of Tim's departure, the speed at which Andy turned out written material for the Manual sped up exponentially. Although the material was still subject to a second set of eyes in Legal, the "editor" now would be Snake himself, a veteran of advanced underwriting. But Snake's attitude on content was to give Andy the room to move, so long as what was printed was not inaccurate. Snake put the burden on himself to prove if something in the Manual was inaccurate; before, the burden was on Andy to prove that what was printed was accurate. By the end of 1983, the FPC Manual had been approved for printing and distribution to the field agencies as the quintessential text on tax, estate, and business planning, many chapters using life insurance as the funding vehicle.

Because of the starkly improved workflow and cooperation between legal and marketing in the post-Pershing era, Slavin was somewhat stifled in his insistence on control over the advanced underwriting process. Frank had used this very *Marketing Counsel* position title for his advanced underwriters at Commonwealth Mutual, and so there was at least some precedence for this enhanced title. George bought into the idea because it did raise the professional image of the Unit, needed after the intra-department civil war that had gone on the year before.

So, while Slavin opposed the name change to Marketing Counsel, because it implied that people in marketing were "counseling" on tax matters (thereby suggesting the 'unauthorized' practice of law), a deal was struck in negotiations between FX and Slavin, refereed by George Forson, that while legal had the authority to ask this Unit for consultation and periodic reporting to it in order to assure that the unauthorized practice of law was not involved in marketing, it would acquiesce to the new position and Unit title, Marketing Counsel. A number of new protocols were established and agreed to by marketing in order to make sure the Unit was not acting as legal counsel:

- The position title Marketing Counsel would be reserved for those in the Unit who actually were lawyers; non-lawyer advanced underwriting consultants, if any, would not be afforded that title.

- Any written materials, letters or otherwise, and any conversations about so-called live cases, had to couched as hypothetical. So, if an opinion letter were written by a member of the Unit, the advice would not be directed specifically at the live case at hand, but termed as if the consultant were being asked generally about a tax planning principle.
- Any written communications, even the FPC Manual, had to have a disclaimer that the material was not dispensing legal advice; that "any legal or tax advice particular to a client's situation should result from consulting a competent and qualified attorney of the client's selection."
- Sales literature intended for distribution to clients or their advisors were to go through a higher level of scrutiny by the legal department prior to distribution. Training materials, for *internal use only* in training agents, would not be so scrutinized, but had to have a disclaimer on the material – such as the FPC Manual – "for internal use only."

None of this was objectionable to FX or anyone else in the Department. It was precursor to the kind of regulation that self-regulating organizations (SROs), such as the NASD (National Association of Securities Dealers) or SEC (Securities and Exchange Commission) would impose in future years on anything related to the sale of securities products.

Andy wasn't totally satisfied, but went along, as the new job title was an enhancement in professional image over the former "Advanced Underwriting Consultant," and so long as his work was overseen by Snake Samuelson, he was confident that he would be accorded the proper professional deference of someone who knew what he was talking about. And so Andy and Sue became "Marketing Counsel." Eventually a third "Counselor" was added to the Unit, Carol Blum. She was mainly a pension expert, but AMLIC was slowly going out of the pension business and concentrating more on non-qualified executive compensation plans, where life insurance was more prevalent as a funding vehicle. Boomer Parker left for a field position in the local agency in Northern Virginia by the end of 1984, and pensions, such as it was, were consolidated into the work of the Marketing Counsel Unit.

Frank Meaney's Marketing Services Department was fashioned into five distinct units:

- **Field Training** – both sales skills training (as AMLIC was at that time a career company that took new people into the business and trained them to sell) and product training. Andy would come to use the term "Big T" training for sales skills training and "Little T" training for product training. Boomer headed this for a time in transition between the end of the pension unit and his move into the field.
- **Marketing Counsel** – the former Advanced Underwriting Unit.
- **Sales Support** – the use of the product illustration system, specifically, and how to design product solutions using that computer-based system. This Unit would eventually be headed by one of FX's new hires, Tony Quarles, or just "Q," as he was known (like the tech guy with all the MI6 gadgets used by 007 in the James Bond films).
- **Product Development** – a discipline in which a marketing person, often FX himself, and a pricing actuary reporting to Chief Actuary Janeesh Rau, would get in a room and hash out the specs of any new product – the marketing guy worried about the top line (sales) and the actuary worried about the bottom line (margin and profit).
- **Marketing Communications** – all of the collateral sales literature and regularly scheduled communications with the field. This was not the same as the Corporate

Communications Department, which sat in the Executive area and performed the public relations function for the company. The Unit had a parade of leaders, ending up with some stability when a staffer, Marie Frame, took the leadership position in early 1985.

Marketing Operations, run by Howard Crowe, was where the flow of commissions and other payments to the field agencies and agents were handled, and was separate. The same for the distribution channel itself, a career agency, managerial system in which the company retained profit-and-loss responsibility over a series of owned-and-operated agencies (20 of them at its peak in the mid-80s), the agency managers reporting to one of four "regional vice presidents" who in turn reported to George Forson.

As 1983 opened, Atlantic Mutual was simply a carrier of life insurance, annuity, and retirement plan products, designed primarily to serve the Civil Service and military markets that traditionally dominated the Washington, D.C. area. But as the industrial and labor pools in D.C. began to change in the early 1980s, so too did AMLIC have to alter its own strategic positioning in the marketplace. No one was more aware of this strategic shift than CEO Wayne Madison and his COO Elliott Kelleher. While AMLIC was a nationwide insurer, its home base was also one of its largest sources of sales – D.C.

It was not just D.C. that was changing. By the mid-80s, most of the growth in employment opportunities came from small businesses, not large corporations. And financial advisors – including insurance agents – found going after the large corporate accounts was extremely competitive and with extremely long gestation periods to a sale. At the same time, affluent members of the Baby Boom generation – in their 30s and 40s by this time – were allergic to doing business with "life insurance agents." They sought a more broad-based portfolio of services and products from their advisors.

This led to a strategic shift in the approach of AMLIC. During 1983, the company acquired a mutual fund company, Chesapeake Investments, which specialized in socially-responsible investing. This meant that the funds in Chesapeake's product offerings screened investments for things like environmental friendliness and positive labor-management relations. It also screened out firms invested in apartheid South Africa and the tobacco industry. Many skeptics criticized Chesapeake as "tree-hugging softees" investing with their liberal hearts. "How can you get the highest returns on investments by creating a set of screens totally unrelated to financial performance?" would be the critical refrain.

To be sure, the AMLIC management team was not politically in line with this socially-responsible approach. But they wanted into the investments business and this was a firm that was available for sale, locally-based, and so the political angle was discounted. Good thing that it was… It turned out, in case after case, that socially-responsible investing eventually paid off in the long term; when apartheid fell in South Africa, those companies heavily invested in that regime lost out; when the tobacco industry was sued by state governments and class action plaintiffs for billions of dollars, being invested in tobacco didn't look very smart. By the same token, those firms that managed their labor relations well avoided unionization which would have raised the cost of production significantly higher, and those that did not pollute the atmosphere or water avoided some rather nasty sanctions by government regulation and court cases.

Chesapeake also owned an NASD-member broker-dealer which, after acquisition, would be renamed The Investment Group (TIG), offering a full service securities brokerage to individual and institutional clients. This would be AMLIC's entry into financial planning. TIG was, among other things, an SEC RIA (Registered

Investment Advisor), which allowed it to perform financial planning services, for fee and/or commission, for individual and business clients.

One more opportunity came in 1983 when a brief loophole in the scheme of regulating life insurance companies allowed AMLIC to charter and establish Atlantic Savings Bank, a one-branch commercial bank based in Northern Virginia, Annandale, to be specific.

The result: by the end of 1983, AMLIC was reorganized into a parent company for a group of brands under the banner of Atlantic Financial Group (AFG), a fully diversified financial services firm offering a wide range of products and planning services, targeting the so-called mass affluent population around the country (household incomes between $75,000 and $250,000), ages 35-55, many of whom were either middle to upper managers of their employers and/or owned small, closely-held businesses of their own.

And/or, because many in the target market "double-dipped," or moonlighted at more than one occupation. As an example, in the military market that AMLIC nested in for decades up to this point, many military personnel – especially officers – would be career military in the post-draft era that was the 1970s and 1980s. Career military had the benefit of a retirement on 50% of the last three years average salary for 20 years of service, 75% for 30 years of service. This ***20-gets-you-50; 30-gets-you-75*** strategy applied to countless thousands living in the Washington area. Some joined up at age 18. After 30 years of service, they retired at age 48 on 75% of pre-retirement pay. No one actually ***retired*** at age 48. They would take their valuable skills learned while on active duty – the military was becoming more a high-tech training ground and less a grunt-dominated infantry, artillery and armored core – and went into consulting. These retired military officers were often called "Beltway Bandits," after the ring road circling D.C., and consulted with their former employer as "defense contractors," for much more per hour than they ever got in uniform. Meanwhile, they collected their 75% pay. This was a pretty lucrative way to afford putting your children through college without loans, buying a second home, or building an additional nest egg for the "real" retirement that would come perhaps 15 years or so later. This assumed, of course, that you knew what to do with the extra money coming in; that's where the financial advisor came into play.

Likewise, the civil servant at the federal level, the GS11 trademark attorney for example: If he/she started right out of law school, at age 25, in the Patent Office, they built up a pension that credited 2% of final three years average salary for each year of service to the Government. By age 55, that civil servant was due 60% of pre-retirement pay; stay until 65 and it was 80% - a nice retirement.

Given that the civil service and military markets were the core of Atlantic's client base already, it was not a stretch to move into these markets as financial planners. A common retirement strategy used at that time was called **Pension Maximization**, in which an employee with a defined benefit pension plan for retirement would fund a life insurance policy outside of the pension that allowed the employee and spouse to take a full "life only" annuity settlement at retirement, avoiding the 10% - 20% reduction in monthly benefit for the assumed "life and 50% survivor" option. The death benefit, insuring the employee, would be an income-tax-free, lump sum payment to the spouse should the retired employee die, replacing the forfeited 50% survivor benefit. In the meantime, the couple lived on a higher payout from the plan for having taken the life-only option.

In 1984, the Retirement Equity Act made this a little more complicated as all pensions were required to pay out the life and 50% survivor option to protect the spouse, unless the spouse signed a "pension waiver" giving up the survivor option.

In 1987, this technique became even more difficult as the Civil Service Retirement System in the federal government froze the defined benefit pension plan and put new employees into a 401(k) style plan in which the retirement benefit would depend upon the accumulation of funds in the employee's account over time – a defined contribution plan where the benefit was not known until retirement.

By the 1990s almost all private sector employers had moved away from defined benefit pensions and toward 401(k) plans, reducing the attractiveness of this planning technique. But in the time frame of the repositioning of the Atlantic brand, these developments were not yet known.

In any event, the home office staff as well as the field sale people needed to get ready for this huge change in orientation. No longer were the sales people "agents;" they were now "account managers." Everyone wanting access to a myriad of investment products needed quickly to get licensed to market and sell securities. This required one or more NASD licenses, called Series. A Series 6 allowed one to sell mutual funds and variable insurance products. It was accompanied by a Series 63, the state sales exam so that sales in the individual states were possible. Those charging a fee for financial planning needed a Series 65. Those wanting to sell individual stocks and bonds, like a stockbroker, needed the dreaded Series 7 – Registered Representative. The Series 7 was the toughest of all the securities exams; a 6-hour paper-and-pencil exam given on the third Saturday of every month. For those managing, hiring, firing, and supervising the activities of these "Registered Reps," one needed to be a broker-dealer principal and pass the Series 24 exam. These licenses were all in addition to the typical state insurance license needed by agents.

In June of 1983, several of the staff in marketing, including Andy, took a week out of their working lives and sat for a five-day intensive training and preparation seminar for the Series 7 exam, to be given, of all places, on Andy's home turf – George Washington University. Of the 12 staffers who took the exam that Saturday in June, 6 passed; 6 failed and would have to take the exam again. Of the 6 who failed, all but one never took the exam again and opted instead for a simpler and easier Series 6 registration. Andy was one of the 6 who passed the exam. He could have opted for the easier Series 6 path. However, he wanted ALL of the qualifications he possibly could muster, and the Series 7 meant the broadest possible set of sales qualifications in the securities business.

Meanwhile, the company had developed a new variable universal life policy (VUL), a securities-based product in that the cash value could be invested into a menu of mutual fund-style accounts of the client's choosing, instead of relying on the company to invest the cash value into a general account and pay the client an interest rate that was net of a spread between the company's investment portfolio (mostly bonds) and the "rate-in-the-window" interest being credited to the policy. Selling VUL required at least a Series 6 license.

At the same time, in early 1984, the new AFG reached a strategic alliance with a firm in California, called Financial Profiles, a vendor of financial planning software that was sweeping the industry at that time. It was a template for offering financial planning services to clients, for a fee. With Financial Profiles (FP), the field began to be trained not only in how to perform financial planning with this software, but in the art and science of charging a fee to a client. As part of the package, FP wanted an advanced version of their software for affluent financial planning clients, together with a text manual outlining various planning techniques that advisors could use with such clients. That text manual they used was the FPC Manual, which had been completed by Andy just months before. It would then be periodically updated not only as the FPC Manual for Atlantic's field force but as an FP value-added, private-label product for it to vend to other financial services firms along with their base software. This was all part of the strategic alliance between the two firms: Atlantic got the software cheap with unlimited distribution; FP got the technical expertise in the business and estate planning markets to add value to its product.

How to charge a fee to a client... This was something new to the field sales people. They had always lived for commissions on product sales only. Now they were being trained that they had been "giving away" their expertise, their advice, and should charge up-front for that service. There was a lot of resistance to this approach, this *fee-plus-commission* model. But this was where the company was going and they set up a compensation schedule that rewarded fees as well as commissions, called Equivalent Client Dollars, or ECDs. No longer would agent productivity be based simply on "net new premium" sales, which in 1983 stood at $19 million nationwide for AMLIC. Now, all sales of all kinds of financial products – insurance, mutual funds, financial planning fees, etc. – were pegged with an ECD factor for each, representing the relative value each product line had to the profitability of the company.

One last addition to this new product model: Kelleher and Madison recognized that AFG account managers could not position themselves as truly objective advisors if the only products they could use to implement the plans they were writing for their clients were proprietary, Atlantic product. So, where an Atlantic insurance or annuity product was not best suited to the client's needs, the account manager (AM) had a menu of co-called Class II products with which the company had made distribution deals with other carriers to complement the proprietary line. These also carried an ECD factor.

With all these changes, AFG hoped to be at the forefront of a sea change in the entire industry. And Andy enjoyed the advantage of having come out of a profession (law) in which charging fees were the order of the day. This gave him a strategic advantage over others in the Department as far as training account managers in this new paradigm. And in 1985, several members of the Marketing Services Department toured the company's agencies around the country, teaching all aspects of the new business model. Andy was part of that task force.

In addition, Andy had become the head of the Marketing Counsel Unit which, at the beginning of 1985, had himself, Carol, Sue, and a paralegal assistant within its ranks. While Andy and Sue almost never spoke to each other, Andy and Carol had become allies and friends – at least until the announcement of Andy's promotion. Carole saw Andy's promotion from her peer to supervisor as changing for the worse their friendship, especially when Andy had to provide performance feedback or dole out assignments to staff. Andy was finally in a position that had authority as well as power, but he learned he could no longer be one of the staff.

Nevertheless, the task force that travelled around the country in 1985, introducing the field to FP, fee charging, new products, and the like, managed to complete a tour of over a dozen cities by the early summer.

At that point, Andy and Q – who had also been part of the task force – were invited to an offsite retreat in which many in the home office and among the most loyal field people were included. It was part of a wave of meetings that would become known as Communications Lab. Part of the paradigm shift at Atlantic *cum* AFG had included honing the relationship skills of marketing and sales people in the company, with the idea of making them better at their respective jobs. It started when Wayne Madison hired a couple of psychologists; one, an inside employee named Steven Merker; the other, a consultant named Al Thibault (Dr. T). While Merker oversaw the human relations development of the company generally,

Dr. T specifically came with a seminar package he had developed. He called it Behavioral Dynamics, and it took the seminar participant through a myriad of exercises and thought processes designed to break down barriers and develop positive relationships – at home with family, with friends, and with business associates and clients. To give Tim Pershing his due, he foresaw some of this in trying to bring Vivian Yellin into the company – right idea, wrong person, wrong timing.

In mid-1985, Dr. T began a series of these Communication Labs at which a group of perhaps as many as 2 dozen employees were chosen to travel to a remote location and engage in this week-long seminar. On the one hand, staffers would scoff at this seminar, one said "You can't leave until you cry," as a way of demeaning its purpose. Another common criticism was that it felt like brainwashing, the way the group assembled at remote retreat locations, preferably with Spartan accommodations, no television or radio, no newspapers, as closed off from the outside world and 1985-era technology as possible, in order to eliminate distractions. On the other hand, an employee of AFG felt left out and neglected if not invited, fearing that he or she had no future with the company if not invited to participate.

About 6 or so of these retreat seminars were held in 1985, all within the first eight months of the year. Andy went to the second-to-last one held, in early August. Held at a remote and weathered "resort" in the horse country of central Virginia, Andy found immediately that there weren't even any phones in the hotel or meeting rooms to call home or the office. He was completely cut off from the outside world, only the 24 colleagues and four staffers in addition to Dr. T were available to him. The first two days of the Lab were for sensitivity training, particularly breaking down barriers and defenses that people construct to protect themselves from vulnerability. The whole idea was to get vulnerable, personally as well as professionally. Attendees were encouraged to discuss their innermost fears and feelings, about themselves, their families, and each other. Confidentiality was assured, all were told by Dr. T. There were also relaxation exercises and each session was moderated by Dr. T or one of his staff.

Andy realized early on that there was no escape. And during one session he had heard loud and clear from one female colleague from the recently acquired Chesapeake Investments about his arrogant and pompous tendencies when dealing with her. It is true that Andy came on strong, sometimes intimidating, using that loud radio voice and facial gestures that could scare a monster when he got angry. Of course, Andy was mostly bark, little bite, but people who knew him only casually would not know that. When the Chesapeake staffer got up in general session and tore a verbal hole in Andy where the proverbial sun don't shine, all looked at Andy to see what his reaction would be.

"You come at people like a 'bull in a china shop'," she commented in front of all 24 attendees. "I really can't stand your arrogant approach to people."

Dr. T interjected, "How do you know that Andy comes on like that to 'people.' Why don't you keep the comment to how he interacts with you, specifically?"

"Fine! Andy, I think you're simply a pain in the ass and don't think of anyone else's feelings, especially mine."

"Thank you for that input," Dr. T replied, and turned to Andy. "Do you have any response to this comment, Andy?"

And Andy knew that while he felt slighted and embarrassed in front of colleagues, he needed to show a softer side. "I accept your comment. Let me take it under advisement and see what I can do about it." It was a rather formal reply without vitriol that those assembled who knew Andy was surprised to hear. They expected an angry outburst; maybe one that would have harkened to the way Shel used to ball out recalcitrant salesmen at Canada Dry.

Later that day, Dr. T pulled Andy aside and told him, "you were very gracious in there, Andy, and I appreciate the constructive way you took the criticism." In fairness, Andy was not learning new skills at this Lab. He had simply learned how to "game the system," to tell them what they wanted to hear.

Andy never cried *per se*, as cynics say you have to at these things, but more than one of his colleagues opened up enough and shared personal stories that left not a dry eye in the house. The one thing Andy learned from all this:

1. Listening to others' stories, especially from colleagues you work with every day, and not judging them, does lead to closer friendships; and
2. Andy came away from the Lab thinking he must have had a better and more normal and nurturing childhood than he thought, after listening to the childhood stories from others.

Andy returned from Communications Lab on a Friday in the middle of August. When he arrived back at the Home Office that afternoon, he was immediately confronted with resignation notices from his two associate Marketing Counselors. Sue, who had never been to Communications Lab and was 6-months pregnant saw the handwriting on the wall and decided to drop out of the workforce for her baby and let hubby be the provider. Carol, a one-time friend, had gotten an offer with a pension administration firm in Virginia and decided her prospects were better elsewhere. By the end of the month, both were gone.

Sue and Carol seemed to know something Andy did not know and got out while the getting was good. On the day after Labor Day, 1985, while Andy was on the Metro subway on his way into the office, he opened the morning *Washington Post* business section to see the headline: **Atlantic Mutual to Layoff 1/3 of its Employees Today**.

And when he arrived at the office he came to find several staffers in marketing with pink slips, packing up their personal items. Frank as well was on his way to transferring to a sales manager position in the Northern Virginia agency. Q had gotten caught in the RIF as well and would soon land a position in a field agency as well, but with another company. George Forson was still there, and he called Andy into his office.

"Andy, don't worry about the cutbacks. They won't affect you. We have plans for you…"

Andy waited with baited breath.

"We're going to have you transfer out to our Potomac agency in Silver Spring [Maryland]. You're going to be an in-house financial plan writer. You know how to handle the fee end of the business well, so you'll do fine. You'll be paid 20% of all fees generated in the agency."

"20% of all fees," Andy repeated.

"Well, a few of the veteran account managers in the office will be exempted from sharing fees with you. They already have a developed book of business. You'll be working with the newer account managers, and the ones that Walt Christopher, the manager, will be recruiting in our new system."

"When will this all take place?" Andy asked.

"After the end of the year," George explained. "We'll need to transition over the next few months into this new system, phase out Marketing Services, and all that. In the meantime, you can hold down the fort in the Department. Meaney will be there as well; his transfer happens same time as yours."

And a dejected Andy left Forson's office in a daze. Going out to Potomac was a non-starter. For one thing, walling off the veteran agents there from sharing fees with Andy meant cutting him off from most of his income potential. The "new-bees" as they were called will never generate enough fees to replace Andy's income.

Andy was also aware of some of the shenanigans that went on in that agency. The manager, Christopher, was embroiled in a revolt quietly going on in the agency. The year before, a sales contest was run to qualify the most account managers for the famed Million Dollar Round Table (MDRT), a well known club of top sales agents in the life insurance business. Bonuses were to be given out to the agency with the highest number of qualifiers at the end of 1984. To help the agencies marshal the production from its AMs, a staffer in the home office was assigned to each of the four Regional VPs to the task. Andy had been assigned to Billy Carl, the RVP who had the Potomac office in his portfolio. Andy worked with Billy to go after production from Billy's best agency in his territory, Potomac. There, Andy found that Walt Christopher had made deals with his top agents that involved his sharing the manager's bonus with each agent who qualified for MDRT. 14 AMs qualified that year, the most of any Atlantic agency in the country, and a special bonus kicker went to Christopher for winning the title.

However, Walt apparently got amnesia about what he promised and never paid out his winnings to the qualifiers. Excuses, delays, distractions went on for most of 1985. By the time of what has become known in Atlantic corporate folklore as the ***Labor Day Massacre***, AMs in Potomac had become thoroughly disenchanted with Christopher. By October, they had gone to Billy Carl with their complaints. Then there was further delay in resolving the issue: Carl had resigned from Atlantic at the end of October to take a Senior VP position in marketing and product development with a large mutual company in Philadelphia. This left the mess on George Forson's desk. But then Forson himself left the scene in November when he transferred to Orlando, Florida to take on a semi-retired consulting position with the company. So, the matter sat on Elliott Kelleher's desk.

But Andy knew what had happened. He heard loud and clear from the AMs in the office what had been done to them. Andy knew that Christopher's days there were numbered and that in the meantime there would be chaos there and a loss of productivity, which would have further debilitating effect on Andy's income.

What had happened, unbeknownst to Andy, is that a strategic plan had been devised during the year that would, beginning in 1986, divide the marketing functions of the company into a geographic Marketing East and Marketing West. Kelleher would run Marketing East; Benny Baskin, who had been running the Los Angeles agency and was very influential with Wayne Madison would take on Marketing West. There would be no centralized marketing going forward. This was political payoff by Madison to satisfy the aspirations of Baskin, much to the loss of position for Kelleher and Greene, for that matter. The divide almost looked like the division of the Roman Empire into Rome and Byzantium.

There was some talk of Andy joining Kelleher in Marketing East. But confidential communications between one of the Regional VPs, Dean Waterman, and Kelleher, led Elliott to conclude that Andy would not be welcome on the team. One day that Fall, a note was sent through inter-office mail, anonymously, to Andy. It read:

"You're not seen in good favor with some. In a meeting with field managers, Dean Waterman was heard to share with Kelleher, 'Greene is a very knowledgeable guy who knows his stuff. He's also fat and dresses like a slob. Not in keeping with our look.'"

Andy never learned for sure who had sent him that note, but it was a tipoff in the fall of 1985 that there was no room at the inn for Andy.

Chapter 5: Flying Without a Net

With an emerging fear, Andy faced a thug in the neighborhood who had bullied him several times in the past. The thug was on a bicycle, coming up the sidewalk at the far end of the courtyard from where Andy stood. The thug was peddling hard, headed straight for Andy. As the cycling bully came within striking distance, Andy pre-empted the attack. This time, the thug was in for a surprise. Andy reached out with his left arm and clotheslined the thug, taking him off his bike and hitting the ground, fortunately for the time being on his side, not his head (no helmet). Andy now seized the moment, and jumped on the bully, furiously punching, kicking, spitting, anything to vent his pent up anger at this representation of every bully he ever encountered in his short life.

The thug began to bleed, from the head and arms, eventually out of his mouth, and there was every reason to think that this might wind up as a homicide. Eventually, the thug stopped resisting. He apparently became unconscious. But Andy didn't stop. He knew that any chance the bully had to recover would result in a counter-beating without mercy; so, he showed no mercy instead. Off in the distance, Andy could hear police sirens, coming closer, but Andy got up and instead of running, continued to kick the helpless thug in the torso with his somewhat dirtied pair of PF Flyer sneakers. When the cops arrived and saw the scene, they were ready to handcuff Andy. Two officers pulled Andy aside. Andy was out of breath and shaking with a combination of fear and anger. An ambulance pulled up to the sidewalk less than a minute later. A pair of paramedics surveyed the thug's condition. The thug wasn't moving. One of the parameds looked up in Andy's direction, though aiming her look at the officers holding Andy by each arm.

"No good," the paramedic said. "Call the coroner."

The two cops took a look for themselves at the dead bully. One muttered, "This is that Grillo kid that's been terrorizing the neighborhood for years."

"I guess what comes around goes around," replied the other.

Andy stood motionless and watched the scene. He slowly gathered his wits and calmed his shaking.

"You did this?" called one of the cops to Andy. "You'll be considered a hero in this neighborhood. Bobby Grillo was the head of the famous Sutter Lords gang."

"I didn't know his name," Andy mentioned in a half whisper.

"We should arrest you. But no one around here would ever convict you of anything. You're a nice kid; good grades, lawful family, cause no trouble. We'll call this self-defense and leave it at that."

Andy did not have a mark on him, other than sweat from him and blood from his victim. He turned to look back at the courtyard. It reminded him of home. His garden apartment was in the far left corner of that courtyard. Somehow, he felt vindicated...

...A hornblast at the intersection reminded Andy that the light had turned green. And he proceeded to step lightly on the gas pedal at the floor of his Honda Accord and ramp up through the intersection. Andy had been daydreaming. He sometimes did this when faced with what he saw as a personal humiliation.

The farming of Andy out to a local and corrupt agency, being turned down for Marketing East because of his personal appearance, these were personal humiliations for Andy, especially because colleagues in the field and home office knew of the situation. In those times of humiliation, he sometimes recalled fights he had as a child, in Howard Beach, where fist fighting was a way of determining where you stood in the pecking order among the boys on the block.

In each recounting, Andy revises what actually happened and comes out on top. Andy gave as good as he got as a child, but he was not a fighter; not by talent, not by temperament. Andy never worried or remembered the fights he lost. Instead, he remembered darkly the fights he ran away from, where he lost face in the eyes of the other kids in the neighborhood. This was made worse by the fact that having been Captain Greene of Company A, Andy was the highly visible leader of the group.

Now, driving home from the office on an unusually bitter cold day in early November, Andy started running through alternative scenarios in his mind. The one he kept coming back to was to open his own financial planning practice. This was a chance to run his own business, be his own boss. Some of Andy's bosses over the years would come to the same conclusion about him: "Andy doesn't really report to anyone. Andy reports only to Andy."

Like some of his relatives, he wanted his own little shop to run. But not a shoe store; not a hardware store; not even like the flower shop his mother, Stel, had opened in Rockland. Those were goods products being sold. Having been a lawyer; having marketed insurance and investment products for the past three years, Andy knew this would be different – a professional practice, financial planning, operated much like a law office.

Andy had been reading a book from Andrew Rich, *How to Start and Build a Financial Planning Practice*, and began to imagine implementing much of the game plan from that book. Because no one was really minding the "store" – the home office marketing department – by the fall of 1985 (what was left were lame ducks placeholding for Marketing East and West), Andy had some freedom to build a business plan for this financial planning practice. He attended a seminar put on by the book's author, explaining in detail how to get in on this new profession.

"As to credentials," Mr. Rich explained, "you'll need not only Series 7 and 63 licenses, you'll need a life and health insurance license as well. It is also helpful to be a CFP, Certified Financial Planner, as this is the certification that seems to be emerging as differentiating a 'real' financial planner from a 'faux' financial planner. The CLU and ChFC designations are nice to have, but the public doesn't recognize them as professional differentiators, so don't worry about them. You will want to file a sample financial plan with the IAFP's Registry of Financial Planners. Their approval of your plan means a 'Good Housekeeping Seal' of approval from the association backing the financial planning profession."

Andy had the credentials already. He had mastered - let's face it, taught others – to use FP. So, Andy would adopt that software as his template for writing financial plans. He felt confident that the Registry would quickly approve his specimen plan and admit him to its rolls.

During November, Andy worked through a 10-page business plan for the practice, calling it **Northern Virginia Financial Group**. For the logo (he paid a marketing communications colleague at Atlantic to develop the logo as a favor) the F in Financial was represented by a British pound symbol. The letters were green, except for the pound symbol, which would be in gold leaf. This logo would be authentically engraved (not heat pressed plastic) onto his business cards and letterhead, both in buff-colored stock. Why? Lawyers would always check to see how a firm's logo appeared on a business card – engraving meant you were "for real." Andy might not be in law practice *per se*, but he was never very far from it.

Having gotten the British angle into the logo, his plan explained that the geographic-centric name made it clear that his target market was the Northern Virginia suburbs. He discounted D.C., which had mainly the very rich and the very poor living within its tiny borders. As to Maryland, Andy suffered from "Potomac Fever," the phenomenon in the Washington area in which Marylanders did not like to cross the River into Virginia and *visa versa*. Maryland was "South New York." Virginia was "the South," period. Many in the deep South kidded Andy when he would travel there doing training meetings in Atlantic agencies, saying with his slight New York accent that he was "from the South," just like them. The audience would graciously point out that Virginia was "up north, there" compared to Atlanta, Birmingham, Jackson, and New Orleans, where Atlantic had agencies. And for that matter, Virginians treated Northern Virginia with suspicion. Much like upstate New Yorkers do not consider New York City to be part of New York, some downstate Virginians refer to anything north of the Rappahannock River (Fredricksburg) to be the "People's Republic of Northern Virginia." But also like upstate New Yorkers, those downstate Virginians sure did like the tax money that came into the state capital from that suspicious part of the state.

Andy might have grown up in New York, but having married a Virginian and put down roots in Virginia, he considered himself a Virginian. His first born son, Robert, 18 months old when the Labor Day Massacre occurred, was born in Virginia. The Greene family was Virginian as far as Andy was concerned. And being somewhat of a Civil War buff (as all Virginians seem to be), naming the firm Northern Virginia Financial Group harkened to the Army of Northern Virginia, the name of R.E. Lee's Confederate army. No thought was given to any racial overtones. At that time, associations with the South in the Civil War – the War Between the States as it was officially called; unofficially The War of Northern Aggression – were always couched by Virginians in the states rights argument, not in the slavery issue. This led to the anomalous situation that when Virginia adopted Martin Luther King's birthday as a Holiday in the 1990s, that third Monday in January was already a state Holiday – Lee-Jackson Day, after the Confederate generals. Thus, the state legislature straight-faced passed a law naming the new Holiday: **Lee-**

Jackson-King Day. None of the racial anomalies raised by implicit reference to the Old Confederacy dawned on Andy; he was, after all, a Virginian, and issues like that never came up in polite conversation.

The next issue in planning this business was the money. Andy would take whatever severance the company was offering as an alternative to transfer – just as he did at ACP – and add to it a cash-out of his entire 401(k) balance at Atlantic. The severance would turn out to be less than $2,000 after-tax (one week for each of the three years Andy had completed in service to AFG) and about $8,000 after-tax from the 401(k) cash-out. Andy could add but $2,000 in savings to the working capital. The rest would be raised by an equipment loan from a bank, funds borrowed by pledging the office equipment purchased as collateral. The office equipment comprised:

- Two computers, both Gateway, one with a built-in hard drive, and one with a primitive modem to dial into a stock quote service Andy would use;
- A three-station phone system from Northern Telecom, with connection to a Philips stereo system Andy brought with him from home to play music through the phone's intercom speakers so there would be background sounds in the office at all times;
- A conference table and six chairs from Scan, a Danish contemporary furniture retailer, that was really a dining room set (Andy loved the rosewood finish on this rectangular table and it meant a full dining set at home if the business did not do well);
- An 8' sofa and wing chairs perpendicular on either end, with a coffee table in front;
- Andy's desk of course, a Duke of Marlborough writing desk from The Bombay Company;

- A more utilitarian desk for Andy's assistant in the outer office;
- Rolling executive chairs for each desk;
- Work stations for both computers; and
- Various and sundry other small items, not the least of which were pictures to hang on the wall.

For the pictures, Andy would bring various scenes from Northern Virginia, not D.C., to enhance the local nature of his target market. This included a 1935 image of Tyson's Corner, as it existed before the area was developed in the 1960s into one of the premier suburban shopping and office districts in the country. It also included a 1903 image of the Colvin Run Mill along Route 7 in Great Falls. And no Northern Virginia office would be complete without a poster of the "Taverns of Alexandria," referring to the major watering holes in the Old Town area across the Potomac from D.C.

Andy allowed for one Washington image. When he worked at ALG, it was in the National Press Building on 14th St., NW, walking distance from the White House in one direction and the Capitol in the other. On Friday, August 7, 1981, the week after Andy and Sallie returned from their honeymoon on the Outer Banks of North Carolina, the famous evening newspaper, *The Washington Star*, printed its last issue, after 128 years in business. Andy happened to arrive early that day and got one of the coveted copies of that last issue before they all disappeared. He had the front page framed and hung it in his office wherever he worked, a great conversation piece for anyone visiting. Andy also made sure that all of his earned degrees and designations were framed in coordinated fashion and would be hung facing the sofa in the office, where all prospective clients having an initial consultation with Andy would see it when not looking at him. Andy would call this the "I love me" wall, implying some advanced knowledge on the part of the planner; expertise from which the client should be thankful to profit.

Now, it was time to find office space. Andy secured a 5-year lease on about 750 square feet on the first floor of what used to be the Prince Street Schoolhouse in Old Town Alexandria. He negotiated the lease to only $12/foot, making his monthly rent $750, utilities and evening maintenance included.

The value of the equipment and furniture purchased was valued by the bank at $20,000 and issued Andy a loan for that amount. They were generous in their valuation and terms, as the bank was one that Sallie had a longstanding relationship with in her law practice, and by association they looked favorably upon Sallie's husband.

In December 1985, Andy met with Elliott Kelleher to give his decision. He would not go to the Potomac Agency to be an in-house plan writer. "If I'm going to write plans, I'm going to be my own boss."

"You'll be flying out there without a net," Kelleher commented. "With us you'll have an instant flow of income and a support system."

"Elliott, with all due respect, your alleged flow of income is mythical. You've taken the best producers in the office and excluded me from them. You have no idea what is really going on in that agency. I have little confidence in the ability to recruit new people to that office. As for support system, I **am** the support system in this company. I taught the field how to be financial planners. I'm just going to apply what I already know."

The lack of a comeback from Kelleher indicated to Andy that there was little disagreement with the points he was making, and that there was little value Kelleher and others placed on Andy's services going forward. If Andy wanted out, "don't let the screen door hit you on your way" was the unspoken answer. What Kelleher also didn't know was that Andy had negotiated with an agency manager from another company to be its detached office in Northern Virginia. John Davies, from Free State Life Insurance Company, was a well-known "general agent" in Towson, Maryland, outside Baltimore. Free State wanted into the D.C. market and got a foothold in suburban Maryland, but penetration on the other side of the River would require some innovative thinking, and that's where Northern Virginia Financial Group came into play.

Elliott did however ask about what Andy knew of the situation in Potomac. "Do you know something about the Agency I should be aware of?"

"It's just a feeling I get, nothing specific," was Andy's cop-out answer. Now that he was leaving – Kelleher had not made any counter-offer to get Andy to stay – there was no obligation on Andy's part to impart any intelligence debrief to the COO of the company. He was still smarting from not having been selected to head advanced sales in Marketing East, and the high handed way that he was discounted by management.

Kelleher did not pursue the matter. His opinion of Andy was limited to his obvious knowledge of all manner of advanced underwriting and financial planning, not to managing sales people or the distribution channel. This came to be one of Kelleher's greatest but unknown mistakes he would make in his career. Andy was, quite simply, a nobody, as far as senior management was concerned. "Who cares what the head of advanced underwriting says about the field? He's an egghead lawyer with no sense of distributing product. Why bother with him?"

On Friday, January 3, 1986, Andy opened Northern Virginia Financial Group. The day was full of celebration; an office warming party was held in the early evening that included Sallie, the toddler Robert (Bob), Renee Adams (the newly hired assistant), Willie Sherman (Andy's one-time RA in the dorms at Oneonta who happened to take the bar exam in Virginia at the same time as Andy and went into sole practice), and a host of colleagues, friends, and a few prospective clients that Andy was trying to cultivate. Included were the members of Andy's informal Board of Directors: Willie, Sallie, and Frank Meaney (FX) – Andy's former boss and mentor in the home office.

FX had the good fortune to be in the right place at the right time – no sooner did he arrive in AFG's Northern Virginia Agency than the manager there was forced to retire on disability – a degenerative disk in his back that made it impossible for him to pursue a full managerial schedule. Frank would then succeed to the manager position himself and run that agency for the next 8 years. As to his ongoing relationship with Andy, he would provide advice and counsel, as if a sales manager, but his real agenda was to be there when – he assumed – Andy's venture would fail, and Frank could bring him into his own operation as a full time Account Manager.

Willie Sherman, for his part, was someone Andy had looked up to in college. Willie was a good time RA in the dorm. A year older than Andy, Willie looked after the social novice and made sure Andy had a place to go and someone to talk to when things got slow, when things got lonely. Willie was a bartender part time in one of the many watering holes in Oneonta at the time. Back home in the summers in the Albany area, Willie also tended bar; this is how he earned enough to get through school. Willie and Andy temporarily lost touch after Willie graduated. They reunited when both were in the same Bar Review class in the Winter of 1978, and both sat for the bar that February. Then, on and off, Willie would attempt to recruit Andy into law practice with him. Willie had set up in the Adams Morgan section of D.C., and ended up in general practice –

specializing in criminal defense and debt collection. But it was a hard go for Willie, and to supplement his income, he continued to tend bar in the evenings at Columbia Station, a bar on Columbia Road, NW, that in the late 70s catered an eclectic mix from the neighborhood – part Black, part Hispanic, and part white liberal refugees from the anti-war movement (Students for a Democratic Society, or SDS, used the place as a meeting hall at times).

By 1986, Willie was still trying to convince Andy that nothing short of law practice would be up to the professional prestige Andy should strive for. But Andy was too far away from considering law practice by that time, and Willie's law practice, a hand-to-mouth existence at the edges of the profession, was not the best example to put forth as an argument. Nevertheless, Willie not only attended the office warming; he served as bartender at the event. And he was waiting in the wings, in case Andy's business failed, to take him into his own law practice.

Sallie had hoped that the "practice" as she liked to call it (still pretending that Andy was a lawyer) would be sufficiently successful that she could drop out of practice herself and stay home with Robert and (who she hoped would be) a second child. She had become somewhat burned out after 10 years in law practice. Her practice was mainly domestic relations (divorce), very big in Fairfax County civil practice and fairly lucrative, but emotionally draining and occasionally dangerous. The office Sallie maintained was just a few miles south of Old Town Alexandria, near where her parents lived. It was convenient for her to have child care for Robert take place at her parents' as her mother could stand in when the sitter was ill or could not make it in to work. Sallie's office was a two-person affair, like Northern Virginia Financial Group. She had a secretary, Mollie, who "wo-manned" the front office, took phone calls and managed Sallie's calendar. Sallie's office was in the back, but like most attorneys had a back door exit out into the parking lot – in case there was a need to escape a volatile situation with a client, or the client's spouse. You see, Sallie had been threatened many times by angry ex-spouses of her clients. She liked to say that she preferred representing husbands, because "they could afford to pay." But 2/3 of her clients were wives and mothers. When the divorce would become acrimonious, as it did all too often, there were occasional threats directed at the wife's lawyer; some by letter, some by oral epithet (the B-word seemed in common parlance), some by phone. The police could not provide cover for Sallie, as no one had yet tried to enter the office and carry out a threat of revenge against a former wife's lawyer. But sitting in an office, open to the public, with only two unarmed women inside, created a tempting target. Oh no, keeping a gun in the office was never an option for Sallie, a poster child for liberal causes, including gun control. By 1986, Sallie was looking for an honorable way out…

The office warming party went off without a hitch and that weekend there were high hopes for the success of the new business. It's a funny thing, what happens the day after an office opening. During the day of the opening, the new entrepreneur is totally unconcerned with getting business in the door. This business owner is basking in the glow of the new office, all clean and gleaming bright. Everything in its place! It is the second day that panic sets in, and that Monday was the beginning of panic for Andy. He began to look at the bills that would begin to come due shortly and wondered where the business was going to come from.

Andy's business plan included a lot of marketing techniques learned by watching the better agents at Atlantic do their prospecting stuff. Cold calling – the practice of dialing numbers of people one had no prior relationship with – was still commonly taught to new salespeople. But no one wanted to rely on that; neither did Andy.

So, the Plan called for a three-pronged attack of the market:

1. First, Andy participated in a direct mail campaign with a business reply card included. The initiative was sponsored by John Davies, the Free State general agent in Towson, who used but did not finance directly his Northern Virginia office, Andy's office. The direct mail was an appeal on almost all financial fronts – insurance, investments, retirement planning, and included a check-off box for financial planning. Andy would get all the financial planning responses as leads.
2. Then, Andy set up a series of selling seminars, some of which were put on by his local broker-dealer, Central Investments, where Andy would be the technical expert and would share the revenue from clients procured from those seminars with the other people involved in the "show."
3. Andy also split cases with other producers at Free State in Towson, when an agent needed a technical expert or financial planner.

In other words, most of what Andy did to market himself at first was done in sharing prospecting leads with others. Soon, he found that while he was meeting many new clients, the revenue from each was very thin when it had to be shared with others.

Andy then decided on an initiative of his own: he would join various professional associations in the community and network with other business people there. The first one he joined was the Fairfax County Chamber of Commerce. The local Chamber was mainly a meeting place for business-to-business (B2B) networking; luncheons held every month featured a speaker hired to present on a topic relevant to the business-centric audience, but the main event was the opportunity to exchange business cards with other business owners. These other business owners ran small organizations, called closely-held, because there was only one or a small number of owners of a business that was privately owned (not traded on a stock market).

These business prospects were right up Andy's alley of advanced underwriting expertise. Everything he had been writing about in the FPC Manual – everything he talked about at agency meetings and consultations – would be solutions he could bring to business owner problems. And when newly joined to the Chamber, Andy got a chance to rise at one of these monthly luncheons and introduce himself to the entire audience, giving him the opportunity to give his "elevator talk," or "9-second diamond," to the crowd.

"I'm Andy Greene, and I own Northern Virginia Financial Group. We're in the business of providing financial security and independence to business owners, such as yourself. If you're interested in financial security and independence, I'd like to have the opportunity to talk with you further. Thanks for giving me the time to introduce myself to the Chamber membership."

And Andy was off and running, collecting at least a dozen business cards from attendees at that luncheon. He would diligently follow up by phone with every one of them. And he would continue to network each month, exchanging cards with anyone and everyone sitting at his table for the meeting. In April that year, the Chamber held its business networking forum, a full-day meeting of speakers and presentations in the form of seminars. Andy paid for a booth in the exhibit hall of this event, allowing him to get into conversations with all sorts of business owners in Northern Virginia. At the time, the Northern Virginia business community was dominated by a few lines of work: real estate developers, Beltway Bandit government contractors, lawyers and law firms, and…other financial advisors (insurance agents, bankers, and people like Andy) vying for these other businesses as clients.

As competitive as it was, Andy surmised that there was another avenue he could go down that would be less intense with competition. While there were many "financial planners" in Northern Virginia, not many of them were also active members of the Virginia State Bar. So, Andy joined the Alexandria Bar Association and began going to their monthly meetings, cocktail hours held at the close of the business day in a building next to the City Courthouse on King Street, the main drag in Old Town. Andy could walk the five blocks from his office to these meetings. There, he traded business cards with other Bar members, never saying specifically what law he practiced, although it was clear from his Northern Virginia Financial Group card that he seemed not involved in active practice. Because being an active member of the Bar meant having to get at least 12 hours of continuing legal education (CLE) each year, Andy also had the chance to network with other lawyers attending various CLE seminars, trying to earn the required credits to renew their licenses.

Andy was anything but lazy in his prospecting. Learning from agency managers in the Atlantic system that prospecting was the number one problem agents faced in the business, Andy saw to it that this would not be the reason he failed at this venture.

Yet, Andy faced some challenges with his approach. For the Alexandria lawyer crowd, he found they would not accept his approach to them once outside of the monthly cocktail parties. Andy hired a telemarketer recommended to him by John Davies. This telemarketer, Andrea, had done some work for John with other agents up in Towson, with considerable success – success at getting appointments for the agents. She simply took the business cards and other contact information the agent would supply her and called the number that appeared there. She was persistent and was known for calmly disarming the objections of the prospect on the phone. She was compensated by the appointment, so her revenue did not depend on an actual sale but simply getting the agent or advisor in the door.

So, Andy set aside a Tuesday in June for Andrea to come down first thing in the morning. She got 68 business cards that Andy had collected from lawyer members of the Alexandria Bar Association, all people Andy had met at monthly cocktail parties and CLE seminars (so they knew at least vaguely who Andy was) and she began calling each one. Andy had stepped out that day to put on a lunchtime selling seminar on charitable giving strategies to wealthy business owners in Tyson's Corner, and left Andrea with Renee in the office to make the calls. She had Andy's calendar by her on the desk to fill in the appointments she would get.

At about 3:30pm, Andy called into the office from a pay phone at the Marriott Tyson's Corner, venue for the seminar. The seminar had ended. Andy had stayed to chat up a few stragglers from the meeting who were looking for some free advice. Andy had stayed that long hoping to snag a couple of appointments with some of the attendees. When he called Renee answered.

"Hi Renee. How's it going there?"

"It's been better. Your telemarketer has had a rough day with the leads you gave her."

"Let me talk to Andrea."

"Sorry, bossman, Andrea's gone. At around 3 o'clock she banged down the phone and started crying."

"Why? What are you talking about?"

"She not only didn't get any appointments for you by that time, she got some angry replies to her calls."

"Wait a minute," Andy interjected, "these are lawyers, professionals. They couldn't have been that bad."

"According to Andrea, they were. A couple of them apparently said they thought you were playing 'bait-and-switch' with them, pretending to be a lawyer when you were just an insurance agent.

One said they were considering complaining to the Bar Association about your misleading role at meetings."

"They were all like that?"

"No. It seems that most simply wouldn't let her get past the receptionist and talk to the lawyer. A lot resulted in messages left that were never returned."

For six-plus hours of work, the telemarketer had scored a big zero for Andy. Andy thought of the zero sign George Forson had made when he explained Jerry Ciccolo's firing to him. Andy did try and call Andrea, who did not answer the call but later left a voicemail message for him late that evening that apologized for her "failure" but that this wasn't the job for her. "Had this incident tore Andrea away from the occupation of telemarketing?" Andy thought. He never knew for sure because John never spoke of the matter to him, but Andy would never have any contact with her in the future.

As to the Chamber of Commerce leads, Andy did develop some working relationships with some of the members. Andy would make a point of "doing business with those that do business with me," and said so to some in the membership to hit home the point that if they expected business from him they needed to at least give him a shot at their business. And Andy found a modicum of success here. For one thing, the Washington area was known for having low barriers to entry into the market. The Metro Washington area was very transient; unlike New York, you could find few people who had been born and raised in the area. This meant that there was relatively little loyalty to established brands. Of course, the converse was also true; people had little loyalty to your brand once established. There were exceptions, but they were few, especially in the financial planning business. Agencies and practices came and went; many established in the 80s were gone, subsumed, or acquired by the 90s.

With the Chamber leads, Andy found that the ratio of 10:3:1 certainly applied. This was the Rule offered by most sales managers and trainers in the business. It takes 10 initial consultations with a prospect to get 3 to agree for you to propose a plan or solution to them and 1 of those three to buy product from you. Andy knew about this Rule; he simply believed that it took 10 phone conversations and handshakes in which he delivered his 9-second diamond to get 3 to at least pay a fee for a financial plan. He could live with only one of the three buying product to implement the plan because he had already earned a fee for his expertise.

During that year, Andy rapidly developed what turned out to be 49 "clients," people who had signed a fee agreement and paid for a financial plan, almost one a week. Andy would charge anywhere from $500 - $2500 for a financial plan, depending on the time he foresaw in complexity of the client's situation. The average fee for the 49 clients in 1986 came to $850, totaling $41,650 in financial planning fees for Andy that year. The breakdown of financial planning clients went like this:

- 20 from the Chamber
- 10 from selling seminars
- 8 shared with other agents at Free State
- 3 from referral from friends and colleagues known before the office opened
- 8 from personal observation – just getting into conversations with folks.

The problem was not writing financial plans for people. The problem was that not enough revenue could be derived from just that service. The fee paid was a one-time event, although small fees were charged for annual reviews. The fee-plus-commission model required that the client implement the plan with Andy, so that financial products funding the recommendations in the plan would be bought, generating commissions to Andy.

In addition, Andy had been tracking a new law that was going through Congress at the time: The Tax Reform Act of 1986 (TRA86). Designed to simplify and create the closest thing to a flat income tax structure the country would see in Andy's lifetime, it had a couple of provisions meant to partly offset the lower marginal tax rates that would take place beginning in 1987. One was the disappearance of the tax deduction for interest paid on debt, EXCEPT for homeowner mortgage interest. This would mean that none of the interest payments on individually-owned life insurance policy loans would be tax deductible going forward. Another was the end to everyone getting an up to $2000 tax deduction for deposits to an (Individual Retirement Account) IRA – from now on that deduction would not be available to his clients who were covered and participating in an employer-sponsored qualified retirement plan. But the biggest issue for Andy was the limitation, going forward, on deducting financial planning fees as tax advice. Beginning next year, that deduction would only exist to the extent it exceeded 2% of the client's Adjusted Gross Income (AGI). Add to all this that the highest marginal federal income tax bracket was going down from 50% to 28%, and this meant trouble for how much Andy could charge a client for a financial plan. For example, Andy's approach had been, "The fee for the Plan is $1000, but don't worry because it is all tax deductible and in your tax bracket, Uncle Sam is paying half for the Plan, so it's only $500 after tax." Now, a nondeductible fee would mean the client would pay the full $1000 after tax in most cases. Few planners in the business foresaw this eventuality in pricing their plans; they all felt that "the fee is the fee and the client will pay it for the expert service and advice." Andy was not so sure.

This was especially important, as Free State was not providing any financial support for Northern Virginia Financial Group. Andy wanted it that way, so that he could have the freedom to do business with whatever product providers he wished. This included his not associating with Free State's broker-dealer, but connecting with Central Investments, a small broker-dealer in Tyson's Corner that catered solely to Northern Virginia registered reps. But this meant that the only financial incentive to Andy for associating with the Towson agency was that Free State provided a healthy "training allowance," known in the business as TAP, for new agents. The TAP was based solely on life insurance production, and proprietary production at that. Only life insurance sales with Free State qualified for a training allowance that more than doubled the commissions earned by an agent in the program. TAP was available to new agents in the first three years in sales, and could turn the usual base commission of 50% of first-year premium on a new life insurance policy into more than 100% total commission.

What he also gave up was any secretarial allowance or expense allowance offered by Free State to offset the fixed costs of running an office like Andy's. Again, Andy's penchant for keeping himself independent, part of the business model to be able to market himself as a truly objective financial advisor to clients, meant he could not participate in these programs – they were reserved for so-called captive agents, those that sold only proprietary product.

Still, Andy did try and guide clients to the life insurance recommendations being made in almost all of his financial plans. One such plan was done for a client who came to him through that shared lead, direct mail program with John Davies' people in Towson. Theotis "Theo" Pulliam was a civilian employee in the Pentagon, former military, leaving the army after only four years active duty. Theo was single, African-American, age 28, living in D.C.

Even though D.C. residents were not in Andy's target market, by May – when Theo showed up on his radar screen – Andy had become hungry enough not to scoff at anyone who could "fog a mirror."

When Andy called Theo at work to follow up on the direct mail card Theo had sent in for financial planning, Theo immediately took an appointment with Andy for the week before Memorial Day. When the initial consultation was held, Theo immediately signed on for a financial plan, and wanting to strike while the iron was hot, Andy for his part began taking Theo's financial and personal history using his standard factfinding form, furnished by Financial Profiles. Theo would have to forward a few financial account statements, like bank balances, last year's 1040 form, and any outside investments he had. Andy knew the Civil Service Retirement System like the back of his hand, no need for further information there.

During the factfinding session, Theo revealed his marital status and indicated that he had no children and that his intended beneficiary would be a male friend of his. Theo not only signed off on a life insurance application but also on a disability income policy Free State also provided, to insure against loss of income from sickness or accident.

Andy had been counseled by the Free State home office to be suspicious of D.C. residents. In 1986, almost all life insurance carriers had stopped doing business in the District of Columbia. This was due to the law there that would not allow agents to ask a prospective insured any questions related to AIDS or HIV. D.C. residents seeking life insurance, or disability income protection for that matter, could not buy policies in the District.

However, laws involving life insurance and disability income policies were and still are governed by the law of the state in which the applicant signs the application, not where the applicant lives (the exception is for variable insurance which is a securities-based product and governed by the SEC and NASD, federal authorities). So, it was not uncommon for D.C. residents to cross into Maryland or Virginia to purchase insurance. In those states, there was no restriction on asking about AIDS or HIV, so the carrier could underwrite the policy based on fully disclosed statements of the applicant.

When the factfinding was done, Theo said, "I think I'd like to get the insurance started now."

"Well," Andy replied, "that's a good idea. I would recommend applying for disability as well as life insurance, as you are single and there's no one to back up your income should you get sick or injured."

"That's fine. What amounts are you recommending?"

"For life insurance, I usually recommend whole life as the premium stays the same for the life of the policy. And I would recommend no less than 5 times your current salary as a baseline… Let's see, your current income is $50,000 a year, so we would apply for $250,000. For disability, we would want to go for the upper limits of what you can buy given your income, perhaps $3,000 a month benefit."

And Andy took a moment out of the room to generate and print computer illustrations of both products. When Andy returned, ready to show Theo the illustrations with premiums, Theo did not say anything about the cost, but simply asked, "Is there a lesser amount of both of these I could buy without a medical exam. I don't have much time for this and I just want to get something started that will get me some insurance the simplest way possible."

"I understand… I can put you into a life policy for $100,000 of benefit with nothing more than your application statements and authorization to go into MIB [Medical Insurance Bureau] for your medical history."

"That's fine. But I'm not interested in cash value in the policy. You'll generate wealth for me in other investments, right? So, let's make it term insurance."

Andy didn't like selling term. It was cheap and generated very little revenue to his office. He also bought into the saying that term was "renting your insurance; permanent is owning your insurance" because it builds equity, just like buying a house.

Theo would not be moved, and as Andy needed the sale, he did not press the point further. A $100,000 annual renewable term policy was written and bound by receiving the first quarter's premium which Andy was authorized to accept and give Theo a "conditional receipt" meaning that Theo was insured pending underwriting. "If you get hit by a bus walking out of this office, you have the insurance," Andy morbidly stated. Andy also bound a disability policy for $500/month benefit; again, the limits of coverage without a paramedical physical.

On both applications, Theo directed the answer to the question, "Are you HIV positive or been diagnosed with AIDS," as "no." It was one of the easier insurance sales Andy would make that year.

As the year grew older, Andy became concerned about cash flow. His "burn rate," the velocity through which Andy was using his working capital, was reaching critical proportions. By late summer Andy could no longer be sure that Northern Virginia Financial Group would generate enough revenue to survive the year. While financial planning fees were on target, maybe even above target, getting people to implement their plans with product purchases were proving difficult. By Labor Day that year, Andy's premium production in life insurance was about $10,000. Securities sales were better; after all, this was 1986, and everyone was buying stocks and mutual funds. The country was in its fourth year of recovery from a recession. But securities sales generate only a small fraction on the dollar of what life insurance premium generates, and the TAP was rarely "tapped" into by Andy because it depended upon life production, not equities sales.

During that summer Andy tried to gain access into one or more strategic alliances. One came from a referral from Shel, Andy's father, who put Andy in touch with a stock broker in Manhattan who was cultivating Shel as a client. Tony Cameron (Camerlengo, but Anglo-sized to de-emphasize ethnicity) had been calling Shel every month. This started out a year earlier as a cold call, but they got into discussions that had little to do with the stock market and investments. Shel was nearing retirement age and appreciated Tony's repartee to the extent that he didn't try and move too quickly toward opening an account. Tony was, if nothing else, patient. When Tony learned from Shel that his older son was "in the business," Tony saw an opportunity.

"You mean he's a broker, Shel?"

"Not exactly… He calls himself a financial planner. I don't quite understand it. He came out of the life insurance business. That's his expertise. And he's a lawyer. That's also his expertise."

"Wow, Shel, I didn't know." And the wheels in Tony's head began to spin. "You know, I work with a lot of clients who need insurance, but we don't provide anything like that here. In fact, the brokers, me included, should have our own insurance looked at. We probably need more than what we have. But we have no one with that expertise."

"Let me have Andy give you a call," Shel offered.

And a week later, after an initial phone call, Andy made the trip up to Wall Street to visit Tony in his branch office. The conversation seemed promising: Tony was offering to have Andy first survey the brokers in the branch for their insurance needs. Once that was completed, "we'll start sending you our clients as referrals. But first, I want to see how well you do with us in this office. That will put us in the position of giving testimony to your ability with these products. O.K.?"

"O.K." What else could Andy say? This seemed to be a gift from heaven. A referral from family is almost as good as getting business from family.

Andy never did any work in insurance or investments with family, but not for a lack of trying. Shel, who'd known his son from birth, simply didn't have the capacity to take financial advice from his "kid." If nothing else, Shel felt he knew how to take care of his family financially and no son of his was going to tell him how to handle his money. To some extent, though he never said so to Andy, Shel felt a bit of a conflict of interest in doing business with Andy, as his son was a potential beneficiary of the father's wealth.

Shel's attitude was that he knew more than Andy about money. So, any advice Andy would try and give was dismissed. One thing that Shel felt he knew better about was how to handle his impending retirement, which included a pension plan from the folks who eventually bought out Canada Dry. "A defined benefit pension," Andy thought. "You don't see many of those in the private sector these days." And Andy immediately started into his Pension Maximization talk.

"Don't need help there, kiddo," Shel cut him off. "I already have that set up. Mom signed off on the pension waiver so we could enjoy a higher income with the life-only benefit."

Stel, a two-time cancer survivor over the past decade, was believed by Shel to probably be the first of them to go. Shel was in excellent health, even dropping his entire "balcony of affluence" (50 pounds) once he retired. He played tennis three times a week. It was assumed Stel, who had battled both breast and lung cancer, had a limited period of time. Therefore, it made no sense to worry about a survivor benefit from the pension for his wife. Shel would outlive her and was mainly focused on making sure there was enough money coming in for both of them to enjoy life for however long they had, together.

The alleged alliance between Andy and Tony never materialized. While talk of coming up and working with the brokers in the office on their insurance needs continued to come up in conversation between them, Tony had in the meantime won Shel's confidence and hence his investment account, which was modest but still slightly north of $1 million. In other words, Tony didn't need Andy anymore; he'd won the client over and that was his goal. So, when Andy tried to raise the issue and schedule time to come up to the Big Apple, Tony kept putting him off. Tony did not want to piss off the son of his new client, so he never said he wouldn't go through with the deal. He just kept making excuses to postpone any action on the alliance.

Meanwhile, Andy was running out of time. So, he kept trying different combinations of initiatives, thinking that the law of large numbers would have one of them work in his favor. He began a strategic alliance with a "stock picker" at Central Investments. Brad Cunningham was billed as a "wiz-kid" in managed equity accounts and provided four different portfolios to clients, depending upon client risk tolerance and time horizon. Andy began inviting Brad to speak at monthly client cocktail hours in the Northern Virginia Financial Group office, where Brad would present quantitative and qualitative (technical and fundamental) analysis of his chosen stocks for each of the four portfolios. The most popular portfolio was called "Galapagos," after the Islands and the Galapagos turtle – slow and steady. All of Andy's clients and some prospects as well would be invited to hear the latest insights into the investing world. This added to Andy's reputation as something more than just a life insurance agent. Andy and Brad would split commissions on placed equities from these clients.

However, the commission flow from these trades was very small. A $10,000 trade, for example, was likely to generate no more than $100 to Andy, even at full broker prices. And most of these trades did not exceed $10,000. For 49 clients that year, perhaps half entered at least one trade this way.

For 1986, Andy's GDC (gross dealer concessions) from Central came to less than $25,000, net of one alliance that drove Andy's commission level higher, although generating no more net income to him. One of Central's product wholesalers approached Andy in September with an introduction to a new registered rep with the broker-dealer. His name was Danny DeLessio, and he ran a small boutique financial planning agency, similar to Andy, but in Tyson's Corner. Danny had a problem in that he had not yet gotten life and health licensed in Virginia but he had several clients who wanted to roll over some qualified retirement plan money (mostly 401(k)) to an IRA product. Danny wanted them in a variable annuity IRA that

Central was pushing as one of their prime products. Central's people wanted Andy to front for Danny and write the annuity contracts; then later, after commissions were earned on the contracts, pass the commissions by separate check back to DeLessio.

By state law and NASD rules, writing these contracts and putting one's name on the applications as the rep for these clients meant that Andy took on the responsibility for the clients; they were now Andy's clients, not Danny's. But DeLessio had no intention of handing over these clients to Northern Virginia Financial Group. And the clients had never met Andy, had no idea who he was. The idea was that later, the rep on these accounts would be changed to DeLessio, once he secured the proper licensing.

Though the transactions proposed were just a technicality, supervised by the same broker-dealer, they were clearly illegal. Shill transactions like these, if known to authorities, could result in removal of both parties from the securities business, and the insurance business. But this kind of thing, in 1986, was commonplace to get around regulations. Central wanted the business; it wanted Delessio's business; it knew Andy was struggling; and Andy was hungry for anything that would raise his GDC percentage. These transactions involved close to $50,000 in GDC and would move Andy from 25% commission to 40% commissions on his other securities business. Funny things happen to ethics when you're hungry, and Andy took the deal, writing these contracts as they were sent from DeLessio to Andy's office. But just as the $50,000 came in the door, it went back out a month later; under the unwritten deal between Andy and Danny that these commissions were payable back to Danny. Andy got to keep none of the revenue generated. And for his trouble, he took a big risk. But Andy was still in many ways a novice in the practices of marketing and selling investments.

In July, Andy also tried to raise his professional image by submitting a sample financial plan to the Registry of Financial Planning Practitioners at IAFP. It was a fairly exhaustive plan which Andy was sure of would earn him a place in the Registry. Mysteriously, however, by year end, the Registry had not ruled on Andy's sample financial plan. Calls to the Registry people got nowhere, and Andy wondered what the holdup was. Years later it would be reported that the Registry was a "pay-to-play game," in which those CFPs making the largest donations to lobbying and other activities of the IAFP got preference in admission to the Registry. The IAFP would be reorganized in the 1990s into its current Financial Planning Association. The Registry itself was by that time totally disbanded.

Also, in July, Andy worked with one of the leading producers in the Towson office for Free State, and they got into a seminar selling situation, presenting Pension Maximization to the USMC recruiters in the Baltimore and Washington areas, at a Columbia, MD, hotel. The Marines were all in full uniform, all buzz crew cut hair. Andy in those days left his hair rather long, just shy of shoulder length, and was dressed in his best suit and wing tip shoes. The Marines were all trim and fit, as you would expect them to be. Andy was showing a little paunch in the mid-section.

The meeting opened as all Marine meetings do, with the Marine Corps hymn, sung by all in uniform. Andy felt out of place; he had not served a day in the military, and he wondered whether his SDS friends from Columbia Station would disown him for hanging with the military. Then, during his presentation, the 35mm slide projector Andy was using broke down, leaving Andy with no visuals to use. This was a real problem, as the concept is hard to show without numbers illustrating how the money flows.

"I guess it's just a case of Murphy's Law here," Andy tried to joke his way through. But there was little in laughter and it would be the last time Andy would be asked to do a joint seminar presentation with one of the Free State agents. Andy chalked it up to, "there are good days and bad days in business." This was one of the bad days.

Not that John Davies – the GA at Free State, Towson – was unsympathetic to what Andy was trying to accomplish with Northern Virginia Financial Group. Davies had a disability wholesaler in his agency, Felicia Eckhart (she went by "Effe"), but she lived in Northern Virginia, Annandale to be exact, one town west of Alexandria from the Potomac River. Effe needed a base of operations close to home. Davies set her up in Andy's Northern Virginia Financial Group office and made a small contribution to the office rent as compensation.

Andy and Effe began working together, on some cases involving Andy's clients, though a disability insurance (DI) sale has a gestation period from opening discussion to writing an application to collecting the first premium that is usually longer than that for life insurance, due to the complexity of options in designing coverage that a non-cancellable, guaranteed renewable, DI policy can have. More important in the short term is that the two Free State "producers" became friends and industry allies during this time.

Effe was married with three small children at the time. She would often commiserate with Andy over the trials and tribulations of family life in the Eckhart household. Her husband, John, was not especially supportive of her career goals of building an insurance wholesaling practice. She also donated a lot of her time to the local Life Underwriters chapter in Northern Virginia, the leading fraternity of life insurance sales people in the industry. She would, in the early 90s, become the first woman President of the Northern

Virginia Chapter of the National Association of Life Underwriters (NALU) and ran twice, though unsuccessfully, to represent Virginia as a state delegate to its national convention.

To complicate things further, Effe was a stunning beauty. At 5' 9", 34 years of age, long legged with long blond hair, blue eyes, and a smile to die for, she was always a sexual target in a male dominated industry. Effe had been the victim, at least once, of an inappropriate approach by one of AFG's leading Account Managers while Andy was Marketing Counsel in National Headquarters. But Andy did not know of the incident at the time; Effe would not file a complaint or go public in any way with such matters. She always wanted to stay above the fray and not compromise her standing in the industry with a "he said, she said" scandal.

Lastly, Effe was a victim of her own warm personality. She liberally hugged and kissed on the cheek all manner of brokers and other agents, both in NALU and colleagues at Free State, including Andy. It was all-too-easy for some of the sales people in the field to get the wrong idea from Effe's innocent flirtations.

It was only during her time housed in Northern Virginia Financial Group that Effe shared with Andy her problems at home and in the business. Her winning personality and outstanding good looks allowed her to succeed well in attracting brokers to Free State for disability products. But her dual problems – at home and in the field – made her quite vulnerable to a softer approach from a male coworker. Andy felt drawn to Effe, but resisted temptation. For her part, Effe came to trust Andy completely; she appreciated his not trying to turn their friendship into something more. Effe may have been unhappy at home; she may have had daily challenges working through the sexism that permeated all levels of her industry. But she remained loyal, like a good Catholic wife and mother, to her husband and family.

In late September, Dan Zimmerman, from DAZ International – the recruiting firm Andy had had some dealings with at Atlantic – gave Andy a call.

"Hey, Andrew Greene. This is Dan Zimmerman from DAZ. Do you remember me?"

"Yes. I remember you. How are you doing?" Andy replied.

"I'm doing great!"

"Zim," as he was sometimes called, was always doing great. It's important when selling to always have a positive outlook. Andy could tell he was selling today.

"And how are you doing, my friend? I heard from some folks at AFG that you opened your own agency."

"Yes, a financial planning boutique shop, actually."

"And how is that going?"

"We're doing well, about 4 dozen clients already and some good reviews and contacts in the community." Andy avoided getting into revenue numbers.

"Well, that's great to hear. So, I guess you're not interested in hearing about a career opportunity that seems to have your name written all over it."

"Dan, I'm always listening." Andy tried to moderate his interest but by late September, anything was looking good. "What's going on out there?"

"I have a new client, a nationwide insurance firm, a life insurance subsidiary of one of the largest global property-casualty insurance firms, and they're looking for a head of Advanced Sales to lead their marketing efforts to small, closely-held business owners and affluent estate applications." Dan waited for a response from Andy.

Andy said nothing for a moment… then, "Interesting. So tell me about this company."

"Well, you know I can't reveal the company identity at this point. You know the drill… If you're interested, you send me a resume. I put it in front of their people. They decide if they want to pursue you. At that point then we get into specifics."

"Can you tell me where the position is?" Andy meant where on the organizational chart. Dan thought he meant geography.

"That's the hard part of all this Andy, my friend. It does mean relocation out of D.C. You know that if you're going into a home office again, relocation is a must. There isn't anyone but Atlantic in D.C. and you've already played that one out."

Andy had been diverted now from org chart to geography. He wasn't too keen on relocating, but he was desperate. "Where, exactly, is this company located?"

"Southern New Hampshire," as if putting in "southern" somehow made it seem not as far away from Virginia as the 500 miles up the coast it would be.

"So, you mean like Manchester?" Andy, having roots in New England, knew the geography and Manchester, the largest city in New Hampshire, was just an hour's drive north of Boston.

"A little further up than that… More like Concord."

This meant the state capitol. The only thing Andy knew about Concord, NH, was that every four years it became – for a week or so

– the center of American Presidential politics, being the home of the New Hampshire primary.

"I told them the little that I knew about you," Dan continued, "and they want to talk to you. But I also warned them that the book on you is that you would not leave Virginia."

"Dan," Andy was trying to play it cagey, "you're right. But I never turn down a conversation out of hand. I'd be amenable to a meeting with them."

And so, during the last week of September, Andy flew into Manchester airport and a limo was waiting to drive him to the home office of Lambert LifeAmerica located walking distance from the state house. Concord was the sleepiest town Andy could imagine, especially considering it was a state capitol. The town reminded Andy of Oneonta, maybe only slightly larger, a throwback of local shops and small bungalow, clapboard houses, Cape Cod style mainly. The big chain retailers were almost completely absent from this town.

The Lambert home office was a rare modern campus in Concord, all 16 acres of land and a sprawling four-story building in the middle, surrounded by a parking lot so big that in the middle of the day it was nevertheless only half filled. The little Andy knew of Lambert going in was that it was mainly known for high end property and casualty insurance coverage. For example, your house had to be appraised for at least $1 million for Lambert to even consider insuring it. Only high end luxury cars could qualify for insurance from Lambert. The company had begun dabbling in the life insurance business at the beginning of the 1980s; not organically by growing its own but by acquiring a string of small life companies: Union Life was the insurer that was originally based on the land that Lambert eventually developed into its LifeAmerica home office. It also owned Colony Life in Parsippany, NJ; Lambert's property-casualty home office was also in that area. Finally, in 1985, it bought Appalachia Life, Chattanooga, TN, a company that had huge success in universal life products, the kind that Atlantic had also marketed.

In the home office, the lobby floor was spacious and decorated beyond the imagination of most of the local residents of Concord. The second floor housed Lambert Securities, their broker-dealer. The third floor was mostly for operations of the life insurer, and the fourth floor was executive offices and the marketing area.

The interview was with several people, the key being the hiring manager, Marilyn "Lyn" Randolph. This would be the first time Andy would be reporting to a woman. In 1986, this was still a rather new phenomenon. But Andy found Lyn easy to talk to. She was a daughter of the South, from North Carolina, transferred from Chattanooga as part of the Appalachia acquisition.

"Why would you ever want to move up to New 'Hamster'" Lyn liked to call it. Andy could see behind her a window showing the woods at the end of the campus, and the fall foliage there, something that wouldn't appear in Virginia for at least another month.

"I have family in New England. And I'm a Boston sports fan because of that family," Andy answered.

"Well, it can't be because of the weather… They say here, 'if you don't like the weather, wait 5 minutes.'"

"They say that about a lot of places."

Andy and Lyn hit it off almost immediately. Lyn was a Southerner, but she wasn't aristocratic about it. She would remind Andy years later of the late Ann Richards, former Texas governor. Lyn had that working class sense of humor. It was disarming. But make no mistake about it; Marilyn Randolph did not get to be Vice President of Product Marketing at Lambert by just making jokes. She was known to outwork almost every one of her colleagues, and so won the grudging respect of the field sales people, some of whom were very old school and didn't care much for a female interloper coming into their "club."

Within a day after returning to Alexandria, Zim was back on the phone to Andy. "Well, my friend, you made a great impression on them up there in New Hampshire."

"Really?" Andy was playing it close to the vest.

"So, are you ready to move up there? Have you talked to your family about this?"

"Are they making me an offer at this point?"

"That will probably come in a few days. For now, just know that it is your job to lose."

By mid-October, Andy had received an offer letter from Lyn at Lambert.

Meanwhile, conversations had started between DeLessio and Andy. Danny wanted to buy Northern Virginia Financial Group; not as a going concern, but he wanted to expand his client base. He was impressed by Renee and wanted to hire her as well. He also was interested in some of the equipment the office had. This was perfect timing – a new job with enough cash from the sale of the business to pay off all of Andy's debts and leave him free and clear.

Now came the time to convince Sallie that this was a good move.

"I really have concerns about moving all the way up there, away from my family. And giving up my practice…"

"Wait. I thought you had enough of law practice; that you wanted out of it. Here's your chance."

"But to move so far away…"

The couple took a scouting trip at Lambert expense to Concord. It did nothing to alleviate Sallie's concerns. "This is so different from anything I've known before."

"If I stay with the business, it is quite likely that I'm going down with the ship. I don't see surviving the year. I've gotten some clients but they do not drive enough revenue and I'm out of cash. Even if I could find a way back, it will be years before I get to bring any money home. Are you prepared to be the sole breadwinner for us?"

"You know I can't do that. I barely make enough to support myself. And who is supposed to take care of Robert? Are you going to stay home with him?"

It was disconcerting to Andy. Somehow the argument had changed from Sallie being burned out and wanting out of law practice to him staying home to care for their toddler. In any event, by end of October, Andy had both accepted the Lambert offer and signed a contract to sell the assets (not the shell or name) of Northern Virginia Financial Group to DeLessio Financial, Inc., to be completed by end of 1986.

And then something happened…

In November, some of the insurance business that Andy had been praying for began to come in. By December, Andy had doubled in the last two months all of his production in life insurance sales for the entire year. But in October he could not see that, and now he was committed to the move to New Hampshire.

In December, another headhunter came calling on Andy. A Canadian life insurer, Royal Life, had decided to open a U.S. marketing operation, based in the Torpedo Factory (a WWI armory rehabbed into an arts and business center in the 1980s) in Old Town Alexandria, and did Andy want to apply for the advanced sales position there…

Chapter 6: In From the Cold

The money from the sale of Northern Virginia Financial Group was just enough to pay off all of Andy's debts for the venture. A few additional dollars were raised by "fire sale" of the remaining furniture and equipment that DeLessio did not want, including that dining *cum* conference table Andy loved.

In December, Andy travelled to Concord to start his new job at Lambert. He would come home on weekends, and the company arranged 90 days of relocation benefit so he could stay in a local hotel in town at company expense.

Sallie began to wind down her practice, but it would be the following May before the practice was totally closed. In the meantime, she made a couple of house-hunting trips to New Hampshire, with Robert in tow. That winter was an unusually snowy season and there were times that the family was touring real estate in 4 feet of packed powder. Sallie had her eyes set on perhaps building a new house, something that she dreamed of, especially given the lack of upscale housing that Concord offered at that time. So, one day, in February, the family arranged to meet a realtor at an open lot in the nearby town of Bow, on top of a mountain known as White Rock Hill. When Sallie got out of the car with Robert, the little one got stuck with his boots in the snow and could not extricate himself. Sallie, then trying to pick up Robert, also became stuck. Andy, coming around the car to help, likewise became stuck, the snow was so deep. As the three of them stood there, all stuck in the snow, Andy could see someone emerge from the woods, away from the road.

"Hi there," a voice called out. "You must be the Greene's." The voice emerged as a young man with snow shoes on his feet that looked more like tennis rackets. It turns out it was not a realtor but a contractor who had bought the land they were on, subdivided it into three two-acre lots, and was prepared to build what he called a "custom spec house" on each. Custom spec meant that the buyer would either bring plans or pay to have house plans created, and would contract with this builder to build to those plans and then sell the house and the lot back to the buyer when completed.

In 1987, New Hampshire had become the refuge for people from Boston and other parts of Massachusetts looking to escape high taxes, overcrowding, and crime. "Flatlanders" is what the locals called these people. But the locals sure liked the money that these Flatlanders brought with them. The flight from Massachusetts was fast and furious and would peak in 1987, during the so-called "Massachusetts Miracle" that spilled over into New Hampshire and caused a real estate boom that the area had never experienced before and probably not since.

There was still the matter of Royal Life and the new U.S. headquarters in Alexandria. Here was a chance to not have to relocate. But the timing was such that by the time Andy got to interview with the new chief marketing officer (CMO), Brandon Kessler, it was January 1987 and Andy was at least a month into the new job at Lambert.

Brandon eschewed any nicknames. He projected flawless manner, upscale attire. He projected an image of billionaire success. And it was intentional. When Brandon met with Andy the first time, it was at the Morrison House, a well-known B&B in an historic building in Old Town. Brandon was not from Virginia; he had no accent, and Andy never really learned where he was from. That was never the topic of conversation. His success stories were; his opulent possessions were. Brandon seemed more concerned with whether Andy could "fit in" culturally with the rather reserved and soft spoken Toronto crowd that dominated Royal at that time, as opposed to Andy's technical knowledge. Andy caught on quickly that his gregarious New York ways would come off rather "cheeky" to the Midwest Canadians in Royal's home office. Although Toronto was not the site for this operation, Toronto was a critical influencer on hiring decisions.

"What we're looking for Andrew," Brandon commented, "is for someone who can project the image of understated class as well as marketing acumen. No room here for 'loud.'"

"I understand. It is too easy to 'over-market' a brand. You want *suggest* over *overt*, yes?" Andy was trying to stifle what was left of his New York accent.

"Precisely. You seem to get where we're coming from. There will be an opportunity for you to meet the people in Toronto as well. They will want to get to know you. But one advantage is that you are local in Virginia. No relocation needed here."

"Well, Brandon, I have started a job up in New England. But my house here in Alexandria has not sold yet, so I suppose it's safe to say that."

When Andy went to visit the Royal home office in Toronto the next week, it was his first time in Canada. The volume of sound in the office was deafening silence; you could hear a pin drop. This was starkly different from the noise at either AFG or Lambert, where it seemed bodies and paper were flying around the office constantly. At the same time, Q, who headed AFG's sales support before the Labor Day Massacre, also interviewed for the same sale support role on Brandon's marketing team in Alexandria. Q – asked at Communications Lab, "where do you see yourself in this company in 5 years," answered, "CEO" – was a little too brash for the Toronto crowd and did not get the job. But Andy put enough of a lid on his New York side that by the end of February, Brandon was ready to talk offer.

When the offer was made, it was for slightly more money than Lambert was paying. Andy felt pangs of guilt over his disloyalty in even considering the offer. He had already made a commitment to Lambert, and was already developing working relationships with the home office and field.

Andy decided that the only thing to do was to come clean with Lyn and explain that while preparing to move, this situation with Royal had come up; that "my wife has some concerns with settling in New Hampshire." Andy was putting some of the excuse on family as the reason he felt he needed to consider this opportunity in Virginia.

Lyn, for her part, did not flinch. "I know that a southern gal like Sallie would find life up here a bit different," and laughed at the understatement she made. "Hell, it's a shock to my North Carolina system as well. But don't make any decision until you've talked to Don."

Don, as in Don Wasserman, was the CMO for Lambert LifeAmerica. He was Lyn's boss. He had come up through the field force. He was from 1983-85 the number one regional vice president in Lambert's distribution channel. This channel was different from what Andy experienced at AFG. Distribution of financial products here was through independent agents, called personally-producing general agents (PPGAs). They were geographically assigned to one of 12 RVPs (regional vice presidents), company wholesalers who recruited producers to Lambert and ministered to the existing PPGAs in his/her region.

Don's region had been New England, based in Boston. When Lambert was busy buying up small life insurance carriers around the country, Lambert LifeAmerica's President, Paul Swift, needed a CMO, and fast. In 1986, he brought Don in. Now where Paul was a native of the Granite State, reserved and somewhat formal and bland, Don was a flamboyant salesman, died-in-the-wool marketer, with a gregarious attitude to boot. Like Brandon Kessler, he liked the finer things in life, and showed it off in his clothes, cars, jewelry, etc. Unlike Brandon, however, the manner of presentation was loud and unmistakable. Unlike Brandon, whom Andy never heard utter a swear word, Don cussed like a longshoreman. Brandon tried to project an air of old money. Don was "new money," all the way. Nevertheless, Brandon, at age 45, was clearly the younger to Wasserman's 60.

"How the hell are you Andy," Don called out as Andy arrived with Lyn for his meeting with the CMO. "Lyn, Andy and I need to talk one-on-one…Would you excuse us for a minute?"

"Sure, Don," Lyn answered as if somehow she had suddenly been reduced to being a secretary.

Andy wondered, "Why isn't my boss in on this conversation?"

"Thanks, doll."

And Lyn closed the door behind her. "I'll bet you're wondering, 'what the fuck is he doing pushing my boss out of this meeting.' Am I right or am I right?" Don's voice level was just a bit too loud for what Andy thought was proper. But what did he know after three years of working with southerners at AFG?

"Well," Andy started, but Don piped in again…

"Lyn's been great. You know I brought her up here from Chattanooga. I made her a V.P. This is the first woman marketing executive we've had at this company, and I made it happen. I have great respect for Lyn; she ain't no bitch, that's for sure."

Andy was waiting for the other shoe to drop. "That's good to know."

"But I want to talk about Andy Greene, and his future here." Andy perked up a bit. "You've made a great impression here so far, kiddo, and I appreciate that. I liked you from the first moment you got here. You have the credentials to walk into a room and command instant respect. But you seem to get that credentials don't mean shit once you open your mouth. The field guys need to know you're one of them. I don't know if it's your family background or the year you spent in the field with that Financial Group thing you were doing in Virginia, but you have the balance of technical knowledge the agents need with the empathy for their job that tells me you have a bright future here."

"Don, I really like it here. But I can't ignore my family's preference to settle permanently in Virginia. My wife's family is from there. My son knows nothing other than Northern Virginia. This has been a tough situation for me."

"Andy, I get it. I also want you to understand that we kind of pulled you out of a losing proposition down there… Oh, yes, we figured you wouldn't move up here in the first place if your agency was doing well. We heard that 'you can't get Greene to move north.'"

"Well, I do have roots in New England, sort of."

"Sure. But here's what I want to put in front of you: I can't put it all on paper right now, but we have a Regional guy in the middle Atlantic area – we call it the Coastal Region – includes Virginia – who is 63 years old. Phil McPherson, you know him?"

"Yes, I know Phil… Good guy." Andy projected some weak praise here. "I've already done a meeting in Baltimore with him, a couple of weeks ago."

"I heard. You killed, down there… That's a good thing, kiddo."

"Thanks."

"Don't thank me. Phil is bonkers for you. He'd like to see your ass down there more often."

"I can do that."

"And you will, Andy. But here's the thing. Phil is getting close to where he will want to retire. **He will want to**, I am sure, if you get my drift. At that point, we'll need a new RVP down there to take over. Phil will have some input into a replacement. But mainly it will be based on relationships with the PPGAs in that region. If they know you; if they have confidence in you; you're in. Do you understand me, Andrew?"

"I think so… Don, does Lyn or Phil know anything about what you're planning."

"Planning? Fuck no! There's no plan here. This is just two guys talking. As time goes by, what I want is for you to embed yourself in that region – not taking anything away from the other regions – and make yourself indispensable there. If you can do that, the regional choice will be simple for me to make. And in the meantime, you'll have budget to travel in and out of that region as often as you need to for our joint benefit. Good?"

"Don, over what period of time are we talking about? I heard there is no set retirement age for RVPs here."

"And there is none. But Phil is getting to the point where he is coasting. And when that happens, it's only a matter of time."

"Any way you could be a bit more precise in your projection, Don?" Andy didn't want to push the matter too far, but he had to bring a plan home of some kind. "I need something to tell my wife about my career plans here."

"Don't communicate this any further than between the two of you. I'm thinking 2-3 years, tops. But don't mention this to anyone in the company, not the field, not Phil, not Lyn. O.K.?"

"Well, you've given me a lot to think about, and I appreciate it."

"Shit, man, I don't want you to think about it. Continue your move up here. Anything you buy in this market is going up 10-20% a year in value. If you move in three years back to D.C., you'll make a few bucks profit in the meantime. And tell those *schmucks* at Royal you're staying with us." And he laughed loudly at his own Yiddish vulgarity.

By early March, Royal had its answer. Andy, in a phone call, told Brandon, "I just can't turn my back on this new commitment I made to Lambert. I have to see it through."

"I appreciate your integrity, Andrew. Perhaps, we'll run into each other in the future," was Brandon's only comment in reply. And the move to New "Hampster" continued on.

By the middle of 1987, while Andy and Sallie were overseeing the building of their 2200 sq. ft., cedar clapboard, stick-built, two story colonial in Bow, matters back at AFG were changing fast, and not for the better. The Marketing East and Marketing West split had failed, mainly due to some of Benny Baskin's penchant for personal spending on the company expense account. Atlantic had become a playground for folks who used it as an ATM for their personal lifestyles and public relations image building. Baskin had begun paying for an upgraded company car and a Los Angeles area apartment (to house his mistress) by laundering expenses through the L.A. Agency as technical support fees, reimbursing himself under a phony corporation purporting to do IT maintenance consulting. He kept the ruse going for longer than he should have been allowed because the Agency Managing Director, Johnny Wales, was also participating in some of the revenue from the phony consulting firm. Johnny, a protégé of Benny, also practiced some of the same opulent money laundering. There was insufficient control over budgets in Marketing West, which ran almost without fiscal oversight from D.C.

Other practices, which would become hallmarks of unethical behavior by insurance agents in the 80s and 90s, were evident out West as well. One of these practices was to put in place a life insurance policy for a client for one year, allowing the agent (AM) to get full commission and bonus credit for things like the annual sales meeting (in an exotic location) and then replace the policy with one from another company the next year. Sometimes the agent helped finance the initial year's premium for the client. Another practice was to fill in application questions for the client that the client had not even been asked or had answered, allowing the agent to purport the client's health and financial status to be other than truthful, to say the least. One other was to use unlicensed personnel to bird-dog for clients and even write insurance applications; then signed off by the licensed agent-supervisor without bothering to re-validate the client's information on the application.

In Marketing East, the unethical practices were less evident, but another phenomenon was taking hold. The field force was paying less and less attention to writing life insurance and more and more attention to the investments side of the practice, and the financial planning fees. The new people being recruited into the business, many of them young people in their first careers, were drawn to AFG agencies, called Financial Centers by that time, by the lure of being in the financial planning profession, not the life insurance business. These people had no intention of focusing on the product line that was the lifeline of profitability for the company. Of course, these same people soon learned, as Andy learned first-hand, that the margins paid to the producer of investment sales and financial plans is far less than for life insurance. Many did not survive their first or second years in the "practice." The 3-year retention of new AMs in an AFG Financial Center during the late 80s dropped from 1/3 to less than 10%; the company's life insurance production paralleled this trend as well, dropping each year from the peak in 1984 to a trough ten years later of less than $5 million in net new premium, now called life ECDs.

The drop in production and the unethical spending patterns were not immediately known to Atlantic Mutual's Board of Directors. The Board was led by Wayne Madison as Chairman, both Kelleher and Baskin had inside director positions as well. The three were able for a time to hide the deteriorating financial situation from the Board. They controlled access to information and the outside Board members were kept fairly in the dark, at least for awhile.

Madison, for his part, also participated in some less than ethical practices. One was to use company funds and resources to conduct charitable campaigns, with Wayne, personally, as the benefactor. An example of this was his personal support for the Boy Scouts of America, funded by the company but in his personal name. This was also done with the United Way Campaigns that happened each fall; staff in the home office were pressured into making periodic donations directly from their paychecks. They were told that the company was aiming at 100% employee participation, and anyone looking for advancement in the company knew better than to refuse to sign up. Another example of how people can rationalize bad behavior – Wayne Madison would later claim that it was all fine because it was for a charitable cause.

Wayne also funded some activities within the home office that seemed to be alien to what a diversified financial services organization would embark upon. One such venture was to put Wayne's son-in-law, Steve Ronkowski, into a new venture: building a fully tricked-out video studio inside the home office building on Capitol Hill. Ronkowksi had been a staffer in the Marketing Communications Unit under Frank Meaney's Marketing Services Department. Steve was known as a good-time guy, got along with everyone, joked with everyone, liked by everyone, respected for his marketing and management sense by few. But he dated and in 1985 married the only daughter of the Madison family. In the Labor Day Massacre, Steve was protected, and so it was dreamed up that he would develop and staff a full-service video and audio studio on the 5th floor that would be used for in-house productions and marketed to outside organizations wishing to produce training, compliance, and marketing videos.

The fact that Atlantic was not a publicly traded stock company did help the concealment. As a mutual company, the stock was held by the company's policyholders. There was no outside set of stockholders to serve. This was a major brand marketing advantage: the company could say that it existed to serve the policyholders themselves, not some outside investors. As opposed to Lambert, a stock company, AFG was owned "by its customers." But by being a mutual, Atlantic did not have the same oversight by the SEC that publicly traded companies did – it did not have to file financial reports to the same extent as stock companies.

The mutual form of doing business can still be an advantage, as long as your customers all own life insurance with your company. But as the makeup of the company's customers began to shift from life insurance to investments and other products, the customer base began to separate from the owners. A declining percentage of the customer base was policyholders. And those policyholders were financing the activities outside of the life insurance product line: the mutual fund offerings from Chesapeake, the development of Atlantic Savings Bank, the proliferation of the broker-dealer (TIG) as the central touch point for marketing and compliance with the field, and so had less and less influence over the company's direction. Essentially, the life insurance book of business in force at Atlantic, very profitable as it was, became an "ATM" for all the other product lines that were far less profitable. But in 1987, Atlantic still had a very large though aging book of in-force life insurance to its credit. The revenue from recurring premiums from this business helped the bottom line of the company and so helped screen the oncoming problems from Board scrutiny.

At least this was the case for a time. In early 1988, a few of the stockholder-policyholders began to ask questions about the company's direction. There were rumors, though at that point unproven, of some shenanigans going on in the field. One of the younger outside Board members began a secret investigation of his own. Aiden Jacobson, AJ to his friends, was a successful entrepreneur in Bethesda, MD, outside D.C. He specialized as a management consultant, fixing up failing companies for rehabilitation or eventual sale. His expertise was corporate finance.

But his aspirations went beyond pushing numbers across a page. In 1981, he developed a past-time of playing ice hockey. This was just after the 1980 Olympics and the Gold Medal earned by the "Miracle on Ice" U.S. Team. At that time, novice amateur hockey leagues for adults were springing up all over the country. AJ joined the National Novice Hockey League, which began as a training camp for new adult skaters and could take a novice in 8 weeks (two nights a week) from "can't skate" to playing hockey. The league in the D.C. area played in skating rinks all over the Metro area; Fairfax, VA and Rockville, MD were two common venues for games. The games would take place on weeknights, starting at 10:30pm, after the more profitable general skating sessions were over. This meant a young executive like AJ had to be very dedicated to the sport, as the games generally ended around 1am. Sleep would be at a premium for those wishing to start work bright and early the next morning. Also at the same training camp, and eventually the same team, was Andy Greene, who in 1981 had just gotten married and was looking for some after-hours activity to stay in shape. Andy and AJ thereby developed an acquaintance even before either of them was associated with Atlantic Mutual. Andy would join Atlantic a year later; AJ would join the Atlantic Board in 1985, around the time of the Labor Day Massacre.

AJ knew of Andy's departure from AFG. He watched as Andy thrashed about with Northern Virginia Financial Group. He knew of Andy's expertise in advanced underwriting and his marketing knowledge. The two stayed in touch only occasionally after they both stopped playing hockey, in 1984. But they knew how to reach each other.

AJ correctly surmised that Andy knew of some of the inside games that were being played in the home office and the field. Andy for his part had stayed in touch with a couple of his colleagues who stayed on in National Headquarters, especially Marie Frame, who at that time ran the Marketing Communications area for both Marketing East and West, one of the few units that still transcended both marketing areas.

On many of Andy's trips to the Coastal Region for Lambert LifeAmerica, he would get together with Marie to run a portion of the Potomac bike trail, as it ran along the River from the Memorial Bridge down to Old Town. Marie was just a friend, no more, but a confidant. By 1987 she lived near Old Town. And she would regale with stories of the management excesses in the home office, especially some of the promotional materials she was having to put together for the Boy Scouts and United Way Campaigns – having nothing to do with company business. She also passed along rumors of the spending practices that went on in L.A.

In January 1988, AJ reached out to Andy, inviting him to lunch at the Columbia Country Club in Chevy Chase, MD, where AJ was a member. Andy scheduled a regional trip down there with time to make a side trip to see AJ. He waited for AJ in the parking lot. The two shook hands and entered a huge dining area that was just off to the right of a classically outfitted lobby area. Columbia was at heart a golf club, and a "restricted" one at that time – no Blacks, no Jews as members. In fact, it had only recently allowed women to have membership in their own right, as opposed to a spousal membership. Andy knew he was dining in the enemy camp, but never let on to AJ.

The conversation started with a little friendly rehashing of their days playing hockey. AJ wasn't half bad. A natural athlete, he took to skating quickly and was a winger on the first line of the team. Andy was also a winger, on what was called "the checking line," euphemism for "these guys won't score; their job is just to try and keep the other side from scoring." The checking line is where you put your lesser skaters. They joked about their hockey exploits.

Eventually, AJ got to it. "Andy, I think you have an idea of what I want to talk about here."

"I have a vague idea that you're worried about what's going on at AFG, right?"

"Exactly, my friend." Andy had learned that when someone says "my friend" reach for your wallet.

"Aiden, you know, I left the company over two years ago. Why do you think I would know much about what's going on there now?"

"Because I assume you've kept in touch with some people there. I know you were close with Frank Meaney in Northern Virginia. He was your boss, right?

"Yes. But that's history."

"Sure. So let's start with the history. No one has ever told me about what happened to you and the others in '85."

And Andy began to tell AJ about the Labor Day Massacre, about Marketing East and West, and why he was excluded from consideration for the new marketing team.

"And then you started your own company."

"Northern Virginia Financial Group."

"Yeah, I can see from your sweater." AJ pointed to the logo that appeared on the maroon colored, V-neck, woolen sweater Andy was wearing over his starched white shirt and bowtie. Andy still had pride in the company he had started and wore the remnants of the brand whenever he could. You might think it was off-putting to do that in front of Lambert PPGAs at regional meetings. But the opposite was true. It was a reminder to the crowd that Andy had once run his own "PPGA-like" operation; he was one of them.

"How did that go?"

And Andy recounted the tumultuous year he had with the business, the sale to DeLessio, and the move to New Hampshire. "I got a letter from DeLessio about three months after the sale had been completed. He was angry, saying I hoodwinked him on the deal. He claimed I'd left him with nothing but a bunch of clients I had already sold whatever there was to sell to them."

"But he had no recourse against you, did he?"

"No man, and I never heard from him again after that. My assistant who had gone to work for him quit after two months; the guy was abusive to his staff. And he was only a little better to his clients."

"So, Andy, he got what he deserved and you got out with your ass intact. That's what I do for a living. I take a losing corporate situation and try to salvage something good from it."

"You do have that reputation." Andy was proud to see that AJ got why he had told the story about DeLessio's letter – to show he got the better of the acquisition deal.

"So, what about now, Andy? What do you know about Atlantic now?"

"AJ, I keep in touch with a few people." And Andy commenced to telling the stories he'd heard about Baskin in L.A., and what Wayne was financing in the home office. "Clearly, you need to keep my name and those I associated with out of the conversation."

"You can be sure of that. I'm on the Board now, as you know."

"Yes, I know. You came on just as the Massacre was happening."

"I'm also concerned about the way the mix of business is shifting so rapidly away from life insurance. But I'm going to start on the low hanging fruit – the clear mismanagement that can't be denied. Keep your head down and your ears open, my friend."

Andy thought it advantageous to stay in touch with such a "captain" of Washington industry. He had already thought ahead to when – not if – he was coming back to the area. Andy always had a plan; sometimes the plan changed, but he always had a plan. So, the two kept in loose touch over the next several years, each watching the other's progress in his respective careers.

In October 1988, there was an AFG Board meeting to review financial results for the third quarter of that year and to sign off on next year's budget. During that meeting, Aiden Jacobson released a file full of documentation indicting Wayne Madison of mismanagement. The previous week, the Board's Executive

Committee had recommended the firing of Benny Baskin and Johnny Wales. Wayne was allowed to resign and retire on a handsome exit package. A retired CEO for Atlantic Mutual, still on the Board, would take over as interim Chairman and CEO, while a replacement for Madison was found. Marketing East and West were collapsed into one marketing department, once again, with Elliott Kelleher as CMO. Kelleher had won by being less bad than any of the others. This "we suck less" attitude would be a joking mantra in the halls of National Headquarters for the next six years.

Andy went back to his tasks, officially as Lambert's Director of Advanced Sales – unofficially as assistant RVP in the Coastal Region. Because advanced marketing was such an integral part of Lambert's life insurance approach to the market, Andy became involved in all manner of marketing, even including product development and sales literature, to support both product and concept in the marketplace. There were others in the Product Marketing Department under Lyn Randolph – Tim Samson and Ed Scher – both Product Marketing Consultants. And they were more than competent. Before Andy showed up, both covered the advanced sales area themselves. Though not lawyers, they knew at least enough to be dangerous. In Chattanooga, the company still had Lester Jones, a long time Appalachia Life employee, who was also a non-lawyer CLU who dabbled in the advanced markets. Lester was a Southern Gentleman through and through, but it also meant that he harbored some prejudices from his heritage. When word came down that Lyn was hiring Andy, Lester speculated, given Andy's New York background, that he probably was Jewish. Lester did privately ask Lyn, "what are you doing hiring a Jew?" He pushed off the bigotry, blaming it on the Congregationalists in New Hampshire who would never accept a Jew in their midst.

Lester never let on his predisposition about Andy, and over time they came to a mutual respect. Lester got to meet Andy's parents when Shel and Stel met Andy at the airport after a sales conference that both Lester and Andy had helped host – in Monte Carlo, of all places. And Andy was a sometimes dinner guest at Lester's home in Chattanooga when Andy travelled down that way. Most everything Andy learned about Chattanooga, except the famous Civil War battle and Union victory that led eventually to the fall of Atlanta, was from Lester.

As to Tim and Ed, they could barely keep their jealousy of Andy to themselves. They both felt an interloper had come and taken some of their turf away – advanced marketing. Nevertheless, all three attended a conference hosted by the American Society of CLU in Tucson, AZ, in the winter of 1987. Known as the Arizona Institute, the conference was a week-long affair and was attended by about 100 or so mainly field agents from around the country and around the industry who specialized in advanced underwriting with their clientele. Andy, Tim and Ed were three of only five home office people who attended this annual meeting. Andy was so impressed with the quality of the information given by top notch speakers at this meeting that he made sure it would be on his calendar almost every year for the rest of his career. This would be the last time Tim and Ed would attend. But also attending was none other than Jerry Piccolo, who had hired Andy into Atlantic 5 years earlier. Jerry had moved to Phoenix and was an in-house advanced underwriting expert for agents in a large insurer's regional office there. So, Andy and Jerry were able to get reacquainted. And Andy was able, once again, to tell the story of what happened at Atlantic after Jerry left.

Andy also got dragged back into Northern Virginia Financial Group, at least for a moment in time. While at the Arizona Institute, a claims officer from Free State Life left a voicemail message on

Andy's home phone back in Virginia. "This is the Claims Department from Free State Life Insurance. We're calling you because you have a client, Theotis Pulliam, who has made a claim on his disability insurance policy that you wrote him about a year ago. You need to call us ASAP to discuss the claim. Thank you."

And Andy excused himself from the morning coffee break during classes that day to phone back East to the Free State home office. "What's up?" he started, when he reached a claims officer there, apparently the very one who left the message at home.

"Well, Mr. Greene, it seems the insured on this policy was diagnosed HIV positive just before he signed the application on this policy. He's now in the hospital with full blown AIDS."

"You can deny the claim if you want. It is within the two-year contestability period, right?"

"Let's not get ahead of ourselves. We have a life policy that we assume we'll have to contend with as well. The problem, sir, is that you signed off on two applications in which Mr. Pulliam states he was not HIV positive at the time."

"That's right. I remember that."

"Well sir, it seems he was obviously lying to you, and us. My question to you, sir, is 'Did he actually answer that question himself?' In other words, did you take down his answer as he told it to you?"

"Of course!" Andy was feeling a little defensive at this point.

"We need to be sure of this, because you bound us to both policies, collecting premium and giving a conditional receipt, and we were not in the room when he made out this application."

"Look. I don't know what you're implying." Putting his lawyer cap on, "Your own underwriting regulations, in your own underwriting manual, clearly says that I am not allowed to have the applicant fill in the answers himself. I have to ask the questions on the app and fill in the answers, then ask him to check it over for accuracy and sign it."

A little indignant, "I know what the manual says, sir, you do not have to repeat it to me, counselor," getting the hint that Andy was making what sounded like an oral argument to a judge. Did he know of Andy's legal background? "We know what the rules are. We simply want to know if you followed them. Specifically, did you let him answer the question, or did you answer the question for him?"

"It was his answer. I took down his answer."

"You didn't coach him or prompt him on how to answer?"

Andy knew of the practice, that some in the field used to tell the client that unless he's sure he has to answer yes to a health ailment, the answer should be "no."

"I did not coach him or prompt him. It was his answer."

"Then I guess you were just ignorant instead of culpable in all this?"

"What do you mean by that?" Andy was getting more defensive by the minute.

"I'm sure you're aware that he is a D.C. resident. The guy comes over the River to Virginia to apply for insurance. He knows he can't get the insurance in D.C. Then, he's faced with the reason why, the question on the app about HIV / AIDS. So, he lies. He comes to you to buy the insurance within three days after he's diagnosed, before his diagnosis shows up in MIB, so we don't know about it, until it's too late."

"Mister, you're inferring a lot in that scenario. Are you saying that Mr. Pulliam knew ahead of time that no one was writing life insurance in D.C.? That's pretty sophisticated knowledge, my friend. Are you saying that the only reason he came to my office was to get the insurance? Did you not consider the fact that a month before he answered a direct mail offer for a free consultation toward a financial plan; that he did not know that the plan would have an insurance recommendation in it before he came to see me; that there was no way I could do anything but put down the answers that he gave me?"

"Please calm down, Mr. Greene. We simply want to establish the facts before we decide what to do about this claim."

And an affidavit was eventually signed by Andy specifying the circumstances under which the insurance applications were taken, along with a copy of Andy's financial plan for Theo. Pulliam died in October that year. In the end, the amounts of disability benefit and life insurance – being small enough to run under the requirement of a paramedical physical exam (and blood test) – were paid out to Theo and his companion-beneficiary. Free State didn't want the negative publicity of denying the claim of a gay man dying of AIDS. The amounts paid out were calculated by Free State's legal department to be less than the cost of litigation over the claim. The very next year, the D.C. City Council passed a bill removing the restriction on asking the HIV / AIDS question on insurance applications. And the life insurance industry re-entered the D.C. market.

One of the perks of being in marketing at Lambert LifeAmerica was that some in the department got invited to attend the annual sales meeting for the company. This was called the White Mountain Club, consisting of PPGAs who qualified to attend because of their level of production for the company. The meeting was essentially a vacation for the agents and their spouses (mostly wives), but in order to make the cost of the meeting pass IRS regulations – that it was educational, not taxable to the attendees – these meetings had to have a business component to it.

This is where people like Andy came in. As head of Advanced Sales, there would always be an advanced planning topic that would come up on the program. Andy's qualities as a presenter at these meetings did not go unnoticed by senior management, especially Don Wasserman, who oversaw the invite list for home office. If asked to attend the meeting, it was likewise important to make sure there was documentation that the home office attendee was there on a business purpose. And it was common practice to invite the home office employee's spouse as well. So, there would be an invite letter that would go to the employee, specifying the business nature of the meeting, and the employee's and spouse's duties in entertaining and hosting events at the conference for field people. Again, this was a way to avoid taxing the company's cost to the employee.

In fact, while Lyn and Andy always took these responsibilities seriously, this was a thinly veiled front for providing a non-taxable perk to favored staff at the home office. You were considered upwardly mobile at Lambert if you received an invitation to "Club." The 1987 meeting in Monte Carlo, a hugely opulent and expensive affair, included Lyn, Lester, and Andy from Product Marketing. When Tim and Ed were left to "hold down the fort," their disappointment and hostility toward Andy increased.

These "Club" meetings always had a day off without a business meeting, and the home office staff would usually team up with field people for any manner of outings. Golf was always the favorite daytime activity for the field. And to the extent that home office marketing attendees had originally come from field sales positions, it was easy to create foursomes in golf that had a mix of field and home office. In fact, home office attendees were instructed not to allow a group of field people to go off and do anything without a home office person in tow.

The point was less to keep the field agents out of trouble as it was to use the "quality" time to forge lasting loyalty relationships between the home office and field. But the need to supervise some of the more adventurous, sometimes lascivious, producers was a close second in purpose. Usually, a PPGA at Club would not embarrass themselves in front of a home office executive. But left alone, the alcoholism, drug abuse, and "whoring," would sometimes cause problems.

That did not prevent incidents the home office people created for themselves, such as the night in Monte Carlo when Lester Jones and his wife decided on a late night bit of fresh air – after a few minutes of unbridled marital passion – and went out onto their hotel room balcony in little more than bathrobes. Unfortunately, they inadvertently locked themselves out when they closed the sliding glass door behind them.

This was simply not acceptable for a Southern Gentleman – forget his compromising situation – to have his wife out there as well, scantly clad. Stuck outside on the balcony, in the middle of the night, with nothing on but their robes, Lester swung into his chivalrous role and decided to shimmy down the barrier fence on the edge of the balcony and work his way down from their third floor room to either the second floor room below – perhaps there was someone home – or eventually to the lobby level.

However clever this plan was, Lester was no longer a young man, and he was not completely sober either. He lost his grip on the barrier and tumbled two stories to a row of bushes that broke his fall. He was little the worse for wear, other than the indignity of lying in the bushes with just a robe on. He did break a wrist and had some minor contusions to his back. It did wake the other Lambert attendees and bring hotel staff to Lester's rescue, so he did save his wife any further embarrassment. But the broken wrist was a several weeks reminder to everyone who saw him of what had happened. And so it became the stuff of Lambert folklore.

Because Andy did not engage in this kind of behavior, he was a perfect candidate to keep others from doing so as well. And Andy was not a golfer, which meant he would be in charge of all the offsite activity that was other than golf; touring the sites, playing tennis, bicycle outings, jogging, swim and massage at the spa, all were part of normal off-hours time where Andy would be in attendance.

Sallie did not accompany Andy on these trips. She suffered from ear infections whenever she travelled by plane. She also did not relish the idea of having to "kiss-ass" as it were the field producers, which was a major role of any home office spouse at these meetings.

The 1988 Club meeting was in Hong Kong, while the British still held the colony. Andy especially liked this one because it was not a front for golfing. It was a shopper's paradise, especially if you came with lots of American cash rather than credit cards. And Andy filled an empty suitcase with gifts purchased in shops along Nathan Road, including the first jewelry he bought for Sallie since the wedding – two strands of pearls; one fresh-water and the other cultured. To make sure he did not get taken for a ride on these purchases, Andy went to at least six different jewelers, all giving him various aspects of an education on pearls, before he made a purchase decision. Andy also got to go on a day trip into the Chinese Mainland that had just recently opened up to tourists.

In 1989, it was off to Puerto Rico, where Andy had a run of good luck at the Blackjack tables in the casino at the El Conquistador. But the attendees also got a first-hand look at the poverty in most of San Juan, as the bus taking them from the airport to the resort went through the poorer parts of the city. During one of the general business sessions, a local band playing Latin music suddenly broke into a Latin version of "Dixie," to play to the Southern producers and the home office management from Chattanooga in attendance. It was common Southern tradition that whenever "Dixie" was heard, to show your Southern heritage, one would stand with hand over heart, just as if the National Anthem was being played. All of the Southerners in the audience, all white, immediately got up, as expected. Andy, believing he was a Virginian, felt an urge to stand with them. Then he had second thoughts, and remained seated. It appears Andy was only a sometime Virginian.

In 1990, the Club meeting was in Bermuda (notice how the distances from New Hampshire seemed to get smaller with each new meeting, no coincidence as the financial people became concerned with how much was being spent on these conferences). There, Andy learned that Bermuda is for couples, not for going stag, and Andy felt a little left out without Sallie there.

In between Club meetings and the annual Arizona Institute, Andy travelled extensively throughout the country. Lambert had the whole country covered by Regional Vice Presidents. Often, he would spend a week with an RVP, going to do meetings in various cities throughout the region. In Keystone (Pennsylvania), it would typically start in Philadelphia on Monday, a travel day to Harrisburg and a meeting there on Wednesday, another travel day to Pittsburgh for a meeting Friday morning. In Great Lakes (Michigan and Ohio), the barnstorming would start outside Detroit, then a car drive in Ohio to either Columbus or Cincinnati (Cleveland was mysteriously rarely on the schedule), stopping for some great BBQ on the way. In the Dixie Region, it usually started in Atlanta, then on to Charlotte, maybe ending in Raleigh.

In New York City, Andy ran into a small snafu, when he "tipped" the waitstaff at a dinner hosted for some prospective new PPGAs – with the RVP in attendance – like a New Yorker (20%), instead of the company guidelines of 15% (it was protocol that the home office always paid for these dinners on its respective budgets, further encouraging RVPs to have home office representation when wining and dining prospects – to make the home office pick up the check). After Andy filed his expense report, the CFO, Barry Lemon, apparently pulled the form for spot audit and found the heavy tip, and sent Andy a note reprimanding him for excessive spending. Andy, believing that Lemon was micromanaging, as "green eye shade" finance guys will do, sent back a padded envelope with 118 pennies in it, representing the $1.18 at issue, with a note, saying, "My apologies; I do not want the company to be out any money for my tipping in New York. Please accept this as reimbursement."

Lemon wrote back an inter-office memo in reply, stating, "Thanks for the 118 pennies…Petty cash needed the coin." And inside the inter-office envelope was a plastic card, called "The Tipper," showing the target amounts to tip at various amounts of check, with the 15% column circled with a Sharpie. Andy seethed about it, but eventually had a laugh over the whole thing. He shared the matter with Lyn and she cracked up so loud that Tim and Ed overheard outside Lyn's office, came in and they all had a laugh over it. The "case of the missing tip money" quickly became folklore around the home office, making fun of Barry Lemon and stressing – maybe more than was justified – the high road, the "graciousness" of how Andy played the whole thing out.

Of course, Andy spent more time in the Coastal Region than any of the others. This usually involved a meeting in Wilmington (Phil McPherson's regional office was there), then onto Baltimore, then ending somewhere in Virginia (either Northern Virginia or Tidewater).

Everywhere Andy went, the PPGAs got a good show and learned something. They valued even more the possibility of getting Andy's advice on live cases. Sometimes, especially in Coastal, Andy would actually make appointments to go out with PPGAs on calls and help, as Andy would put it, "with the laying of hands over the plan" the producer was recommending to his/her client and the client's advisor (attorney or accountant) in attendance at the meeting. Andy continued to observe the protocol of not giving advice directly to clients on live cases. He would instead try and give his recommendations to the PPGA or to the client's advisor, so it could not be said that Andy was the client's attorney.

Andy continued to take advantage, when in Northern Virginia, to take the necessary CLE classes to maintain his active membership in the Virginia State Bar. He often took Sallie with him on these trips, by car rather than plane, with Robert in tow. By 1989, they had a second child, Jackson (nicknamed Jack).

Life at Lambert LifeAmerica was not all fun and games. On October 19, 1987, the stock market crashed, depleting many of Lambert's clients of much of their wealth in a single day. The clients weren't the only ones losing that day. Many agents were heavily invested in equities, often with high leverage in the form of margin accounts. They got to trade *sans* commissions in their own accounts at Lambert Securities, and took full advantage of the *largesse*. October 20 dawned with one PPGA in Tampa, Florida, dead of a self-inflicted gun-shot wound. It was a sure suicide – gun aimed below the chin and fired upwards through the head. Friends of the deceased agent would later share that he was greatly in debt, had a bad cocaine habit, and "Black Monday" – as the day before would come to be known – was simply "the straw that broke the camel's back."

Andy would hear from top agents, "We work hard, and we play just as hard." Here was a case of playing into oblivion. And it was a shame, too. Within a week after Black Monday, the stock market had recovered all of its losses. The smart financial advisor in the business was reminded that clients invest with their advisors for the long-term, and what goes down soon comes back up, if you give it time.

Andy also used the time to stay in touch with his colleagues from AFG: Marie, AJ, Q, Frank Meaney, and others. Andy learned that in early 1989, Atlantic had hired a new CEO, the Managing Director from their Pittsburgh Financial Center, William "Tab" Davenport. This was rare in the financial services business, to put a sales and marketing person in charge of the whole company. Across the industry there was a deeply held suspicion of marketing people in the top spot. These people were considered spendthrifts with the company's money. Conventional wisdom: A financial institution, like an insurance firm, should have a "bottom" line person in charge, usually a finance or investments person, sometimes an actuary, occasionally an operations person...but not a sales and marketing person. In the last decades of the 20th century, the situations in which a marketing person succeeded to the CEO position in a financial services company was usually only when the Board had become desperate to protect or build market share, where the top line of the income statement was the problem. At AFG, the top line was a big part of the problem. The Board had gotten rid of the bad apples that misspent for personal gain, so the bottom line was secure. But the problem with shrinking production in life insurance was seen as the overriding imperative now. At AFG the top Financial Centers in the late 1980s were always Phoenix, then Pittsburgh, then Northern Virginia. But only Pittsburgh was still doing more than 25% of its total ECDs in life insurance. So, the company took a successful Managing Director out of what he did best and promoted him into a job for which he had no background.

At least Tab Davenport knew what he didn't know. He felt he needed someone who knew the history across the sales force. So, he kept Elliott Kelleher on as CMO. Everyone assumed Elliott was a goner, so the staff were surprised when he was kept on. And Elliott in turn decided to hire a new head of Marketing Services, Brian Saunders, who in turn hired a new head of advanced underwriting, Dave Manning. Elliott would concentrate on managing the field force; Brian would be head of all the in-house marketing areas, even the marketing operations area, where commissions and expense allowances were paid and ECDs were calculated for keeping track of the personal production of each AM.

In early 1988, Concord, NH woke up. For maybe a month, the city was inundated with politicians, their handlers, and the press in anticipation of the "First-in-the-Nation" New Hampshire primary. This was the one time every four years that New Hampshire gets to be the center of the country. It also helps the local economy, so this was a huge deal on many levels. In late January, Kansas Senator Bob Dole had surprised everyone by winning the Iowa Republican caucuses. He was figured to be a distant second to Vice President George H. W. Bush. Suddenly, Dole's people saw an opportunity to beat Bush in his own backyard. While Bush boasted that he hailed from Texas, this was only half true. The fact was, the entire Bush family originally hailed from New England. Bush's father, Prescott Bush, was a Senator in his day from Connecticut. And everyone savvy in American politics knew that the Bush's vacationed in Kennebunkport, on the Maine coast. New Hampshire was assumed to be Bush country. But now Dole saw his chance to dislodge Bush from the front-runner position.

Dole for his part, had recently served as ranking Republican on the Senate Finance Committee. During 1987, Dole and his Committee pushed through Congress a tax bill, which, among other things, revamped the definition of life insurance in the Internal Revenue Code. Life insurance policies known as "single premium" policies would lose most tax shelter advantages. Dole famously came out against the practice of loading up a permanent life insurance policy with so much premium that a single amount could buy the minimum amount of death benefit and the policy would continue in force indefinitely (until the insured's death). The new tax provision called these policies Modified Endowment Contracts (MEC), and excluded them from the FIFO taxation on withdrawals. Dole and others had become concerned that life insurance was being sold more for its tax shelter than for the benefit of "widows and orphans."

None of what went on in Congress was lost on Andy Greene. The single premium product at Lambert LifeAmerica had to be re-designed to fit within the MEC rules, effectively ending its sale-ability. Dole was right; selling permanent coverage had become more of a matter of tax sheltering the cash value and its treatment on withdrawal than about the death benefit protecting families from the loss of its breadwinner. But it nevertheless irked those in the business, like Andy and Lambert's Product Development Department, that one of its best products had effectively been outlawed.

So, when – flush from victory in Iowa – Dole's people decided to "double down" their efforts in New Hampshire, his entourage hastily scheduled an appearance in the Lambert home office, in its cafeteria, for the Thursday afternoon before next Tuesday's primary. Someone in the entourage should have foreseen the potential problem of Dole appearing in the cafeteria of a life insurance carrier. No one did. Dole appeared with Elizabeth, his wife, at around 3pm that afternoon. The appearance was well attended by Lambert employees and the press. After a brief set of comments, first from Elizabeth and then from the Senator himself, Dole's campaign manager in New Hampshire, the very popular Senator Warren

Rudman, opened the meeting for questions from the audience. A silence fell over the room. The employees had been very cordial to Dole; applauding though not enthusiastically at his presentation (they actually liked "Libby," his wife, more). No one seemed to have any questions.

"Someone, anyone, here's your chance to ask the Senator whatever you want," repeated Rudman.

Then Andy slowly raised his hand. Those sitting near him had an inkling of what he was going to ask. "After all," Andy would later say, "we asked the "A" question when Gary Hart appeared in the home office." "A" for adultery (Sen. Hart was embroiled in the sex scandal that would doom his candidacy on the Democratic side). Certainly, "Dole had to know the 'T' [tax] question was coming."

"Senator," Andy began in his best Washingtonian press corps style, "Welcome to Concord and to our offices."

"Glad to be here, sir," the Senator replied, graciously.

"Being that you're in the home office of a nationwide life insurance company, I wanted to ask you about that tax provision you helped put into last year's tax bill that outlawed single premium life insurance. What was your thinking there and why should any of us support you after you pushed the thing through the Finance Committee?"

Dole was known for his temper, and he turned slightly from his right side, protecting the hand he lost use of as a wounded veteran of WWII, when he served in the 10th Mountain Brigade in Italy. His face went from smile to contempt. "I didn't come here for a legislative quiz," was all he said, and Senator Rudman quickly stepped in to move the Q&A to someone, anyone else. There were no other questions. Dole was clearly insulted at Andy's question, but the look on the Lambert employees' collective face was truly historic. They had never seen anything like what Andy pulled off in front of one of the country's best known political leaders.

When the session broke up, some came forward to say hello and shake the hand of the candidate. Andy did not. He instead made his way back to his office at the other end of the floor. As he arrived back at his office, a colleague ran behind him and called out, "Andy, Senator Rudman is looking all over for you. He says he wants Dole to have a chance to give you a more complete answer to your question." Surely, Rudman, if not Dole, knew that the candidate's answer was a public gaff, in front of voters and the press.

"If the Senator wants to meet with me, tell him to give me a call and set up an appointment." Andy was showing a little self-righteous indignation of his own.

Neither Rudman nor Dole ever followed up with Andy. However, over the next five days leading up to Tuesday's primary, Dole never seemed to recover from that gaff at Lambert. This foul mood of Dole's continued on, culminating in the famous comment after the primary was clearly lost, when Dole accused Bush, "tell him [Bush] to stop lying about my record." From then on, it was local folklore at Lambert and in Concord, that Andy Greene had single-handedly ruined the Presidential candidacy of Bob Dole in 1988.

By 1990, Andy had firmly established himself as an institution in his own right at Lambert. Known well by all the PPGAs and RVPs in the field – respected, sometimes envied, in the home office – Andy was well thought of, more respected and occasionally feared than liked. His bowtie and braces had become his trademark. He fashioned a moustache to add to his individuality as well.

Andy used to say to Sallie, "My best work is in the field." This was usually in response to Sallie's complaint of being left alone in New

Hampshire to look after Bob and Jack on her own. To be sure, when Andy was home, he was HOME – and took his turn at everything from changing diapers and potty training to mowing the lawn and other yard chores. Sallie, who had done some part time "of counsel" work for a local law firm when they arrived in New Hampshire, had given it all up to stay at home permanently when Jack was born.

Sallie was a good lawyer; let's face it, a great lawyer. And as a leader in the feminist movement in Northern Virginia she took great pleasure in beating the "good ol' boys" in Fairfax. When she was in practice, she use to explain to Andy, "There are three kinds of women lawyers in practice today. The first I call the 'Sweetie Pie,' who uses her looks and flirtatious style to get what she wants. The second is what I call the 'Superbitch,' who tries to be an Alpha-male in a dress. The third is the 'Neuter Gender.' That's me. I try and remove gender from the equation and look pretty much androgenous."

Andy thought to himself, "I guess Effie Eckhart would fit the first category if she had a law degree."

What Sallie wasn't as good at was being a homemaker. She found she missed the action in law practice. She wasn't much of a cook, and less inclined to clean up. While Andy wasn't much of a cook either, he usually was the one to do the cleaning. He was particular that way. He'd say, "Kitchen and bathrooms, they are the most important rooms to keep clean at all times." Sallie meanwhile was so focused on being a full time mother that nothing else was allowed to creep in. The major problem for her now was being stuck in New Hampshire. She came to really hate the place – the snow, the black flies in May; the ruralness of it all.

And the people… In the South, where small talk is an art form, people will not let a social moment go by without conversation – even it is idle conversation – which it usually was. In New

Hampshire, if people had nothing to say, they said nothing. An example was an invite from a neighbor to barbeque in their backyard. The men, Andy and the neighbor, would sit on the porch on rocking chairs, and watch the sunset, rocking back and forth, perhaps saying nothing for several minutes at a time. Andy must have learned this habit from his grandfather. It drove Sallie crazy, and she often raised that as an example of how she could not figure out how to get along with "these people up here."

Andy knew that staying in New Hampshire would be bad for his marriage. A plan to get back to Virginia at some point – at least south of here – "was what we needed," he thought. And yet, Andy enjoyed his time in the Granite State. It meant he could root for the home team in Fenway Park or the Boston Garden. When Bob was only 4 years old, Andy took him to his first NFL game, at the then Foxboro Stadium south of Boston, with local hero Doug Flutie at QB taking revenge against the Chicago Bears for the Pats crushing loss in Super Bowl XX two years before. Bob would quickly become a New England Patriots fan from then on.

Andy became comfortable enough by 1989, when Jack was born, that he took on a part time second job at a local radio station, WKXL," the voice of Southern New Hampshire." Here he served as a weekend DJ and brought in the Boston sports games – Red Sox and Bruins especially – on the satellite. When, in the summer, the full time on-air guys took vacation, Andy arranged his schedule to fill in at "PM drive time," the first and last time Andy would work on-air during peak listening hours anywhere.

Sometimes Andy would bring Bob to the studio on a Sunday afternoon for the beginning of his 6-Midnight air shift and have the boy, then age 5, sit on Andy's lap while he pushed various buttons and moved various tape machines, bringing in CBS News or Sports reports each hour, and spinning records and CDs (compact discs, not certificates of deposit) in between Red Sox games. Eventually, little

Bob learned the timing enough that Andy let him push buttons on his own to move from one program item to the next on the log. This was to be the last dance on radio Andy would have, though he didn't know it at the time. By the mid-1990s, radio had gone totally digital, run by computers – no more cart machines and two-track reel-to-reels; no more turntables and CD players. But in 1989-90, this was a fun way to earn a few extra dollars to help pay the mortgage without financial help from Sallie. For her part, Sallie would often come down to the station in the early evening, with baby Jack in tow, sitting in for a few minutes while Bob tried showing off to his Mom what he could do on the control board. Then, Sallie would take the two boys home by nightfall while Andy continued his shift until station went off-air.

In order to make time for the radio job, Andy began cutting back on his travels a little. He was also concerned about leaving Sallie alone with the boys. She couldn't even see the next house from any window in theirs; the distance between homes in this rural enclave was ¼ mile on either side, through dense forest, with a slope down a hill to the back of the woods where the Greene's lot ended. The driveway was 200' feet long to the roadway, unpaved with only a coat of Bluestone Hardpack gravel to show the way. When the children went outside to play during deer hunting season in the fall, Sallie had them wear blaze orange vests, to make sure they could be seen by any hunters who hunted in the area and may not have yet learned that someone built a house on this hill. In late March each year, when the weather would finally allow for temperatures above freezing, the large volume of snow accumulated over the winter would all melt within a couple of weeks, creating an almost impassable mess on that driveway – Sallie's car, a Ford Taurus station wagon, more than once got stuck in the mud.

In March of 1990, Lambert was preparing to put on its annual Lambert LifeAmerica Variety Show, an event held in Concord High School's auditorium. Proceeds from the sale of tickets and other donations went to various local charitable causes. But this was not just a charitable event. Attended by almost all employees at Lambert, their families and friends, and many acquaintances in the community, the Show became an opportunity to lampoon the company, its managers, and the industry, as well as take a light and comic look at life in New Hampshire. Employees not only locally in Concord, but around the country in the Parsippany and Chattanooga offices would make the trek to New Hampshire and stay for the Show, held on a Friday evening in the middle of the month.

The Show consisted of everything from musical reviews to demonstrations of special talents, but the best parts were the comical skits the employees put on, taking a good-natured but satirical look at life at Lambert and New Hampshire. For the past three years, the show had been hosted by Tim VanEckland, a zone VP in charge of half the country's field RVPs. Tim had a gregarious personality about him and was a natural mouthpiece MC for this Show, which usually started like something out of the Tonight Show with Johnny Carson – a 10-minute comic monologue, geared to warm up the audience. Then, after each act, Tim would return to the stage, clad in tux and black tie, to entertain the audience while the stagehands behind the curtain changed the set to make way for the next act. The Show usually went on for about two hours. The senior management, ironically egged on by President Paul Swift himself, would actually encourage the employees writing the sketches to roast the senior management and other officers of the company, even giving the sketch writers-actors information / ideas about what to make fun of in performance. Swift made sure that officers of the company, including himself, always sat in the front rows as obvious targets to be "roasted" by the performers. It was all in good fun, totally PG – a family affair. Swift saw it as a morale booster.

In 1990, VanEckland found himself unable to be MC, due to a family commitment. Who would be MC for the Variety Show? In stepped Andy Greene, a bit of a characature in his own right. Having made a name for himself, turning esoteric tax concepts into light comedy – "information retention is higher when you laugh about it," Andy would philosophize – the home office welcomed the change of "talk show hosts" for this year's Show.

Andy was able to put together just about 10 minutes of comedy monologue. He knew that he could not use some of the field humor he and Lyn were using when travelling around the country, wholesaling Lambert product. Things like "Lambert Life, the most fun you can have with your clothes on," or other bawdy statements about the company's target market clients - the locals in the audience wouldn't get the humor.

But the field would… And so Andy decided that the Show should, for the first time, be videotaped, in its entirety, and sold, afterwards as a second source of charitable dollars. Andy had some dealings with a local videographer in Concord who was looking to cultivate Lambert as a corporate client to produce its training and marketing videos. Andy had been taking his crew down to the studios in the AFG home office in D.C. and renting the video equipment and personnel to produce those kinds of videos for field training, compliance, and sales ideas. Andy had even used local television talent in the Washington market – the weekend weatherman at Channel 9 – to be the narrator of the productions. This videographer hoped to win the business away from AFG. Andy gave him an opportunity by letting him "donate" his time and equipment to show what he could do for Lambert. The videographer "bit down hard" on the opportunity, agreeing to donate a two camera setup in the auditorium, with full audio reproduction through the microphones above the stage and a wireless "lav" on Andy while he performed. And the agreement included a master of the video, in 1" wide tape format used commercially at the time, from which Andy would have hundreds of reproductions made for sale to the PPGAs and RVPs in the field, or as souveniers for the live audience and performers at the Show.

Andy worked with two young marketing people, Carl Tewksbury and Jeff Palomino, in the home office, putting together the sketches and other acts for the Show. For his own monologue, Andy "borrowed" from some of his favorite comedians: Woody Allen, Steven Wright, humorist author Lewis Grizzard, and added in what he could of his own. "Stealing from one source is called a crime; stealing from multiple sources is called 'research,'" Andy would say.

Andy knew he didn't have enough material to do the monologue to start the Show and also fill in between acts. So, he arranged with the videographer to pre-tape some comedy bits – fake commercials – and play them on a large screen at one end of the stage, as a way to supplement Andy's own material between acts.

The evening of March 15 was cold but clear in Concord, and the auditorium was strictly SRO. Andy wore his cream colored linen suit, with purple braces and lavender tie (no tux for this dude). He added his signature cordovan wing tip shoes. As the Show got within 5 minutes of starting, Andy became so nervous that he "lost his lunch" in the school's boys room. After cleaning himself off sufficiently, he headed for off-stage left and waited for the opening announcement over an off-stage mic by Palomino. A colleague from Lambert Securities saw the sick-looking Andy Greene, and came over to lift his spirits, "You're gonna be great," and began massaging his shoulders and neck through his linen jacket.

"*And now, ladies and gentlemen, a man who believes Split-Dollar is the salvation of Western Civilization… Andyyyyy Greeeeeene.*" [Applause] Emulating David Letterman, one of his talk show heroes, Andy ventured out onto the stage, wireless lav clipped to his tie with the transmitter in his left pants pocket. He rarely bothered to button the jacket, but tonight was special…

"Good evening, folks, we have a great Show for you tonight." And Andy proceeded to introduce himself, as if the audience had never heard of him before. Paraphrasing Danny DeVito as Louie DePalma in *Taxi*, "When you hear my name mentioned, and people talk about what a pain in the *you-know-what* I am, that I can be scary, that I can intimidate people… Pay attention; they know what they're talking about." The audience ventured a nervous round of laughter, and Andy was on his way.

There was the elevator story taken from Woody Allen's old standup act in the 1960s, about a talking elevator that punishes him for having beat up on a television set that wasn't working right. There was the Steven Wright bit about Bizzarro Airlines, "where you can book a flight on any Monday and they'll have you arriving the previous Friday, that way you still have the weekend."

Andy then launched into his "I'm really a Virginian at heart. I was 14 years old before I knew that Damn-Yankees was two words." But with a touch of New York accent, the audience laughed at the reference. "Oh, you don't believe me?" Andy then channeled a Grizzard routine: "I'll have you know that my great-great grandfather, Colonel Beauregard Greene, [audience laughter] was sent by General Robert E. Lee himself to defend Miami Beach from the Yankees…" [more laughter] "And apparently he didn't do a whole lot of good because today it's crawling with Yankees." [punchline quality laughter]

All mild stuff, nothing anyone could find objectionable. About the most to-the-edge-of-the-envelope Andy got was an old advanced sales routine Andy had used often in field meetings.

"I'm just a poor country financial planner from Virginia," he started, in the best southern accent he could come up with. "I surely don't know about all these sophisticated tax concepts. My idea of estate planning is this married couple I know. I worked with the husband on his estate plan, and he brings the plan home to his wife to go over how all of his things will get to her if he dies first. The wife says, 'but what if *I* die first?' And the husband replies, 'What do you mean?'

""'Well, if I die first, are you gonna get married again?'

"'Well…I guess so,' he nervously answers."

"'That's O.K., I'd want you to have someone if I'm not around.'

"'That's very sweet of you to think of me, darlin.'

"After a few seconds, the wife then says, 'Now, if I die first, are you gonna let her wear my fur coat?'

"'Well… I guess I would…'

"'That's fine, that's fine… I don't mind…' [Pause] 'Now, will you let her wear my jewelry?'"

"'Well… I guess I would…'

"That's fine, that's fine… I don't mind…' "After a few more seconds, she says, 'Now about my golf clubs… Are you gonna let her use my golf clubs?'

"'Oh no,' the husband says, 'No way that will happen.'

"And the wife stops him there. 'Wait a minute. You'll let her wear my furs; you'll let her wear my jewelry. She can't use my golf clubs? What the heck is it about my golf clubs you're so attached to?'

"'Oh, it's not that. It's that she's left-handed.'"

And it was the biggest laugh Andy got all night on his own. He also pivoted between acts to a pre-taped video with three girls rapping a parody of the Beastie Boys song, "You've got to fight… For your right… To work at Lambert!" Another video featured a close friend and travel colleague of Andy's pretending to be Panama strongman Manuel Noriega, shouting to his followers with sword in hand in broken Spanish and hawking Lambert Funding, a financing program using securities on margin to pay life insurance premium, a favorite securities based product of Lambert Securities.

There was the Concord Businessman's Sychronized Marching Drill Team, with eight people in business suits and briefcases, marching to a Souza tune, all but one a male; the female playing Groucho Marx style fun with the whole seriousness of it.

There was the sketch about three women interviewing for a secretarial position at Lambert, each one from another part of the country representing each of the sites of home offices for Lambert – the gum chewing Jersey girl from Parsippany; the work-boots and flannel shirt wearing hick from New Hampshire; the parody of Scarlett O'Hara representing Chattanooga.

There was one act that Andy played a part in: playing bass guitar behind a quartet performing a Pink Floyd tune – Andy had dusted off his violin-shaped bass from his days in England and gotten it a full setup in order to play for the first time since college.

Most entertaining to the audience was a rather long sketch emulating "Weekend Update" from *Saturday Night Live*, in which Carl and Jeff riffed irreverently about all manner of company personnel and policy.

The Show finished in true SNL style, with all players coming out for bows, including Andy, while the P.A. played "Still Crazy After All These Years," by Paul Simon.

The whole Show was caught on video and over 100 copies would later be sold to supplement the funds raised through ticket sales at the live performance. The amounts raised, given virtually no expenses in producing it, set a Variety Show record, and pleased Paul Swift no end. Andy had barely a cordial relationship with Mr. Swift, he being too serious and studious to make conversation with the gregarious marketing manager that Andy had become. But Andy's stock went up after the Variety Show; Swift could appreciate the effort, especially when it raised his own stature in the community and a record amount of charitable funds, which were also used locally. Swift even toyed briefly during this time of running for Governor, after the somewhat pompous but unforgettable Governor "Big John" Sununu (Andy and Sallie jokingly referred to him as "Sunono") left Concord to be Chief of Staff in Washington for President Bush (41). The Show's fundraising results certainly wouldn't hurt Swift at all.

The very next week, Andy was on the road. Every March – around St. Patrick's Day – it was time for Andy's annual trek across Pennsylvania with RVP Michael McDaniels, a true-to-the-core Irish American, a member of the Sons of Hibernia no less. On the drive from Philadelphia to Pittsburgh (this time they skipped Harrisburg), the two had plenty of time to talk – there's nothing like six hours stuck in a car with someone to get really well acquainted. Mike knew Andy about as well as any RVP knew Andy at that time.

"I heard about the Variety Show and your part in it… Good work, Andy. I ordered a copy of the tape for myself, and I wanna clip parts of it to use in some of the regional meetings."

"Thanks, Mike. I appreciate the compliment and the help with funding the charitable causes." Andy quite frankly couldn't remember what charities the funds were going to, and he didn't really care. Neither did McDaniels.

"I don't really care about the charity stuff, man. But you've become quite the showman. That's why you're a favorite in regional meetings; everybody loves your *shtick*."

"*Shtick*? Mike, you're learning Yiddish from me well. I hope the Sons of Hibernia don't throw you out of the Club for hanging with a Jew." Andy chuckled to make sure McDaniels did not get insulted by the comment.

And McDaniels laughed out loud. "You ever play that game, 'who do you want playing you in the film about your life?'"

"Yeah, but I never gave it much thought."

"Well VanEckland and I were joking around the other day and we decided who we think should play you…"

With anticipation, "Who did you two pick for me, Mike?"

"Ernie Kovacs." The way you play up the meetings like they're a comedy show, complete with funny slides and your moustache and bowtie, it reminded us of Ernie Kovacs, the pioneer of TV comedy and trick photography."

"Man, I know who Ernie Kovacs is." Andy was actually a bit flattered that they hadn't picked some fat slob like Jackie Gleason. "But Kovacs is dead. Aren't you supposed to pick someone who is still alive?"

"Are you still alive, Andy?"

"What do you mean by that?"

"Are you ready to go up the ladder to the next stop in your career? You know you should be in the field with us, where the real money is. I've heard rumors that you're up for the Coastal slot when McPherson retires, and that he's retiring real soon."

"Where did you hear that?"

"Don Wasserman said something about it to VanEckland when he was drunk at some party, and VanEckland said something about it to me when he and I got drunk one night a few months ago."

"Interesting speculation, Mike, but Wasserman is out, you know." Don had been forced out of the CMO position and sent back to Boston to run his old region. This happened just before the Variety Show.

"Yeah, Swift is calling the shots now, and you're one of the few marketing people he likes. The Variety Show must have helped you with him; that thing he considers his baby."

Andy said nothing for a minute, so McDaniels continued, "Can I offer you some coaching, my boy?" The "can I offer you some coaching" was a common expression in the business for "I'm now going to give you some constructive criticism, for your own good."

"O.K." Andy cautiously replied.

"Not often, but sometimes, when I'm talking to you, you seem to look like you're not there anymore, like you've tuned out. You're looking at me, but you're not listening to me. It doesn't happen often. But if you do that with other people, and I suspect I'm not the only jerk you do this to, you're going to have problems with field relationships once they report to you rather than entertain them.

"You see, it's one thing to perform in front of a group of agents, it's another to have to build relationships with them one-on-one, which is at the heart of recruiting and developing PPGAs in our business."

"I get it, Mike. Didn't know I was doing that."

"I don't know if you really are. It just looks that way sometimes. Be careful with that. If you can overcome that, I see no reason why you wouldn't be a great regional."

"Thanks for the advice." Andy did not really take it personally. He understood that McDaniels was just trying to help, to mentor him.

Mike, age 58, had been in the business for 30 years. Andy, now in his late 30s, had been in the business 7 years plus. He still had a lot to learn, and one thing he did learn was to let people mentor him. Frank Meaney used to tell him, "More senior people in the business, they love to mentor younger folks coming up… Let them. It will help your relationships with them and you might actually learn something in the process."

But the secret promise that Don Wassrman had made to Andy three years before, to get Andy to stay at Lambert, could no longer be made good. Don was back in his region. His only comment to Andy when he was packing up to leave the home office was, "Kiddo, I put in the good word for you with Swift." And he winked at Andy.

Meanwhile, Swift had put in the head of Lambert Securities as interim CMO. Andy did not have a warm relationship with Victor Malmsteen, and "Vic" confessed to know nothing of the deal between Andy and Don. Wasserman had been cast in disfavor by Swift, Malmsteen, and other "suits" in the home office as too rough around the edges. And Don's after-hours behavior, which included an affair with his one-time regional assistant, virtually out in the open where his wife could not deny what was going on, really hurt Don's reputation. Actually, it confirmed Don's reputation as a second-class personality, with little sense for propriety and ethics, who cared little what other people thought. But so long as Lambert was exceeding sales goals, Swift could not get in Don's way.

Then in 1989, production began to level off. And the beginning of 1990 looked no better. To be sure, the country was in a mild recession by that time. And in Don's home turf, the Massachusetts Miracle had gone bust, along with the real estate values and capital to buy lots of life insurance and other financial products. Once the numbers were no longer there, Swift saw his opportunity to push Wasserman out, and gave him an honorable way to accept his fate by firing the regional who had taken over in Boston (who wasn't doing that well anyway) and install Don back in "the only job I ever really loved," Wasserman would announce when he prepared to leave Concord.

As a side issue, the affair had become public, and so Don quickly settled with his wife, completed a divorce, and by the end of 1990 had married his once-again regional assistant. The conflict of interest of having your wife – a trophy wife at that, as she could barely type, but she looked good – as your regional assistant was obvious to everyone in the company, except Don. By 1992, Don was forced to retire on disability due to his lung cancer from smoking two packs a day, eliminating the problem for Swift, for good. Don passed away in 1994.

While Andy waited to see if there was any chance to resurrect the "deal" he'd made with Wasserman, Andy's phone rang... It was "Zim," calling once again...

Chapter 7: Moving On Up; Moving On Out

"Hey there, Mr. Greene."

"Hi, Dan, how are you doing?"

"How's life up there in the frozen tundra?"

"I'm doing well, sir. Can't say the same for my family."

"Your wife not taking to the 'Northern Exposure' lifestyle? You kind of thought that might be the case when you accepted the Lambert job."

"Yeah, right… I remember… And if I ever forget, she's there to remind me."

"Well, guy, fear not." Andy figured some career opportunity was coming. "I have an opportunity for you that you might want to consider, if you're up for it."

Andy had used DAZ International to fill an advanced underwriting position under him at Lambert the year before, so Andy and Zim were in regular contact. But Andy soon learned that companies looking to save money relied primarily on "personal observation" for candidates to fill anything but senior level positions. Personal observation meant working your own network of acquaintances to fill positions. Using head hunters was expensive, often 30% of the offering salary. So Andy figured that if Zim had an active search, whether retained or contingent, it must mean a step up by a company willing to spend. "Tell me about it."

"It's a director of advanced sales, but at a higher level of visibility, position title, and compensation. This position is at the elected officer level."

Andy was an appointed officer at Lambert. *Appointed* meant that management could put you in the position without Board approval.

You were an officer, but you still had little access to inside information; that was left for the *elected* officers, who were approved for their positions by the Board. As an example, a Director (Andy's title), even an Assistant VP, was usually an appointed officer position. A true corporate Vice President would be an elected officer; comp, severance package, bonus structure, all more generous for those elected as opposed to appointed. The Hay Company was the foremost executive resource consultants in the industry at the time and their template for corporate organization was repeated in nearly every financial firm in the country.

"I'm listening," was Andy's tentative response.

"This company is going through a lot of change, a whole new management team is coming in, and they want new blood."

Andy cut to the chase. "And where is this company located?"

"They have two home offices. The formal corporate office is on Wall Street; the operational center and where you'll be is in Piscataway, New Jersey."

Andy knew his geography, but could not recall where Piscataway was. "Where in New Jersey is that?" Andy sometimes confused Piscataway with Parsippany.

"It's in Central Jersey. Go to Rutgers and make a right, ha, ha. Figure it's about 15 miles south of Newark, 15 miles north of Princeton."

"Princeton?" Andy thought Sallie might go for such a highbrow town after spending three years with people who think work-boots are fashionable.

"Do I have your updated resume?"

"I'll fax it to you straightaway."

"Good. Let me get your material in front of these people and go from there."

Andy figured it would be months before an offer would ever come from this company. It turned out it was Empire Life. Andy had heard of Empire. They were, at one time, one of the top 50 mutuals in the country. They had one of their largest agencies: The Warren Financial Group in Bethesda, MD, just north of D.C. Everyone in the D.C. insurance and financial planning market knew who Bill Warren was – he was a legend. He drove the model of what a modern General Agent should be in running an insurance agency.

"So, who is running Empire now? Andy asked.

"They brought in a guy from the field. Imagine that. Insurance companies never do that. Bill Warren. You may know him because he's from D.C."

And Andy became more interested. He'd lost out on working for a field guy President in the AFG deal. He certainly didn't want to lose out again. "I know him by reputation, Dan; stellar reputation in D.C."

But the hiring manager would not be Warren. He had a COO, Dick Sheridan, who was brought over from the famous Northern Mutual Life agency in Richmond, Virginia. This was getting better and better. Sheridan had hired a CMO and Senior Vice President (SVP), Sam Roberts, to run the marketing and distribution areas, including hiring into the Department. Sam had been a wholesaler for a west coast carrier, based in Santa Barbara, CA. In other words, the entire reporting line, from advanced sales to the President's office, was former field people. Andy surmised that this would be the kind of environment in which he could succeed, big time. And it meant returning to a mutual company. And the job would at least get the family out of New Hampshire, halfway back to Northern Virginia.

Andy stalled as best he could about this opportunity, stringing out the schedule of interviews for a few months, in order to give the new Lambert management team time to decide what to do about the Coastal Region.

Andy got his answer about six weeks after the Variety Show. A new CMO had been hired, and no decisions would be made about any regions or RVPs until the new guy got his feet wet in the position. The new CMO: Brandon Kessler.

It turns out that the Alexandria operation for Royal had not worked out as planned, and Brandon was blamed by the Toronto people for not getting the operation more effective sooner. Brandon seemed to suffer from being diverted from the task at hand. It was not attention deficit disorder (ADD). It was more Kessler's taste for the finer things, wine and women (Brandon was married, sort of), that did him in. However, in true insurance industry form, no one outside of Royal learned of Brandon's dalliances or alcoholism. His departure from Royal was done as a voluntary resignation, "to pursue other interests." In such situations, the HR department is always instructed not to give out any information about the severed employee other than start and stop dates of employment and position title. In order to get the terminated executive to agree to sign a "covenant not to sue," he/she was usually given "an offer that can't be refused," in the form of a handsome "golden parachute" out of the company – an obscene amount of money – some might say "hush money."

Brandon's somewhat formal style and elegant manner impressed Paul Swift. It was markedly different from the rough and gruff style of Don Wasserman. Brandon brought a quieter personality to the marketing area, and this was what Swift was looking for.

In early May, Andy scheduled a meeting with Swift to give him his resignation. As Andy waited outside Swift's office, he viewed – for the first and last time – some of the collectibles and artwork that Swift had accumulated over the years. Swift may be from the Granite State, but this did not water down his penchant for fine art. As he was called into Swift's office, Andy entered to sit in a wing chair on the other side of Swift's desk. Swift pushed a button on his desk and the door to his office began to slowly close behind Andy. Andy had never seen such a remote controlled door device before. Swift did not rise to shake Andy's hand. He seemed to know something was up.

Andy explained to Paul the matter of leaving Lambert, blaming it partly on his family and partly on the need to move up in his career. "I would stay, Paul. I had an informal agreement with Don that I would eventually take over the Coastal Region when McPherson retires. That seems to be by the boards at this point."

Swift said little. "You know that what Don told you and a buck would buy you a cup of coffee," is all.

Andy realized that even mentioning Wasserman's name was not a good move. And Swift accepted the resignation without much more than a wish good luck as he pushed that button again and the office door opened for Andy to leave. Later, Andy would be told by colleagues that Swift was saying, "Greene just isn't one of us," as a way of explaining the departure to the RVPs.

However, when the field continued to criticize home office management for letting Greene get away, the story changed. They had to find someone to blame for losing Andy. Andy's boss was a convenient target. Lyn, being one of only two women among the elected officers at Lambert, Concord, was probably being picked on for more reasons than Andy's departure. In fact, working with Lyn had been one of the highlights of Andy's time there. But management wanted someone to blame. A few months later, the Product Marketing Department was reorganized and Lyn was demoted by Brandon. And a few months after that, Lyn was back in North Carolina, having been given "an offer she could not refuse" to accept a bag of money in exchange for her "voluntary" resignation.

Andy's last day on the job at Lambert was Brandon Kessler's first day at Lambert. Brandon was keen on renewing a former acquaintance and asked to see Andy before he left. The first part of the meeting was a perfunctory recollection of their meetings in Alexandria, when Andy was up for the advanced sales position at Royal. Brandon did not make much of an attempt to explain his departure from Royal, only to say that "this Lambert opportunity is a once-in-a-lifetime chance." Why, he did not specify.

Then, Brandon took a document from his new desk. The document had several pages listing each RVP at Lambert, a picture of each, and some CV-style history on each one. Brandon asked, "I'd like to get your review of each of these guys in the field, your opinion of how they're doing."

This was the first time anyone had asked Andy for his opinion of field personnel. So they went through, one by one, and when they came to McPherson, Andy recounted the story of his informal deal with Wasserman; that he would not be leaving if that arrangement was going to happen; that no one now would commit to that. "So, I have no choice but to pursue other options."

Andy was hoping that maybe Brandon would hold out hope for the RVP slot in Coastal. Instead, Brandon simply paraphrased what he said to Andy years before in Alexandria. "Well, we've met up again here, and maybe we'll run into each other yet again. You never know. This industry is a small world. Good luck to you and your new position." And he shook Andy's hand, flawlessly firm but gentle. And Andy closed the book on what he would later describe as "one of the most fun periods in my career."

When Andy arrived at Empire, the day after Memorial Day, 1990, he was immediately faced again with two staffers in his Marketing Services Department that were none too happy about this interloper from New Hampshire. During the interview process, both of them – Larry Faulk and Tom DeBroglio – were on Andy's dance card to meet. But at the time, Larry and Tom were told by Sam Roberts that Andy was being considered to run the advanced sales operation, only, working side-by-side with them. No problem there: Larry had come with Dick Sheridan to occupy the field training slot. Tom was a 10-year veteran of Empire, and headed up the sales support unit (as Q had done at AFG).

Andy also interviewed with Max Fortunoff, Marketing VP for Empire, based on Wall Street. Max was likewise a veteran of Empire, a holdover from the old regime, before Warren, Sheridan, and Roberts arrived to take over.

Max's understanding was that Andy would report to him as head of advanced sales. But during the interview process with Sam and Dick, a different position emerged. Andy was comfortable at Lambert and would not move to New Jersey without the position having more than just a few more dollars in it. Since Sallie was no longer working, it was now Andy's sole responsibility to provide for the family (despite all attempts at being a modern couple when they first got together, Andy and Sallie had managed to fall into the traditional *Leave It To Beaver* roles). Andy now had to consider not just the dollars up front, but the more lucrative bonus and severance packages that came with a higher position. Andy was trying to work all the angles.

"Sam, I really would like to come and be a part of what is happening here at Empire" Andy said in the interview with Roberts. "It's a very exciting time. But I can't go home to my family with a move to New Jersey without something more than continuing on as an advanced sales guy, only."

"Well, Andy, what is YOUR idea of where you would fit into our organization?" Sam was not too impressed with Max Fortunoff as his head of marketing support. Max was old school, with an age to match (although Sam would never admit it). Moreover, like most incoming executives, Sam did not relish the idea of managing people he inherited. Sam believed, "One of the exciting jobs when you come into a situation like this is to have an opportunity to hire your own people, ones that will be loyal to YOU – not the old regime."

"This is what I see happening, Sam." And without regard to who was being pushed aside, Andy drew a five-pronged Marketing Services Department, essentially along the lines of what Frank Meaney had at AFG. FX had been Andy's first real mentor in the business, and he wanted to succeed at the same job Frank had. The five prongs:

- Field Training & Development (both "Big T" and "Little T")
- Marketing Counsel (introducing that controversial title again)
- Sales Support (the computer illustration system and other technology sales aids)
- Product Development (negotiating with the pricing actuary over design of new product)
- Marketing Communications (all the collateral sales literature and other communications with the field)

And Sam saw an opportunity to pass off the obligation of leading old guard people to someone below him. So, a deal was struck: Larry Faulk in training and Tom DeBroglio in sales support would now report to Andy. Andy would personally lead the advanced sales function, inheriting one advanced sales attorney, Frances (Fran) Early with budget to hire at least one other attorney in that unit down the road. Andy would represent Marketing at the product development table. And a head of field communications would be found to fill that slot. As to Max Fortunoff, he would continue to oversee the rest of marketing support from Wall Street. He had a pension sales and administration operation there, run by Cameron "Cam" Dowd, a 30-year-ago immigrant from Dublin, Ireland, who managed to keep his brogue intact, especially when *schmoozing* past any difficult personal situations with Americans. Fortunoff was relegated to overseeing Dowd's work.

During the week before Andy's arrival, the staff were made aware of the change in organization. It did not go down well. Max complained that his "hire" in advanced sales had been taken away from him. Larry went straight to Dick Sheridan and threatened to quit; Dick talked him out of it, for the time being (Sheridan was Larry's mentor and so had great influence over him). Tom told his own staff, three sales support consultants, to "Start a file on this guy. We're gonna drive his arrogant ass right out of here."

Andy, using Frank Meaney as his model, willingly took on the challenge to "win over" the staff he inherited, rather than push people out so he could hire "his own." After two weeks on the job, Andy scheduled an off-site "retreat" of his management team, which at that time was only Larry and Tom, to plan out strategy going forward for the new Marketing Services Department. The meeting also had on the agenda an opportunity for the three of them to spend some quality time together, away from the office, and get acquainted. Andy was sure he could use Meaney's mastery of leadership to smooth over any ruffled egos. And ego it clearly was; no one suffered any loss of income or position title because of Andy's arrival. Only the reporting lines had changed. The "retreat" was held in the hotel Andy was temporarily staying at, just down the street from the home office in Piscataway. The meetings were cordial; Andy was careful to listen more than speak – all of the things Frank Meaney had taught him were applied here.

Larry and Tom were cordial, smiled a lot, and little changed in attitude. Tom was still hell-bent on foiling any attempt by Andy to supervise him, making up false status reports about progress on illustration system upgrades and other projects when little or nothing was getting done. Larry had started contacting his Rolodex network, mostly from Northern Mutual, to see where he could land, with his dignity and income intact, back at his old company.

Max Fortunoff was more gracious. Was it because he was a "Landsman"? Andy was not sure. But Max accepted his fate without any obvious dissent. This may have been because at this point in his career – Max was 62 at the time – he was more concerned with just making it to retirement rather than stir the pot for career advancement. Yet, he too, allowed nothing to get done in pensions; he allowed Cam Dowd to use his Irish brogue to get past anyone questioning the work in the pension department. Cam as well was in his early 60's, and he too seemed more interested in coasting to a retirement than making waves in the office.

Marketing Services, the title Andy created from his AFG days to represent the generic marketing support functions, did not include any line authority over Empire's career-managerial distribution system. Empire had in 1990 some 18 agencies across the country doing about $20 million in new premium a year. As career-managerial, the agencies were owned and operated by Empire, the agency managers were employees of the company and profit and loss were managed from the home office.

By 1990, most career agency companies were converting their agencies to what is called "general agencies," with "general agents"

(GAs) in charge. The GA would still be an employee of the company, but now he had responsibility for profit and loss. The GA was paid a gross override to run his/her operation and from that the expenses of the agency – rent, utilities, administrative salaries – were paid. If the agency made a profit, the GA kept it.

The problem was that few if any career-managerial agencies in the industry were making a profit by the 1990s. A concept sometimes called "transfer pricing" had come into vogue. Transfer pricing involved charging off a portion of fixed as well as variable expenses from the home office's operations to the distribution channel, which in turn was charged against the agencies. When the company applied transfer pricing to the managerial agencies, it found that few if any could at least break even. Breaking even was all the distribution channel could hope for, but it couldn't even do that. Why? Because of the same anti-life insurance disease that had taken over AFG's field force had infected the entire industry. Sales people no longer wanted to be in the "life insurance" business; they wanted to be "financial planners." This meant that focus on the highest margin product line was gone. Insurance companies could tolerate this in the short term due to huge reserves of in-force policies accumulated over the decades. So they "kicked the can down the road."

Career agency companies by 1990 had moved to off-loading the P&L responsibilities onto these GAs. Unlike PPGAs, they were company employees. But the result of getting rid of responsibility to manage the field force to break even was the same. Just as the soft drink industry had gone from O&O plants manufacturing finished product to working with independent bottlers, a parallel phenomenon was taking hold in financial services.

As a college professor years later, Andy would lecture, "Some companies are good at making stuff; some companies are good at selling stuff; some companies are good at servicing stuff; few if any are equally good at all three. So the resulting rule is 'do what you do best, and outsource the rest.'"

But in 1990, Empire continued to struggle with overseeing a career-managerial system. This meant that agencies had budgets with oversight from the home office. All expense items got a second pair of eyes in the home office to make sure they were legitimate; at least that was what was supposed to happen.

Three phenomena grew out of this setup. The first was that a very few agencies still managed to generate enough life insurance sales margin to operate at least at break even. The Warren Financial Group throughout the 1980s had been able to do this, even through the early stages of the reorientation toward financial planning. These agencies got a lot of leeway to run themselves as if they were general agencies. This meant that if the manager, acting like a GA, wanted to make outside agreements to broker other companies' products, the home office looked the other way. The manager-GA in this way created a mini-Empire, a company within a company, with revenue flow from sale of these other products totally outside of company oversight.

Payments to field managers for the sales of insurance products were called *overrides*, in that they were payments to the managers of the people actually making the sales. The overrides were not a portion of the agent's sales commission. Instead, they were payments in addition to the agent commission for supervising and supporting the sales people. Within the career system, there were override percentages for sales managers, people who had sales units and reported to the manager or GA, and there was a separate percentage payment made to the manager-GA him or herself. They were variable compensation payments, paid only upon sales completed.

However, when taking on the brokering of outside products, the GA often took the entire override himself, unless he'd appointed someone in the agency to oversee that part of the operation.

At Warren Financial Group, these outside agreements with other companies were overseen by Bill Warren's younger brother, Alan "Bud" Warren, whose sole job it was in the agency to manage the brokering of products outside the Empire official system. At AFG, the company tried to manage these outside agreements by fashioning a set of company-wide Class II deals with carriers offering product that the field needed but Atlantic did not manufacture. At Empire, there were attempts at the same thing, but they were blunted by the lobbying of the leading managers in the field to "stay the fuck off my income." Fairly cheeky were these manager-GAs who felt the company was there to service the field, not the other way around.

The second phenomenon that grew out of transfer pricing was the practice of some managers in the field to "double dip" expenses. They would, for example, authorize an expense into the home office from the agency that they never incurred. An example of this was the common practice of making an agent pay for his/her own computer in the agency; then taking the paid receipt from the agent and putting it in for reimbursement through the agency's home office budget, payable back to the manager – as if the manager had incurred the expense, not the agent.

One such practice occurred in Empire's Bay Area agency outside San Francisco. The manager was Felix Biggio. Felix had been part of the former management at Empire that Warren, Sheridan, and Roberts had replaced. When Sheridan came on board, he was replacing Biggio in the COO slot. Sheridan, in an attempt to show compassion to the outgoing executive, offered Felix the open slot running the Bay Area agency. Felix was originally from Northern California, so he accepted Dick's graciousness. Then, he repaid it by bilking the company out of tens of thousands of dollars by double-dipping expenses. He even had a home office mole, a close associate on his former management team, who was paid by Felix to falsify reimbursement to agents for completing CLU and ChFC courses under the company's tuition reimbursement plan; the agents having never taken the courses. The money was sent to Biggio's budget, who then withdrew it for his own personal expenses.

The home office should have instantly caught on to it, given Felix's opulent living style that he'd taken to when he got to San Francisco. But it took a random audit by Roberts and his new hire to run the distribution channel, Blake Lesser, to reveal the extent of the damage. Lesser came on board almost at the same time as Andy, and the two were to run marketing for Roberts, together as a team. Andy would be the inside guy; Blake would handle the field.

Lesser got wind of expenses running through the Bay Area agency that seemed out of line with what other agencies of similar size were experiencing. The audit went on for several weeks. The mole in the home office was unceremoniously arrested, "perp walked" out of the building in front of everyone, for embezzlement. Somehow, some of the other veteran managers and agents, many loyal to Felix from the prior administration, talked directly to Warren, and Biggio was allowed to resign, with the severance package he would have gotten from his previous home office COO position, and physically disappeared from the industry. Any criminal charges were dropped.

Roberts and Lesser were at least able to play muckrakers in this incident and won Sheridan's praise for removing a "cancer" from the company. Warren had little to say about the incident.

The third phenomenon was a "bait-and-switch" of recruiting new sales people into the business by telling them they would be professional "financial planners" when in fact they were insurance salespeople. This syndrome would raise its ugly head in particular at Warren Financial Group.

On the heels of the Bay Area audit and removal of Biggio, Blake Lesser began to "feel his oats," and took the aggressive position that he was actually the chief marketing officer at Empire. Of course, he wasn't. Sam Roberts was. And in Sam's presence, Blake was careful not to go there.

In his dealings directly with Andy Greene; well, that was another matter. "Staff serves the line," Blake would say, meaning that Andy was in charge of staff, whose responsibility was to serve the sales force and distribution channel.

"We're all line, here, Blake," Andy would answer.

Clearly, this would be another contentious relationship for Andy. Lesser would sometimes invoke his military background (USMC) as leverage for his leadership qualities. "I've seen war. I fought in Viet Nam. I know what leading men into battle means."

"How about the women?" Andy would joke.

One day, Blake took the argument a step further. "Stop making light of this. You know what I mean. While you were safe at home, in college, I was out in the jungle, protecting you. What did you do in the war Andy?" and Blake looked at Andy's slightly too long hair, mustache, "balcony of affluence" and bowtie. Oh, he had Andy sized up all right. Andy got as close to war as protesting the War in the early 70s, in England and in Oneonta; although truth be told, Andy later regretted that he didn't do more to oppose that War.

"While you were off fighting in 'Viet-fucking-Nam,' Blake, I was fighting the other war, the one to get the damn Government to bring you home in one piece." And Andy, for dramatic effect, paused for a moment. "In fact, sir, I'm probably responsible for saving your sorry ass by getting you home from that War." Another short pause, "You're welcome!"

The irreverence of Andy toward a veteran was too much for Blake to take, and he began to lunge at Andy, but failed to make contact, as Andy slipped slightly to his left, like a boxer, and simply waited for Blake's next move… Which never came; so, Andy left it at that.

These episodes would occur only rarely, but drew the line between them. Andy had made another enemy at Empire. And the two of them dared not bring the animosity to Sam Roberts' attention – "the first one to complain usually loses," Frank Meaney would say.

Blake and others in the home office concluded early on that Andy Greene was simply a blowhard, arrogant, SOB. They may have been right. But as Andy would remember his torts professor in law school saying, "You can't sue for son-of-a-bitchery." He felt that so long as he had good relations with the field and with senior management, he was untouchable.

Andy made one more enemy in the home office, and this was the General Counsel and the Law Department. As at AFG, the corporate lawyers could not get behind Andy's name for advanced sales being "Marketing Counsel." And unlike having Frank Meaney to run interference for him, Sam Roberts was less inclined to intercede on Andy's behalf. Nevertheless, Andy forged a fairly close relationship with Dick Sheridan, who also felt like he was being treated as an outsider. Dick came in from another company, a direct competitor, with a lot of ideas that ran counter to "the way we do business here at Empire." Sheridan had an intellectual demeanor and professorial style, rare for a former GA in the field. Andy would later find out that Dick Sheridan inherited the Richmond agency from his father: Dick, Sr. There's a saying that "few family businesses survive the second generation of owners," and that saying was somewhat appropriate for "Sheridan & Son," and their agency in Richmond.

But in 1990, fighting the Law Department, Blake Lesser, and his own reports, Andy was fighting a three-front war, and he looked above his own boss for help. Sheridan felt empathy for the interloper role Andy had been cast in. He forced the issue. Warren, not being a lawyer himself, did not see what all the fuss was about. So he didn't fight on Legal's side. So, a similar deal was struck using AFG as a template: lawyers in advanced sales could be called Marketing Counsel; non-lawyers could not. And a set of AFG-style protocols were put in place as well.

Part of what made the "medicine go down" for the Law Department was that the Marketing Counsel Unit was going to build a true advanced underwriting manual for the field. This would bring a higher level of understanding tax planning concepts to a field force the Law Department feared were giving advice that was inaccurate. They did not want the job of writing the manual themselves; none of them knew policyholder taxation as a specialty. So long as Andy's people would write something accurate, they were fine with "fobbing off" the job so they wouldn't have to do it. Sam Roberts and Dick Sheridan had seen a copy of the FPC Manual from AFG when Andy came to interview. They were impressed, and quickly tasked Andy with the job of fashioning something similar for Empire.

But Andy was not going to source write the Manual himself. He was in management now. He felt his job was travelling around the country and rallying the field force to the new Empire Life. He knew he was part of a management team hired to "shake things up." This Empire field force had rarely seen advanced sales guys come out. The prior head of advanced underwriting didn't care to travel that much and preferred to write articles and sales literature to communicate his message to the field, and to network with other home offices so he'd always have a full Rolodex of industry contacts in case he needed a new job.

Now, Andy saw his chance to mold a new model for advanced sales, and began travelling around to the agencies, giving talks and doing "the Doctor is in," similar to what he'd done at AFG and Lambert.

This meant that his staff back at headquarters would write most of the Manual. And so the author's job fell on Fran Early. Fran had been at Empire for 6 years, important to her because she had just last year become fully vested in the company's 401(k) plan. Fran had been doing advanced underwriting for almost two decades, but had rarely travelled to conferences or taken continuing education courses, other than CLE to renew her Bar license in New Jersey. She had fallen behind in the state-of-the-art of advanced marketing. Fran was 58, and she was tired. And she was not the best speaker to represent the Unit.

When Andy approached her to assign her authorship of the first few chapters of the Manual, she accepted it without resistance but then seemed not to progress with the work very well. By the fall of 1990, Fran had not yet completed even one chapter of the Manual. Andy was in the process of hiring another Marketing Counsel, but in the meantime was at a loss to know how to motivate Fran to get going with his signature project for the year in advanced sales.

So, in discussions with Fran, when she seemed a bit lost on what Andy was looking for, he shared with her the FPC Manual from AFG, as an example of what he was going for. Now, everyone in the business accepted the fact that there are just so many different ways you can explain an advanced underwriting technique. But Andy never expected that Fran would simply copy, word-for-word, everything in the FPC Manual.

Three weeks after Andy had given Fran the FPC Manual, a draft of the first chapter, on Executive Bonus, was complete and delivered to

Andy. Andy began reading the material, without the FPC Manual next to him. It had been some years since he had written that Manual, but he assumed he knew what he'd written. This was a big assumption, especially since Financial Profiles had purchased the right to use that same material.

As Andy read Fran's draft, he saw what he wanted to see, things like $B=P/1-t$, and such. It was comfortably written, he thought. "I like what I see here," he said to Fran. Fran never revealed that she had simply cut-and-pasted whole pages and sections from the Manual and put it in her draft.

Two more chapters were written and edited that same way. All three went up to the Law Department for sign-off. The lawyers decided to check Andy's history, and looked at his CV, seeing AFG and Lambert in his pedigree. They decided to contact both companies to retrieve materials in advanced sales that were in use there and compare to what they had in front of them. What they retrieved, including the FPC Manual, showed them the copying from other companies' material. All companies in the business claim at least a common law copyright over any original work produced by its employees for consumption by the field or the public.

Law saw its opportunity to cut Andy down a peg, even get him shown the door, and marked up the draft and its comparison to the FPC Manual and walked it over to Dick Sheridan and Sam Roberts. Andy was called into Sam's office as soon as the lawyers were done with their presentation to management. This, the lawyers figured, would be the end of "Marketing Counsel." Sam showed Andy the copied material. Dick was sitting to the side of Sam's desk, left of Andy, whose face went white with embarrassment.

"Sam, I had no idea this was going on." At that moment, Andy had a decision to make, perhaps two decisions. The first was whether to tell his bosses that this was the work of his subordinate, and try and pass responsibility down the organizational chart. The second was whether to offer his resignation.

"Andy," Sam started, "how could this happen?"

"Sam, I don't know. I must have not been looking at my old material and simply said the same thing I'd said before." Andy would not implicate Fran in the plagiarism. Sam and Dick were unaware that Fran had written this rather than Andy himself.

"Did you author this yourself or did your staff do this?" Sam asked, with Dick simply watching.

"Sam, it doesn't matter who wrote it. I had the responsibility to edit it, proof it, and know that it was original. I'm really sorry about this, and thank G-d that we caught it before it got published and sent out to the field."

"Got that right. But **we** didn't, Law did."

"Guys… Do you want me to resign over this?" And Andy was almost to tears at this point.

"I don't think we have to go that far," Dick piped in. Dick and Sam understood that there are just so many ways you can write about Executive Bonus. Sam was embarrassed at having Law come in and suggest plagiarism of his staff. But he was not a lawyer, and did not see what all the fuss was about. Dick, as a non-lawyer as well, was relieved that the material had not gone out of the house.

"Andy," Dick said, "Let's talk no more about this. Go back and have the material re-written" revealing Sheridan's belief that Andy was covering for the real author. "I'm sure this time you'll see to editing more closely, right?"

And Andy smiled meekly and left the room.

After Andy left, Dick commented to Sam, "This stuff was clearly written by his staff, not Andy. But Andy didn't try to pass the buck. He fell on his sword. He gets what 'failure to supervise' is all about."

"So, you're O.K. with letting Andy continue?" Sam asked.

"Are you?"

"The guy has great rapport with the field. We don't want to lose that. He's probably overwhelmed with all the work in front of him."

"Let's not make excuses for him. But I think he learned something from this incident, and I don't think he'll repeat the mistake."

"Agreed."

And no further repercussions from the incident occurred. "Marketing Counsel" continued as the Unit name. Fran would not lose her job either, at least not yet.

Once a month on average, Andy made it a point to take the commuter train into Manhattan and spend the day with Max, Cam, and other home officer staffers in the Wall Street office. It was partly his attempt to forge some kind working alliance with Max. It was partly to get out of the Piscataway office for a day. The trips that Andy took into the City projected to his management team – who rarely went into Manhattan – that he was important enough in the company to have to make that trip at all.

On his first trip there, within a month after being hired, Max got the opportunity to tell Andy a bit of Empire folklore.

"The former management team will always have a place in my heart, but not my whole heart," Max began. "We were all set a few years back to merge with Golden State Mutual Life. The deal was practically done."

"I heard something about that." But Andy in fact had heard nothing about this 1986 planned merger of mutuals. He was too busy hustling Northern Virginia Financial Group. "How can two mutuals get together? I heard that legally it can't be done. There are no stockholders to price the value of company stock."

"They can't be acquired, that's true," Max continued. "They can merge."

"But we all know there is no such thing as a true merger," Andy objected. "It's always just a front for acquisition by the larger partner."

"True enough. The 'merger' was hyped so much as Empire being the predator and Golden being the prey, and we sort of believed after awhile that we were the senior partner."

"How could you buy off on that? Look at the size of Golden versus Empire… Golden is far larger." Golden had been doing $60 million a year in new premium through a combination of career agencies and some recently formed regional offices working with brokers.

"With mutual companies, that's a hard thing to measure, not a lot of data points there. We had acquired over the last 20 years a lot of assets. Forget about the debt taken on to buy those assets. Cam's pension department is part of what the company did – acquire business in force in order to raise the size of our asset base. Asset base," Max repeated, "not net worth or life insurance in force."

"Why would you guys do that?"

"Because management wanted to keep Empire on the top-50 list of mutuals, when measured by assets, which is how the trade press measures mutuals these days."

"Fair enough. So everyone here thought the company was bigger than it was…"

"Right!"

"So, what happened to the 'merger'?"

"What happened was that one day a team from Golden's home office came to Piscataway to hold a series of meetings with our home office. That morning, a general session was held where the Golden rep says, in front of our employees, 'Hi. Let us introduce you to your new management team.' And the place went bonkers. For the first time, the home office realized that this was a takeover by Golden of Empire."

"Well, home office staffers alone can't kill a merger."

"No they can't. But the field can. And within minutes calls were going out to field managers and top producers about what was really going on here, and they put a stop to it."

"How did they do that?"

"They simply threatened to abandon ship, to leave the company, leaving Golden with no additional distribution for its trouble. Golden's people within a week gave up on its plans and Empire stayed separate, much to the gratitude of all of us."

"But if management here knew what the real deal was, and they didn't make that clear to you, weren't they really pulling one over on you?"

"Well, yeah, sort of. I think Vance Nicholson," the CEO at the time, "pulled the wool over his own eyes. He believed that this was truly a merger of equals. But we know it never ends up like that." Then, Max came to the conclusion. "After the merger fell through the

Board retired Nicholson and his guys, and that's when Warren came in."

"Sounds like the field had a lot of power here. It first stops the merger, then it replaces your CEO – sorry, our CEO – with one of its own."

"Distribution is king in this business, Andy. Always remember that."

One of the more formal roles that Andy got involved in when in Manhattan was his product development role. The pricing actuary he negotiated with, Mark Tobin, was based in the Wall Street office. Mark and Andy met the first time to start work on a Second-to-Die whole life policy in September 1990. Tobin treated Andy with some suspicion, as Mark had always been able to fashion product with little interference from marketing. Tobin would look for input from the field himself. But there was little oversight as to the conclusions of market needs that he came to.

Second-to-Die insurance is a creation mainly for the estate planning market. Since 1981, the federal estate tax allowed an unlimited marital exclusion at death. This meant that the deceased spouse could pass as much wealth as he (they always assume the husband will die first) wished to his spouse and not pay any federal estate tax. The individual states usually followed suit on this issue. So, it was common by the 1980s for estate planners to have each spouse set up wills and other assets to go to the surviving spouse first. When the surviving spouse died, then the assets would be distributed to the heirs, usually children and grandchildren. It was at the spouse's death that the IRS would get its bite at the estate. This meant that liquidity to pay any estate taxes would be needed at the second spouse's death, not at the first death. The Second-to-Die insurance would only pay its death benefit at the second of two people to die, timing the liquidity to when it would be needed.

Usually, these policies were owned by an irrevocable life insurance trust (ILIT) so that the death benefit would not in turn raise the value of the surviving spouse's estate. One of the side benefits of this kind of insurance is the cost. Since it took two people to die for the insurance to pay off, the pricing was based on requiring two deaths, not one, making the odds of claim in any given year far less. Thus, the premiums would be lower, much lower, than providing insurance on both spouses separately.

Notwithstanding all of this, Empire had no such product. And Mark Tobin was unconvinced that the field would be able to sell such a product, given that it would only work for clients wealthy enough to need protection from estate taxes. Tobin believed that few Empire agents were working in that end of the market.

Andy saw it differently. He surmised that armed with the product, the agent would gravitate toward that market now that he/she had a solution. He was vaguely aware that some of this business at the Warren Financial Group, for example, was going out to other carriers because Empire had no such product; at least that was the rumor among brokerage wholesalers in the D.C. area. And such a product would be a huge achievement in moving the field force closer to the advanced markets, where Andy's core expertise lived.

When they first met, both Andy and Mark decided to get some coffee outside the office, down Wall Street at a little coffee shop Tobin knew of.

While sipping hot coffee on a hot September day, Tobin made his position against a Second-to-Die product clear. When Andy tried to explain his thinking on the subject, Tobin cut him off.

"Look, if you think I'm going to roll over and do whatever marketing wants, you're very much mistaken." Andy tried to get it back to the issue of product development. But Tobin would have none of it. "I have been in charge of product development here for years, and I'm not going to let Dick Sheridan change that. You can tell him that."

"Mark," Andy responded, "I'm not going to tell Dick anything. I'm going to suggest to you that Empire has fallen behind the times and I can't imagine you want that moniker on your resume for having run product development all these years."

"Don't patronize me," Tobin barked back under a false whisper.

"I'm not patronizing. I'm trying to help you." Andy then held out his hand to offer a handshake.

Ultimately, what came out of negotiations was a compromise. It would be a Rider on Empire's whole life policies that allowed the beneficiary to elect to defer payment of the death benefit until she died. Called a BIO Rider (after Beneficiary Insurance Option), Andy built an entire campaign around this new product, and hired additional staff in marketing communications and training to push the product out to the field. By 1992, only 6 BIO Riders had been placed on new policies sold. The product was a dud.

But Andy would not be perturbed by the lack of enthusiasm for the BIO Rider. In February 1991, Empire held a manager's meeting in Kissimmee, Florida, near many of the major league baseball training camps going on at the time. Andy was on the agenda to roll out the new product. Also in attendance was the recently hired head of Empire Securities, the company's broker-dealer. Kevin Millner was a rather athletic but rotund President of Empire Securities. Andy immediately sought his friendship when he learned that Millner had played minor league ball in the Boston Red Sox organization as a young stud, in the early 70s. In fact, Millner made it up to the big club on one of those 21-day contracts they give minor leaguers when the major league rosters are allowed to swell from 25 to 40 players. Andy was impressed that Kevin still had his Red Sox uniform from that short stint as a catcher in Boston.

One night, after a dinner with the field managers, some of the guys started playing a little pickup baseball at a field next to a golf driving range, just down the street from the dinner. Kevin went back to his hotel room to get something he had packed as a lark for the trip – his home team white Red Sox uniform, #43. He also had his catcher's mitt in hand. Why he thought to do this he never revealed. But he caught "first pitches" from several managers present. Then Andy got a turn just as the managers were through.

"Stay there a moment, Kevin." And Kevin waited to receive a pitch from Andy on a makeshift mound that did seem to be regulation 60' 6" from the plate behind which Kevin crouched. And Andy threw the best fastball he could throw, given it had been age 16 since the last time Andy had "pitched" a real hardball. In the dirt…

"Low and outside," Kevin joked.

"How do you know it was outside instead of inside? Is the hitter left or right handed?" Andy replied with a laugh.

And Andy finally got to pitch to a "member" of the Red Sox. Not exactly what he dreamed of, but close enough to cross it off his bucket list.

That September, the day after Labor Day to be exact, Andy organized what he called a "barnstorming trip." He assembled a group of his staff to go from agency to agency, giving presentations on various products, programs, and sales ideas, to stimulate production from the agents. This trip was to be through the South: Sunday night: fly into Nashville, for an agency meeting there Monday morning, part of their weekly sales meeting with the agents. Andy would rent a car at the airport to use all week; a Lincoln Town Car no less (Budget used to have a $39/day Town Car offer one way in those days). After the meeting, and the requisite "Doctor is in" session after lunch, the group would pile into the car for a drive south to Birmingham, Alabama for a meeting Tuesday. Same agenda. Repeat for a drive further south to Jackson, Mississippi, for a meeting there on Wednesday. Then, on to New Orleans for a meeting Thursday. Take Thursday night off and fly home Friday morning.

Andy chose carefully who would be in the presentation group. By this time, Larry Faulk had left Empire for an agency job in Philadelphia. Andy had hired from the field a young agent whose main experience had been pensions – Nate Paglio. Nate showed promise as an effective and empathetic presenter. Andy did not put him in charge of the Field Training and Development Unit right away, but he was being groomed for the position and this trip was a test to see how he could handle himself in front of a group of sales people. His job was to push the BIO Rider.

Andy picked out two of Tom DeBroglio's team for the trip: Dara Welch and Zach Goodman. Dara was hailed by Tom as his protégé, and she had mastered the computer illustration system. Andy chose Dara and Zach over Tom's objections, feeling very territorial with his staff. Like Nate, Dara was married with two small children, so travelling was always a challenge. Zach was the youngest of the group, 25, single, with some non-lawyer knowledge of advanced markets. He was one course shy of earning his CLU designation. Like Andy and Nate, he had an NASD securities license (although

Series 6; Andy had earned his status as a broker-dealer principal, getting Kevin Millner to sponsor him for the Series 24 exam).

Andy picked his new Marketing Counsel, Sheila Borders, to come along with some advanced planning ideas. Andy would, for the first time, play only the role of MC. The rest of the team would do the presenting. Sheila was being tested to see if she was ready to assume the lead role in advanced marketing in the Department. Her main sales idea was to use non-qualified deferred compensation plans as a way to avoid FICA (Social Security) tax. Andy would then be free to consult more with the management of each agency, forging closer working ties and alliances.

Part of Andy's agenda was the idea of putting a group of disparate characters together in a car for a week and see what happened. Either they would drive each other crazy or they would create lasting friendships; Andy was hoping for the latter. He was also hoping to create an alternate intelligence channel into his own Sales Support Unit, around Tom, who continued to prove outwardly cordial but tight lipped and short on any cooperation with Andy.

The barnstorming trip was going off like clockwork. All meetings were well received; all destinations arrived at with little fuss. Everyone seemed to be getting along on the long drives from city to city. When Thursday evening arrived, it was time to relax and review the week among the group. Sometimes, when a trip like this ends on a Thursday, folks like to catch a late flight home to be with family and perhaps even take Friday off as a travel day. But no one argued about the item on the agenda for Thursday night, called "Post Mortem Trip Review & Attitude Adjustment." Attitude Adjustment was euphemism for "let's all have a stiff drink, or three." Post Mortem meant a review-and-reflect on what went well and what could be improved on future trips, along with insights into what each member saw going on in each agency (Andy was to be debriefed by Sam when he returned).

During the evening festivities, in the hotel bar where the group was staying, everyone got a little loose; everyone began celebrating the end of a successful road trip. The alcohol flowed and began loosening tongues a bit. Dara, with a Jameson's on the rocks in hand, eventually came over to where Andy was sitting, with exactly the same drink. Zach came with her. Dara waited until Andy was sitting relatively alone. Zach seemed to be her backup. Dara started, "I need to tell you something about what is going on in my Unit."

"What's that?" Andy inquired.

"If I tell you, you can't say it came from me."

"O.K. It sounds bad."

"Tom is not your friend." And she paused for a reaction.

"Tell me something I don't know."

"When you came on board, he immediately had a meeting with us. He told us to 'start a file on this guy. He's not going to be around very long.'"

"I see."

"Tom's been hiding the progress on the new illustration system. We really haven't made much progress on it. It simply doesn't work. He doesn't want you to know that so he's been stalling on releasing it to the field."

"I haven't really gotten much of an update on it, true."

"And he was really pissed when you pulled Zach and me out for this trip."

Then Zach chimed in, "But I'm glad we went on this. It's great getting out into the field and seeing what's really going on."

Andy got a little bold now. "Well, Dara, fuck him if he can't take a joke."

And Dara added, "This road trip is the first time I've been treated by management as a real professional. Tom thinks you're not going to be around long. Is he wrong?"

Within a week after the barnstorming crew was back, an announcement came down in a home office associate meeting held by Bill Warren. It seems that rumors were spreading that another merger was in the works. Some employees had seen some people they didn't recognize show up in suits and go into the executive offices. These people were actually consultants from Deloitte Touche.

"I brought you all here," Warren began, "to bring you up to speed on some corporate news that you need to know about. Empire is in the midst of studying a possible merger with Gadsden Life, based in Arizona. The Board has authorized management to study the merits of the merger with Gadsden versus a scenario of investing in building organically as a standalone company. We don't know what the result will be, but you will see some people here and on Wall Street over the next few months and I don't want you to be concerned. Any merger we would make would be in the best interests of all of us, policyholders, employees, etc."

There were a few mild questions that revealed the real agenda of everyone in the room: Protect My Job!!

Meanwhile, Dick Sheridan pulled Sam, Blake, and Andy into his office. "Warren has put me in charge of putting together the standalone scenario, which is, by the way, the result I'd like to see happen. That's what the consultants you are seeing around here are all about. They are going to advise the Board about which way the company should go. We're going to have a strategy meeting next week, off-site. All elected officers under me will be there, and we will put together an organizational plan to move forward with a standalone scenario.

And sure enough, one week later, the elected officers, *sans* Warren, convened at the Mohonk Mountain House, upstate New York, to plan out the standalone scenario to give to the Board. During the several meetings, various pieces of an organizational plan started coming together. In between several breakout sessions, there were what Andy recognized from the past as team building, Communications-Lab style sessions designed to build rapport and human relations skills among the several people there, many of whom were in a cold war with each other up until that point. The idea Sheridan had was, "the in-fighting needs to stop, and now. We have an existential threat to all of us from this merger and we need to band together."

The outline of the marketing area was slowly coming together. But it included a consolidation and elimination of positions in the Department. A mock-up of an org chart, with position titles but no people identified in them, was put together on a white board. Andy noticed that the chart seemed to be missing one position; there was going to be one less elected officer position in this new organization. Someone was going to lose his/her job. But who? Who would be stupid enough to stand up and say, "Take me off the org chart"?

Andy was... In front of the whole lot of elected officers at the next general session, Andy got up and offered himself, saying, "I can see that someone has to go in this new organization. There appears to be no room for me."

Everyone looked at Andy in disbelief. He was going to commit "Hari-Kari" in front of everyone? Wasn't the goal to make sure you had a job when all this falls out.

The session ended with no firm resolve, just Andy's morbid offer to kill his own career left out there with no real response from anyone. Andy left the room and wandered down a narrow hallway to the restroom. Reappearing in the hallway a minute later, Andy saw Dick and Sam talking to each other. Andy slowly made his way near the two to enter the conversation.

"Andy," Dick whispered out for only Andy and Sam to hear, "What you did in there was nothing short of heroic. And I'm not going to forget what you said, don't you worry." And as the session restarted, the box on the org chart labeled Marketing Services suddenly disappeared off the Board, as if it had never been there. No comment about it was spoken.

About a week after that, Andy got a call from one of his favorite agents in the field. Darrell Witherspoon was one of only four agents in the Warren Financial Group who had made Club in each of the last three years. He was age 32, Black, just recently married, and very religious, a Seventh-Day Adventist, meaning – like Jews – he celebrated a Saturday Sabbath. Darrell could make a living working with clients in his own ethnic group – D.C. was majority Black, and suburban Maryland had a large African-American presence, especially in Prince George's County, where Darrell lived. But Darrell was too smart to be pigeon-holed into being the financial planner for the Black community. He managed to cross-over and work with a diverse group of clients – something that he would say was a key to his success.

Warren Financial Group had fallen into a disappointment in the three years since Bill Warren had left for the home office. He put in his place his sales manager, Rod Peek. Rod had been the fair-haired most likely successor to Warren. He was tall, at 6'3". He was attractive and well groomed. He was married, no children yet. But he had no real management ability. His stature had declined as manager of the agency. This wasn't helped by Bud Warren, the brother Bill had left behind to manage the outside production of the agency. Bud had little regard for Rod; the two of them maintained an icy relationship while Bill was there. It only got colder after Bill left.

Rod had been found to partake in some *bait-and-switch* when recruiting new financial advisors to the agency. He would put ads in newspapers and job postings for "financial planners." When going through the interview stages, these financial planner candidates were told that they would be professionals, meaning that they would be part of this new financial planning profession, stressing objectivity and client service.

Then, when these recruits came into the office for their first day of training, called pre-contract, they found out for the first time that they were going to be life insurance agents; that the life product line was what got them paid and what the agency ran on. Many would go to lunch that first day and never return for the afternoon session – they were MIA, never to be heard from again.

Rod was also not an advanced markets kind of guy. So, he brought little to the table for the veteran agents, most of whom did the bulk of their work in the advanced markets, like estate planning and business insurance applications.

"Hey Andy, this is Darrell…Witherspoon, man."

"I know Darrell. I was just messing with you. How are you doing?"

"Well now, Andrew, I have to say 'I had a dream last night,'" as if channeling MLK, Jr. himself.

"Did you, now?"

"Yes, Andrew, *I had a dream last night,*" Darrell repeated.

After a momentary pause, Andy answered, "And what was this dream, Darrell?"

"Andrew, I dreamed last night that you had come in and taken over running our office down here."

"That's quite a dream, Darrell."

"Is it true, Andrew? Are you coming here to save the office?"

"Man, you're making me sound like the fuckin Messiah here."

But Andy knew it was true. Only the day before, Blake had approached Andy.

"You know we have problems down in D.C. The place is practically on strike. The agents are saying they won't write business to help Peek pay his mortgage. And you know when that happens, game over."

"So… What can I do to help?"

For Blake, putting Andy in D.C. meant Andy would now report to him and Andy would be out of Blake's way as a threat. "I don't suppose you'd want to go down there and take over the agency, would you."

Would he? You bet!! But he played it cool. "Under the right circumstances, I would."

And that night, Andy arrived at his home in Princeton with news he was sure Sallie would love to hear. "We're going back to Virginia."

Chapter 8: Flying Again

On November 1, 1991, Andy Greene was introduced by Empire's Zone VP for the East Coast, Ron Parquet, in an all-hands-present agency meeting in Bethesda, as the new manager of the Empire Agency in D.C. Andy faced 28 agents and 12 administrative staff, who seemed to be relieved and welcomed the new manager. Rod Peek had been removed as manager only two weeks before, so Andy's arrival was met with some anticipation.

The very same week that Peek was fired, so was Empire's manager in Baltimore – Norm Appel. Norm had been placed in his position by Felix Biggio two years earlier and fancied himself to be Biggio's protégé, in more ways than one. Norm learned from Felix the methods both used to "double dip" agency expenses. When Blake Lesser learned what had happened in the Bay Area, it wasn't long before he went looking at the expense patterns in Baltimore as well. And what he found were much the same practices, asking agents to pay for their own equipment but then taking a copy of the agent's receipt and putting it through the home office as a reimbursable expense. Appel was so full of hubris that even when Biggio resigned, he continued the double-dipping practices in Baltimore.

Blake was all too happy to remove Appel from the agency. However, the agents in the Baltimore office caught on just a little sooner, not about the double-dipping, but with Norm's conceited and erratic behavior. At times, it seemed he had a drug or alcohol problem, given his temper and moodiness. No one seemed to know for sure. But Norm lost a group of 12 of his most productive agents all at once when a competing GA recruited them away from him and to an agency of Productive Life, just a ½ mile down the road in

Towson, MD. This suddenly left the office with only three agents, one office manager and a newly hired recruiter. Norm went into a deep depression after the exit of this group that he never came out of for the remaining few weeks he was in charge.

Lesser had all the excuse he needed, and then some. But with the home office going through the turmoil of comparing merger versus standalone futures, there was little room for recruiting a new manager for Baltimore. Blake asked Andy if he could handle both offices. This should have tipped Andy off that Blake did not see the situation in the field as long term. But Andy could only see the opportunity to establish himself once and for all as a professional line manager in the "Capitol Area" financial planning marketplace. If successful, Andy would never have to relocate again, as his expertise would now be geographically based, as well as based on technical knowledge. Bethesda and Towson were less than 50 miles or a one hour car drive from each other. Andy got caught up in the excitement of additional production opportunities. He got caught up in the opportunity to run a business in his "home town," this time with someone else's money. So, he did not hesitate to take on the additional responsibilities.

And later that same day, Ron and Andy drove north from Bethesda to Towson to repeat the introduction from that morning with the remaining personnel in the Baltimore office. The reception in the afternoon was not as warm as the one in Bethesda. But then, there were fewer people involved, and the three producers left in the office were either still shell shocked from their colleagues' exit or they had an agenda of their own that was outside Empire's best interests.

In Towson, there was Kate Gerber, a women in her 50s who came into the financial planning business three years before with the idea of being a truly objective advisor to her clients. This led her to be a marginal producer in Empire life insurance sales, but well thought of and impeccably ethical in her dealings with her clients. A CFP herself, Kate considered the exit of her colleagues as a betrayal of their existing clients. There was no provision for allowing these 12 agents access to their clients who had Empire assets in their portfolios. And Kate felt that the 12 who left had gone to "greener" pastures for their own pecuniary interests, not what was best for their clients.

There was Barry Zieman, more of a died-in-the-wool life insurance agent, who was not even NASD licensed, so he did not venture into the investments side of the business with his clients. Barry preferred to concentrate on insurance products, mostly universal life. Barry had struggled with personal issues, including a divorce and ensuing nasty child custody case involving his 10-year-old daughter. The personal problems caused his sales to falter for the past two years.

Then there was Carl Walker, who had developed a full boat financial planning practice, based mostly in the advanced markets, by working with small, closely-held business owners, the very people Andy's expertise could best help. Carl also networked with a couple of sports agents with clients who played in the NFL. The Empire home office had hoped that Andy could have some influence in bringing more of Walker's production to "Mother Empire," for he had been putting a large amount of business through an independent producer group, called Hemisphere, essentially a guild of advanced producers who commit to do at least $100,000 in commissions a year with the group in order to have access to their products and support services. Hemisphere would negotiate directly with insurance companies to garner the most lucrative contracts and pass the higher commissions – at least some of it – on to its members.

Carol Berner was a social worker and married mother of two teenage girls when, about 6 months before the mass exit from the Baltimore agency, Appel hired her to build a roster of recruits for Norm to bring into the business as agent/financial planners. When the mass exodus and resulting firing of Appel occurred, Carol assumed she was also out of a job.

Someone was out of a job, all right. But Andy figured that consolidation of the offices into one working organization would be the right first move. So, he put Carol in charge of recruiting sales people for both offices. The Towson office manager was let go. A receptionist at a lower salary would answer phones in Towson. All Empire business would now go through Bethesda. The production, such as it was at that moment, would be credited as one agency.

However, to the public, the two offices looked to be quite separate. The Bethesda office was renamed Commonwealth Financial Group. At first, the agents complained that the name sounded too Virginian. "We are in Maryland, a state, Andy; not Virginia, a Commonwealth." But because "Commonwealth" suggested "wealth," as Andy explained, the sales force eventually relented and accepted the new name.

In Towson, Appel had used the trade name "Maryland Financial Group." And Andy decided to keep that name going. Separate 800 numbers to each organization were maintained. And each office had its own sales manager. In Towson, Andy asked Barry Zieman to take on that role at least on an interim basis. He resisted taking the job until he realized that Andy intended to let Barry continue to work his own book of business and simply supervise the others, earning an override on the others' business.

In Bethesda, Andy had lost the existing sales manager to another agency with another company the day he arrived. This "recruiting" – O.K., call it what it was – stealing – talent from one agency to another had become commonplace, especially in the D.C. market, where company and employer loyalty were relatively low. So, Andy looked to a relatively new producer, but someone who could still be a model for the "new org" sales people Andy was hoping to hire –

people with less than 3 years in the business. Andy tapped Saul Rosen, son of the wealthy business and real estate tycoon in Montgomery County, MD, Morris Rosen. Saul was the youngest of four sons in the Rosen family: a cardiologist, a litigation attorney, and a CPA – successful all. Saul thought of himself as the "black sheep" of the family, and sought to prove himself in the financial planning profession.

Among the top agents in the Bethesda office were the so-called "3 Wisemen." These were three veterans of the life insurance business, each one with no less than 20 years tenure. Dan Eisenberg was the only one of the three still housed in the agency itself. He was a basic "kitchen table" agent, did no securities business, just wrote at least one life insurance application a week, 50 weeks a year, for 20 years, and so he had built up quite an annuity of renewal commissions and service fees over that business. Dan was 60 when Andy arrived, had raised one son and two daughters with his wife of 35 years, and was stubborn as a mule, but had earned the right to be.

Also one of the 3 Wisemen was Mel Kaplan, as long in the business as Dan, also focusing on insurance rather than investments. But that's where the similarity ended. Mel's office was next door to the agency, just down the hall on the 5th floor of 3 Bethesda Metro (a building sitting on top of the subway station). Mel concentrated on the closely-held business market, worked a lot with doctors and lawyers in the City, and ran a pension administration business in his office managed by his third wife, Wendy, whom he'd married some 12 years before Andy arrived. Mel and Dan once were close friends. Their wives were close friends. But when Mel split from his second wife to be with Wendy, Dan and his wife would have no part of it, and they never spoke directly to Mel again.

The third in the triumpherate was Van Farmer, whose office was still one more door down the hall from the agency, next to "The Kaplan Group." Van was a good 'ol boy from Washington & Lee

University in Lexington, Virginia, who had built a very successful practice with two associates under him. Van also focused on the advanced markets – mainly estate planning. But Van was also a member of a nationwide producer group, The Wainwright Group, which required Van's office to produce at least $500,000 of life premium with the Group to maintain membership. So, he had his associates place just enough business with Empire to keep his office in good standing with the company, allowing him to place the bulk of his production through Wainwright.

In life insurance sales, the 3 Wisemen accounted for 75% of all the Empire Life business that flowed through the Bethesda agency when Andy arrived. Yet, that had become a small number because of the "strike" by virtually all hands in revolt against Rod Peek.

The rest of the agency consisted of a hodgepodge of personalities and agendas. Representing most of the remaining Empire Life production in the office was Darrell Witherspoon, about 20 years junior to each of the Wisemen. In that same age group were a husband and wife team – Grace and Gayle Pierce; a right-wing Zionist who fancied himself as Andy's spiritual counselor "Rabbi" Keith Schumer; a Palestinian immigrant from East Jerusalem who suffered the remaining effects of polio as a child, Yaz Suleil. There were members of perhaps every ethnic group in D.C. among those on the roster at Commonwealth Financial Group.

Andy had a two-fold goal in the short term: Gin-up the production, particularly life production, particularly Empire Life production, among the existing agents; and recruit like crazy to get some new blood into both the Maryland and Commonwealth offices. As to the second goal, Carol Berner swung into action. She was hell-bent on proving she could do this well.

As to the first, standing in the way were obstacles that were quite different in each office. In Towson, it was the hidden agenda of lead producer Carl Walker, which was to build his own Hemisphere office. In Bethesda, the problem was the in-house broker-dealer principal in charge of the investments side of the business there – Gary Cardoza.

Gary was fairly young, age 32, with 7 years in the business. He was securities first and last, never having been trained in insurance products. Warren had brought him in from the bullpen of a stock brokerage office in Bethesda, to manage the securities side, and he did so, very well. Cardoza did so well that the office became the second leading office at Empire in securities sales, while declining in life insurance sales each of the last three years. Andy sought to reverse the trend. He knew that the margin paid on life insurance sales were the only way to sustain the office. Cardoza was not interested in life production. It didn't pay him anything.

Life business did pay Peek a lot however, a lot more than equities, so the agents continued to do equities business through Gary. They were at least making something on the sales. The point was that it was not helping to pay Peek's mortgage. By the end of 1991, the Bethesda-Towson combined offices were 15th in life production at Empire, but 2nd in equities sales.

Andy didn't feel the immediate impact of the lack of life production in his wallet. The deal he made with Blake Lesser – similar to how a new manager starts out – was to take a monthly salary that reflected the flow of overrides that the office had produced for Empire on a last five years average, much higher than if the measurement had been the current year. Still, Andy kept track of how his monthly pay compared to what he would have gotten on the "gold standard," the override formula in effect for veteran Empire managers at the time. Andy's personal goal was to generate a positive variance favoring the formula by the end of 1992; a bold goal that few managers were able to generate at that time. Of all the agency managers at Empire at the end of 1991, only 6 were on the "gold standard." The rest were, like Andy, subsidized with a salary.

During the first week Andy was in charge in Bethesda and Towson, he faced two situations; one personal and one business. Andy lived temporarily in a hotel in Bethesda while Sallie held down the fort in Princeton, allowing Robert to finish second grade before moving. One night from his hotel room, Andy turned on the TV to what had always been his favorite station for local news, only to learn from Anchor Gordon Peterson that Sports Announcer and Gordon's close friend and associate, Glenn Brenner, had fallen ill and into a coma from some sort of brain hemorrhage brought on from physical stress during Glenn's run in the prior weekend's Marine Corps Marathon, the largest and best known running event in D.C. Brenner was a comic as well as sports institution in local Washington television and a TV idol of Andy's during all those years in Virginia – before the move to New Hampshire. Brenner was thought to be in good health, albeit a bit overweight, and the thinking was that his weight was out of line with the stress of a marathon. Andy thought of his own weight and worried that such a thing could happen to him as well. Although not a marathoner, Andy still prided himself on running 3 miles, 3 times a week, along the Potomac River. But being in the field was no place for a serious diet. And there never seemed to be enough time for exercise; the stress in the field from trying to generate business was a 24/7 job. And the stress also meant not taking the time to choose meals wisely; just grabbing whatever was convenient.

In business, Andy was asked that week to meet with three major agents in the Empire field force who were not in his agency but knew Andy from his time in the home office. The three had come down to Washington as members of a Governmental Relations Committee for the Association for Advanced Life Underwriting

(AALU) to strategize on upcoming legislation affecting life insurance. In particular, there was pending a change to the tax law introduced by House Member Pete Stark (D, CA) to take away the tax shelter of cash value life insurance. But also on the agenda of the three agents was to meet with Andy and get a briefing on what he knew about what had been going on in the home office. After all, he had only been in the field for a week; his information was still fresh.

Andy knew little, and he said so, other than that he knew that Dick Sheridan was firmly committed to finding a standalone future for the company. Andy thought that would be good news to the three field people. Instead, they seemed to indicate an antipathy toward Sheridan. They seemed to know, though they didn't admit it, that the merger with Gadsden was a *fait a compli*. And as a fellow agency manager, they were intensely loyal to Bill Warren, and followed his agenda religiously.

Andy commuted on weekends back to the family home in Princeton. He would stop on the way up to New Jersey in Towson, to work there on Fridays. And he spent Mondays there as well, on his way back down to Bethesda. At the beginning of his second week on the job, a letter was waiting for Andy in Towson. The envelope had no return address. But inside, Andy found it to be a letter from Norm Appel. It read:

I hope you're enjoying what's left of that loser agency in Baltimore. You have to be a real sap to think you can build with the three remaining losers I left there. I really stuck it to the home office when I left. The agency cannot be rebuilt without me. Have fun with it, sucker.

And Norm signed his name underneath. It astounded Andy that Norm would testify as to his own incompetence in running the office in Towson. And Andy shared the contents of the letter with Carol and the three remaining agents in the office, as a way to reinforce that Norm's departure was for the best and that this would be a new day. They didn't need the reminder.

During Thanksgiving Week, Dick Sheridan became aware that Bill Warren was conducting a separate campaign that made the merger the only option. Dick decided to seek out a couple of the outside Board members, hoping to lobby for an alternate view on the Board. Dick was on the Board, but Warren was the Chairman as well as CEO.

Warren learned from an outside Board member – from a phone call during Thanksgiving dinner with family – that Sheridan was lobbying the Board for the standalone scenario outside of Warren's knowledge. Bill did not wait until the weekend was over. He called Dick on Friday and fired him on the spot for insubordination. The next week the Board voted to approve the merger with Gadsden, to take place January 1, 1992.

The merger deal, as it was revealed to the public after it was completed, put the current CEO of Gadsden in the Chairman's role for the year he had until his scheduled retirement. Warren would be President and Vice Chair during that time; then succeed to the Chairman's role for the additional year he had until a pre-ordained retirement. After that, the current COO and President of Gadsden, only 50 years old at the time, would be the resulting long-term Chairman and CEO of the combined company. This guaranteed a lucrative "golden parachute" to both Warren and his counterpart at Gadsden, all negotiated in secret with both Boards' respective Compensation Committees, the place where executive compensation packages are designed and proposed to the full Board for rubber stamp approval.

In early December, Warren convened another meeting with home office staffers to inform them of the merger decision. During the meeting in Piscataway, in the Empire cafeteria, the announcement went down with silence, until it was time for Bill to take questions. The first one came from none other than Tom DeBroglio. He asked, "Bill, how badly did you fuck us over?"

The place went wild. The meeting was quickly concluded. Tom's resignation was on Sam's desk within the hour. Tom would go on to be a sales support consultant at another company, also based in New Jersey. Fran Early would retire on disability due to ill health. Nate Paglio would find work with a pension administration firm just before he was to get his pink slip, the next March. Dara Welch and her husband decided to have another child and she dropped out of the workforce, indefinitely.

Zach Goodman saw the handwriting on the wall. Andy had invited him to come down to Towson to tour the Maryland Financial Group, with an opportunity for him to build his own unit of producers and be a sales manager. Zach seemed to relish life in the field, and he did consider it seriously. But by the end of 1991 he had decided that while going into the field might be a good move for him, not with Empire. He stayed in New Jersey and became a financial planner with IDS, soon to become American Express. Sheila Borders stayed long enough to get a severance, which was disappointing, considering her short tenure with the company and that she was but an appointed officer. She ended up hanging out her shingle and going into law practice.

A similar fate awaited Kevin Millner. Since the broker-dealers of the two firms were also being merged, the new company would not need two heads of the broker-dealer. Despite the fact that Empire Securities was larger in retail sales, Gadsden was known for a proprietary family of mutual funds and Millner was made a slightly better severance deal than Borders, as he was an elected officer.

As for Max Fortunoff and Cam Dowd, they were both close enough to retirement to "take the handsome severance deal" that awaited them post-merger, as if they had any choice.

This left Sam Roberts and Blake Kessler, who agreed to stay on during the transition to help integrate the Empire field distribution channel into the one operated by Gadsden. They each walked away in July of 1992 with two year's salary as a "golden parachute," along with a one-year bump in employer deposit to their 401(k) accounts.

Commonwealth Financial in Bethesda, and Maryland Financial Group in Towson, continued on as if nothing was going on at the corporate level. Andy continued to be supervised by Blake Kessler. In March of 1992, Andy was invited to a joint meeting of Empire and Gadsden agency managers, overseen by Kessler's new boss, Clark Carlsberg, who came from running Gadsden's career agency system.

In the meeting, Sam Roberts had the chance to take the floor and went to great lengths in his presentation of the merger integration to introduce Andy as the newest manager in the combined companies. During Roberts' session on "best practices" in the new **Gadsden Financial, Inc.**, Andy raised his hand to ask about the new company's philosophy regarding managers also producing their own book of business. Many of the large mutuals, nicknamed the Eastern Mutuals by the staff at Lambert, prohibited sales managers and agency managers from producing their own sales. They said it was a conflict of interest with their role of stimulating production from the agents themselves. Empire had always allowed personal production from its managers. Thus, Andy had prided himself on writing the odd policy now and again while running the agencies, so the agents could see his own name on the sales board that hung in the office. Andy believed in MBE (management by example). He certainly did not want to lead the agency in sales, just show that he still knew how to do it.

Also in attendance at the meeting, held in Orlando, Florida, was Fred Fidler, manager of the Gadsden agency in Rockville, MD, the next town north of Bethesda. The Fidler agency was much smaller than Commonwealth Financial Group. It had but 12 agents, only two were perennial Club qualifiers and MDRT members, and had not recruited any new agents in two years. Its life production with Gadsden was less than $500,000 in 1991. Andy knew all this and had handicapped the situation as non-threatening to his own future. He also had been told by both Kessler and Roberts that nothing was in the works to combine the agencies; that they would run parallel to each other for the foreseeable future.

After the Roberts session in Orlando, the meeting went into a short coffee break. Andy got to mix with some of the other managers, several of whom came from Gadsden. One such manager – a real GA with Gadsden – was the industry-famous Sid Goldstein, from Philadelphia. Sid had appeared many times at industry meetings; MDRT, CLU, and the like, as a guest speaker. He was looked up to as one of the most successful GAs in the industry. At 55, Sid was at the peak of his fame and fortune. No one, not the least of whom Clark Carlsberg, got sideways with Sid.

During the coffee break, Sid eventually made his way up to Andy and pulled him aside. They shook hands and introduced themselves to each other. Sid was short of stature, at 5' 6", if that, but long on bravado. Andy had seen Sid a few times on telecasts and videos from the American Society of CLU meetings, but never in the flesh. Andy was impressed, but not awestruck.

"Andy," Sid began, "That question about managers personally producing…"

"Yeah. I didn't exactly get a clear-cut answer on that one."

"Kid," Andy was not even 40 yet; so he was "kid" as far as Sid was concerned. "Always remember one rule… Always have fuck-you money. Always make sure you have your own book of business. The company can take away your agency, but your clients are your clients and if you take good care of them they will follow you wherever you go. They are your best fuckin asset."

This was true enough. Even though an agent may not have a "vested" contract, meaning that the insurer claimed ownership of the policyholder if the agent left the company, a good agent could always pull his/her clients to a new company. The client usually was more loyal to the agent than to the company. And despite home office attempts at many firms to cut off terminated agents to protect the in-force business it had, the majority of clients followed their agent to the agent's new company. The agent – not the company – was the face of life insurance to the client. This was especially true of insurance brands that were not household names to the public. Gadsden, Empire, Productive, Golden, Lambert, Atlantic: none of these brands would be on any insurance customer's list of known companies. The agent sold to himself, not to the brand, at these companies.

After the coffee break, the managers went into a seminar workshop put on by some of the Gadsden home office crowd, most particularly its General Counsel, Donna Oldham. Donna was a married mother of an only son, a driven and ambitious lawyer *cum* corporate executive. She wanted to demonstrate to the field that she understood the agent's job, and she wanted to show her marketing "chops." What she did was develop an approach talk, a script of how to handle an initial consultation with a prospective client, and place it in Gadsden's training manual. Andy watched with curiosity as she demonstrated the script by role play with one of her staff. In the role play, she made several references to the target market that Gadsden believed it was successfully targeting, the Baby Boom generation, individuals aged 30-50, with families. What she did, however, was to refer to the client as a "Baby Boomer."

Andy knew this was an absolute no-no. Having been in charge of Field Training as part of his Marketing Services portfolio at Empire, he understood that clients want to be thought of as individuals, "as if they are the only person at that moment that you are interested in." Andy would say, adopting the approach of a good radio broadcaster, "you can talk to millions but in second person singular, as if each listener was the only one you are talking to."

Andy raised his hand after the role play had finished. And in front of the entire field management in attendance, he commented, "I don't think you want to refer to the prospect as a 'Baby Boomer.' You might want to change that. Clients don't like to be pigeon-holed as a group. They want to be treated as individuals."

Andy was quite right, as evidenced by the nodding of heads in the audience as he spoke. But he was not correct. Andy had embarrassed the General Counsel of Gadsden Financial and Donna cast a particularly angry look Andy's way, similar to Bob Dole several years before. But unlike the Senator, she did not respond, either way. She went onto another question from the audience and tried to ignore Andy's comments.

Andy was slowly getting more comfortable and confident in his role as head of the two agencies he'd inherited. In April of 1992, Carol Berner had managed to recruit six new people in Bethesda to a training class that Andy oversaw himself, to make sure there were no bait-and-switch allegations from the trainees. They knew that they were financial planners. But they also knew up front that the life insurance was top priority. Andy shared with the trainees his 9-second diamond of being "in the business of financial security and independence; financial security comes first – that is the life insurance – because you can't build a house without first building the foundation."

In Towson, Carol had a harder time, but there were three new-bees going through training there. No doubt in both places that demand for salespeople were higher than the supply of qualified talent in the marketplace. Managers fairly well accepted anyone as an agent who was willing to sign a contract and live with mostly variable compensation in the form of commissions.

Yet, good selection was a skill that the local GAMA (General Agents and Managers Association) Chapter in D.C. called "a top priority to successful agency management." So spoke the 1992 Manager of the Year, Oliver Winters, at the Chapter's Annual Awards Dinner in Bethesda in early April that year, a meeting at which Andy attended, along with his sales manager at Commonwealth, Saul Rosen. Andy was still working on weaning Saul away from the investments side of the business and concentrating more on the life production; hence the invite to the GAMA Awards Dinner. During the cocktail hour, Andy got a chance to shake hands with the evening's top honoree. Oliver Winters managed the Productive Life agency in Bethesda, was a past president of the GAMA Chapter in D.C., and was well known in insurance industry circles in Washington, though maybe not as well as Bill Warren.

Winters managed in his brief encounter that evening with Andy and Saul to impart one bit of advice. "If you can sell, or you can recruit, you'll always have a job in this business." Productive was a company that forbade managers from maintaining their own "book" of clients, so recruiting was Winters' personal claim to fame.

At only age 54 but 15 years running his agency, Oliver Winters was one of the old-time agency managers in Washington. The average tenure of an agency manager in the Washington area in the early

1990s was little more than two years. The D.C. insurance market had become a war between the major GAs and managers from each company. Managers would poach talent – both sales agents and sales managers – from each other. It had gotten to the point that most GAs in the area had stopped coming to GAMA meetings where they would have to sit at the same tables and "break bread" with each other. Winters joked that soon GAMA would have to have metal detectors at the door of meetings to make sure no one walked in with a lethal weapon. In fact, it was worse than that. The 1992 Awards Dinner would be the last one held by GAMA in D.C. By 1994, the Chapter had ceased to operate due to lack of membership and attendance at meetings.

April 1992 would render a major victory for Andy and the combined Commonwealth and Maryland Financial Groups. Measured against the other Empire agencies still running in the new company, the D.C. / Baltimore agency, as it was officially called inside the home office, had grown to 4th place in proprietary life production that month, from 15th just five months before. True, most of it came from the 3 Wisemen in Bethesda, who had turned the spigot of production back on. Darrell Witherspoon also had a good month, and a few of the other securities-oriented producers in the office began to pitch in some life production as well. Morale in both offices started to rise, as Andy stopped the practice of managers working on live cases with agents for a piece of the agent's commission. Andy's philosophy had been that he was earning an override on the entire operation's production and unless he was asked to essentially take over the case from an agent, he would not insert himself into the agent's commissions. He enforced this with his sales managers as well. Managers were to go on sales calls for their overrides only. This was especially helpful to those in the offices who wanted to use

Andy as their advanced sales attorney and take him to close a deal with a high income client and the client's other advisors.

Andy was thought of as generous and fair with the agents. So they spoke highly of him in the office, which also raised the morale of the administrative staff. In Bethesda, where Jean Smithers was the office manager (Andy liked to call her the "Sergeant Major", after the highest non-commissioned officer in the Army – Andy's childhood military background in evidence here), she gained confidence with each passing month that she could manage the administrative staff in both Bethesda and Towson. And she and Andy developed a confidence in each other over these months. Jean's only concern was whether Andy would last in his position as manager.

"I've seen them come and I've seen them go." Jean said in a one-on-one meeting they had in Andy's office at the end of April. "Are you here for the long term, really?"

Looking directly into Jean's eyes, Andy stated, "Jean, I'm not going anywhere." Then, after a pause, Andy took Jean's hand in his over Andy's desk. "Do you trust me?"

After a short pause, Jean answered, "Yes, I do trust you."

Meanwhile, Bud Warren continued to manage the outside brokerage agreements that filled the agency's product line with products Empire and Gadsden did not manufacture. These agreements named Andy Greene as the GA for each company. Now that he had two offices, Andy was an even bigger target for these outside companies to do business with and the overrides flowed at an even higher rate than under Bill Warren in his time. Andy shared the overrides with Bud Warren, but found checks coming in from these various companies for which Andy did little to generate other than be the GA in the office. Bud would collect the GA override checks, Andy would endorse the checks, sign the deposit slips, and Bud put the checks into a private "Commonwealth Financial Group" account with Andy as the sole signatory. Gadsden and Empire had nothing to do with this part of the operation.

Since Andy was used to a home office salary, the flow of income was way beyond his imagination. Though he did well as a corporate "suit," his income now was twice what it had been. Andy was careful, however, not to spend the cash flow from these outside agreements. He made sure he lived within the Empire salary agreed to with Blake Lesser, which itself was a pay raise over his home office salary. Andy was looking into the future. He saw the war going on between the major GAs in the area and felt he would need a "war chest" to fight for his share of available talent.

In Bill Warren's time, if he wanted to sign a young agent into the business, there was usually a problem with the new-bee being able to finance him/herself until enough commission and TAP came in. Most companies, including Empire, refused to finance a new person in the business, believing, as Lesser would say, "Financing finances failure." The philosophy was that if you were good at selling you would quickly turn a positive cash flow. This meant that the home office avoided financing losses with field people who washed out after a year or two, never validating their contractual commitments of production to cover the financing the company provided.

Warren knew that while this all sounded good from the home office perspective, it was a losing proposition in the field. A desirable talent – let's face it, most anyone who could fog a mirror was a desirable talent in the 1990s – would be able to find a company offering financing. So, if you wanted that recruit for your agency, you had to come up with some money to float the recruit until the sales began to flow. The home office looked the other way at some of the under-the-table deals the managers would make to snag a good recruit. Bill Warren was no exception. He would ask the recruit to make a list of all his/her monthly expenses, getting it down to the minimum the recruit needed to live on while he/she got started in the business. Then, Bill would open the drawer of his desk, the drawer that had the outside, private checkbook, and would take out a pen and write the recruit a check for the amount tabulated in the budget the recruit had put together.

Bill would then say, "Here, this will get you started, and I will continue to write you these checks for the next 12 months… Provided you sign this pre-contract paperwork and do from this point forward whatever I tell you to do. I don't want any resistance or objections from you for the next 12 months. Do as I say, and in a year you'll be in good shape."

Bill didn't even make it a loan. It was like a private salary. If the recruit turned out to be good, Bill would make back all of what he'd paid out in overrides on the recruit.

The lesson Bill set in the office was not lost on younger brother Bud, and he went to great lengths to explain Bill's entire approach to recruiting. He told Andy, "Tell the recruit that they're in business for themselves, not by themselves. The check was part of the 'not by yourself' in the deal. But this meant Bill owned the guy from that point on. If the guy worked out, he'd be forever loyal to Bill for getting him his start. If he didn't work out, the outside overrides financed the cash flow and Bill was no worse off than if he'd stayed within the lines of Empire's hiring policies."

And Andy listened intently. For one thing, letting Bud carry on at length about his big brother, his idol, drew Bud closer to Andy. For another, there was something in the merits of this recruiting approach, something worth trying that they don't teach you at GAMA.

So far, Andy had been able to gin-up production in the agencies without having to resort to financing agents privately. The loss of revenue that Andy experienced from not putting his hands in the agent's pocket for a piece of the agent's commission was, for the time being, enough to show the home office he was putting the agency on the right track. The outside overrides paid to Commonwealth Financial Group would, for the most part, sit in the account, unused.

Andy did indulge himself two discretionary expenses. The first was the purchase of a 1987 Mercedes 420sel, white with red leather upholstery. A GA in the field, recruiting and selling, could not be seen with a Honda Accord. And the car came with a story: It had previously been owned by Tom Clancy, the author and Bethesda resident.

The second discretionary expense was purely personal. While Sallie was still in Princeton, looking after the kids, Andy picked out a ruby and diamond ring to give her for their anniversary. When they originally got engaged, they had little money. Being prudent with a dollar, Sallie insisted they forego the usual engagement ring, and opted only for wedding bands at the time. Andy promised her, "Someday, when we're doing better financially, there will be that ring."

Andy knew that Sallie's favorite gem stone was a ruby. To help shop for the right ring, Andy sought the assistance of his old friend and colleague, Effie Eckhart, and she was the only person to see the ring before he brought it home to Sallie. The ring would become a family heirloom from that point on.

April turned into May. In the Gadsden home office the integration of Empire into Gadsden was well underway. It was not just the dismantling of Empire's home office personnel that was happening. A folklore was developing about certain personalities at Empire that fed a self-serving narrative about who did and who did not fit into the new company. The interlude in Orlando between Andy Greene and Donna Oldham clearly put Andy on the "don't side." Rumors that Andy "is a loose cannon" spread throughout the Gadsden home office.

Nevertheless, Andy was unaware of the rumors. Or he wasn't listening. So long as Andy had Commonwealth and Maryland moving in the right direction, Andy felt he was untouchable. The Gadsden agency in Rockville was tiny compared to Commonwealth and Andy saw only blue skies ahead.

When the monthly sales numbers for April came out during the first week of May, life production was up, securities sales were flat, and this irked Gary Cardoza, Commonwealth's head of the investments side of the house. That week, Gary tendered his resignation. He had secured a "principal's" position in another agency. Gary was unhappy about the new direction of the agency and wanted out before it went any further. But when a copy of his resignation went into the home office, Bill Warren was alerted, and called Gary to talk him out of leaving.

Bill promised, "Gary, there are going to be some changes made in the agency. I think you'll like them. I can't give you details at the moment, but I'm asking you to hold off on this resignation."

"Bill," Gary replied, "I can't pass up the offer I have in hand if I have no idea what you're planning."

"Hey, man, just sit tight. I pulled you out of a 'boiler room bull pen' in a wirehouse, hawking stock tips to anyone who would listen, and gave you the position you have now in that damned agency. You owe me this." Almost LBJ-like, Bill Warren knew when to put the pressure on a reluctant colleague.

And Gary waited…

Then, the phone rang the Friday afternoon before Mother's Day. "Hi Andy, Blake Lesser here." Andy rarely got a call from Blake. "Andy, I'm flying into Dulles on Monday and I'd like it if you'd meet me at the airport."

Andy knew from experience watching other distribution heads what this meant. "Blake, what are you trying to tell me? Am I out?"

"I can't comment now. Meet me Monday morning. My plane gets in at 11am."

"Blake, just tell me… Are you taking me out of here?"

And in a rare feeling of empathy for Andy, Blake said, "Yeah, that's about the size of it."

Andy hung up the phone. He was devastated. He didn't know what to do. So, he went down the hall from the Commonwealth office and went in to visit Mel Kaplan. Andy and Mel had become good friends. Mel used Andy frequently on live cases. Andy used to joke that the very short Mel Kaplan, with his gregarious manner and boisterous tone, reminded him of Louie DePalma, the Danny DeVito character from *Taxi*, one of Andy's all-time favorite television sitcoms. Andy used to say, "I am but a mere Alex Rieger to your Louie DePalma," paying homage to Mel's biting sense of humor and false callousness toward the world.

Andy sat down across from Mel's desk and told Mel, "They're taking me out, Monday."

"Yeah, I know," Mel replied.

"How do you know?"

"Rumors in the home office have been going on for a week."

"I had no idea."

"Yeah, that's the way those bastards do it. They prepare everyone but the victim for the fall." After a moment, "don't go crying in your beer, man, follow me."

And Andy followed Mel out into the hallway and down another door to "The Farmer Group," Van Farmer's office. Mel waltzed through the reception area as if he owned the place. Andy followed meekly, apologizing to Van's receptionist. Mel entered Van's office, ushered Andy in, and closed Van's private office door behind Andy. Van was sitting on a love seat sized sofa, with a coffee table in front of it. His desk was on the opposite side of the room. It looked like Van was just relaxing with a cup of coffee, reading the Wall Street Journal, not a care in the world. "The stock market must be up today," Andy thought to himself.

"Andy, my boy, good to see you," and Van held out his hand for a handshake, without rising from the sofa.

It looked to Andy as if Van was expecting him. But Andy nonetheless launched into his tale of woe.

"Looks like I'm out of the picture guys," addressing both Mel and Van.

"It may be your lucky day, Andy," Van said.

"What do you mean?"

"The shitheads in the Gadsden home office were going to take you out eventually anyway."

"Why? We did good work here."

"They don't care about that. They've decided you aren't one of them." Andy thought of the same comment he'd heard when he was leaving Lambert. "They're going to put their own guy in here. Shit,

I hate that, but it won't really change anything for people like Mel and me. We'll go on, whoever is the manager."

"Good for you…"

"Andy," Mel jumped in, "Don't be a wuss about this. It happens."

"You mean 'shit happens'?" answered Van, and they both broke out in laughter.

"Man, I brought you here for a reason, so listen up!" was Mel's instruction.

Van started, "I do a lot of production though Wainwright… You know that, right?"

"Yes, Van, I'm aware of that. I know we never talk about it, but it's an open secret."

"I've never tried to hide it, Andy. But that's not what I'm talking about now. Do you know the carrier that a lot of that business winds up with?"

"Well, Wainwright was the brainchild of a major producer with Golden State Mutual Life, I seem to remember."

"That's what I'm talking about! Mel, this guy is not as dumb as the home office thinks."

"Yeah, listen up Rieger," Mel's *Taxi* nickname for Andy.

"Golden is looking to expand their brokerage presence to the East Coast. Their guy, Jack Harrelson, called me not three days ago, wanting a referral to candidates in this area for a regional brokerage manager slot in a start-up office in D.C. Are you interested?"

Andy could barely contain his joy, and he recalled George Harrison's line when The Beatles were offered their first chance at recording while they were in Hamburg, Germany, "Yes, well I'd be quite well prepared for that eventuality." And all three broke out in laughter.

"O.K.," Van continued, "I'll give Harrelson a call back this afternoon. It's just lunchtime out in California. Do you have a resume I can fax him?"

"I'll get you one out of my office. Give me 5 minutes."

On Monday, Andy met Blake at the airport. The severance paperwork was in Blake's briefcase. They rode together to the office in Bethesda. Waiting for them in Andy's office was Bill Warren himself. He had come down separately to keep the agents and staff calm in the face of this change in management. The deal was that Andy would continue earning his monthly salary through the end of June, at which time Fred Fidler would take over a combined Rockville – Bethesda office. Towson would be disbanded for lack of production. Carl Walker had announced his exit from Empire-Gadsden that same day. He was on his way to building his own "empire" within Hemisphere. The others would find new homes in other agencies.

Bill Warren made a personal appeal for Andy to stay with the agency in personal production. Later that week, Andy received a phone call from Fidler, again asking Andy to at least stay through a transition period to help him and the agency get comfortable with each other. It was going to be a few months, Andy surmised, before Golden State was ready to make its move, so he agreed to stay on.

Fidler and Andy harbored no ill will toward each other. Was it that they were Landsmen? Fred Fidler had grown up in Brooklyn, Mill Basin to be exact, so there was commonality there. Andy did write a little business in his months with the new agency, for which Fidler was grateful. At life underwriting chapter meetings, to which many of the life insurance agents belonged, Fred and Andy would organize an agency table at the luncheon. There, during the invocation, they stood silently. When a senior member of the Chapter would come to the podium to deliver an invocation – to say "grace" with liberal reference to Jesus – Fred and Andy would recite to themselves the *Schma,* the universal prayer of all Jews, and secretly smile at each other as the invocation ended, each knowing what the other was privately doing. Reference to Jesus was about the only thing "liberal" in the insurance industry – it seemed difficult to find a Democrat among the membership at times, even in D.C. And along with the conservative lean, the membership took the opportunity to put G-d into business conversation whenever it seemed to fit – and G-d in this case was a New Testament G-d.

Chapter 9: Someone Else's Money

Andy flew out to Santa Barbara to meet with Jack Harrelson from Golden State Mutual Life. They first met offsite at the Conference Center at Pepperdine University, so they could have some offsite privacy.

"You come very highly regarded by Van Farmer," remarked Harrelson.

"That's nice to hear. I think the world of Van, one of my top producers in the agency."

"Well, we think pretty highly of him as well." Jack Harrelson was a tall, thin man with features and a speaking pattern that vaguely reminded Andy of John Wayne. Harrelson was big in the California Republican Party and lived in Orange County, just south of L.A., the West Coast "capitol" of conservative politics. This created a very long commute to north of L.A. And Jack maintained a bungalow in the hills north of "the Valley" for during the week, putting him closer to the home office.

For Andy's part, he had given up the too-long hair style and gone a bit more conservative. But the braces and wing tips still gave away his East Coast orientation. Maybe that was what Harrelson was looking for – his notion of what an East Coast "go-getter" brokerage manager ought to look like.

"Golden State is expanding, Andy," Harrelson explained. "We have a multi-year plan of building up this brokerage distribution system. Traditionally, we have been a West Coast company. Now, we're going nationwide. We're going to open three new regional brokerage offices a year, until we've covered the country. The three on the list for 1993 will be Philadelphia, Cincinnati, and Washington, D.C." (he pronounced it as 'Warshingtun').

"Sounds exciting."

"We think so." And Jack then looked down at the copy of Andy's resume he'd gotten a few days earlier. "So you worked at Empire Life."

"True. You know the company?"

"Oh, yes I do," And Jack launched into Golden's side of the 1986 merger fiasco. "Seems Empire though it was buying us." And Jack took the liberty of a little laugh. "How could that two-bit company, going downhill, think it was buying us. It was the best merger that never happened. After the deal fell through, this idea of converting from a mostly career agency company to more of a two-level brokerage came into being."

"Two-level?" Andy asked.

"Some of our top producers decided to start their own producer group, using Golden product."

"You mean 'Wainwright.'"

"Yes. You know about that? Oh, sure, Van brought you into the loop on that I'll bet."

And after a pause, Andy decided to break up the "dead air" in the room. "And the other level I guess is this brokerage system you're talking about."

"Exactly. And we know that this is fairly new. When we open a new regional office, we go in with the idea that we know we're going to make some mistakes, we just need to learn from the mistakes to get better. You would also find me saying to you often that you will not have an expense problem, we'll take care of that. What you'll have is a revenue problem; getting the production in the house."

Then Jack proceeded to take Andy through a bird's-eye view of the compensation structure for the brokers Andy was to recruit. The standard contract allowed Andy to award a broker any level of commission on first-year premium, from 50% to 85%, without home office (meaning Harrelson's) approval. The way it worked was that the base commission would always be 50% up to the "target" premium, defined as the premium for which full commissions would be paid. Then, an expense allowance as a percentage of the base commission would bring the broker up to the compensation level agreed to. For example, a 75% contract meant 50% commission plus a 50% expense allowance (EA) on the base, or another 25 points, to equal 75%. An 85% payout, the most common contract Andy would offer, would be 50% plus a 70% EA to get to 85%. Beyond 85% required home office sign-off, and Jack explained that there would be no approvals beyond 90%.

On the expense side, any EA payouts below 70% would go to offset branch office expenses. Thus, there was an incentive to contract brokers at less than 85%.

Andy would be paid a straight salary for the first three years, then be weaned onto the "gold standard" of an override formula that would give Andy significantly more income if the office were successful.

What Andy did not know at the time was that Andy was not Harrelson's first choice to open this new D.C. office. After the Empire merger fell through, Golden did get an opportunity to grow larger in its asset base – its major interest in Empire – by acquiring a smaller insurer in California that had gone into receivership and was ultimately taken over by Golden. The bankrupt insurer – Western Life – was sold to Golden by the State of California Insurance Department on very favorable terms to Golden. Western had a GA in Bethesda, MD, Harry Soules, who in turn had a steady flow of production from about 12 brokers who were very loyal to Soules. When Western was acquired, Harrelson saw the opportunity to bring

Soules into this brokerage distribution channel. But Soules resisted, not wanting to lose his GA autonomy and become a "company man." As a GA, Soules was independent, and he could represent multiple carriers simultaneously. As a brokerage manager, he would be an employee of one company and carry only that proprietary line of products.

Harrelson saw Soules as his "fair haired boy," and often admitted so. But when Soules could not be "bought," Harrelson decided to put the pressure on Soules by bringing in a brokerage manager and letting the "new guy" crowd what had been Soules' clear field of providing Golden State products in the Mid-Atlantic market. That's where Andy came in. He was the pressure.

Andy's notice to Fred Fidler in late October, that he was leaving Commonwealth Financial Group, came as no shock to Fred.

"I knew something was up," Fred admitted. "The Golden State home office called me to check work history. Apparently you had listed me as contact at Empire? Probably not your best move. I knew you were looking for another job at that point, so I don't hold it against you. I appreciate your help during the transition."

"Fred Fidler was a *mensch*," Andy thought.

And on November 1, 1992, exactly one year from his appointment as head of the D.C. and Baltimore agencies of Empire, Andy became the founding manager of the Washington Branch Office of Golden State Mutual Life Insurance Company.

Office space needed to be found, and fast. Andy knew exactly where he wanted to be, in the Tycon Tower Building in Tysons Corner, VA, about a 10 minute drive from the house Andy and Sallie bought in Great Falls earlier that year (using the Commonwealth

Financial Group private "war chest" for the down payment). A 750 sq. ft. space was found on the 12th floor. Andy worked with Golden personnel in California to pick everything from carpeting colors to furniture for the office. Andy had been given an allowance in his budget to spend on such items.

This was the second time Andy would outfit an office – he had done so with Northern Virginia Financial Group – but this time with someone else's money. And Andy's interior decorating style was pure "law firm." The conference room had inset bookshelves stocked with all manner of official looking books. Rosewood and mahogany were the woods used for most of the furniture. The idea was that brokers would actually come to this office to not only turn in business but to meet clients, where Andy could play his usual role of advanced underwriting expert to the client's advisors.

Andy hired an office manager, Ruth Wood, and a receptionist, Carla Smithson. Ruth had most recently been an administrative assistant in Frank Meaney's agency for AFG, though Ruth did not come referred by Frank. Ruth was tall, and big, very big, with a personality to match. Carla was slight of build, had not been in the financial services business, ever. But she could "give good phone," using the Don Imus reference.

The office contained a couple of spare offices. These were designated to house a couple of brokers who needed office space themselves. Andy would in fact "rent" one of the offices to two different brokers at different times in his tenure as Branch Manager. But there was always one that remained empty. Here, Sallie would often come by and leave the boys, Bob and Jack, in Andy's care while Sallie ran errands or got some precious "me" time in an escape from full time motherhood. Andy was more than happy to oblige, and the spare office became in time a play area for the boys, now 9 and 4.

Andy also hired a "sales support consultant," Jane Perkins, who assembled sales proposals and other sales materials for the brokers to use with their clients. Jane had been an agent with Productive, in their Sterling, VA office further out in the suburbs. But she had had a rough go of it in personal production, and found more success in preparing others to close a sale.

By 1992, Lambert LifeAmerica had started to hit a snag in its sales growth. The life insurance marketplace had become saturated, and sales became a zero-sum game of taking market share from other companies. Products had become somewhat commoditized. Everyone offered pretty much the same product line. Conventional wisdom, that "distribution is king" in this business, caused many companies to find ways to build either more distribution or more productive distribution. While Golden was going for "more distribution," putting on brokers all over the country, serviced by O&O company brokerage shops, companies like Royal and Lambert decided to pare down the number of direct contracts it offered with producers and go after big agencies that could each deliver large amounts of business, allowing the insurer to need fewer "company men" to recruit and develop relationships with the field. In 1990, Royal had only 85 GA contracts in place around the U.S., but each one delivered over $1 million in sales a year, the minimum commitment to get a GA contract with the company. If you weren't big enough for your own contract, you were put under someone else's GA contract and produced business for which the GA would receive an override. This allowed Royal to outsource most of its need to manage a sales force; the GAs took care of that.

Now Lambert LifeAmerica tried the same approach, urged on by the cost of managing a PPGA system that had 1600+ contracts with 16 RVPs by 1991. So, Lambert began looking for RVP candidates that had "portfolio," meaning the candidate had a Rolodex with big name

GA agencies which would open its doors to the candidate due to pre-existing relationships. In the summer of 1992, while Andy was reduced to being a rank-and-file agent for the Gadsden-Empire agency in Bethesda, Phil McPherson announced his retirement from Lambert.

Phil was what Brandon Kessler called a "steak-and-whiskey regional." Phil was great at the back slapping and golf foursomes that built relationships with field producers. But he aimed at lone wolf PPGAs, small sales offices with one or a handful of small time agents. If you could do at least $25,000 of sales with Lambert, you could have a PPGA contract.

Brandon, having come from Royal and its 85 GAs looked to change all that. His formula was to bring to the table RVPs who in turn could bring real value to sales people in sales support, advanced sales knowhow, and marketing technique. At the same time, Brandon viewed his ideal RVP candidate as being able to attract the large GA office that had many brokers under contract so that each GA contract could deliver several multiples in sales of what the small offices were now doing for the company. So Brandon wanted all of what Andy offered in marketing knowledge and technical expertise, but he also wanted the guy with the big relationships, not necessarily in that order.

When Andy heard that McPherson was retiring – he heard this from remaining contacts he had in New Hampshire – he immediately contacted Tim VanEckland to see if he could resurrect his candidacy as the next RVP of the Coastal Region.

But things were already changing at Lambert and Andy was seen as too old school, with small time contacts operating under an old distribution model taught to him by Don Wasserman, Phil McPherson, and Lyn Randolph.

Enter Randy DeSilva, who came from a large Midwestern stock insurance company and showed Kessler what Brandon believed was a deep "Rolodex" of big name contacts in the Mid-Atlantic area. DeSilva was long on relationship, promising to bring all his GAs from his current company. He was somewhat short on technical knowledge, but he got to Kessler but good. They struck up an immediate liking for each other.

Andy was seen by Kessler as that "advanced sales" geek from Alexandria who – with decent mentoring – could probably do the job. But Brandon Kessler wanted results, and now. He was feeling the heat from Paul Swift who in turn was feeling the heat from Lambert Corporation's home offices in New Jersey, the Board Chairman and major shareholder Percy "Pete" Lambert often saying, "My shareholders could get a better return by buying CDs than holding this 'LifeAmerica' investment."

In September 1992, Randy DeSilva was named Lambert's RVP for the Coastal Region. Andy, named Washington Branch Manager for Golden State Mutual two months later, it was only a matter of time before they would run into each other – despite DeSilva maintaining the regional office in Wilmington, Delaware while Andy was about 100 miles southwest in Tysons Corner, VA.

The first run-in happened the following Winter. After New Year's Day, DeSilva started cutting contracts with dozens of Lambert PPGAs who DeSilva had earmarked as small time producers not worthy of a direct contract with Lambert. DeSilva had devised a plan, endorsed by Kessler, to consolidate existing producers into groups under one GA contract, held by whomever Randy believed had the best potential to manage the others. Often, the resulting GA was someone who had a Series 24 Principal's license with the NASD, so they could sign-off on securities trades with the broker-dealer and take on compliance functions with these producer-reps.

As the contract terminations came in, these long time PPGAs began calling McPherson to complain. McPherson could not help them; even though for 12 years he had been the face of Lambert in the Coastal Region, he had retired and knew he had no clout with the home office anymore. Then, the calls started coming to VanEckland, who was attentive in listening, but also offered little help. Tim knew that he was a figurehead in his position at this point. The strategic plan was strictly between Kessler and DeSilva, and anything Kessler wanted from Paul Swift during this "honeymoon" period of Kessler's tenure at Lambert was his for the asking.

Then, looking for a sympathetic voice, these former PPGAs, now brokers under a mega-GA, began calling Andy Greene in his Golden State Mutual brokerage office. The calls helped Andy recruit because many of them ended up signing contracts under him with Golden. Andy wanted to do this recruiting on the up-and-up, however. Andy knew that they were calling first to see if he could have any influence in Lambert's home office to save their contracts with that company. They would sign up with Andy to produce business for Golden, but their emotional ties and service fees for their in-force block of policies with Lambert made it clear that Andy should try to lobby for them there first; if for no other reason than to demonstrate his loyalty to these agents BEFORE he took their business away from Lambert.

Andy put a call into VanEckland, who forwarded Andy's voice mail message to DeSilva who then called Andy himself.

"Hey, Andy Greene. This is Randy DeSilva, the RVP for Lambert in Wilmington."

"Yes. Randy. Congratulations on your new position." Andy could hear a lot of traffic noise in the background on DeSilva's end of the line, and surmised he was using his car phone, causing him to speak rather loudly into the speaker in the car.

"Yeah, Andy, man, I hear you've been calling my home office asking about these producers at Lambert we have in your area."

"I was just inquiring on their behalf if there was any way that their contracts could be left as is…"

DeSilva cut Andy off there. "These producers and their contracts are my business, not yours. You need to stay the fuck out of my business."

"I hear you, Randy. They called me, not the other way around. So I felt that from past loyalties, I'd inquire on their behalf."

"Hey, asshole, you don't go into my region and mess with my producers. You don't go to fucking VanEckland behind my back and get him to change things. This is none of your fucking business, twerp."

"Randy, I meant no disrespect…"

"Well, dickhead, you disrespected me, big time. I know about you. You were the inside guy for this RVP job and you lost out to me. That should tell you something. You have no business here. Stay the fuck out of my region! Stay the fuck out of my business, or else!!"

"Randy, hold on there." Andy was thinking, "Keep your cool Greene. Remember what FX used to say, 'the first guy to lose his temper, loses completely.'"

"I'm in this job for a reason Greene, a reason you could not duplicate. That's why you're a brokerage guy and I'm working with big time agencies."

"O.K., Randy, I just wanted to inquire before I start signing these guys up myself."

"Don't threaten me, you *schmuck*! You can have them if you want. They're worthless to me, not enough business from anyone to bother with. You can have them and the expense of supervising them if you want. But I don't want you calling me or the home office anymore. You are not with this company and you need to GET LOST!"

"I didn't call you, Randy, but I get the picture. You don't need to go dick swinging with me over it."

And DeSilva tried to cut Andy off again and continue the "dick swinging" tirade. But Andy hung up.

Andy thought, "Well, I just found my first batch of producers for this new office." And over the next 30 days proceeded to sign most of them up with Golden.

Golden State Mutual had devised a marketing package and product around a concept that became very big in the 1990s – the Private Pension Plan. As an offshoot to the single premium life insurance that had been effectively legislated out of existence by Bob Dole and the U.S. Congress, the tax shelter of life insurance cash values nevertheless had become the major attraction point for clients buying permanent insurance policies.

The concept, technically, followed this logic. Take a universal life insurance policy. In it you can pay as much or as little as you like, up to a high ceiling of contribution beyond which the policy became a MEC (Modified Endowment Contract) and lost its tax shelter. But that ceiling was very high.

Why would anyone want to put more money into a life insurance policy beyond what was necessary to fund the death benefit? Because any funding beyond the minimum necessary to pay the insurance charges went into the cash value account in the policy, where it sat earning tax deferred interest.

"And, if you know the smart way to get money out of a life insurance policy," Andy would say in his presentations of the concept, "the money can be accessed tax free." Then he would go on, half-jokingly, "You know there's three ways to get money out of a life insurance policy: The Smart Way, the Dumb Way, and the Sad Way. The Sad Way is you die, and your family gets the death benefit. The Dumb Way is you surrender the policy for its cash value, lose the entire death benefit, and pay tax on the gain as ordinary income. The Smart Way is that you withdraw your premiums from the cash value – the first withdrawals are a return of premium (FIFO) and so are not taxable. When your basis has been reduced to zero – all your premiums have been returned – you switch to loans, and borrow cash values. If your policy, like ours at Golden, has a 'zero-spread' loan provision, you are borrowing at no interest. And loans are a non-taxable event."

That was the concept in a nutshell. Yes, the withdrawals and loans decreased the death benefit, but the client didn't buy the policy for the death benefit. The tax law after 1987 defined how much premium you could put into each dollar of death benefit and still get the full tax advantage of the cash value. Conversely, you could take a set amount of dollar contribution the client wished to commit to his/her Private Pension Plan (PPP), and the computer illustration system would figure out the minimum, not maximum, amount of death benefit it could buy. The death benefit still served as a self-completing feature in the event the client never got to enjoy the cash value later on, such as at retirement. It usually only took about 5 years of this level of contribution before another life insurance definition test, called DEFRA (after another acronym for another tax law) stepped in and cut off contributions. But the ceilings created in these definitions of life insurance (see IRC Sec. 7702 and 7702A) were so high that there was plenty of room to fund a policy principally as a retirement supplement – a tax sheltered retirement supplement – and less so as protection of widows and orphans from the premature death of a breadwinner.

What was so attractive about this concept was that it now meant an agent could sell to greed instead of need, a much better motivator. And it meant that agents could stop dealing with scaring clients into buying insurance to protect against "death."

"There's a reason they call it 'life insurance,' not 'death insurance,'" as Andy would usually close the presentation. And he would demonstrate with an illustration of a male non-smoker, age 45, putting $100,000 a year into a Golden State universal life policy for 5 years, generating a starting and necessary death benefit of a little over $500,000 (the death benefit would have to rise to keep the policy within the definition of life insurance), but creating a retirement fund at age 65 of $100,000 a year coming out tax free until an assumed death at age 95. "Five years pay-in, 30 years of pay-out. How'd you like that?"

And the sales agents loved it. The PPP became the leading sales concept for Golden State and its D.C. brokerage office in 1993 and again in 1994. This allowed Andy to attract quickly a large number of producers to his 85% contract. It also allowed him to sell several such PPPs through his office that he exceeded his sales goals and E/R (expense/revenue) ratio in his first full year.

The original E/R goal for 1993 in his branch office was to be 2:1; $2 of expense to $1 of production credit. Andy was at $1.25. In addition, Andy went from a zero start to having contracted 43 separate producers (brokers) by the end of the year. Andy felt he was a hero and expected accolades from Jack Harrelson when he came out to California for his first annual review in January 1994.

Instead, Harrelson spent most of the time finding fault with Andy. He cited that Andy got too much of his production from just a handful of large cases from one broker. Harrelson did not like Andy's swagger when he came out for his review, and decided to cut him down a peg.

Andy tried to remind Harrelson that back when he was being hired, Harrelson had said that once the office got going, Andy could hire a second line sales manager to build on the momentum. Jack had said at the time, "We won't do that yet, because we don't want a case of the 'blind leading the blind.' But once you get the hang of the job, we'll fund a 'sales director' position in the office for you."

When Andy brought the subject up at the review, Harrelson angrily cut him off. "Don't tell me what I promised you. Don't call me a liar."

"Jack, I not calling you a liar."

Harrelson went on, ignoring Andy's reply. "I'll put a sales director in there when I think you're ready. If you start calling me a liar, this is going to be a very short conversation."

And Andy repeated, "Jack, I'm not calling you a liar. I just thought we were there at this point."

"You're not there, Andy, not by a long shot. I'll tell you when you're 'there.'"

Andy already had in mind who he wanted to hire. Lyn Randolph, his boss at Lambert, had been let go, via RIF (reduction in force, to borrow the Federal Government terminology). She was getting ready to sell her house in New Hampshire and go back to North Carolina. Her husband was a public school teacher and could have gotten a job wherever Lyn landed. Andy wanted her to land in

Northern Virginia, feeling that he learned the PPGA business partly from her.

Andy did not treat his job at Golden as if he were a brokerage manager. He treated it as if he were an RVP of a PPGA distribution channel. The difference was more a matter of size of production from each producer than anything else. A PPGA would at least commit to a steady flow of sales revenue, even if it was not enough for the new Lambert model. A broker was an occasional producer, a transactional one at that, who used product lines of various insurers with little if any loyalty to one company. It was a matter of degree of relationship: broker at the extreme transactional end; GA at the most loyal yet independent end; PPGA in the middle.

Andy knew only two distribution channels: career agency, where agents were "captive" employees of one company; and PPGA, independent, small scale, but with some company relationship. The career agent, Andy learned, was a promiscuous relationship with the insurance company. Most career agents would not allow themselves to be true "captives," certainly not once they'd become established producers of business. They gave their career company enough business to validate their contracts, and put the rest outside, where the commission rates were much higher and they could suggest to the client an objectivity of not providing just one line of products. In this way, the career company was the "wife," and the outside companies were "mistresses." At least that was the way managers in the business termed it, always in some sort of sexual terms.

So, Andy would apply the PPGA model to his job as Branch Manager, casting himself as a *de facto* RVP. And he began to show the swagger of an RVP who had proven himself, like the guys at Lambert used to do. Jack Harrelson was having none of it. Nevertheless, at the end of the review meeting, Jack did say to Andy, "But you did have a good first year," and shook Andy's hand in congratulations. Afterwards, Jack, Andy, and a couple of Jack's minions from the home office entertained Andy with a dinner at a local steakhouse near the home office, where the minions took Harrelson's lead, drank themselves silly and ragged viscously on the new President, Bill Clinton, and the Democrats.

In 1994, Andy found it hard to build momentum on what he'd done the previous year. Although continuing to sign up new "brokers," production lagged a bit behind. In addition, problems in the office began to emerge, as turf battles between Ruth, Carla, and Jane broke out into cat fights at times. These were initiated by Ruth. She had been the first one hired by Andy and felt she ran the office and all the people in it. She was also going through a nasty divorce, and kept approaching Andy at the end of the day looking for sympathy, and maybe a bit more. There was no physical attraction there for Andy. But Ruth would revisit the possibility from time-to-time, never coming right out and propositioning Andy, but the personal offloading from Ruth would always occur after hours, when they were alone in the office, and Andy started to become uncomfortable.

When Andy finally did what he neglected to do initially, call Frank Meaney and get the low-down on Ruth's tenure with the AFG agency there, he became even more concerned. Ruth apparently had been fired, a detail not disclosed by Ruth on her Golden job application or in her interview with Andy. Frank's office manager finally brought Andy up to speed – she had been an internally disruptive force in the office, pitting one of "the girls" against the other. It seemed Ruth was a "drama queen" and lusted after the intrigue of office politics and personality clashes.

In spring 1994, Andy – struggling to build the production of his region – got a conference call from a two-person financial planning office in suburban Philadelphia. They wanted to sign a contract with

Andy's office to do business with Golden. Golden had opened a branch office within a 15-minute drive from these producers, in West Conshohoken. Andy, feeling it was only right and proper, disclosed to these prospective brokers, who were on the phone together with Andy, that Golden had an office right in their backyard, run by George Pennington, who had been hired at the same time as Andy.

"Yes, we know about George. We did business with him at a prior company. It didn't end well. We'd rather do business with you."

Andy replied, "Well, we can do that." Andy had been told that even though the branch offices around the country had geographically-centric names, there were no territorial limits on where a branch manager could go to recruit and develop business. "But I think it's only fair that I let George know that I'm contracting you guys. In the meantime, I'll send you the necessary paperwork."

"That's fine," they both answered at the same time. And a package went out that day to these new brokers.

Andy immediately phoned George Pennington. "Hi George, Andy Greene, here, how are you?"

"Doing fine, Andy. Just trying to drum up a little business here. How's it going down in D.C.?"

"Same here. Always recruiting."

"What can I do for you Andrew?"

And Andy let it out of the bag. "George, I got a call from these two producers in your area." And Andy revealed their names.

"Yeah, I know them from my prior company. We did some business together. What are they doing calling you?"

"Well, George, they say they want a contract with Golden, but through my office."

"Shit, man, that ain't right!"

"I told them about you. They admitted they knew you. They insisted they wanted to go through me."

"So, are you contracting them?"

A little hesitantly, "Well, yes. You know Harrelson told us there was no such thing as territories in this system here at Golden."

"That's not fair, Andy," George complained, childlike.

"Maybe, but the company doesn't want us to lose business over this."

Then Pennington turned ugly. "I really resent you recruiting in my backyard. You stay out of my territory. You have no business taking over my relationships with agents."

"George," Andy reminded him, "They called me, not the other way around." Then, a hollow offer. "But I'll tell you what… I won't send in any contracts to the home office until you've had a chance to talk to them. Maybe you can convince them to you. O.K.?"

"What chance do I have with you already telling them you'll take them on. This is fucking backstabbing man. I won't forget this. I have relationships in your area, man, and if you do this, I'll come down there and recruit out from under you."

Now Andy got his back up a bit. "George, that's up to you. Bring it on…" And Pennington hung up on him. They never spoke directly to each other again.

About a week later, Andy prepared to follow up on a luncheon visit with a small insurance agency in Leesburg, VA, about 15 miles west of Tysons Corner. The shop was a two-person partnership, a referral from a former Lambert PPGA Andy had put on when Lambert started going after bigger fish. Andy got to know one of the partners well, had visited the office in Leesburg a few times, and was ready to close the deal. In his briefcase, he packed the entire contracting package he would need to put the agency on through his office.

First, Andy called to reconfirm the appointment before heading out. "Just calling you to confirm I'll see you at your office with contracting paperwork in hand."

The partner Andy knew responded, "Don't need to do that Andy. Congratulate us! We're already contracted with Golden."

"What do you mean? I haven't processed any paperwork for you, yet."

"Don't need to Andy. My partner is long-time friends with your brokerage guy in Cincinnati, and we signed on with him."

Apparently, these brokers had no idea how the Golden distribution channel worked. They thought no matter who they signed with, it was all the same. They didn't realize that the branch they sign on with is the one that gets the credit for their Golden sales production.

Andy then called the branch manager in Cincinnati, now playing the role of the spurned wife. "What do you think you're doing? You know my branch is less than a 30-minute drive from their office."

"Andy, I knew these guys from before I came to Golden. And you know we have no set territories. We go wherever our relationships take us."

"You didn't think to tell me you were going to do this? Did you tell them of my existence?"

"They knew your existence. You were working with the other partner. I guess I was in the office at the moment they made the decision to sign on with Golden. I have no responsibility to you, you know that."

"This isn't right, man. We can't be doing business this way."

About a month later, Golden held its annual branch manager meeting, where managers are brought up to date on the latest and greatest from the home office, including a good dose of motivational "brainwashing" to keep each branch manager focused on the goal.

Andy decided to take matters into his own hands. He organized a separate meeting with the other branch managers, about 15 of them. Twelve showed up in a small conference room in the hotel where the big meeting was taking place. Andy used a coffee break in the formal meeting agenda to bring the group together.

Andy put on his best home office exec manner, with a hint of Vito Corleone in his voice to try and stop the in-fighting going on between branches. In the first 10 minutes, Andy learned that other managers had similar incidents with each other like Andy had with "Philly" and "Cinci."

"Guys," Andy started, "There's plenty of business out there for all of us. But if we spend our time fighting with each other, we're not going to be effective. We need to agree to a set of protocols when we enter the vicinity of a brother "regional" (using Lambert terminology)."

Some of the branch managers felt Andy was being a bit "bold." He'd only been in the job 18 months. Some in the room had been doing the job for many years. But that never stopped Andy. The merits of what he was saying, given that many in the room had their own tales of being "stolen" from, kept the meeting from getting nasty. Some preliminary agreement about contacting the local branch manager before putting someone on in his "region" seemed to gain a tacit consensus.

After the meeting, late that afternoon, Jack Harrelson called Andy aside as the big meeting closed for the day. Jack began, "Andy, I hear you've been meeting with the other managers and stirring up trouble." Apparently, one of the managers had "ratted out" Andy. "We can't have that. You know the branch offices have no territories. We want it that way. Survival of the fittest. Whoever has the better relationship, wins."

"But Jack-" Harrelson cut him off.

"I don't want to hear it. You haven't been here long enough to start changing the rules of engagement. We have our ways; we have our rationale for doing things the way we do. When you're the top branch manager in the system, we'll talk. Until then, shut up and do your job. Got it?"

And that was the last time Harrelson and Andy would speak of the issue.

At AFG, by 1993, things had gone from bad to worse. Elliott Kelleher was unable to build back the life production Atlantic needed to thrive. Tab Davenport attempted to build assets for financial strength, similar to what Golden State Mutual had done with the Western Life acquisition. In 1992, the Commonwealth of Pennsylvania had come in and taken over one of its domiciled insurers, Keystone Mutual. Atlantic made a bid to buy the company; lock, stock, and in-force policyholder base. But Pennsylvania turned down the offer, wanting it to go to another carrier based in the state. Time had been wasted by Davenport and the Board. They had not been paying close enough attention to the negative direction the in-force insurance block was heading into.

Meanwhile, the home office management team continued to be distracted from the task at hand. In 1992, Dave Manning was found dead on a NE D.C. street in the middle of the night. The police had concluded that it was a drug purchase gone bad. Brian Saunders, Manning's boss, admitted after the criminal investigation was completed, that he knew Dave had a drug problem; that Dave would sometimes go into the worst neighborhoods of D.C. to make his cocaine purchases. Saunders nevertheless contended that he did not know the full extent of Manning's drug problem.

Sure. Saunders was busy with other issues, such as his relentless romantic pursuit of Marie Frame, his head of marketing communications. Brian Saunders was a confirmed bachelor. At age 40 by 1992, the fact that Saunders had never been married suggested that either Saunders was gay or weird, and most in the home office joked that they "didn't know which was worse."

Marie Frame, for her part, also age 40 and also never married, was likewise the subject of speculation in the home office. And Andy Greene, who still sought Marie out as his running companion whenever he was in Washington, was unaware of Marie's preferences in that area, and knew enough never to ask.

But she did share with Andy her unease about Brian Saunders, who periodically would suggest to colleagues in the field and home office that Marie was his "girlfriend." It wasn't true; Marie had no romantic intentions toward Brian. By today's standards, this was sexual harassment. In 1992, the whole situation of how two confirmed single people handle such a situation was very murky. If Marie had refuted the suggestions, she still had to deal with the remaining explanation of why she "did not have a man" in her life. So, as uncomfortable as she was, she let the remarks slide because, after all, it would just raise more speculation than it was worth and it was nobody's business.

But it did mean she began to distance herself from Saunders, who took the distance personally. It caused a slow deterioration in the working relationship, not only between the two of them, but within the entire Marketing Services Department at AFG. Marie confided in Andy mainly because she knew she could trust him – not only to keep her confidence, but not to repeat Brian's mistake of assuming a relationship between them that didn't exist.

By the middle of 1993, with sales of life insurance continuing to slide, repeated demands by Davenport for more life production going ignored, and more recruiting of securities-centric Account Managers, Tab had had enough. In June, he forced Elliott Kelleher to resign. Ironically, Elliott's next stop in his career was with Royal Life in its U.S. Headquarters in Alexandria, taking over for Brandon Kessler, who had gone to Lambert LifeAmerica a couple of years earlier.

Davenport took the Board and the AFG management team through an exhaustive process of finding a replacement CMO. Tab knew he needed someone with a life insurance orientation, not another financial planner. Initially, Tab thought of drawing on the man who had replaced him as manager of the Pittsburgh agency, James "Jamie" Keane, a one-time leading AM in the agency. Jamie was on the young side to be an agency manager, at only 35. He was as wide as he was tall, but he had a way of winning people over to his thinking by great human relations skills. The Pittsburgh office had continued to do well under Keane after Davenport left.

The problem was two-fold. Jamie suffered from the same disease as Andy did years before – he didn't look the part. In fact, compared to Andy, Jamie's "balcony of affluence" was quite more pronounced, and some wondered if Jamie would live to see age 40. The second problem was that despite Jamie's urgings of more life production in Pittsburgh, the percentage of ECDs going to life insurance sales was still declining. Jamie would say he was "agnostic" on the issue of life versus securities production. He once said that "an ECD is an

ECD, regardless of where it comes from." Keane was spot on right, but not correct. The ECD value system was supposed to equate the currency with its value to AFG's bottom line, but it didn't really work that way. Political pressures from the field pushed an artificially high value to securities, in order to satisfy the need for recognition by a securities-centric field force.

Then Davenport found out that Billy Carl, the RVP that had been Davenport's boss in the 80s, before the Labor Day Massacre, had left his senior VP position with another carrier and was available, for the right reason, to consider coming back to his old company. Jamie thought the fix was in – his old manager was head of the whole company now, and would certainly not turn his back on his hand-picked successor in Pittsburgh. But Jamie had not counted on Billy Carl, someone who had the knack for out-schmoozing even the likes of Jamie Keane. And in July 1994, Tab Davenport announced that the Board had chosen Billy Carl to be CMO of Atlantic Financial Group.

Billy had been quite the "steak-and-whiskey" RVP in his earlier days. He lived off of his human relations skills, which was the hallmark of his ability to sell anyone anything. The folklore on Carl was that "30 minutes with Billy and you'll see G-d." And it wasn't far from the truth. While away from Atlantic, Billy had gone through a nasty divorce which embroiled his twin daughters and cost him a fortune. He had also lost face in the eyes of mutual friends when the ex-wife declared that she was "coming out of the closet."

In the face of all this, Billy Carl found G-d, and became somewhat of an evangelist and student of New Testament. He became essentially, "born again," though never liking that title.

While Billy was settling in, he found that "Snake" Samuelson had risen in the Law Department to General Counsel in his absence. He also found one of his beloved AMs in the field, Nelson Soris (known as "Nellie"), from Northern Virginia, had come into the home office part time to act as a wholesaler across the country for life insurance production. Nellie was built similar to Jamie and had a personality to match. Andy would come to nickname Nellie "Soris Maximus" and Nellie nicknamed Andy "Green-O-Matic." Nellie shared the wholesaling responsibilities with Anthony "Tony" Marconi, from Pittsburgh, also part time. Tony acted like a mafia "don" at times; Pittsburgh was his territory. When you came to Pittsburgh, Tony took care of you and made sure you knew he knew everyone in the City. Part time meant they still serviced their own clients, and did the wholesaling as they could fit it into their schedules. They both reported to Saunders.

In marketing operations, a veteran of Atlantic Mutual, Howard Crowe, was still there, churning out the commission statements, paychecks for the field, and managing the calculation of ECD credits. Howard was already 55 when Billy Carl took over, but he didn't look a day over 35, with no gray hair (at least none he allowed to show).

During many of Andy's Friday afternoon runs with Marie, she kept Andy in the loop; that Kelleher had been shown the door. Then, she briefed him on the Jamie Keane candidacy. Finally, in July 1994, she told him that Billy Carl had been brought back to AFG, along with a Messiah complex from Davenport that Carl was going to "save the company from itself."

By July 1994, Andy's relationship with Jack Harrelson had gone totally cold. In his first year, Andy would get weekly calls from Jack, just to check in and see how Andy was doing. After the manager's meeting in the Spring, the phone calls totally stopped. Meanwhile, Ruth Wood had turned against Andy as well. In an early visit from Harrelson to the new branch office, Jack had pulled

Ruth aside and privately told her, "Now remember, you don't work for Andy Greene, you work for Golden and me. I want you to keep an eye on what's going on here and let me know if you see anything untoward."

Ruth took the admonishment as an opportunity to punish Andy for not being more "empathetic" and responsive to her needs. Particularly after Andy learned that she had been fired by FX at the local AFG agency, Andy had been starting to build a case for firing Ruth there as well. But Ruth, sensing trouble, beat him to the punch, and phoned Harrelson to make a somewhat embellished case of Andy being more concerned about babysitting his kids in the spare office than in paying attention to business.

The chess match continued. Andy, sensing things between him and Harrelson were not going well, reached out to his old colleague, Billy Carl, as soon as Billy moved into his new position at AFG. Andy and Billy reminisced over the 1984 MDRT sales campaign and other old times they experienced together a decade ago. They agreed to meet in mid-August for an "informal" discussion of opportunities at AFG.

Meanwhile, the curtain came down on Andy's tenure at Golden State Mutual in mid-August. Jack Harrelson came out, without revealing his true agenda. Andy thought that maybe Jack was investigating his own gripes about Ruth Wood and his desire to fire her. But after almost an entire day interviewing the staff in the branch office, privately, without Andy present, Jack finally, at the end of a Wednesday afternoon, entered Andy's office and closed the door. Jack sat in a wing chair astride a chrome and glass coffee table Andy had in the office. Andy came out from his desk to sit in the other wing chair on the other side of the coffee table.

Harrelson started the conversation. "Andy, I wish I was here under better circumstances." For the first time, Andy was now sure what

Harrelson's true agenda was for his visit. This was always the way a firing interview started. "The Company has decided that it would like to end its relationship with you. We can do this one of two ways: You can resign or I can fire you. If you resign you save face but you may have problems with an unemployment claim afterwards, since you terminated voluntarily. If I fire you, you preserve your unemployment claim, but you have a forced termination on your work history."

Actually, both options were being positioned somewhat falsely, and Andy knew it. A resignation only creates an unemployment claim problem IF the employer decides to report it to unemployment as a "quit." This, most employers don't bother doing because they don't want to rub salt in the wounds of an already pissed off former employee. As to firing, it was home office policy that if a future employer called in to verify the work record of a former employee, the human resources department was never to reveal the reason for the employee's exit. The response would be limited to dates of employment and position title.

Jack continued, "I'll be here for a few days. Why don't you think it over and call me tomorrow and let me know how you want to play this. And thank you for your time and effort with us these past two years." And Jack got up, shook Andy's hand, and left. Andy was given until the end of the month to clear out, but he was no longer the Branch Manager from that moment on.

Andy spent that evening with Sallie, giving her the awful details. Her reaction was not good. This had not been the first time Andy had lost a job. Whether by his own fault or circumstances beyond his control, Sallie lost patience with the "roller coaster" she said Andy had her on. "What are you going to do?" was all she could come up with at the end of their discussion, privately, in the master bedroom of their home.

Andy already had a plan. The next day he met with Billy Carl at AFG – the "informal" interview. They immediately hit it off, as if 8 years had not passed since they last worked together. No promises were yet made, and Andy did not yet let on that he'd been sacked by Golden State Mutual. As Andy left the building after the meeting and went to his car, Brian Saunders was coming into the building and spotted Andy. They had never met before, but Brian knew of Andy by reputation and surmised that something was up.

Brian Saunders and Billy Carl never quite hit it off. For Brian's part, he was a bit too stiff and preachy. Brian believed he was a finished product, needing no mentoring or development by anyone in the business. Billy, for his part, felt Brian needed all sorts of mentoring. In fact, that was one of Billy's requirements. "Can you be coachable?" Andy's answer was an unqualified "yes." Brian's response was equivocal.

Two days after Andy's meeting with Billy Carl, Brian came into Billy's office with a resignation letter which, in addition, asked to be moved into an RVP slot supervising some of the agencies in the AFG system. Billy accepted the resignation part, declined the request for RVP, and Brian Saunders' time at AFG came to an abrupt end. That day, Marie phoned Andy to let him know that Brian had resigned. Two hours after Marie's call, Billy called Andy inviting him in for a second interview.

The fix was in, at both ends. Andy decided to let Harrelson treat his removal from Golden as a firing. At the end of August, Andy learned that Harry Soules had accepted the Branch Manager position in Tysons Corner. Soules stopped by Andy's office while Andy was clearing his personal items out of his desk. Soules was surveying the furnishings to determine how he wanted to change the office. That day, Andy also found out that Ruth Wood had been fired a couple of days after Andy's termination.

When Andy ran into Soules, Harry commented, "Well, it looks like I'm becoming a 'company man.'"

"Interesting development, Harry," Andy responded. "I thought you'd never come into the company full time."

"I have you to thank for the change of heart, Mr. Greene." Harry meant to be a bit sarcastic with the "Mr." reference.

"What do you mean?"

"This office was cutting off some of my Golden production. I couldn't draw any more brokers to my GA contract. Something had to be done."

And Andy realized at that moment that he had been used by Jack Harrelson to put the squeeze on Soules. Harrelson never intended to deal with Andy Greene long term.

Meanwhile, Andy was named AFG's Vice President of Marketing Services on October 1, 1994, almost 12 years to the day that Andy had entered the financial services industry. Andy was back with his original company.

Chapter 10: You Can Go Home Again

Andy had several meetings with Billy Carl in September 1994, before a formal offer was made. Billy wanted to make sure the field and home office would welcome Andy back after an 8-year hiatus. In meetings with Frank (FX) Meaney and other agency managers (now called Managing Directors at AFG), the news was overwhelmingly positive. Just as with Billy, the field that remembered Andy felt that the company was returning to its glory days. The AMs (Account Managers) were a little less enthusiastic. They did not want Billy or Andy tramping over their securities-oriented practices, turning everyone back into "life insurance agents."

The same ambivalence came from most, not all, of the home office. In the marketing area, Andy's return was hailed as the "prodigal" son returning home. Outside of marketing, there was some trepidation that marketing was taking over the entire company: a former field manager as CEO; his former RVP as CMO; and the return of that arrogant SOB from advanced underwriting; all in a straight line of authority.

In one of the sessions between Andy and Billy, Andy was asked to map out what a department would look like for him to run. Andy did not hesitate to go back to the Marketing Services template that FX had some years back and that Andy used at Empire. This meant, once again:

- **Field Training & Development** – Here Andy would install Nellie Soris, taking him out of the Northern Virginia agency entirely and moving him out of a life product wholesaler role he played under Saunders.
- **Marketing Counsel** – Now that "Snake" Samuelson was General Counsel, there was no opposition to the title, so long as Andy's people observed the previously agreed-to rules of

engagement. Andy would recruit a woman who served with Andy on an industry advanced sales committee, Susan Blanque. She was well known for having lead advanced underwriting at Royal Life in Toronto, though Andy had never met her there.

- **Sales Support** – Andy wanted to bring back "Q," but in the meantime, Q had become a stay-at-home father. His wife was earning a good living as an IT consultant under lucrative contracts with several area companies. The couple had three daughters, two of them adopted, and lived in Columbia, MD. Q had become quite settled in his child-rearing role and could not be persuaded back into the "rat race." So, here Andy looked to DAZ and Zim to find suitable candidates. The one Andy settled on was Tim Wheaton, a former broker in the field and freelance computer consultant.
- **Product Development** – Andy would assume the role representing marketing. Janeesh Rau had survived the many reorganizations at Atlantic and was still the Lead Actuary for the company. But he had long since stopped "doing the math." He preferred to position himself to become the next CEO, hobnobbing with the Board whenever he could. So, he designated his second-in-command, Henry Barton, to represent the "bottom line" in product development negotiations.
- **Marketing Communications** – Marie Frame stayed on to manage that area.

Billy looked over the organizational chart for the revamped Department. He recognized the design as very familiar. He asked, "What about Marketing Operations? We had Howard Crowe reporting to your predecessor."

Here Andy remembered some advice he got while going through his MBA program at GWU, to the effect, "Don't overextend your dominion of control. You can sometimes get more points in alliances than by control."

Andy guessed that Howard did not entirely enjoy reporting to Saunders. Andy further guessed that Howard would consider it a promotion if he were to report directly to the CMO. And Andy had little experience in managing the commissions that flowed through a field compensation system. "Billy, I think Howard would be better as part of your Senior Staff, alongside me instead of under me, reporting directly to you."

As far as Billy was concerned, Andy had just passed the test. Billy was worried about Andy making this new job too much of a power grab, rather than being part of a larger team with a mission to save AFG. Andy's comments about Crowe assured Billy Carl that Andy was a "team player."

"Sounds like a plan to me," Billy assessed, and he immediately approved the Department plan. Andy would join the "team," called the Senior Staff. The Senior Staff also consisted of two Zone VPs, who managed the Managing Directors in the field. But the two who were there when Billy arrived would soon decide on a different direction. Clayton "Clay" Ferreira was from Texas, and wanted to go back there. He and his family had had enough of D.C. So he simply fired the lowest producing Managing Director in his Zone who happened to be in Dallas, and appointed himself Managing Director there.

A somewhat parallel move was made by Clay's colleague, Jonathan Vollmers. Vollmers had come to D.C. after being a sales manager in the Pittsburgh office. He came into National Headquarters along with Tab Davenport. But he longed for what he thought was a more autonomous existence in the field. Frank Meaney (FX) had decided to retire at the end of 1994, and Vollmers saw the opportunity to appoint himself as the next Managing Director in Northern Virginia.

The Senior Staff now had two holes in the roster, but not for long. Oliver Winters had retired from his agency manager position in Bethesda for Productive Life at the end of 1993. But he became bored with being retired and wanted back into the game. He had originally applied to be considered by Tab Davenport for the open CMO position when Kelleher departed. When Winters learned that Billy Carl had been selected for the position, Winters swallowed his giant pride and sought out Billy for consideration for a Zone VP slot in the new marketing organization.

At the same time, Jamie Keane, Managing Director in Pittsburgh, also passed over for the CMO job in favor of Billy Carl, decided to put in for one of the open Zone slots he became aware of when Jonathan Vollmers told Jamie he was not coming back to Pittsburgh but would take over the Northern Virginia agency.

In both cases, the discussions that Jamie and Oliver separately had with Billy included some vision for the future. Tab Davenport had recruited Billy back to AFG on the promise that after a decent interval Billy would be named COO, heir apparent to take over as CEO and Chairman when Tab decided to retire.

Billy was always thinking of who would move up as he moved up. Both Oliver and Jamie were given the impression that each would be under consideration for the CMO slot as Billy moved up, maybe even to COO as Billy became Chairman of the Board.

But Andy had been given the same talk, too. "Andy, there is room for advancement here. I don't expect to stay in this position forever. As I move into higher responsibilities, I'll be looking at who can succeed me in this position, and the Senior Staff members certainly have the inside track there."

The result was that three people on that Senior Staff came away with the impression that each of them were in line to move up with Billy

Carl. Three people fighting for one future position; a true formula for rivalry...

In the meantime, there was the matter of saving AFG which, by 1994, could produce less than $5 million in life ECDs across 16 agencies with less than 300 Account Managers. The numbers of agencies had been fairly constant over the past 8 years. Recruiting new AMs and generating life insurance sales was another matter.

Because Andy had been hired a few months before Ferreira and Vollmers departed for the field, Andy got used to sitting at the opposite end of the long conference table from Billy, the new CMO, in the conference room Billy used for Senior Staff meetings. When Winters and Keane arrived, Andy did not change his assumed seat. To Oliver and Jamie this looked like the marketing area was being run by Andy and Billy as the major partners. This immediately irked both new Zone VPs, who were trying to create the impression of partnership with the new CMO for themselves. And both separately spoke to Billy about the "boldness" of the VP of Marketing Services positioning himself as the assistant CMO.

Then Winters began to lobby Billy to move the Field Training and Development Unit to his domain, arguing that Training is an agency function and so belongs with field management. "Marketing Services is a staff function, and staff serves the line," he would argue. Andy would use the refrain he used at Empire, "We're all line here."

Billy, for his part, wanted peace among his Senior Staff and tried playing "Solomon" in splitting the issue. He went to Andy, explained the complaints he'd been getting, and asked for Andy's cooperation and sensitivity. Andy agreed not to occupy the end of the conference table, but asked Billy to consider, "When that seat is empty, watch who occupies it. That'll tell you something about who's into the power grab."

"I know the whole thing is silly," Billy replied, "but I need you to get along with these guys. Don't win the battle and lose the war."

"Is this a war, Billy?"

"You know what I mean." Yes, Andy knew that Billy had set up a fight to the death among three competitors for the CMO slot. Did Billy realize what he'd done? But Andy did not speak these thoughts to Billy.

At the next Senior Staff meeting, Andy arrived earlier than usual, and occupied a seat along the long side of the table. Jamie was next in the door and seeing the empty seat at the end, grabbed it before Winters got there. Oliver was again seething at the result when he arrived, just in front of Billy, but said nothing. Andy took a quick glance at Billy to see if he recognized what had happened, as if to have a private chuckle with Billy, at the others' expense. Billy noticed, but did not give Andy the benefit of a look back.

As to the Field Training issue, Billy asked for a consensus solution. So, Andy privately approached Oliver and invited him out for a drink after work to discuss the matter. A local watering hole, Senators, had become a favorite lunch and after work hangout for AFG home office management. It was only a couple of blocks away from the office and was the only place in the City that featured memorabilia from the two failed American League baseball franchises that had played and left Washington for greener pastures. Since 1971, D.C. had been at once one of the largest and richest entertainment markets in the country and surely the largest market without a baseball team. Andy – being a baseball fan himself – especially fancied this venue.

When Andy and Oliver met at Senators for their "talk," Oliver was straightforward in saying he felt the field training function was an agency function. In a strict career agency distribution channel, he may have had a point. Agency managers and GAs would dispense training in their offices for new agents. Oliver was old school. To the extent that agent training included the "Big T" of skills training – not just product and sales concept training – Productive had its "agency department" handle the issue directly with the managers in the field.

However, earlier in the day, Billy mooted the issue a bit by telling Winters that "We're not moving Field Training" for now. Andy was aware of the comment and felt he was in the stronger position; that it was just a matter of getting Oliver over the defeat. Turns out that Soris Maximus had expressed his preference to stay in Marketing Services rather than going to Agency, having a somewhat contentious relationship with Winters. But Winters was undeterred. "I'm going to continue to lobby for this move."

"That is, of course, your decision," Andy responded, putting on his best "Vulcan" detached logic. Then, he offered, "Let's try this... You need some help in management development as well, right? How about you drive management development in the field and leave agent training with me. Of course, you'll always have input into the agent training piece, you and Jamie."

"I'm going to continue to argue for moving the entire training piece to 'agency.' That's where it rightly belongs."

What Oliver did not yet know was that career agency was not going to be the only distribution channel for AFG going forward; not if Billy Carl had anything to say about it. Within a few months after all three new members of the Senior Staff joined AFG, Billy realized that career agency was a dying distribution channel for all but the very largest "Eastern Mutuals." Trying to convert these managerial agencies into general agencies, with entrepreneurial general agents managing their own P&L, would probably result in mass exodus from the company.

Billy decided that a "complementary" – not "alternative," he refused to use that term – distribution channel needed to be added to the way AFG distributed insurance product. The decision came from Billy's realization that the field as it currently existed was simply not in the life insurance business. Yet, the only way to grow AFG profitability long term was to rebuild the company as a provider of life insurance and related products.

So, a two-pronged approach to the marketplace was developed. First, AFG needed to develop at least one or more insurance products that reflected the needs and greeds of the insurance consumer at that time. The insurance consumer was still that Baby Boom generation, upscale breadwinner or closely-held business owner, panicking both over protecting his/her family and building a financial supplement for what was becoming a longer and more active life after retirement. The time was the mid-1990s, a time of a stock market boom, full employment, and rapidly developing high tech industries, with the advent of the internet. Interest rates had been steadily falling throughout the 80s and 90s, so traditional universal life was no longer offering the high interest rates it did 15 years before, making it less attractive to consumers. The result was to develop a securities-based life insurance product, generically known as variable universal life (VUL).

Second, this complementary distribution channel needed to be based primarily in the insurance market and be independent, so that the home office was not on the hook for losses in the field. As an example of how bad the distribution losses had gotten at AFG, by 1994, the leading Financial Center in the AFG career system was in Phoenix, AZ, doing almost 20% of all ECDs in the entire field force. Yet, because most of the ECDs came from mutual funds, bank CDs, and other low margin product lines, the Financial Center was running a $4 million a year deficit. Not a single agency in AFG's system was running at break even. It was just that some Financial Centers – Pittsburgh and Northern Virginia, for examples – ran less of a deficit. This gave rise to Jamie's use of the term "we suck less," whenever Managing Directors would compare their own losses with those of Phoenix.

Billy's decision was to start a personally-producing general agency (PPGA) system, alongside the career distribution system, partly to build insurance sales from a more "target rich" environment, and partly to challenge the career Financial Centers to step up lest they be relegated – like at Golden – to the "dustbin of history."

Despite the depth of field knowledge of Billy, Jamie and Oliver, it was all in career agency. No one on the Senior Staff had experience outside of career agency; except one person. And of all the members of the Senior Staff, none had any background – not even a Series 24 principal's license – in securities; except one person. On both scores, it was the same person – Andy Greene.

So, in December 1995, Atlantic Mutual released its new VUL product: Investor 2000. Built on a universal life chassis, the policy provided a series of two dozen different mutual-fund-style options for investing the cash value. This was like Golden's Private Pension Plan, on steroids, because the policyholder could now play the market with the cash value, instead of relying on the insurer to invest the equity. Of course, the policy was not for the faint of heart. It took on more risk than a conventional UL or whole life policy because there were no guarantees of return. Andy negotiated with at least 6 different mutual fund families to provide insurance "clones" of their retail mutual funds to offer in Investor 2000. The product had the advantage of being a re-entry of the career AMs back into the insurance business without asking them to reorient their securities-centric thinking. Selling the product required a securities license that most AMs already had from selling retail mutual funds. And the product itself was priced quite competitively, with relatively low cost compared to other VUL products in the marketplace. After all, Billy Carl argued, "we need to be playing offense here. We have to grab market share, not only of clients but of agents in the field we want to attract." Billy was always thinking distribution as the way to sales, not anything direct to the consumer.

And in late 1996, AFG rolled out its new PPGA distribution channel, Andy Greene leading the way, together with six new Regional Representatives, geographically dispersed throughout the country. The "Regional" was hired under a sliding scale financing arrangement, where there was a declining salary paid to him/her during the first three years of building the region. The Regional would additionally earn overrides on all business placed in his/her region. By the end of the third year, the region would be self-sustaining and the salary would go away, the Regional now on the "gold standard" of earning the overrides only. Andy added another wrinkle: In the first three years, the Regional would be called a "Regional Director," and be promoted to Regional Vice President (RVP) only when totally on overrides, hopefully by the 4th year. Andy worked with Howard Crowe and his people to fashion an entire compensation system for PPGA – for Regionals and for PPGAs – which resembled the Lambert LifeAmerica model that Andy learned from his days in New Hampshire.

There were only a couple of problems with this two-pronged approach. First, TIG, the broker-dealer charged with vending the Investor 2000 product to the career field force, was not much interested in the product. Elmer "Bud" Knowles, a young go-getter of a President of the broker-dealer, saw little profit to his enterprise from this product and less interest in helping the "life company" save itself. Bud was aggressive, gregarious, with a winning personality. He was generating a nice profit to "Mother Atlantic" and didn't want to hear about taking one for the cause. The margins paid to TIG on sales of the "house" product were smaller (to make the product more competitive to the consumer) than for the other VULs that TIG reps (AFG AMs) could sell. Moreover, selling the proprietary Atlantic product conflicted with the AMs image (and TIG's as well) of objectivity.

Second, Billy and Andy might have looked at what was happening at other PPGA-style distribution channels as forecast for the degree of success Atlantic might have at this channel. In 1995, Lambert LifeAmerica was sold to a competitor insurer, who was much further along in developing big agency relationships than Lambert. The ROI at Lambert LifeAmerica, at half of the return from Lambert Corp's property and casualty operation, was not up to Lambert Corp. standards. The market for solid, established independent agents in the life insurance industry was becoming ever more competitive, as the age demographic of such agents was getting older. New people were not coming into the business at a sufficient clip to replace the retiring ones. Those that remained were not loyal to one company – they went with whatever carrier was offering the best product, and highest agent compensation. PPGA relied on a regional rep that earned loyalty from his/her regional field force. This was becoming harder and more labor intensive than was envisioned in the job description for most of these people. In the RVP, an insurer was also dealing with an aging and disappearing number of successful people – people who could recruit loyal producers to do a steady business and made few demands on a regional's time.

On the other hand, Lambert LifeAmerica might not have been a good example of what was happening to PPGA distribution channels in the industry. Brandon Kessler continued his "play hard" philosophy at Lambert, preferring power over results, women over life insurance sales. Randy DeSilva, meanwhile, found a "bromance" of sorts with Brandon. The two travelled around the country, DeSilva being what Kessler touted was a model RVP to the rest of the field. And DeSilva's responsibilities included travelling with Kessler on many "barnstorming" trips through the regions. This not only meant that DeSilva was not paying close attention to his own Coastal Region, but it gave Brandon a drinking and "whoring" partner when they travelled. It was not uncommon, for example, when the two would fly into Logan Airport in Boston on their way to Concord, for Brandon to have a stretch limo waiting for the two of them outside baggage claim, from which they would make a brief stop in the Combat Zone, downtown, to pick up a couple of the "ladies" and tag team a quick blow job while the limo roamed around the block a few times. After all, Brandon needed to wind down after a tough week of drinking and partying before going home to his family. And Randy became Brandon's sidekick, wingman, if you will, going along with whatever Brandon indulged in. Brandon would end his CMO career with the sale of Lambert, as most of the Concord home office were terminated shortly after the sale. But Brandon cried all the way to the bank, the golden parachute sufficient to carry him and his family all the way to retirement. Randy would never be a Regional again, and his exit from Lambert was not quite as profitable. He continued to thrash about for years afterwards, offering himself up as a field sales consultant to various insurers, with little success.

Andy proceeded forward with his Lambert model in any event. While he hired a couple of Regionals at first among those that were somewhat "long in the tooth" in experience, he did reach out and hire Lyn Randolph, his former boss at Lambert, to run a region in the Southeast, based in Raleigh, NC. This would be her first attempt at becoming an RVP. And Andy's loyalty to Lyn was repaid many times over. The same for that friend in New Hampshire playing the Manuel Noriega role in the Variety Show sketch about Lambert Funding; Darrell Torrence wound up with AFG's California Region.

As to Investor 2000, the product did sell well. Andy rallied all his Marketing Services staff to build complete promotion programs. Andy and Nellie Soris lead the way in canvassing the country, wholesaling this product to every Financial Center in the AFG career system, even building role plays they would perform in agency meetings to highlight the product's saleability. "Soris Maximus" got to lay out some good skills training in the process, using Andy in a role play of how to present the product to a client. Andy got to salt in some advanced sales ideas to fuel interest in using this product with closely-held business owners.

The product was sufficiently successful that in mid-1996, AFG came out with a companion variable annuity (VA) called Investor Annuity 2000, also developed by Andy, in partnership with the actuaries.

Meanwhile, Andy had left behind a Commonwealth Financial Group in Bethesda that was not doing so well. Whether it was Fred Fidler's management or something external in the marketplace, the agency had once again fallen in production. Clark Carlsberg was leaning heavily on Fred, putting pressure on him so Carlsberg would not be seen a fool for having put Fred in the manager's chair three years before.

Fred Fidler suffered from some of the same occupational ailments that many in the industry suffer, not the least of which was an ample "balcony of affluence" earned over years of overeating and a lack of physical exercise. Fred had sleep problems, a pre-diabetic condition, and he wasn't yet 45 years old. The pressure from Carlsberg made Fred's condition even worse.

Then, in early 1995, Carlsberg sent his zone VP down to Bethesda to put Fidler "on probation" for lack of production. This was supposed to motivate Fred to better performance. The fact was there was little Fred could do to reverse the downward spiral of an agency that just didn't want to be in the life insurance business anymore. And without much background in advanced marketing, he lacked the one thing that had earned Andy Greene the respect and loyalty of the "3 Wisemen."

On Good Friday, 1995, Clark Carlsberg arrived in Bethesda to take away the manager's position from Fred. The meeting, starting with, "Fred, I wish I was here under better circumstances….," at least offered Fred the option of staying on as a producer.

Fred wanted only to manage that agency. "Managing the Bethesda office was my lifelong goal," he used to tell Andy.

"Can I at least have the privilege of telling the agency myself that I'm not going forward with them?" Fred asked Clark.

"Of course." It was tradition in many career agency companies that the manager "fall on his sword" in a farewell to the agents and staff that shows there are no hard feelings toward the company. In a way, this is supposed to send the message that the company will keep the agency in good hands.

And so, Fred convened the agency in the bull pen area, as Andy had done three years before, to let everyone know there would be a change in management and that he was leaving. Unknown to Carlsberg there was little feeling – positive or negative – toward Fred Fidler, and little was said by anyone in response to the announcement.

On Easter Sunday morning, Fred's wife awoke from their bed to a still and lifeless Fred. She could not wake him. She dialed 911, but he was pronounced dead at the scene from a heart attack.

First thing the next morning, Clark Carlsberg arrived at his office to learn by voicemail from Bud Warren that Fred had died the day before. Immediately, Carlsberg tried to erase any documentation that Fred had been fired the previous Friday; he did not want anyone to think that he had any part to play in Fred's demise. A company-wide announcement of Fred Fidler's passing went out within the hour, praising Fred's service and implying that Fidler "died with his boots on," meaning he was still in charge of the agency when he died. Carlsberg wanted any documentation of the firing the previous Friday to disappear – that Fred was never fired.

But it was too late. Because Fred had given the agency his goodbye speech on Friday, the agents knew the truth – Fred had been fired that day – and they let everyone in the D.C. life underwriting and financial planning profession know that "Clark Carlsberg murdered Fred Fidler."

Funny how a man few in the agency treated with much loyalty suddenly became a martyr, given the chance to end the career of a home office "suit" who was found trying to "cover his tracks." And the legend of Fred Fidler's demise at the hands of Clark Carlsberg resulted in Carlsberg's resignation within a month after the incident. Clark would never work in the industry again, but as a Senior Vice President, he had lined his pockets for years and walked out with an exit package that made his ego bruise just a little easier to take. Mel Kaplan – Louie DePalma – was the one who made Andy aware of what had happened to Fred.

By 1996, Andy had two full time jobs at AFG. He was still VP of Marketing Services. Now he headed the PPGA distribution system as well. He could draw upon resources from Marketing Services to feed the new channel, and did so liberally.

Mainly, though, Andy was hands-on when it came to developing the new channel. He would combine trips to Financial Centers with visits to the Regionals in the PPGA Regions. In 1997, Andy travelled 30 of the 50 weeks he worked, putting a lot of pressure on

Sallie at home, with two small sons. There had been on-and-off friction between the couple; if the argument was not about money, it was more often about parenting responsibilities. Sallie wanted control over the rules at home. She felt she had earned the right to determine how family life would occur, even when Andy was home. For Andy, this left him feeling more like a babysitter for the boys. The two were not only lawyers by education, not only first-born children in their own respective families, but they were headstrong and opinionated personalities. This made the friction between them even more pronounced.

Andy had become an attraction point for recruiting veteran producers from other companies. This was part of what put him on the road so much. When Oliver Winters managed to recruit an entire agency away from Carolina Mutual, Andy helped seal the deal with a show of resources from Marketing Services. The agency was in Raleigh, NC. When it came over to Atlantic, it had only 8 agents, including one sales manager, and the Managing Director, Philip Sands.

Phil Sands was 50 years old, on his second marriage (his wife would become the brokerage manager in the Financial Center). He was about average height and weight. The only distinguishing factor in Phil's appearance was his glasses, heavy frames (eyesight rather bad), and he favored a moustache, which seemed to be big in the 1990s, as Andy had one as well.

In 1997, Oliver was hungry to show he could recruit whole agencies, so he took Sands on without a lot of due diligence. Sands sold Oliver on his own recruiting skills and just to prove the point he brought a veteran recruit to the table in the form of Del James, from Jefferson Mutual. Del was thought of as a paragon of ethical practice in the North Carolina insurance marketplace. He'd built his practice on impeccable honesty and attention to the client, first, last and always. By getting Del James to join what Sands was going to build at AFG, Sands' stock went way up in Oliver's estimation. Del was an MDRT qualifier but also had a reputation for doing business the "right" way. Del James was also a committed family man, with a wife of ten years and two daughters, ages 7 and 5. Del was tall, played and coached basketball in college, thin of build, and also sported the fashionable moustache.

Meanwhile, Phil Sands soon struck up a friendship with Andy. They were both "Landsmen." This gave them a simpatico in Raleigh, as the Jewish community there was tiny. Phil often invited Andy down to Raleigh and got him involved in helping some of the AMs in their live cases. Since Lyn Randolph was building a PPGA Region for Andy there as well, Raleigh became a common destination on Andy's itinerary.

When Oliver, Andy, and Phil managed to convince Del James to join the new Carolina Financial Center for AFG, they all celebrated over dinner. But there was a fifth person at the dinner table that evening: Del's sister, Karen. Karen Bruckner was 27 to big brother Del's 35. She had recently separated from her husband of five years and, looking for a new career, decided to come in with her older brother and learn the business. From that evening forward, Karen attended all business meetings that Del had with AFG. She was his closest confidant, maybe even more so than Del's own wife.

Andy found himself immediately drawn to Karen. Tall, young, (bottle) blond, having recently shed about 30 pounds of marriage weight, Karen was attractive to say the least. She was quiet, rarely spoke unless spoken to in these meetings, letting Big Brother take the lead. And she had a wide smile that just barely covered a sadness that both told volumes about her failed marriage and was part of what drew Andy in.

While most of the home office got to know Del as a potential leading producer in the field, few even knew he had a sister in the business.

But Andy knew. While he quickly became an ally and friend of Del, he found himself devoting a lot of available time to mentoring and befriending Karen. And Andy began calling the sibling team Big Brother and Lil' Sister. He even introduced Karen to the Stevie Ray Vaughn song titled by her new nickname, sort of an introduction of Karen to his love of the blues.

While Andy travelled extensively, he did make time for his sons. In fact, it seemed that his marriage was growing away from a relationship with Sallie and more toward a rearing of young children. Both parents began focusing their attention on Robert (Bob) and Jack more than on each other.

Andy became a coach of Bob's Youth Recreation League basketball team in Great Falls, and for 5 seasons coached Bob's team there. To avoid conflicts with travel, Andy scheduled practices on Friday evenings; games were always on Saturdays.

Bob was not an athlete, but he loved the game just the same and would not stop playing, even if he was not one of the starters on the team. Other fathers with sons in the League would volunteer to coach their son's team because the son was a star player. Not Andy and Bob. By coaching, Andy could make sure Bob got his fair chance to play. And as coach, Andy found a place where he could be a Dad without interference from Sallie, who always seemed to find something wrong with Andy's parenting.

One Saturday morning, after a game in a local school gym in Great Falls, Andy and Bob were exiting the building, with Jack tagging along. Sallie had been running errands that morning, missing the game. As Andy loaded the boys into his Mercedes 420sel, he seated Jack in the back, behind the front passenger seat, in his gray plastic booster seat, standard issue for the suburban kid under the age of 8 or 40 pounds. Bob got into the front passenger seat. As Andy was preparing to close the passenger door for Bob and come around the front to the driver's side, Sallie showed up in her station wagon. She had hoped to catch some of the end of Bob's game, but was too late. What she saw – with Jack in the back and Bob in the front – was inappropriate and too dangerous in her mind.

"I want Jack in the front seat," she called out to Andy, loud enough for the other parents in the parking lot to hear, as she approached the Mercedes from the station wagon parked a few spaces to Andy's left.

"I always put the big one in the front."

"I don't care what you always do." And Sallie began her oral argument in front of everyone in the parking lot. "If you're carjacked, you won't be able to get to Jack in the back. Bob is big enough to get out on his own."

"Why are you so worried about carjacking?"

"You're driving that Mercedes. It's a target."

"Really? I've heard that putting a little kid in the front seat could be dangerous because the air bag does not fit a small child if there's a crash." Andy was in the oral argument full tilt now. Other parents watching the two parents argue thought it was like two attorneys arguing a case in court, without a judge to determine who was right.

And Sallie went undeterred by Andy's argument over to the back seat of the Mercedes, pulling Jack out of the car, taking the booster seat with her, and putting him in the front seat of her station wagon. Andy watched the whole thing, including her driving off in a huff.

When both cars and drivers arrived home, the fight continued. "I don't believe what I just went through in front of all the team parents back there," Andy opened.

"I thought we agreed you would do things with the boys as I wanted. You're off travelling all week and I'm left having to do this all myself when you're gone. If you change the routine, the kids get mixed messages."

"I never agreed to do things ***your way*** as you say. I want to be able to parent my children as I see fit when you're not around. I am a parent here, too, you know."

At this point Sallie was screaming. "You want to control everything. You control the money; you're off doing whatever you want. Then you want to override me at home, too? Go to hell!"

"You go to hell!" Both stopped just shy of cursing in front of the kids. Bob had gone upstairs to his room, but he could hear the argument downstairs, which had progressed to the kitchen. The censorship around not being able to use worse language was all Andy could take. In frustration, he picked up a small fry pan sitting on the counter and threw it against a kitchen cabinet above the sink. Sallie, standing on the opposite side of the kitchen, grabbed Jack up in her arms. Andy proceeded to throw a couple of empty Tupperware bowls against the refrigerator to the right of the sink. Sallie took Jack and held him out in front of her, as if to challenge Andy to throw something that would hit him, or her, or both. Sallie never missed a chance to build an abuse case against her husband. Andy did not help matters by losing his cool. This would be the only time Andy would ever throw things in anger. But it would come up for years later in arguments the couple would have. Andy retained just enough control to make sure he did not satisfy Sallie's attempt to have their son hit with anything.

Then, Andy stopped. He went upstairs to the master bedroom. He began filling the garment bag he had used on his trip the prior week with clothes for the next few days. He left with the bag, down the stairs, out the garage door, into the Mercedes, and took off for the

Tysons Corner Marriott he had been familiar with during his days at Golden, occupying that Tycon Tower office just behind the hotel.

Andy was not above calculation himself, even in an emotional crisis, and knew that he was travelling to Raleigh the next week. So, he only needed the hotel in Tysons Corner for one night. He also knew to include enough dress clothes in that garment bag so he was prepared to make his trip without returning home. The trip itself would be by car, not plane, 5 hours south, so he had all of Sunday to get to Raleigh. Toiletries could be bought on the road. Before he ended his trip to Raleigh, Sallie had called him on his car phone and the two managed to disengage enough from the fight that Andy returned home that Friday. After all, Andy had a game with Bob's basketball team coming up and a practice Friday night. But the damage was done.

In Raleigh, Andy could just about put the matter of his domestic troubles out of mind, or so he thought. On Monday morning, Andy arrived at the Carolina Financial Center to work with Phil Sands and his people. Andy had arranged to offer himself to the Financial Center for the entire week, acting as an in-house advanced underwriter to work on live cases with the AMs, even going out on sales calls, all without any cut of the agent commission or manager override. With spaces in his schedule, he offered the same services to Lyn Randolph and her PPGAs in the area. Andy was acting as a hired gun to help stimulate production in the Region.

In one of the live sales calls, a 70-year old widow, mother of three grown daughters, was coming in to review her estate plan, which would include her life insurance situation. The widow was a referral personally to Andy from a long-time friend in Raleigh, so she came in specifically to see Andy. But Andy was not doing personal production at this point. Although licensed to sell insurance and securities, even in North Carolina, Andy was a home office executive now. This was an opportunity to put one of Phil Sands' AMs into the case. After all, who would service this client after Andy had gone back to National Headquarters?

So, Andy brought in Karen Bruckner. The two sat in on the client meeting, behind closed doors, while Andy conducted a fact-finding interview to determine the client's needs. Karen watched diligently but silently, after Andy formally introduced her to the client. Andy opened with a few general questions, wanting to get the widow-client to open up beyond the math and talk a little about how she wanted her assets allocated when she was gone. Still grieving a bit from her husband's passing, the widow began crying as she explained her family situation – the three daughters came from two different marriages, and there was discord among the siblings. This upset her and set her off sobbing. Karen watched as Andy let her have her cry, pulling over a box of Kleenex for her to use, and waiting patiently for her to compose herself. Andy was careful to neither show impatience for the crying but also not to offer too much compassion, lest the interview become a melodrama with no solution to her financial issues.

The widow argued, "But I'm going to pay the taxes eventually anyway. Why do I need the insurance?"

"Because you'll then pay Uncle Sam 'pennies on the dollar' for those taxes. You'll pay only a small fraction in premium what the insurance will provide to your daughters to cover any final expenses and taxes due."

Eventually, Andy and the widow agreed on a path that included some new life insurance to create liquidity in her estate. When it came time for the insurance application to be filled out, Andy excused himself, left the room and let Karen take down the essential information, including collecting the first premium in order to bind the policy. Karen had been well trained at making sure the policy was bound by a premium at the time of application.

Later that day, Andy and Karen congratulated each other on a job well done. "Let's celebrate tonight," Andy offered. "Let me take you to dinner."

"Sounds like a plan," Karen agreed.

Karen knew Andy was married, had seen pictures of his children Andy had taken out from his wallet. Karen noticed that there were no pictures of Sallie in that wallet, which tipped her off that things at home might not be right. But Karen could continue to tell herself that "this is just friends and business colleagues getting together." Karen had no intention of becoming some home office exec's "mistress." Karen was a young version of a grand "southern lady," and such things were just not done.

Dinner in Raleigh is not quite the same thing as dinner in D.C. – not as many fancy places to choose from. Andy and Karen settled on an upscale sports bar, a common watering hole for the AMs at the Financial Center. They arrived around 7pm, after any of the Financial Center people would have left for home, this being a Monday night as opposed to a Friday.

The dinner conversation started out innocently enough, mostly about work and family. Karen fancied white wine. Andy stuck with a local microbrew. Andy noticed that about a half hour into the dinner conversation Karen's speech pattern and accent began to change, almost as if she had taken on a different personality. Whereas Karen normally put on that southern drawl of most Carolina girls, along with the "y'all" and other expressions of the region, the accent seemed to become more subdued and the surface expressions a southern lady used to make small talk disappeared. Andy read this as "now we're getting below the surface."

"My marriage was a disaster. I should have known it would never work."

"Why did you get married, then?" Andy asked.

"I really didn't think I would ever get married if I didn't do it then. It wasn't as if guys were lining up to see me. He asked, so I felt I had to say 'yes.'"

"I don't believe that. A woman as beautiful as you? No options? Not possible!" Did Andy just say that? He could hardly believe his boldness.

"Thanks for the compliment."

"No compliment, just fact."

Then a pregnant pause while both took in another bite of dinner, another sip of alcohol.

"But I sort of understand the feeling. I, too, got married by default. I just figured this is what I am entitled to, no more. And the whole thing is starting to fall apart for me as well." Andy was thinking of the unresolved argument back home.

It's important to stop for a moment and realize that using unrest at home as an excuse to flirt with another woman was only part of the problem. If asked, virtually every 40-something married man in business would face this moment of truth: Whether his marriage could survive such a flirtation. Was this just as much a "mid-life crisis?"

"Can I confess something to you, Karen?" And Andy waited for some recognition that it was O.K. to proceed.

"Sure."

"I have to tell you that I have developed this bodacious crush on you."

"That's sweet. I have appreciated your friendship these past few months," Karen replied, as if he'd said nothing more than something platonic.

Not a whole lot more was said about Andy's confession for the rest of dinner. After Andy paid the check, they both proceeded outside to their cars, parked next to each other. It was time to say goodnight.

Andy then seemingly took the moment away. "I wish I had met you years ago. I'm in the middle of a bad situation at home. But I think that before I say anything more about my feeling toward you, I have to say that I feel I have to go home and work on my marriage."

"Of course you do. You have two boys to think about. They have to come first." Karen was opting out gracefully. This only drew Andy in all the more.

This is not to say there was no desire on her part. It was just that she was too much a lady to admit her feelings. But whether it was the wine itself, or just an attempt to show Andy what he was passing up, she came slowly closer to him and started a kiss on the lips that developed into a French kiss that went on for what seemed to Andy several minutes. Andy began to wrap his arms around the young beauty, and could feel the rush of blood to wherever he needed for his body to prepare for what it assumed was some passionate lovemaking. It felt like something he had been deprived of for an eternity, the feeling of a woman in his arms, and it felt like he didn't ever want to let go. It felt as if he could cry in gratitude just for this moment; someone out there actually wanted him as something more than a friend, more than a meal ticket, more than a baby sitter; as something more than a colleague.

Then, Andy, while still in lip-and-tongue lock, began to realize where this was going. "This might actually happen," he thought. And he backed away, slowly, gently, but feeling like a coward. "Don't start something if you're not going to finish it," he recited to himself.

But Karen offered no objection or anger at the aborted tease. They would never talk of the moment again with each other. "Whatever happens or does not happen, I want you to know I am your friend," was all Andy said at the time.

Karen nodded in agreement, and that was that. They each took off on their own. But they continued to work together, as if nothing had happened.

The next day was devoted to working with Lyn Randolph, Andy's hand-picked Regional in Raleigh. As they drove in Andy's car from visiting one PPGA office and heading to another, Lyn mentioned, "You have a real shit-eating grin on your face. You get laid last night, or something?" Lyn meant it only as a joke.

"Almost." And Andy recalled what had happened with Lil' Sister the night before.

"Geez, man, you're actually beaming as you tell me this. You're fuckin' beaming!"

"I am?" Andy never spoke in sexual terms, at least not in business. This was all new territory to him. "But I chickened out, I'm afraid."

"Give yourself a break, man. I know what this is, from the other side of a marriage, and you may have just saved yours. You didn't chicken out. You thought of your family first…as you should. Don't be like those assholes when they travel. Don't be like Brandon Kessler and his minions."

"You know about that?"

"You bet. All of Concord knows about his exploits. All of Concord blames him for playing while Lambert LifeAmerica 'burned.' They think they all lost their jobs because he couldn't keep his pants zipped and pay attention to the task at hand."

Then Andy turned the conversation away from Karen and toward something else more germane to the relationship in the car at present. "Lyn, I always felt bad that you took the blame for my leaving Lambert."

"Stop it! You're not to blame. Those pansies were going to get rid of me one way or the other. For all of his faults, Don Wasserman was at least with it enough to give a girl a chance; without trying to fuck her, I might add. Brandon Kessler was a walking dick."

"And DeSilva as well."

"Randy DeSilva is worse. He's an empty suit. He pretends to be working, looks good in a coat and tie, but brings nothing to the table. He's in it for power only, and to get it will kiss whatever ass he has to. Brandon at least got his position without being someone's sidekick. I was pissed when they didn't give you the Coastal Region. I could smell the stink on DeSilva a mile away."

"They didn't kill Lambert in Concord by themselves."

"No, of course not. But they didn't help. And a lot of folks got hurt needlessly because of them; people in the home office."

Andy continued to work in the Carolina Financial Center from time to time throughout the year. And he had a couple of occasions to intercede on behalf of Big Brother and Lil' Sister. In one situation, Del had mistakenly placed a mutual fund order before getting the sign off from the client. This wasn't as bad as it seemed to most, but it was because of Del's stellar reputation for ethics that it troubled him that it had happened. Instead of opening the issue for the whole Financial Center and home office to review, Andy signed off as Principal for the order and then worked with Del to make sure the client gave his O.K. to the order retroactively.

In another situation, Lil' Sister had written a small annuity contract. The application had been put into a common inbox bin, as all insurance applications in the Financial Center were placed, until the new-business clerk could get to process the application and send it into the home office. Karen left the application in the bin at the end of a workday; the clerk would not get to it until the next morning. Over the intervening evening, one of the sales managers in the office, one of the original 8 who had come over to AFG with Phil Sands in the agency acquisition, had gone in and altered the agent's report on the application, putting himself on for 20% of the commission on the case. The sales manager, Beau Burleson (BB, as he was known), was nominally the supervisor for Del and Karen, though they needed little if any supervision – Del provided the training for his sister, and they both used Andy Greene as a direct channel into the home office for any problems that would come up.

Karen did not realize what had happened until she got her commission for the case. All agents calculate their commissions, at least in their heads, when making a sale. They don't wait around for the commission statement that comes at least a month later. Karen was no exception, and she noticed what appeared to be less commission than she expected.

Karen took the matter to Big Brother. She did not want to trouble Andy with this. They both decided to take the matter up first with BB and Phil. In a meeting with the four of them in Phil's office, Phil explained, "Now you both know we operate on the MDRT system of commission splitting." And he went through the percentages, "20% for each of five roles played in any given case. BB provided advanced sales assistance in developing the presentation to the client."

"No he didn't," Karen indignantly blurted. "He didn't do anything."

"Now, Karen," Phil tried to mollify Karen, paternalistically, "Sometimes it is not obvious the role someone plays in a case. Beau is your sales manager and he felt that he provided assistance in the case."

Beau said nothing. Del had something to say. "Phil, this isn't right. If Karen said Beau did nothing on the case, I believe her, and you should, too."

"Beau, did you even know about this case?" Karen asked in inquisitional fashion.

"Yes, of course, Karen. I followed you through from start to finish."

"How so? You didn't provide me the referral. You attended no client meetings."

"Well, I must have misunderstood." BB sheepishly relented. "I'll take myself out of the case."

Del seemed to end the meeting with, "Please see that you do," as if he, not Phil, were the GA here.

But Del James was not finished. He called his friend Andy and relayed to him what had happened. Usually with something like this, it would go from the GA to the Zone VP, which was Oliver Winters. But Del did not have the relationship with Oliver that he had with Andy.

Andy in turn took the matter up with Oliver. Though Winters seemed somewhat perturbed that this did not come to him from the field, but through "his staff" in the home office, he initiated an investigation of agency practices in Carolina, and found that sales managers were frequently altering applications and putting themselves in for a piece of the agent's compensation.

The result ultimately, after months of investigation, was the termination of both Phil and BB. Had the Financial Center done more in sales, there would have been a temptation to make this all go away without fanfare. But when the production did not come as Sands had predicted, there was no flack from the home office in terminating the Managing Director for, euphemistically, lack of supervision.

Then, the shit really hit the fan. As the Carolina Financial Center was falling apart, other problems came to the surface. As Phil was leaving, he tried to collect what he felt were funds due him for having financed the acquisition of recruits into the agency. A bit different from the practice at Warren Financial Group, Sands would get approval of some funds from the home office to finance a special deal for a recruit he really wanted to get. Winters' policy had been to approve the financing as a special deal, but make the Managing Director sign an IOU for half of any financing losses incurred if the recruit did not work out. Sands in turn would assign the recruit to a sales manager, such as BB, and make the sales manager sign an IOU indemnifying Sands for half of Sands' obligation to the home office. BB would in turn ask the new recruit to sign off on an IOU indemnifying BB for half if HIS obligation back to Sands.

Del and Karen had come on board with just such a financing arrangement. Sands and BB were terminated just as Del and Karen were also leaving the Financial Center. They had decided to take a PPGA contract through Lyn Randolph and be otherwise independent. The IOU's, other than the one the Managing Director gave the home office, were all private deals, without home office involvement or obligation. When Winters went to Sands to demand repayment of his half of the financing losses from Del and Karen,

Sands went to BB for his half of the half, who went to Del for his half of BB's half of Sands' half.

Del refused, "You don't get repaid for anything after you did what you did." BB then did not have enough money to pay back Phil, who pleaded poverty to Oliver Winters. In actuality, there was some question whether there was any real financing losses owed back to BB by Del or if BB were again using some fast-and-loose math to cover losses created by others who were leaving and BB just saw a deeper pocket in Del and Karen, who had been the most successful of the AMs in the Financial Center. But Del did not stay for any calculation of numbers – BB had no credibility with him – and BB never pursued the matter any further.

"Not good enough," was Oliver's response to Phil's plea of poverty. Having put himself and his reputation on the line to recruit this agency to AFG, Winters now wanted to be sure that Billy Carl did not suffer the sting of financing losses from Winters' failed expedition into Raleigh. Oliver also made an example of Sands to show Billy he had a backbone. And he made an installment deal with Sands but nevertheless made Phil pay back what amounted to $18,000 over a period of one year. Sands never saw any indemnification from BB or from Del. The Carolina Financial Center was officially closed in the middle of 1998.

Back at National Headquarters, operations in Marketing Services had become routine by the end of Andy's first year on the job. Andy had initiated an audio newsletter series – Radio AFG – in 1995, first as a cassette release; later as a CD. It would be sent out to all full time Account Managers in the field. The AMs could put the piece of plastic into their car stereos on the way to sales appointments and learn the latest and greatest about products and sales ideas from the members of the Marketing Services team, who acted like news correspondents, interviewing various leaders in the company about all manner of issues relevant to the field. The series was a production of Marie Frame's people in Marketing Communications. They packaged the covers and participated in front of the microphones as needed. But Andy, using his radio background, produced the series. And, using his passion for music, hired out a top flight recording studio in Alexandria for the project. Andy's sister, Gail – a graduate of the Berklee School of Music in Boston – even wrote compositions for the theme music and bumpers used between stories.

By using audio only, the series could be produced relatively cheaply and quickly. By sticking to audio, the "correspondents" only needed articulate voices; looks didn't matter. Sound effects, harkening back to the golden days of radio, were often used to spark the imagination of the listener.

And Radio AFG had the side benefit of being a project everyone in the Department could take ownership of, building an *esprit de corps* among the staff. The series won accolades across the company, especially when Andy had stories done about other areas of the home office – the Underwriting Department, Actuarial, TIG, Chesapeake Funds; everyone got into the act. Even Tab Davenport was given a chance, by interview, to occasionally give a visionary message about the direction of AFG. And Andy took the series on the road as well, doing stories featuring "heroes" in the field, success stories in sales that fellow AMs would surely want to hear about.

In Marketing Communications, Marie also had the responsibility of putting together the annual incentive meeting for top sales people. Known as Leaders Club, this was the weeklong vacation, masked as a business conference, for the best AMs and Managing Directors the prior year. And as it was at other companies, home office managers vied for an opportunity to help "host" the meeting. In 1995, it was

Cancun; in 1996, a Carribean cruise; in 1997, the Inn and Links at Spanish Bay, CA; and in 1998, St. Andrews in Scotland.

Since Marie had put the site in front of Billy and the Zone VPs for approval, meaning she had to participate in a site inspection, she also had to be on hand at the meeting itself to monitor the agenda, attend to all the details, and be a sometimes "go-fer" to manage the last minute demands of field attendees, their spouses, and the home office brass.

Meanwhile, Nellie Soris had developed quite the knack for serving as MC at company meetings. His off-the-cuff humor and on stage banter with audiences was at once a comedy act in itself and a nurturing forum for celebrating the successes of each field person. Soris Maximus took great pains to perfect his "act," even making sure he knew something special about each field qualifier as they were called up to the stage to receive their award for qualification, to rousing applause by all in attendance. Nellie got so good at this that no one could envision doing an incentive meeting without him as MC. So, it was natural that he would assume that role at all meetings. And he did so, with so much enthusiasm that many even forgot that this was not his official job description. Andy, himself with a modicum of experience at MC, did not oppose this role for Nellie when it was proposed to him by Billy. Andy saw the talent in Soris Maximus and knew that he was little more than a straight man compared to this almost Jackie Gleason character.

Andy got to go to these meetings, ostensibly to represent product releases and/or advanced sales techniques in the business sessions that were required to be held to comply with IRS rules for the taxability of such meetings. This might have irked Susan Blanque, the lead Marketing Counsel in Marketing Services, but Susan not only didn't mind; she didn't want the responsibility of schmoozing with the field for five days non-stop. Susan knew advanced underwriting as well as anyone, but as an attorney, she stayed above the "sales" fray. And she wanted no part of the corporate politics she felt was surely going on at these meetings.

Susan had her own annual meeting to contend with. Andy brought forward from his days at Lambert and Empire the concept of an Advanced Sales Forum, designed for continuing education of the field in planning techniques and ideas in the estate and business markets. Filed for CE credit for state insurance licensing and CFP certification, the Forum became the major advanced marketing meeting of the year. Top experts in relevant fields, many of them attorneys themselves, were hired to give educational presentations. Susan, Andy, Nellie and others in the home office would do various breakout workshops. Wholesalers from some of the fund families represented in the variable products Andy had developed for AFG would be recruited not only to offer educational presentations, but to contribute financially to the event by taking exhibit booths at the meeting. The exhibit "hall" was the place for all manner of firms trying to win the business of the field; to build relationships with the AMs and PPGAs. And TIG and Chesapeake worked to recruit their own relationships with various investment firms to help finance the event.

Here, Andy would get to play MC. But the tone of the meeting, while still lending a humorous touch, was more serious and educational. Susan put together the program itself and chose the speakers fairly much on her own. The field people coming to the event came to D.C., most at their own expense (there was a subsidy for Leaders Club qualifiers). There was always an afternoon tour of National Headquarters on the agenda – never missing an opportunity at relationship building. Oliver, Jamie, and other "line" people participated as needed. But this was a Marketing Services show, beginning to end, and it put the Zone guys in a position in which they didn't feel comfortable – the back seat.

Among the people involved in the Forum should have been Tim Wheaton, the head of Sales Support. There was always a new release of the computer illustration software coming out or some new application associated with it to show at some breakout workshop. And for the first year of the Forum, Tim did participate.

By 1996, however, the wheels were coming off in Tim's life. His marriage falling apart, his work suffered. It was found out that Tim was suffering from a chronic depression that would come and go in waves. In the down times, it left him almost comatose. His answer to this was self-medication, so to speak. The prescription drugs became a problem of their own after awhile. And none of Tim's condition had been revealed when he applied for the job; yet, his problems preceded his arrival at AFG. Tim began missing a lot of work, and the work he did do simply was not the quality or quantity that could make the grade of a department hell-bent on "saving AFG." In other words, there was no room or budget to carry someone who was not fully engaged in the task at hand.

Andy held annual Marketing Services retreat meetings each January, in which ALL full time staff in Marketing Services would attend. These retreats were designed to involve all hands in the planning of whatever the department had on its agenda for the year, and to engage in some strategic thinking. The staff loved getting away from the office for a couple of days – these usually went Wednesday to Friday as soon after New Years as could be feasibly scheduled. The non-managers particularly enjoyed the chance to participate, the only forum in which they got to input into the Plan and be celebrated by being taken off site for a few days. Andy chose the sites himself; Marie participated in logistics and negotiating. The sites were always within a bus ride from the home office, intentionally. Andy would hire a bus large enough for the 12-18 staff members to ride together to the meeting; in Alexandria; Princeton, NJ; Outer Banks, NC; horse country in Central Virginia – all places Andy was familiar with – and the bus ride afforded an opportunity for some team building to organically grow.

The Retreat meeting itself was mostly business. Andy was on a tight budget and using this as a boondoggle to reward staff was out of the question. Meetings went Wednesday afternoon, all day Thursday, and included Friday morning. There were impressive dinners Wednesday and Thursday, but nothing like the shindigs at Leaders Club, not even like the Advanced Sales Forum.

In January 1996, Marketing Services met the bus for its planned annual Retreat to the Outer Banks, a five hours plus bus ride from D.C. to a location that, because it was way-off-season, was practically given away to Andy and his crew to stay there for two nights. Everyone gathered at the home office early that morning, but Tim Wheaton was missing. When his own staff person, Barbara Harmon, called his home to find him having overslept, Andy was pissed, to say the least. When Tim showed up an hour later, having delayed their departure, he was disheveled and disoriented. Thankfully, he'd chosen the Metro over driving to work that day. But it was soon discovered after the bus left with all aboard, that Tim had left one of his bags with most of his clothes on the subway. So, a side trip for him to restock his wardrobe became necessary.

It looked to Andy as if Barbara was covering for Tim, not only at Retreat but through most of the Sales Support Unit's work. While Andy felt for Tim's situation, the problem could no longer be ignored. One of Andy's first tasks when they returned from Retreat was to have Human Resources intercede. Paula Banks, head of HR, saw to putting Tim on probation and offering counseling and other help to him.

As 1996 dragged on, there was no improvement. Andy's sympathy for Tim's plight had to be balanced against the increasing feeling that Barbara was getting the real "short end of the stick" by trying to keep the work together and getting no credit for the effort. Andy had known Barbara from his first stint at AFG, when she was an office manager for a short-lived Atlantic agency in Atlanta. Barbara made up in hard work what she lacked in credentials – no education beyond high school. She excelled at the art of being a protégé, of learning from others in the business what she had to know and then applying it in practice for herself. She had managed to come into National Headquarters during the Marketing East/West disaster, as an assistant to the training director for Marketing East. When the training unit fell apart, Barb stayed on as a trainer, reporting directly to Brian Saunders. But her lack of education, her lack of sales experience forced Saunders to keep her in the background; "she could not, in her own right, be the Training Director," Saunders assumed.

When Andy got back to AFG in 1994, she was put under Soris Maximus as a trainer. This was a toxic relationship. Nellie Soris had little regard for Barb, less because of her lack of education than for her lack of experience selling in the field. Barbara resented Soris because of his high handedness. "In Nellie's world, there was no room except for Nellie," Barb concluded. Whoever was right, it didn't matter. For Andy, the route to a solution lay in steps. First, Barb was moved to Sales Support under Tim Wheaton.

Now, she had her first chance to shine. Tim was anything but a hands-on leader. It became clear to Andy that she was the next head of Sales Support. But the matter with Tim would have to take time to play out. Given that there was a medical component to the problem, HR counseled that a very slow process would have to take hold, with rigorous documentation of Tim's work by Andy.

Finally, in June 1996, it was time. "Always do a firing on a Monday morning," was what Andy was taught in graduate school. "Never do a firing on Friday afternoon. On Monday, the employee can immediately get immersed in finding a new job. On Friday, he/she has to wait the entire weekend with no way to advance the job search; all the while building resentment against the employer."

Tim was called into Andy's office, where a staffer from HR was also waiting. "Tim, please have a seat."

As Tim sat down on the love seat Andy had in the "parlor" end of his office, perpendicular to the HR staffer, Andy came round his desk to sit next to Tim. Andy, looking him straight in the eye, began, "Tim, I wish I was here with you under better circumstances." Andy learned well from his own experience. "But I'm afraid I'm not. The company has made a decision that it wants to terminate its relationship with you, for the reasons I think you have been made aware of over the past few months. Your situation has simply not improved, and we both have to move on. Margie here from HR is here to go over your exit package and next steps."

And offering his hand to shake, Andy concluded, "I wish you well, Tim."

Tim had lost all color in his face, and did not return the handshake offer. He just sat there as if at any moment he would break out in tears. Andy rose, looked at Margie, and left the room for her to continue the exit interview.

Tim was given the morning to say goodbye to colleagues, to Barbara, and collect his personal effects. He would never work in the insurance industry again. He lost all contact with friends and colleagues in the business. He seemed to drop off the face of the earth. Barbara felt the worst of all, checking obituaries for weeks after to see if Tim were dead. He did not return her phone calls, which she stopped trying after a few days, being caught between her loyalty for her ex-boss and her loyalty to her company.

At the Retreat in 1997, Andy announced to the entire department that Barbara Harmon had been promoted to Director, Sales Support. It was not an easy promotion. Billy Carl had qualms about promoting her with no credentials or obvious field experience. But Andy persisted; Barb continued her yeoman work; and the promotion finally went through after months of viewing her work in action. While Soris Maximus was none too pleased by the elevation of "the girl" to similar status as he on the management team in Marketing Services, Marie and Susan were delighted – they had all become friends during the Tim Wheaton tribulations.

All the while, Marketing Services had become, in the eyes of Jamie Keane and Oliver Winters, a company within the company. They saw Andy as conducting an agenda on his own, outside of the control of "the line." And they both resented it. But as Oliver made his disgust and disrespect for Andy quite well known, Jamie was more cagey at it. He kept on a positive tone with Andy, even teaching him a few tricks of the trade.

Jamie Keane came from the steak-and-whiskey school of managing a field force. But at least he had the good mind to mentor others and deliver some value, sometimes in some unexpected ways. All of these meetings that Andy and his people were putting on – Leaders Club, Advanced Sales Forum, etc. – they created quite a stir in the corporate travel marketplace. As travel agents with local offices in D.C. became more aware of the meetings AFG were putting on, they began to woo the company's travel business, looking to put on the meetings for the company themselves. At least they wanted the destination business.

That, of course, had been Marie Frame's job. And she would have gladly given up that responsibility. It wasn't as if she didn't have plenty on her plate already. But she did well with it and had the confidence of Billy Carl.

That didn't stop Jamie Keane from feigning interest in hiring an outside firm for travel, however. And, with Billy's and Andy's tacit approval, Jamie began to go to some of the exhibit hall booths at industry meetings, where these travel agencies would be exhibiting, getting invitations to their hospitality suites for after-hours cocktails, and pretending to see what "benes" he might be able to get for the company.

On one such venture, he feigned a special top-producer's meeting he said he was putting on. The travel agency was offering some special deals on long weekend group excursions to Ireland, Dromoland Castle to be exact. Dromoland was a huge medieval castle less than a half hour's drive from Shannon Airport, Ireland's largest and most common landing point for Aer Lingus flights out of JFK in New York and Dulles in D.C. Dromoland had been converted in the 1980s into a favorite golf resort for American companies wanting to entertain top clients and salespeople. You could fly out of Dulles on a Thursday night after work, be in Shannon by daybreak Friday, play a round of golf later that day, repeat on Saturday, maybe even sneak in an early 9 holes before catching the afternoon flight back to D.C. on Sunday.

Jamie brought Andy and Marie into the loop on his idea. Marie would put a mock agenda together for a meeting at Dromoland. Andy and Jamie would offer it as proof of their plans. Of course, the travel agent would have to arrange a site visit for the company to inspect the resort. The travel agent offered a site visit for three corporate representatives. But instead of the assumed Jamie, Andy and Marie, it was Jamie, Oliver, and Billy. Andy didn't mind that the boondoggle didn't include him; he was more concerned about pleasing the Zone guys and Billy in a way that did not impinge upon his agenda with Marketing Services.

Andy got his way later when, in 1998, Billy agreed to hold AFG's Leaders Club at St. Andrews in Scotland. Golf resorts would always be favored by a field force and home office execs afflicted with the golfing addiction. But Andy's agenda was as much personal as it was business.

Sallie had never travelled to any of these incentive meetings, although the spouses of home office attendees were always invited. The problem was having to fly, and she complained of ear problems from the changes in air pressure that created ear infections. There was only one solution to the problem, rather Draconian. She could have small tubes surgically inserted into her ears that would relieve the air pressure problem. This is similar to what is done for small children with the same problem. The solution is only temporary, as the tubes eventually come out on their own after a year or two. So, this seemed a far-fetched action to take for a meeting that she frankly didn't care much to attend, having to kiss up to the agents all day.

But Andy knew that depending upon the venue, she might be convinced to take the chance. Sallie's family was originally of Scottish origin and she had always dreamed of visiting Scotland and England. Going all the way back to 1995, Andy had as an agenda a desire to clear the way for one Leaders Club meeting in a place Sallie would surely want to go. And in 1998, this was accomplished. And for the first and last time, Sallie did what she had to, tubes-in-ears and all, and made the trip.

But this did not happen without additional obstacles. By this time, the couple was always thinking about the welfare of their children, Bob and Jack. Andy's mother would watch the kids so Sallie could make the trip. Sallie's own mother was in the middle of a battle with cancer and was not up to caring for young ones. While Sallie wasn't too keen on trusting Stel with the kids – her ways were not Sallie's ways – she reluctantly consented to this approach.

The next problem was that Sallie trusted the safety of air travel even less than the caregiving skills of Stel. She insisted that she and Andy had to travel on different flights. That way, if either of them went down with the plane, there would still be one of them to finish raising the children. Sallie feared making the kids into instant orphans.

Andy actually didn't object to this fear that much. It meant he would fly over to London's Heathrow a day early, giving him the chance to rent a car and stop off in the places where he went to school as a freshman in college. Then drive on up to Edinburg to meet the puddle jumper flight that most of the rest of the home office attendees were taking from Heathrow to get to the meeting.

And the time in Scotland, with a couple of days added on in England, was perhaps the last good vacation – if you want to call it that – the couple would have together.

The meeting itself would be the one that all field qualifiers would talk about with nostalgic pride for years afterwards. And this was the first AFG Leaders Club featuring three qualifiers from the new PPGA distribution channel, to the pride of Andy.

Yet, after returning to D.C., Billy Carl approached Andy with a choice. "Andy, you've done well with this PPGA system you've started. You've gotten 'the rocket ship off the launching pad.' Now it's time to take this system to the next level. If this PPGA thing has a long life in it, it can't continue to be run part time. You're essentially doing two jobs right now, and that isn't fair to you or the company. I appreciate the effort up until now. Hell, we were doing this on a shoestring to prove that it could work. We've proven that. You have to choose at this point."

And Andy waited for the other shoe to drop. Would this really be a choice?

"You can move full time into running the PPGA channel, or you can go back to being head of Marketing Services. It has to be one or the other; it can't be both at this point. Now, I have someone in mind who is available to come in from the outside and has experience with PPGA. But if you tell me you really want to run PPGA, I won't bring him in. It's up to you."

"If you have someone in mind already, Billy, I don't want to interfere. So, forced to make a choice, I'll go back to running just my original department."

And so, in mid-summer 1998, Ian Evans joined the Senior Staff at AFG. There were now three "line" officers, Howard Crowe on operations, and Andy. But there was one more change at the same time. Jamie Keane had experimented with a new variation on the career channel – a small group of producers who were in partnership and were semi-independent but wanted a closer relationship than PPGA offered, maybe for the employee benefits, maybe for the comraderie, maybe out of habit of always having been career agents. In mid-1998, he found one such group in Boca Raton, Florida – three producers sharing expenses and working clients together who wanted to pool their resources and impact with a single company. Jamie brought them on board, with some help from Nellie Soris, to whom these producers grew a close friendship. The group was affectionately called "The Boca Boys," and they became the template for going out and finding other such relationships around the country. Soris Maximus was put in charge of recruiting to this new template, removing him from Field Training and Development. Nellie had always lusted after agency or zone management anyway. He did not want to be "staff" anymore; he did not want to be on the same plane with the likes of Barb Harmon and other techno-geeks.

Nellie was first and foremost an agent himself, and the path to greatness for him was in line management.

In the search of more of these "boutiques," Billy came in contact with someone he'd known from a former company. Richard Cecchi had been a successful agent and financial planner for years in the Philadelphia area. But he was looking for a new relationship, one where his true talents could be leveraged. His true talents? Richard, or "Rocky," as he was known to Billy and would become known to all in the home office, wanted to be nationally syndicated as a radio talk show expert on financial planning matters, much as Ric Edelman (from Northern Virginia) would become in later years. Billy, with Nellie's help, wanted Rocky in the AFG fold. It was time to make a deal.

When Billy wanted a deal, he usually got it. People would say of Billy Carl, "A half hour with Billy and you'll see G-d." And Rocky was not immune to Billy's persuasive powers, his sharing of his vision for that great company AFG would become if only Rocky were part of it. As a player in the industry, AFG looked rather small potatoes, surely not a household brand name. But Rocky could overlook that if AFG would be willing to invest in Rocky's radio venture.

And so the deal was struck. Rocky became part of a second boutique that included his younger brother Joe and his daughter. Rocky began putting business through AFG in big amounts. AFG helped finance Rocky's purchase of paid radio time on a business station (AM) in Philadelphia to get him his start as a broadcast expert – the Rush Limbaugh of investments and financial planning. Andy even made the odd appearance on the show, when the subject turned to planning for closely-held business owners. But the financing by AFG was never revealed *per se*. It was important to the theme of the show that Rocky appear independent; product sponsors would be invited from all places. This was not a paid program of

AFG. And no one, not Andy or anyone, interfered with the program's content.

The Boutique channel, the PPGA channel, the new products, all went into a helter skelter of ways in which Billy Carl attempted to raise Atlantic Mutual from industry obscurity. And it worked, for awhile. By 1998, the life ECD production at AFG had tripled to over $15 million from its low just four years before. And Billy Carl had managed to keep together a team of rivals for that entire time. The Senior Staff members may have thought little of each other in many respects, but the Senior Staff always spoke publicly with one voice.

Chapter 11: Do the Math

A gap in knowledge in the financial community for just how life insurance works has always existed. Other than actuaries and a few technical experts in marketing these products, financial academicians and analysts remain virtually clueless about the pricing and structure of these products and the companies that offer them. Yet, the mechanics of these products – when seen against the backdrop of the macro-economy – is key to understanding some of the ethical issues and eventual consolidation (some would say, decline) of the industry. The products in fact drove, at least in part, the behavior of industry executives, their management decisions, and their frustration with the results they got from marketing these products. Therefore, a time-out to examine the life insurance product and the company offering it is essential to realizing what has happened to the larger financial services industry over the past 35 years.

Before 1980, the life insurance business was quite complacent. The average company offered a combination of whole life and term insurance products to consumers, delivered through a career distribution system closely controlled by the home office. Agents were "captives" of their employers. Consumers did not buy insurance; they were sold insurance. One common mantra in the field was, "We do for people what they would do for themselves, if they knew what we know; but they don't, so we have to go out and tell them."

This is how life insurance agents got their reputation. Consumers did not want to think about their own mortality. Insurance was sold to need, a harder sell than to greed. Insurance was sold to fear – fear of premature death, fear of leaving behind a widow and orphans. And when sold, the consumer rarely had the opportunity to comparison shop. The information to analyze different policies was simply not there. Thus, the agent could sell based on relationship; it was who you knew, not what you knew, that was most important to the life insurance agent. Even if the information had been there, the ability of people to wade through the complexities of a policy would put most consumers to sleep with the variety of moving parts all working to obfuscate the real workings of the policy.

Not that life insurance was a worthless asset…Not in the least. Paying a dollar today that pays hundreds of dollars tomorrow if you die is not a worthless item to have in your portfolio.

Insurance companies historically participated in this obfuscation by making permanent, whole life, insurance so complicated – its details hidden in a black box – most people did not bother to question the cost.

Whole life insurance was based on a philosophy that consumers could not handle their finances without some imposed discipline. The nature of whole life is to keep maximum control of the policy in the insurer's hands. The insured pays a set premium, guaranteed not to change over the insured's life. But that premium MUST be paid somehow, on time, or all bets are off. The premium was based on a set of guarantees: guaranteed mortality tables; guaranteed interest rates; guaranteed expenses of the company.

These guarantees were based on very conservative assumptions: Mortality was based on tables that were usually decades old while life spans of the American public were increasing year-by-year. Guaranteed interest rates in 1980 were usually 4% in an environment of double digit inflation. CDs and money markets paying 12%-15% interest still earned a healthy spread to the banks and other financial institutions offering these demand deposit contracts.

Expenses were a measure of the assumption of what it took to run a career distribution system to sell life insurance. Here, the insurance company was quite willing and able to assume an expense level in the first year of the policy that exceeded the premium paid on the policy. This was often between $1.10 and $1.20 per dollar of first year premium. How could a company take a loss on a new policy? Because to entice agents into the business; to keep them selling; the company offered huge "heaped" commissions, often totaling more than the premium collected by the agent. The company made its money back in the renewal years, offering only 5%-10% renewal commissions in years 2-10; then even less after that.

Selling life insurance is the most complicated and difficult financial asset to sell. Let's face it: No one grows up saying, "When I grow up I want to be a life insurance agent." People were recruited into the business by the money. And for those who made it a lifelong career, the financial rewards were up there with professional athletes and rock stars.

What began to happen around 1980 was that the consumer finally woke up. The consumer was becoming less concerned with premature death. The consumer was becoming more concerned with living too long and running out of money. High inflation rates causing high interest rates made everyone savvy about rates of return, or so they thought. Consumers were no longer going to accept 4% interest in a 15% environment, even with the special tax shelter offered by the Internal Revenue Code for life insurance cash values. Consumers sought more control over their hard-earned money.

The whole life policy was, in fact, delivering some of that enhanced return, through a device called the annual dividend. This dividend consisted of three components, or margins: one was for mortality experience better than guaranteed; another for expenses below what was assumed; the third, for interest that exceeded the guarantee of 4% plus a spread for the insurer to keep, almost like a money manager in a mutual fund.

The problem was that the obfuscation that insurers used to hide the moving parts of a whole life policy – that had served the insurer well for decades – now worked against the insurer. Consumers could not discern in their annual policy statements how their policies were performing. There was little disclosure of all these moving parts; there was simply a dollar amount the policy was receiving as a dividend into the cash value. It was nearly impossible, for example, to understand what interest rate was being credited to the policy or what the other margins were in the contract.

Enter universal life (UL). In this version of permanent coverage, the "black box" of dividends was removed. In its place, the policy statement made abundantly clear, month-by-month, premium dollars going in, loads and expenses being charged, interest being credited, and disclosed the interest rate. In 1982, it was common to see 14% interest rates on these policies. What the policyholder did not realize was that this was based on a 16+% return to the insurance company on its "general account," its bond and mortgage portfolio it used to invest policyholder premiums. The difference, usually at about 2% (or 200 basis points – bps), was the insurer's spread, its main source of profitability. In 1982, it was relatively easy to earn that spread. The policyholder assumed he/she was getting competitive rates of interest, even though inflation was up near 18%, and the policyholder was actually losing purchasing power through negative real interest, the return beyond inflation. No matter, he/she was doing no better at the bank; which was keeping to itself that same spread.

With the stock market going sideways at best – in November 1982 the Dow Jones Industrial Average (DJIA) was stuck at around 800 (today it is above 18,000) – returns on equities were poor compared to cash equivalents like CDs and money markets, and even life insurance. Yes, even net of the insurance expenses in the policy, the consumer was getting huge nominal returns, tax sheltered returns, in the cash value.

It was at this moment that life insurance stopped being solely for the "widows and orphans" and became a greed sale. While it is true that many experts to this day decry the use of permanent life insurance as an investment – they advocate buying term and investing the difference – an investment it became. The NASD and other authorities condemned the reference of life insurance as an investment, which only served to make the insurance agent look even shiftier when he/she would not use the term but investment was at least part of the real motivator behind the sale.

Just as soon as this new paradigm for life insurance was revitalizing the industry, it became a bubble – a bubble that soon burst. As interest rates began to fall, slowly and steadily over the next 30 years, the interest these UL policies could offer began to decline as well. Surely, the insurers would not sacrifice their "spread" of 200bps (a few companies began to shave that spread and did not live past the 1990s to tell the story), so the policyholder got less and less.

And as the years went by, the illustrations of the policies that were being sold in the early 80s were no longer reality. Even the most ethical agent, who refused to illustrate a proposed policy to a client at the current rate, but used an assumed rate between the current and guaranteed, soon found even that was too generous. A 14% current rate with a 4% guarantee – halfway between the two is 9%. The last time 9% was the current rate on a UL policy in the industry was around 1985.

So, by 1990, these early sales of UL began to lapse. Now, I'll bet you're thinking, "Well, if the agent was seeing this going on, didn't he go out and see his clients and advise them of what was happening?"

Well… A few things were going on…

- The policyholder-client had budgeted for the initial premium to be the permanent premium and could not or would not add more money to the policy to bring it back up to where the cash value had been illustrated to be.
- The agent simply believed in letting sleeping dogs lie. If the client wasn't complaining and he was seeing what the policy was doing in the annual statements he was getting, he must be satisfied. No point in upsetting the client needlessly.
- The agent would move the client to a new policy, with what appeared to be lower expense loads in it, to try and revive the coverage, and earn a new heaped commission in the process.
- Most often, the selling agent had left the company, perhaps the business entirely. The insurer tried to reassign the policy to a new agent, but the servicing agent had little incentive to go out and service a policy he had not earned commission on, so he never got in touch with the client. In other cases, the insurer's own reassignment protocol was spotty and the client went without any proactive service.

And all went undisturbed, until the insurer's automated service system detected that the cash value was about to be insufficient to pay the next month's charges. A lapse notice would be generated from this automated system and sent to the policyholder. Then, for the first time, the policyholder would call the insurer's 800 number and complain.

First rule of customer service: "Don't surprise the customer with bad news when they can least afford to do anything about it."

The amounts of money it would take to rehabilitate a policy in force for years that was about to lapse was usually too much for most policyholders to even consider paying.

Funny thing about UL – it's considered permanent insurance, but at the moment of lapse it sure feels like term insurance.

Term insurance, for its part, had become the quick sale of investment brokers and financial planners not invested in making life insurance a major part of their practices. Term was and is cheap. The only problem with it is that it is "actuarially priced not to be in force when the insured dies." This is a famous quote of many in the marketing of these products. Less than 2% of all term policies ever pay off in a claim. Usually, by the time you need the coverage, it has long since become too expensive to pay for. Term insurance has a premium that changes as the insured gets older, to reflect the increasing mortality risk as we age. The policyholder can freeze that premium for awhile, by paying more to make the policy hold its premium for 5, 10, 15, 20 years. The longer you want to hold the premium level, the higher the premium. Pretty soon, it gets to be near the price of a UL policy, which also has a changing mortality charge year after year; hopefully the policyholder has paid sufficient extra premium in the early years so that the cash value builds enough to handle the increasing charges without additional premium contributions; at least that's the concept. Even the IRS has termed UL as "term with a side fund."

So, many companies among the so-called "Eastern Mutuals," whose stock in trade was selling whole life, cheered when their prognostications of the fall of UL began to occur in the early 1990s. Surely, everyone would now return to good old whole life. It was a short sighted view, and a paternalistic one at that, founded on the belief that whole life would somehow outperform UL over time and that the policyholder was a stupid child who needed the "forced savings" discipline of whole life lest he/she have no insurance when it was needed.

What the Mutuals did not foresee was that the marketplace had become more informationally perfect over the prior decade. Consumers were more sophisticated in their approach to finances. The financial planning profession, as a profession, required planners selling these policies to be committed to making sure they stayed in touch with clients and were trained, at least superficially, to understand a policyholder annual statement and see, before it was too late, if course corrections were needed to a policy's funding. The consumer no longer wanted to be "forced" into anything.

What's more, whole life policies were going through a similar dynamic to UL, just not as obvious. Many agents sold whole life with the idea of eventually using the cash value buildup as a way to pay premiums in the future. They used devices such as "minimum deposit," "vanishing premium," and other techniques to show ways to stop cutting checks to the insurer every year.

Take a 45-year-old husband, breadwinner, father of two children destined to go to college. He buys a whole life policy intended to protect his family in the event of his death while the family is still dependent on his income. His premium is designed such that, at current dividend levels, the interest component of the dividend is sufficient that within 20 years the dividend will become larger than the premium each year. The agent-planner makes it even better by telling the client to buy paid-up additional (PUA) insurance with his dividends during those 20 years. The "PUAs" are small increments of single premium insurance that deliver their own dividend margins themselves. Now the illustration of the policy shows the dividend exceeding the premium by year 15. Sounds good? Just as the client is nearing retirement, the planner has given his/her client a pay raise by eliminating the insurance premium from his expense budget.

The problem is that those dividends illustrated are at the current interest rate, which is now declining each year. The dividends, in actual dollars, are still going up, and that is all the client sees in his annual policy statement. But in actuality, the dividend growth has slowed such that the 15-year elimination of the premium using the dividend is no longer valid. Neither the planner nor the client realizes this because the whole life policy statement does not reveal the reality; it only reports the dollar dividend, not comparing it to what had been illustrated. The interest component is buried in the statement, so it is not noticed that the assumptions are off. The planner has a vague understanding that something must be happening; after all, he/she sees what the economy and interest rates across it have been doing. But it is just too easy to ignore the trend.

By the mid-90s, policies were lapsing at an alarming rate at many companies; many others were being replaced by newer versions of the same type that had more competitive mortality and expense assumptions.

So, that is the end of the story? Not quite. Two product issues developed in the 90s that accelerated the problems in the industry.

The first was that many whole life "manufacturers" (yes, insurance companies talk about *manufacturing* a policy) tried to offset the lack of appeal of their products by offering higher guarantees. At the very time long term interest rates were in decline, some whole life insurers developed a series of products that guaranteed as much as 5.5% interest, rather than the customary 4%. These insurers were convinced that the decline in interest rates had gone on for so long that the trend was surely coming to an end. They believed that the evils of UL and its cousin VUL were due to a lack of guarantees in the contract. So, they built policies designed to guarantee higher returns.

Atlantic Mutual was one such company. It decided in the early 90s to scrap its attempts at VUL and concentrate on a new version of whole life with 5.5% interest guarantees. This meant that even if there was no interest margin in the dividend, the contract would still compound the cash value at 5.5%. With the company's bond portfolio still yielding 10% in 1992, this looked like a sure bet to a more competitive product.

By 1996, the bond portfolio had fallen to 7%. Even though the company, like most insurers, had invested for the long term, eventually the falling interest rates hit the portfolio. The bonds would eventually mature or be called, and the reinvestment rates into new bonds and mortgages would be at much lower rates.

AFG still needed 200bps to make its target margins. It saw what happened to some companies that tried to sacrifice margin to stay competitive. But at 7% against a 5.5% guarantee, that was less than a 200bps spread.

The actuaries saw an easy answer. After eliminating all of the interest margin in the dividend, paying only the 5.5% in the cash value, they took the remaining margin needed out of the other two components: expenses and mortality. For reasons discussed in the next section, there was no margin to be had for expenses. So, the actuaries hit the mortality margins, the one place where they were exceeding the guarantees. People were not dying, not as fast as the 1980 CSO mortality table predicted when it was constructed and placed into these policies as the guaranteed mortality assumption. The policyholder therefore continued in the false belief that he/she was getting full value when what was happening in fact was that the 5.5% was subsidized by a less generous mortality dividend than the company was experiencing. This phenomenon would continue into the next decade when the portfolio return less the spread wouldn't even make it to the state insurance departments' non-forfeiture minimums for whole life (usually 2%-3%). At that point, the products were taken of the market and the in-force block of such policies was closed.

Stop for a moment and go back to the example of the 45-year-old male breadwinner. When he bought the policy, he was in excellent health, didn't smoke, so he got the best premium rate the company had at the time, often called "preferred." You might be saying to yourself at this point, "He only needed the insurance while he had dependent children and was working full time. In 20 years he would retire and wouldn't need the insurance. So, why didn't he buy 20-year level term instead? It would have been much less expensive."

This is true enough, except for a few things. Let's say the client in our example buys the policy somewhere around 1988. How could he know at that point that he would in fact not need the policy in 2008? He was going to retire in 2008? Except in 2008 his 401(k) retirement plan suddenly became a "201(k)," having lost half its value in the so-called "Great Recession." He decides he has to continue to work until age 70. Now what does he do when his term policy goes away four years too soon?

But, O.K., let's assume that doesn't happen. Instead lets' assume that in 2007 he comes home from the doctor with a dire diagnosis of a dread disease. Maybe he lives, maybe he doesn't. But the first thing that happens is that his income to pay insurance premiums goes away. O.K., his agent knew enough in 1988 to add a waiver of premium onto the policy so that premiums are waived in the event of total disability (most clients reject the extra premium as too costly, but we'll assume a persuasive insurance agent). The problem now is that his term policy is scheduled to terminate next year and he is no longer insurable because of ill health.

The morale to this story: You simply do not know the future and you need to be prepared for all contingencies. Renting your insurance does not cover all contingencies. So, financial commentators hating permanent insurance because of its high cost and low investment returns need to check to make sure their E&O (errors and omissions, a/k/a malpractice) insurance policies are still in force – "someone's gonna' get sued"! Excuse the editorial; now back to the story...

At this point, you might think that if the insurance companies had gotten the products right, the industry would be safe. The problem was not confined to the products. In part, the pricing of the products were an outgrowth of the changing market environment and refusal of the distribution channels to change with it.

The way a life insurance agent is traditionally paid on the sale of a new policy is to "heap" the commission very heavily in the first year, the acquisition year. Base agent commission starts at 50% of first-year premium, plus bonuses and expenses allowances, and for new agents – training allowance, or TAP. Add onto that the overrides paid to the agent's sales manager and GA, and you can easily exceed 100% of premium in the first year. Then, for the career managerial companies, there are the fixed expenses for the agency itself; staff, rent, utilities, equipment, all at the high end of the market in the most desirable cities.

Actuaries took the assumptions given to them by the "line" officers running the distribution channels and inserted them into the pricing of the insurance products. At Atlantic, for example, the assumption was $1.20 per dollar of fully commissionable premium in the first year. As described before, the company made up for the deficit in the renewal years. Clearly, you don't have to be an actuary to realize a couple of things:

- Keeping the business on the books for the long term is where the profitability lies. This is called "persistency."

- Paying the agent such huge first-year compensation is incenting the exact opposite of persistency. It rewards new sales, not servicing the old ones.

In the 1990s the persistency problem became an epidemic, as agents took business from one company to another, playing on the dissatisfaction of the client with the performance of the policy in place and looking for a better deal. The agent was happy to move the client to a new carrier and earn a new heaped commission. In the securities business we would call this "churning." In the life insurance side of the industry this was simply the nature of the beast created by the compensation system and the declining interest rate environment.

The agent was not doing a good service to the client in most cases by moving them to another carrier. The old policy at least had survived any initial loads and administrative expenses charged only in the first year. To replace the policy would mean the client would have to pay those charges all over again. And with the client now at an older age, he/she would be re-entering the insurance market at a higher initial mortality risk charge than under the old policy.

In addition, the assumption given by the "line" guys to the actuaries – about expense targets themselves – were way off. In 1994, Billy Carl arrived at AFG to find the acquisition expense level of new life business at the company was running at about $1.60. By 1998, with great skill and agonizing distribution decisions, some of which made him a villain in the eyes of many who originally hailed his return to the company, the acquisition expense level hovered at $1.35 and stubbornly would not seem to move much lower than that.

An attempt at getting rid of the problem had been attempted shortly before Billy's return to AFG. In 1990, a revolutionary new compensation system was developed by Howard Crowe. It was known as a *modified levelized* system, and paid the agent a level amount of first-year compensation, but over four years. The comp was not vested in that were the policy to come off the books during those four years, the unpaid remaining commissions would not be owed. Instead of a 50% heaped base, the agent would receive 4 years of 20% compensation on each of the first four years of premium contribution. After that, service fees of 2% would be paid.

The system was a direct attempt at encouraging persistency, at least for the four years it would take to make up the deficit from the first year's acquisition expense. It would lower the acquisition cost and raise the incentive to keep the business on long enough for the company to make up the remainder.

The modified levelized structure was hailed in the home office as a commitment to excellence for client service. It was a true attempt to get at the mismatch of compensation and persistency. Hailed by insurance analysts and commentators in the industry, AFG was "leading the way to a better future for itself and its policyholders," stated one such commentator.

In the field it was condemned and it was avoided, even if it meant driving AMs to place business outside of AFG to regain the heaped commissions that each agent's business plan depended upon. You can imagine the first year loss of income that would immediately result from going from 50% to 20% on first year comp. Despite all attempts by Crowe and the actuaries to "show the math," that this would actually pay the agent more in the long run, even adjusting for the time value of money, agents rejected the plan and part of the demise of Elliott Kelleher was linked to his advocacy for the modified levelized plan. By 1994, the field at AFG was in revolt over the new comp system. However, this was not all because of the system. Had the company kept the old heaped system, it would not have brought more life ECDs to AFG. Many of the AMs simply used the modified levelized system to rationalize their abandonment of the life insurance business in its entirety for the easier sales of mutual funds and other investment products.

While investment products yielded a much lower commission schedule, they could be sold without much fuss. They did not require the kind of intimate trust relationship between client and advisor that life insurance did. It got the agent out from under the stereotyped plaid-suited salesman that was the reason most people run as fast as they can from a life insurance agent.

Billy Carl tried to get behind the modified levelized plan. He saw the math; he knew that it would help financially. But it was impossible to recruit good talent to the field force with that albatross around the company's neck. And like Winters, Keane, Soris, and Greene, Billy Carl was a field guy at heart. After Andy started the PPGA system, with its own version of 95% first-year heaped compensation, the end of the modified levelized system could not be far behind. And when Ian Evans came in to take over PPGA, the hypocrisy of paying heaped commission to independents but levelized to career people could no longer be ignored. The modified levelized system was buried at the end of 1998.

The rivalry between mutual and stock companies in the life insurance industry was also a component of a mythical belief that one or the other was the solution to the industry's problems. On the one hand, a stock company had the advantage of access to the equity markets for capital – selling stock in the company. Tax laws had been changed in the 90s to take away any company taxation advantage for mutuals. And by being a stock company, the open market determined the value of your company. The managing of a stock company, like any publicly-traded firm, was required to be more transparent, due to SEC and other regulatory bodies.

However, as a stock company, the firm was more susceptible to a takeover acquisition by another firm. M&A plans are much easier to execute with two stock companies than with two mutuals. Also, the same "short-sighted-itis," the disease that causes stock companies throughout the American economy to manage quarter-to-quarter, would infect stock life insurers as well.

As a mutual, the stock is privately held by the policyholders – socialism at work. The company operates to offer insurance to its owner-policyholder "at cost." The "profit" of the insurer is paid as "dividends" directly into the policyholder's insurance policy. In financial services, the closest cousin to the mutual life insurer is the credit union, a non-profit bank owned by the depositors. As such, the regulation of a mutual life insurer is less transparent – no SEC interference in corporate management, such as Sarbanes-Oxley (SOX) and other such legislation.

On the other hand, the very lack of regulatory oversight and open market valuation of the firm can and does lead to lazy management. When the senior leaders of a mutual company know that no one outside the firm is looking, all kinds of mischief is possible, as noted with Atlantic Mutual.

And one area where oversight does intrude into the management of a mutual – the financial rating agencies (S&P, Moody's, A.M. Best, etc.) – can cause all sorts of mischief itself. These agencies charge the insurance company a fee to have the company's financial health rated and reported. This is a conflict of interest. The agency has a financial stake in rating a paying "client" with a rather optimistic outlook. This resulted in many firms having top ratings just before they went insolvent – as if no one saw the disaster coming. See the AIG story in 2008 as an example.

For a mutual carrier, financial ratings caused many to hoard dividends in order to pad their available surplus and show a more healthy balance sheet. The policyholder was not getting full value in dividend payout because the insurer was holding back so much surplus in relentless pursuit of the top financial ratings.

Andy would comment that a client should not buy insurance from the top rated carriers, but go to the next tier of carriers. "The AAA rated companies are cheating the policyholder out of some of the dividend to maintain that rating, when it is not needed in order to have a healthy company."

And G-d forbid the mutual that does not pay the fee. The rating agency will often then perform a financial analysis on the basis of what publicly available information there is, such as "10k" statements and the "Bluebook" that insurers file with their home states. This is insufficient information and the agency, having been paid nothing to perform this service, has little incentive to go easy on the carrier.

Having learned from many in the business, Andy would look at an insurer's 10k which has a place in it to list all company employees' compensation that exceeded $500,000 a year. If the top earners in the company were the senior managers of the company, Andy felt this forecasted disaster. The healthy company would be listing its field managers and agents as their top earners, meaning that the people closest to the customer were earning the most money, as he felt it should be. Andy was a field guy at heart.

The squeeze put on the life insurance industry was felt most by agency management in the field and home office middle management. These were places that it was felt some of the "waste, fraud, and abuse" could be wrung out of a corrupted manufacture and distribution of products in the marketplace. Because "distribution is king," a company tread very carefully when it came to messing with agent compensation. So, a different place for saving money was needed.

Andy could feel the squeeze, personally. Each year, at budget time, requests for additional staff would go unfunded. Annual reviews, while always hugely positive, resulted in paltry raises and invisible promotions. "Do more for less" became the annual charge to middle management throughout the industry, and AFG was no exception.

Yet, the years 1994-1998 had been among the most fun and rewarding for Andy Greene. So long as he stayed within budget, Andy had the freedom to come up with all sorts of innovative ways to market the company's products.

Warning to company executives: Don't think that your employees are anything but free agents. If your staff are not properly rewarded for their efforts, you'll get either the bad result or the worse result. The bad result is that they leave you; the worse result is that they don't, but start to dabble in other pursuits.

Andy always had a passion for music. Going back to childhood and hearing his first Beatles record, Andy lusted to play guitar. More than that, to play and write songs. He had dabbled at it, half-heartedly as a teenager and through college. But when law school came, Andy had no time for such idle pursuits. Law school doesn't so much teach you the law as it teaches you a way to think. And in that thinking – concrete analysis – artistic pursuits go by the wayside.

Now it had been 20 plus years since Andy Greene had last played a guitar. But by the mid-90s the influence of law-think had somewhat atrophied from lack of use and the artist in him began to re-emerge. He was not foolish about it. The picking up of the guitar was a slow process. And Andy looked for ways to utilize the music to help his "day" job of marketing financial services.

Andy found that taking a guitar with him on the road was a pathway to social acceptance, as it had been as a teenager. He could bring the instrument to a social gathering on the road, if needed, play a song or two, and be immediately applauded for his efforts.

More often, however, bringing a guitar on the road gave him something to practice in the evenings, after work, in the hotel, keeping him out of the bars and out of the kinds of trouble that a middle-aged, middle manager, travelling 20+ weeks a year could run into. While colleagues might spend the evening getting sloshed on their favorite alcohol and then go to "the ballet" (euphemism for the strip shows in the "gentlemen's clubs"), Andy had something to keep him busy. After all, Andy was not a natural at playing guitar – his was not a gifted talent – so he had to practice every day if he were going to progress from horrible to bad to mediocre to passable.

Eventually, Andy would start composing parodies of popular songs, usually simple I-IV-V blues progressions and change the lyrics to something having to do with financial services or advanced underwriting – something that he could add to his "show" when making presentations to field agents; something to add to his signature bowtie, braces, and cordovan wingtips when on stage. Weird Al Yankovic was his template for parody.

Then, he took the act a step further, salting in an original of his own now and then. One, called *Asset Allocation Town*, was a 16-bar blues in Eb with a Chicago groove that told the story of a financial planner giving advice to his client about not panicking when the stock market is down. The chorus ended with:

You're in it for the long haul,

Money freedom is a high wall,

Your wealth is living in, Asset Allocation Town.

No, it wasn't going to get him to the Cavern Club in Liverpool. But it was a nice diversion.

One day in 1998, Andy attended the annual meeting of what had been renamed NAIFA (National Association of Insurance and Financial Advisors), formerly NALU, in Baltimore, MD's Inner Harbor. Andy had recently begun "going through the chairs" at the Northern Virginia Chapter, and would become Chapter President in a couple of years. He had been recruited by his friend and colleague, Effie Eckhart, who was at that time the first woman Chapter President in Northern Virginia.

The meeting was typically political, delegates being fought over by national Association candidates for office as if this were the Republican National Convention. A large Exhibition Hall was part of the program, where many vendors looking to do business with NAIFA members – insurance brokerages and software vendors – would hawk their products to an audience being encouraged to spend time with the vendors because "they are the ones who help fund the cost of the meeting."

Andy did not spend much time in the exhibit hall. His preoccupation was with any AFG producers who happened to be attending and any Northern Virginia NAIFA members there. So, he did not notice that one of the vendors had a special history with him. But on the last day of the meeting, Andy got into an elevator to go up to his room, collect his things, and check out. Waiting to join him in the elevator was Tim Wheaton, Andy's one-time head of Sales Support. Tim had been tracking Andy throughout the meeting's four days and saw him getting into the elevator alone, with few people around to attract attention. Tim called out, "wait, I'm coming," and without hesitation or knowing who was asking, Andy pushed the "Door Open" button to hold the elevator.

Tim got in. The elevator door closed and the elevator started up. Andy did not immediately recognize Tim. Tim had aged significantly in two years. But then Tim looked Andy in the eye. "Hello, Andy," he said in a monotone that seemed ominous.

And then Andy recognized the voice. "Hello Tim. How are you?"

Tim did not answer, but instead turned around and pushed the "Stop" button on the elevator panel. Turning back to face Andy, he then pulled out a pistol from his inside jacket pocket. Andy, realizing his situation, froze for a minute.

"I have been looking for a chance to do this for some time, Andrew Greene, and now's my chance."

"What's with the gun, Tim?" Andy had no idea how to defuse the situation.

"I'm going to do what I should have done when you fired me, you fucking creep." And Tim pointed the gun straight at his former boss.

It was end-time, Andy thought. The two just stood there for about 10 seconds that felt to Andy like an eternity. Then, Andy got an idea.

"So, you're going to kill me for firing you? Is that it?" Andy dared not show fear here.

"You ruined my life, you son-of-a-bitch! You had no feeling for my personal situation. It was all business to you, wasn't it? That's all you think about, isn't it? Do you have nothing in your life other than business?"

"Tim, we carried you as long as we could…"

"Shut the fuck up, man... I don't wanna hear it. You're a worthless piece of shit!" And tears began to flow down Tim's face.

"So this is how you want to end it?" It was a good thing Andy had visited the men's room before going to the elevator because at this point he was going to be emptying his bladder of whatever was left.

"Shut up! You have nothing to say here. You deserve what you're getting."

"And what's that Tim?" Now Andy quickly decided on false bravado as a tactic. "So I'm a fuck up; I care about nothing but business. So, you want to ruin the rest of your life getting rid of a nothing like me. I'm nobody Tim. You said so yourself. Am I worth the trouble?"

No answer from Tim.

"O.K., then, put me out of my misery if you like. Go ahead, do me the favor. Do it, damnit, DO IT!"

Then an alarm went off outside the elevator, and the elevator started to move. Someone had overridden the "Stop" Tim had pushed. Tim panicked. "What the fuck," were his last words. He turned the pistol on himself, under his chin, and fired once. The whole elevator car was splattered with Tim's blood as he fell backward against the car wall, then lifeless to the floor, the gun escaping from his grip. Andy just stood there, with a deer-in-the-headlights look on his face and blood all over his suit, tie and shirt, as the elevator door opened, back on the ground floor where its aborted trip had started.

Two security guards from the hotel were waiting. One immediately called 911. The other helped Andy, who was visibly shaking, out of the elevator. Because the NAIFA meeting was in general session at the time, there was no one around to see what had happened. People later would testify to a "firecracker" sound coming from one of the elevators. Andy was helped into another car and up to his floor; then into his room, where he got out of his clothes and robotically started the bathroom shower so he could clean up. The clothes would be collected by the police as evidence. Andy prepared to get into the shower, but stopped to open the toilet lid next to the tub and throw up into it. Then, he showered, gargled some mouthwash, changed into clean clothes, and made his way back down to get his car and drive back to Virginia.

Days later, Andy would say he didn't remember much about the incident after the gunshot. He simply went forward on instinct alone, with little emotion. Occasionally, Tim would re-emerge in Andy's dreams...

Chapter 12: Merger, Part I

In September 1998, Tab Davenport announced to the AFG home office that "we are pursuing talks with another company toward a planned merger by the end of the year."

In fact, Davenport was only telling part of the story. Unlike the Empire merger, this was already a done deal, requiring only Board approval to consummate the merger. The merger partner, Banker's American, based in Omaha, NE, was larger than Atlantic, supplying 60% of the capital to the merged firm. Banker's American was also organized as a mutual company. This meant acquisition was not an option. Yet, from the start, to the management team at AFG, it felt like a senior-junior partnership.

Nevertheless, the merger had many desirable outcomes for both merger partners. Banker's American was a cash rich organization, with a huge in-force insurance block of business. Banker's was known in the industry as a strong manager of money once it came into the house.

What Banker's was not as good at was getting new business, particularly outside of individual life insurance sales. It had a weak broker-dealer, and sought the depth of TIG as a way to gain further penetration into the securities business. Along with that came the mutual fund family, and the bank – both of which Atlantic had and Banker's did not.

AFG was at least growing its sales in life insurance, although off of a very small base. Banker's sales in life insurance were larger but stagnant, although it did have group insurance and retirement plan divisions that did well. In other words, each partner brought to the table something the other needed, ideal in a merger.

The next hurdle was whether the management of both firms acknowledged in practice the realization of what the other partner brought to the merger. In many of these deals, lip service is given to the others' strengths during the "courtship" phase of a merger, only to have egos get in the way once the deal is done.

To make sure the ego factor would not overtake the merger, the senior managers from both companies made a commitment to make this a true merger, and actualized it by creating an Executive Office consisting of four company leaders. Tab Davenport and Billy Carl represented AFG, Tab as Vice Chairman of the Board. The CEO and Chairman of Banker's American, Perry Brooks, became Chairman of the merged company, to be called American Atlantic, and Banker's COO – Louis Pershing – would be the fourth member of the Executive Office.

While Tab Davenport was a healthy and active 55-year-old, his counterpart, Perry Brooks, was a chain smoking, stout man of 60 years, with a yellowing complexion that revealed his years of smoking 1-2 packs a day. This was seen by all at both companies as somewhat ironic – a CEO of a life insurance company a smoker, the largest health hazard to long life going in American society. Banker's American maintained a private jet, mainly for Brooks' use when travelling just so he could get around the no-smoking policy on commercial aircraft. He justified its use by allowing the plane to be rented by other "captains of industry" in Omaha when he wasn't using it (no one ever saw Warren Buffet use the plane, however).

Billy Carl had been made COO shortly before the merger. He was then confronted with a counterpart COO in Pershing as part of the new company. Both men learned to put aside their individual egos, at least for the time being, to work as partners in the new American Atlantic, branded in the marketplace as AAFG. Both COO's were 50 at the time of the merger, and so both could do the chronological math and figured that they would figure into the company's future, once their respective bosses retired.

The partnership of this "gang of four," as they were affectionately called by middle managers in both companies, worked despite the members' obvious personality, skill set, and cultural differences. Tab and Billy were East Coast sophisticated, D.C. politically savvy, and were dyed-in-the-wool marketing people. They were first and foremost "top-line" centric; they were best at finding revenue to feed the rest of the income statement. Perry Brooks came from the investments side of the business, good at knowing what to do with a dollar of revenue once it came in but clueless as to how to get the revenue in the first place. Lou Pershing had some marketing background but was old-school Midwest through and through; he hated ever having to come east to D.C. The Gang all agreed that home offices would remain in Omaha and Washington, although the main home office would be in Nebraska.

As further example of the obvious differences between the members of the Executive Office, Tab Davenport had been a rock musician in his early years, playing guitar (his solo on *Johnny B. Goode* was a creditable replica of Chuck Berry's) and singing classic rock tunes. When his marriage dissolved in 1996, he took up the guitar again as a way to re-ignite his youth, and recruited Andy Greene as his bass player in a short-lived company band that played some home office parties at the time. Tab fancied himself as a bit of a rebel. Perry Brooks was anything but a rebel, having grown into his position by conformity. His idea of music was strictly country-western.

Both Tab and Billy were "people-people," in that they performed well as front men – spokespersons for the brand. They didn't really need others to speak the brand for them, although they appreciated "front-man" talent when they saw it, such as in Nellie Soris and Andy Greene.

Perry and Lou did not like the limelight, thought promotion of themselves and the brand to be low class self-aggrandizement, and preferred to have others speak the company line when possible. But that did not mean that they were seen as any less in control in Omaha. Perry and Lou were better on the one-to-one relationships than at the podium. Perry, only half-jokingly, used to say to Andy when he'd see the VP of Marketing Services at company meetings, "Andy, go give the field hell; tell 'em what's what! Tell 'em to sell more life insurance." Brooks didn't want that responsibility himself.

Andy Greene himself had a counterpart at Banker's in the form of Tom Wells, their Marketing Support VP. This immediately created a definition problem, as there were now two departments attempting to do the same thing, with mirror-image units for advanced sales, sales support, and marketing communications. What's more, the Executive Office did not define roles for the two marketing departments, only that they were to work in partnership for the "good of the order," as Billy Carl would put it. Tom continued to report to Lou Pershing; Andy to Billy Carl.

Other areas of each individual company had similar counterpart dilemmas as part of the merger. And the idea was not to cut out staff, if possible; a promise made to the home offices as part of the merger was that cuts in staff were not part of the merger plan. Confusion between home offices did run rampant in 1999 and into the precipice of the new millennium.

The Y2K phenomenon played a role in bringing together parts of each office for a common issue. The fear that computer systems might go dark when the first digit of the year went from 1 to 2 pre-occupied both IT departments. The old Cobalt language that had been used for early computer programs used only two digits, for the last two in the year. Once 99 became 00, no one was sure what would happen. Not waiting around, both offices swung into action early on, re-programming systems into a four digit year so that the chronology of logic would not confound the systems. In fact, the new company did so well that some of the programmers left AAFG mid-year to take high paying positions at other companies desperate to avoid the Y2K monster that was coming. Thus, AAFG did get some relief from a bloated home office staff through attrition.

Over time, Tom Wells and Andy Greene reached a sort of accommodation. While both departments' staffs continued to be suspicious of each other, and it came out from time to time, the department heads began to show a true partnership. Tom and Andy put aside, for awhile, their career ambitions and territoriality, and worked together, keeping the jealousies of their unit leaders at bay as well.

They were in part reflecting the Executive Office which appeared, at least on the surface, to work in true partnership. And the two marketing departments and their leaders began to be a symbol for how this merger should work. Tom and Andy attended several company meetings together, making tandem presentations with their respective staffs. Tom took on the idea of an annual Retreat for his people, but combining it with Andy's Retreat. So, each year they would alternate between Omaha and Washington for a location to meet, jointly. They would then plan tactically to implement the strategic plan given them for the year. Of course, when going to Omaha, the team building exercises after hours consisted of things like BBQ for dinner and go-kart racing for recreation. In D.C., it was a dinner cruise up and down the Potomac, where the Nebraska staff saw the Capitol, the monuments, and other sites live, for the first time in their lives.

In the middle of 2000, Billy Carl was given sole responsibility for individual insurance marketing. Lou Pershing would work with the group and retirement folks. Billy decided at that point that better definition between Tom and Andy was needed. He had a vision of a marketing department that did "real strategic marketing." Billy's criticism of life insurance company marketing was that it was limited to "sales support," more tactical. It did not create a forward looking strategy where market trends could be properly predicted and calculated.

Billy saw this strategic marketing department as something for Tom Wells, who was more of a marketing technician and less of a company spokesman than Andy Greene. In turn, Andy was given responsibility for a merged department of both offices' training, advanced sales, sales support, and communications functions.

Tom was set up with a small staff, picked from his former department, to perform strategic marketing analysis and propose new programs and products that the company was not yet considering, but should. He was to look at new "target rich" environments for the company to explore and exploit. Several of Tom's former staff applied for the few available positions in this new department, though few were fully qualified for the new roles. It's not that Tom really wanted his existing staff to go with him. He saw this new organization as an opportunity to bring in some new blood. He had become tired of dealing with the personalities and peculiarities of some of the people who had been working for him for the past several years. One such person was Jan Daley, a long time Nebraskan who could trace her family's heritage back to the settlers of the mid-19th Century. Jan had been a local beauty queen in her younger days. And you could still see remnants of the model and dancer that she was 20 years before.

Jan had a set of somewhat tumultuous arguments over department direction with Andy, but it was more style than substance differences. When Jan applied for a position in Tom's new department, Andy – thinking she might fit well in his own sales support unit – asked her why she preferred going with Tom. "You're a scary person, Andy," was her answer. "The way you come at people sometimes intimidates me."

"I'm sorry, Jan. I did not mean to scare you."

"I don't think you do it intentionally. This is the way many of you from the East Coast handle yourselves; sometimes disconcerting. And you in particular are so outgoing in your approach; you're just scary."

"Well, I wish you well." The two would stay friends and colleagues for the rest of their time in the company. But the comment from Jan would always stay near the top of Andy's mind when dealing with people, going forward.

As for those who would be made part of Andy's new department, their head of Advanced Underwriting, Ray Dawson, was well known in advanced sales circles. Ray also had his run-ins with Andy occasionally, and figured Andy would seize the opportunity to rule him out of the Department entirely, given Susan Blanque was Andy's Marketing Counsel.

But Susan would leave in 2000. Having served for exactly five years in her position, she left for another company. This was her way. She was what Andy would call years later in business classes at ERU, a "5-year jumper." This referred to the phenomenon of a staffer staying at a job just long enough to fully vest in the employer's contributions to the 401(k) plan. Most companies at that time had set up their 401(k) plans for "cliff" vesting, meaning that the employer's matching contributions to the plan would not become the employee's until the employee had completed 5 years of service, at which time it would all become vested in the employee's account. Many technically savvy staffers would wait until that fifth year and then leave, taking their entire vested account with them.

And Susan Blanque would not leave without some fanfare. Instead of giving her notice to Andy, her boss, she went over Andy's head and resigned to Billy Carl. And in that meeting she had some unkind words to say about Andy as a boss and about most of the rest of the Marketing Services managers.

Worse yet, she repeated some of her critique to a few others in the company. So it was not surprising when this all came to Andy's attention. Andy confronted Susan on her last day on the job, a sort of exit interview.

"I hear you've had some negative things to say about us here in Marketing."

No response from Susan.

Andy continued, "I'm not concerned about what you said. You're entitled to your opinion. But to repeat this to others just poisons the well."

Still no response.

"The very resigning to Billy is not right. It's as if you do not want to recognize who your manager has been these past five years; the person who brought you to this company in the first place. You've never expressed to me your dissatisfaction with what we were doing here, or my managerial style. This is all new to me. I would have thought you'd have the decency to tell me how you felt and not take the coward's path of tossing a hand grenade in the room and then leaving."

Susan just got narrow eyed and tight mouthed, but still said nothing.

"Susan, I've lost a lot of respect for you, the way you've handled yourself here these past few days. Good luck to you."

They would never speak again after that, even though they occasionally ended up at the same industry conferences.

Taking Susan's place, Andy quickly found a tax attorney in private practice in Alexandria, with an office just doors away from what used to be Northern Virginia Financial Group. Roger Carter was a graduate of Marshall Wythe Law School at William and Mary, an army brat whose father, "the Colonel," last posted at Fort Belvoir, near Mt. Vernon. Roger boasted that he'd gone to high school with fellow military brat Jim Morrison, before Morrison left for California to join The Doors. Roger was a veteran of Viet Nam, although as a son of "the Colonel" he never saw combat there.

Roger Carter was anything but military however. In his interview with Andy, Roger revealed that he played piano, and that he fancied himself an amateur songwriter. "A keys player," Andy thought, and immediately surmised the possibility of teaming up with Roger musically. The summer before, Andy had a relapse of the "music bug," when he attended a music retreat in Connecticut called the National Guitar Workshop, and studied guitar in their beginner blues program for a week. Andy was now practicing almost every day, using the guitar as an outlet and release from work and family pressures. Now, he wanted to expand the avocation, maybe even form a band. Roger Carter, a few years older than Andy, was well versed in 60s rock music. It was a match made in heaven, Andy concluded, and hired Roger shortly before the reorganization of marketing departments, without much consideration of other candidates.

Then, Andy and Roger inherited Ray Dawson. Ray was a great technician, but a poor public speaker. He knew tax law well, but put audiences to sleep with his presentation style. Ray was also in declining health, diabetes and other ailments due in large part to his weight and lack of exercise. Roger, on the other hand, could talk, and he looked the part of a svelt and energetic spokesperson for advanced sales – at least that's what Andy assumed, maybe in part because of his belief in Roger's musical abilities. This might have been a halo effect from music to tax law, but Andy saw only more "frontman" abilities for Roger, and soon decided to make him head Marketing Counsel, with Ray reporting to him.

At first, when Ray was transferred to Andy's Marketing Services Department, he worked side-by-side with Roger. The day Tom informed him of the transfer, Ray assumed this finally meant Andy was going to fire him, for the pushback Ray had given Andy in the past on departmental issues. After an email Ray sent to Andy containing a sort of apology for his prior behavior, Andy surprised Ray by asking to see him face-to-face while both were on the road and assuring him his job was safe. Ray, like Jan, felt Andy's demeanor in the past was intimidating, forceful, and hostile to the Midwestern style of doing business. Ray saw something different in Andy Greene from that meeting.

However, when Andy gave Roger the lead Marketing Counsel position, Ray could not accept this result. Ray had been an advanced sales attorney for nearly two decades; Roger was new to the specifics of the life insurance business. And again Ray felt Andy was getting even for the arguments they sometimes had in department meetings. But before Ray could do anything about the situation, he fell ill while on vacation with his family in California. He went on long term disability from the job, and within a month died of congestive heart failure. He wasn't even 50 when he died.

In sales support, Andy had Barb Harmon, who took over the illustration systems for both companies and oversaw the merger of those systems into one. She had a manager of systems reporting to her, Eric Wang, who in turn had a couple of "refugees" from the IT area to work on getting the system out to the field and testing it for accuracy.

Barb was not a computer technician. She was more a field trainer than anything else. In fact, the Field Training and Development Unit that had been a part of Marketing Services at Atlantic was now gone after the merger. Big T training was no longer the order of the day.

The new company was less interested in developing new people in the business than in servicing existing, successful veteran producers. Training was now referred to as "Little T," focused on product training, illustration proposal construction, and sales concepts. That was fine for Barbara Harmon, and the Sales Support Unit absorbed most Little T expertise; Marketing Counsel the rest. Barb fit Andy's need for someone who had Andy's back, who he could depend upon to outwork everyone else, that any lack of credentials made little difference.

In Marketing Communications, Marie Frame shared roles with her counterpart in Omaha, Terry Cochrane. The two forged an alliance of sorts. While Marie had little ego and less desire for power, Terry had ambitions for greater things. However, Terry – all of age 35 and husband and father of three – understood that creating confrontations was not going to be the path to those greater things. Terry also had a side hobby with the guitar, and sometimes played a parody role at company meetings, posing as a country singer, complete with cowboy hat and accent, doing riffs of Willie Nelson songs with the lyrics changed to something relevant to the audience. On at least one occasion he performed at an Advanced Sales Forum in D.C., posing as "Neb Raska" and dueted with Andy Greene as "Big Daddy" (a blues guitarist) to an appreciative dinner crowd of field sales people.

In product development, Andy continued to represent marketing in a reconfigured Product Development Committee. But the actuarial players had changed. Gone was Henry Barton, who left as part of the merger. In came Roman Clay, hired away from a cross-town Omaha rival insurer, to help create state-of-the-art product that would meet profitability goals (Perry Brooks did not want marketing or distribution driving product development by itself, lest the two disciplines run the company into the ground). Roman would be the chair of the Committee and oversee pricing. Andy's job was to bring product ideas to the table for concept testing and analysis.

Roman Clay brought with him some deep experience in product development. He instituted a three step process for a new product. First, there would be an Opportunity Assessment (OA), a 3-5 page statement of the product idea, the market it was targeted at, a defense of why the product would sell, and how it would be sold. The OA was usually developed by Andy, with Billy Carl's oversight. The OA would then go through a concept testing process to see if it was feasible, including a pricing test by Roman's people at one cell, often a 45-year-old male non-smoker.

If it passed this hurdle, judged by the full Committee, the second stage would be a Business Case (BC), a full business plan for the product that included marketing, actuarial, underwriting, and legal input. Sales projections for up to three years were a central part of this document. An up-or-down vote of the full Committee would be taken on the BC.

If it passed, the product would go into prototype development and preparation for release to the marketplace. An Administrative Memo (Admin Memo) would be developed by the pricing actuary that included full documentation of all specifications for the product, including how policies sold were to be administered in the home office.

While Roman Clay chaired the Committee, the membership of the Committee was dominated by Janeesh Rau, the Chief Actuary for AAFG, and Billy Carl, COO. The rivalry between Rau and Carl – legend at Atlantic before the merger – continued in the new company. Even though both came from the Atlantic side of the merger, this would be a major pressure point for getting anything done in product development.

Rau, as said before, was more interested in becoming part of the Executive Office than in managing his current job. His time was preoccupied with schmoozing the newly merged Board of Directors. While not part of the Executive Office, he ingratiated himself with Board members whenever possible. This left him little time for details regarding the pricing and specification for new life insurance and annuity products. He would often show up for Committee meetings unprepared, being unavailable to Roman Clay for pre-meeting briefings. Yet, without his assent, the BC would not be approved to move forward to the Admin Memo.

While Andy meticulously went over all details with Billy before meetings, the process ground to a halt as the product had to be re-taught to Rau. Sometimes meetings had to be cancelled because Rau was unavailable. The gestation period for Investor 2000 VUL in 1995 had been 9 months. Now, the process was taking twice as long.

On top of all this, after the merger it was discovered that the documentation for Investor 2000, its companion annuity product, and all the Atlantic products developed in the 90s had disappeared. There was nothing documenting how these products were priced or how they were to be administered. Systems had been set up, but then nothing written down to remember what was done. Henry Barton, the pricing actuary at the time, was gone. The programmers for the products had left during the Y2K rush to hire Cobalt fluent programmers at other companies. While Rau pointed the finger at Barton for this, everyone knew that Barton reported to Rau through that entire period.

Rau then employed the "Reverse Nuremburg Defense." The Nuremburg Defense, from the Nazi War Crime Trials in the 1940s, went like this, "I was only following orders," when the concentration camp guards were on trial – passing the buck upwards. Rau said the opposite, "I had no idea Barton wasn't keeping copious records of what he was doing. Any actuary knows that there needs to be documentation on pricing and administration. I was unaware he was either not doing this, took the files with him, or destroyed the documentation before he left."

This did not make Rau look good in the eyes of many in the company. However, Rau had cultivated such positive relationships with several members of the Board that the Executive Office, wanting to placate the Board, never let this problem come to their attention. It would be handled internally and no harm would come to Janeesh Rau from all this. They bought off on the Reverse Nuremburg Defense. A lower level assistant, not an FSA (Fellow Society of Actuaries), the sole remaining person once in Barton's department still with the company, was charged with piecing together what she knew from memory for a ghost documentation. The details were a bit sketchy, and she knew to only share what was absolutely necessary, as she assumed this was her job security going forward.

The fact was that the missing documentation came to light when Roman Clay decided to do a profitability audit of Atlantic products, specifically Investor 2000. Andy did not oppose the audit. He was proud of the product. Most had hailed it as saving Atlantic Mutual and it continued to be available for sale at AAFG. It was a favorite of the field force. A significant in-force block of policies were piling up at the administrative center in the Omaha home office.

Investor 2000 was a sophisticated product, with options of 5 portfolios the policyholder could choose from in which to invest the cash value, depending upon the policyholder's risk tolerance and time horizon. The portfolio choices also stressed Modern Portfolio Theory, a Nobel Prize winning theory of economics which, among other things, argued that over 90% of an investor's rate of return on a portfolio is based solely on the allocation of funds among asset classes; not on the individual investments or timing the market. It also stressed that active money management was in most cases not worth the management fees being charged; that the top money managers in any five-year rolling period of measurement almost never remained in the top tier of money managers in the next 5-year period. Therefore, Andy had made sure to liberally pick index funds as investment options in these portfolios, where the management was passive and automatic, and the fees were therefore very low.

This was the kind of attention to detail that suited the securities-centric field force at Atlantic; less so the insurance agent that came to the new company from Banker's American. Nevertheless, all enjoyed the popularity of this securities based product in the securities-crazed 1990s and into the new millennium. The Private Pension Plan ran even more effectively with a VUL than it had with a conventional UL policy, given the high returns investors were seeing at the time. The Private Pension Plan had come under some severe scrutiny by 2000, as some policyholders at some companies complained that their agents had not fully revealed that what they were purchasing were life insurance policies. This forced the renaming of the sale concept to "Personal Retirement Supplement Funded with Life Insurance." But the concept remained a mainstay for "SLOLI" (Sell Lots of Life Insurance), a rallying cry from the home office to the field to get the life insurance sale.

In 2000, the stock market slowed. The DJIA and S&P indexes showed a negative return for the first time since 1991. The financial planning community did not yet realize it but the economy was going into recession. Looking back on it in hindsight, many financial commentators at the time called this the "dot.com bubble" bursting, and the fact was that many new tech companies had been too aggressively entering the marketplace with insufficient target marketing, too much competition, and too little capital. But the reality is that, once again, investors forgot (as they seem to do at the end of boom periods) that every decade the business cycle turns again and a recession hits – 1939, 1946, 1957, 1969, 1973, 1981, 1991. It's just a matter of how soon and how deep.

So, the field sales people, financial planners they were trained to be, all counseled their clients to stay the course. Surely, to sell off now would be selling at the bottom. Use dollar cost averaging to buy more shares with the same periodic investment and lower your average cost of shares. It made sense. Then, the market went down even further in 2001, made worse by the 911 attacks. The financial planning community looked at their Ibbotson models – Ibbotson was and is the definition of investment analysis in the financial planning community. In fact, Ibbotson had been the firm hired by Andy to create the 5 portfolios in the Investor 2000 VUL and VA products. The models showed clearly that there had never been a time, since the Great Depression, of three consecutive years of negative returns in the stock market, except 1939-41. Therefore, the odds of a third year of negative returns were very unlikely, and the planner so advised the client to "stay the course," you're surely going to see a recovery in the third year.

Then, in 2002, the market posted a negative return again, and panic among some investors set in. And some of those investors were Investor 2000 policyholders. And the planner was faced with accusations of incompetence and malpractice; the planner responded that the client had selective memory, that this was a life insurance policy at heart.

Andy's department was charged with the responsibility of managing the panic from the field sales people. All manner of meetings to remind producers of the proper ways these policies were sold originally was reviewed. New sales practices were instituted to bolster proper disclosures, initiated in many cases by the broker-dealer, now renamed American Investments, Inc. (A2I). Many producers moved away from selling VUL and back toward traditional UL. And Andy and Roger Carter performed *Asset Allocation Town* – Andy's song about a financial planner counseling his/her client not to panic from the stock market decline:

You're in it for the long haul,

Money freedom is a high wall,

Your wealth is living in, Asset Allocation town.

During this time, Bud Knowles – head of the broker-dealer – had become disenchanted at the way he had to "cowtow" to the "life company." He sought a securities environment free of domination by a corporate management whose bottom line depended upon life insurance sales. Bud resigned the company in late 2000, replaced by the first African American woman to run a division of either company, Melanie White.

Melanie came into the business in a way not so unlike Andy Greene. First educated as a lawyer, she also had advanced sales experience in life insurance, but gravitated to securities in the halcyon days of the 1990s. She was young for an executive, not yet 40, wife and mother of two daughters, and her family relocated with her from St. Louis, where she had been running a small, regional broker-dealer.

The Executive Office liked Melanie; she understood life insurance and was unafraid of leading an insurance company owned broker-dealer. The fact that they could boast diversity by hiring an African American woman didn't hurt either. Both Banker's and Atlantic had at least one woman running a division of the respective companies – the chief administrative officer at Banker's and the President of Chesapeake Mutual Funds at AFG were both women; both white; one WASP, the other Jewish. And Melanie knew how to work in a team, got along with almost everyone; she could hang with "the Gang" without being "of" the Gang, so to speak.

No sooner did Melanie White take over A2I, than Jamie Keane resigned, leaving for a zone VP position at a competitor company based in Cincinnati, closer to his family's long term home in Pittsburgh. Jamie had been urged by his wife to bring the family back to more hospitable surroundings and away from the social coldness of the Nation's Capital.

In Jamie's explanation to Andy of his exit, he said, "I've been at Atlantic my entire career, 15 years. If I don't get out now I never will and I will never have the broad perspective I need to move ahead in my career." So, the first of the three in the "team of rivals" was gone by the middle of 2001.

Then, Billy Carl decided to leave for greener pastures. Billy had been getting frustrated with the controlling nature of Perry Brooks, and began to feel like fourth in line to manage the entire company. When he was made an offer he "couldn't refuse" by the largest life insurance company in the world at the time, AIG, he decided to relocate as their President of their South Asian subsidiary, in India.

Andy was the first after Tab to learn of his resignation. "I wanted to let you know," Billy started with Andy in Billy's office in D.C., "that I have given my resignation to Tab and I'll be leaving AAFG at the end of the year."

Andy was practically in tears. Billy had been a mentor to him all through their time together at Atlantic. But eventually, Andy started to think, while sitting in a red wing chair on the opposite side of Billy's desk, who would replace him?

"I know what you're thinking," Billy continued. "I haven't told him yet; you happened to be in the office when all this happened. But I have told Tab to put Oliver in charge of all of marketing."

"He's going into the Executive Office?"

"No, not right now. Frankly, I haven't been totally satisfied with any of you to succeed me, but Tab asked for an internal recommendation, and he is the one I came up with. The three of you have all been at each others' throats at times, and that's not true leadership."

"Of course, I'm disappointed," Andy answered, "but I'll make it work."

Billy could see the disappointment on Andy's face. Andy wore his heart on his sleeve; he was no poker face. "Tab and I really want this to work, and you have a critical role to play here. You know stuff." Andy would hear this line again and again to assure him his place in the company. "Just because you're not the one being promoted does not mean we don't value you. It's just that Oliver looks the part and has done the relationship things in the home office that make him the better choice now."

"What do you mean, 'looks the part?'"

"Let's just say he looks more mainstream; more gray hair; more field experience. You haven't done much of the executive entertaining and relationship building you need to do. You are great at networking down in the organization. You're not as good at networking up and sideways. Sometimes, Andy, I get the feeling that you are operating that 'Marketing Services' department of yours as if it was a separate company, like you report to no one. You show up the others on the Senior Staff by holding department retreats; you host the Advanced Sales Forum like it was your own meeting, not giving the other guys much ownership in it. You forget that you have the position you do to make the field guys' jobs easier, and that includes Oliver and – when he was here – Jamie. You did the right things for the right reasons most of the time, but not always, and it always irked them. I got an ear full from time to time from each of them about you."

"You never said much about this in annual reviews or elsewhere."

"I did offer you coaching sometimes and I made clear that as you move into higher positions, it is less about what you know than about what others think of you – how they feel about working with you. I've told you that you do really well with your people; they are very loyal to you. You and Tom have worked well together; you're both models of how the merger is supposed to work. I really appreciate that."

"Thanks for the positives… I was starting to feel like you thought I was worthless." Andy was again thinking about George Forson's 'zero' gesture when he fired Jerry Piccolo.

"Look, man, don't see this out of proportion. We want you to stay with the company. We need your knowledge and your field relationships; the agents love you. So, what can we do to satisfy your need to grow, other than this promotion?"

"Pay me more money?" Andy smiled, half-jokingly.

They both laughed at the remark. "No, really, what can we do?"

"Well, Billy, if you want me to have a growth opportunity, I'd like the company to send me back to school."

"For the LLIF Designation?" LLIF was a designation of LIMRA International, an industry research arm that stood for LIMRA Leadership Institute Fellow, and indicated a company's intention that the recipient was on a senior leadership track at his/her company.

"Well, yes, that would be great. I was thinking of something else in addition."

"In addition? How could you handle your job, the LLIF courses, and something in addition?"

"I can. You know I can. You know I earned a CLU, ChFC, CFP, Series 7, and MSFS degree all at the same time. Remember?"

"Yeah, I remember… What are you thinking?"

"I'm thinking of the company sending me back to school for a Ph.D., in business, majoring in marketing. It will help my contribution to the strategy building functions here."

"Tom Wells is strategy. I'm not against the idea of adding to our bench depth. But I don't get it. Why would you want to do a Ph.D. The only thing you can do with it is teach, right?"

"Bill, you asked me to tell you what I wanted, and this is it."

"Well, let me think it over and get back to you."

And a few days later, Billy and Tab had Andy into Tab's office and made the deal. Andy would be financed in advance for all costs associated with the Ph.D. out of a budget Andy would have control over. By budgeting this venture, it would not be considered compensation to Andy and so he would not be taxed on the costs; this was to be attendance at continuing education functions, just as if he were going to the Arizona Institute. However, Tab and Billy insisted that the research done in dissertation be on a topic relevant to life insurance, thereby delivering an outcome directly beneficial to the company. Andy further agreed that this arrangement was subject to change if tax laws required a different treatment of the costs. Finally, Andy agreed to also pursue the LLIF, again at company expense, in order to align himself more directly than the Ph.D. for future executive assignments.

No contract was signed by anyone. An email reciting what had been agreed to was sent by Tab's office to Andy and Billy. And in September 2001, Andy enrolled at the same school at which he did his MBA, George Washington University, as the oldest Ph.D. candidate the marketing department in the School of Business had ever seen, at age 48. A one-time addition to Andy's executive budget provided the initial tuition cost for that term and amounts for Spring and Fall 2002 were put in place in the following year's budget. This was Billy Carl's last official act before leaving AAFG. Would it be the last time the two would see each other?

No sooner did Billy Carl exit the company, than Oliver Winters began to make his mark on marketing. The strategic plan that Billy Carl had fashioned, with Tom Wells on strategic marketing and Andy Greene on marketing tactics, was made more formal. Oliver wanted to have Andy's area aligned more directly under the line people running the distribution channels. Oliver continued to run career on his own, and hired staff people to help him do so.

Ian Evans continued to run PPGA, but resented having to report to Oliver. Ian felt Winters had no background in PPGA and would not understand the needs of that channel. Ian had also struck up an alliance with Andy, borne in part by a mutual distrust and dislike for Oliver Winters and in part by a mutual emotional attachment to the PPGA form of doing business. This alliance survived the firing and replacing of virtually all of the regional directors Andy had hired, including Lyn Randolph and Darrell Torrence, with Ian's handpicked colleagues from former companies in whom he had greater confidence.

Lyn and Ian never seemed to warm to each other. Years later Andy would come to realize that his former boss and mentor from Lambert suffered bouts of depression, which would render her almost unable to function for days at a time. She hid it at Lambert by taking PTO (paid time off) when it got too bad and outworking everyone else to make up for it when she could function normally. As she got older, the bouts of depression got worse and lasted longer. And in a field management position, there is no such thing as PTO – if you have producers to see, you see them. You can't cancel plans to tour your region because you don't feel up to it. Ian spotted this trend, but did not know of the depression. All he saw – all he wanted to see – was the on-again, off-again performance in the field. And Lyn never revealed her condition to anyone, not even Andy.

Darrell Torrence was a similar matter, but from a source that was different and became specifically known to Andy some time after they no longer worked together. Darrell was a Viet Nam veteran, flew an Army Evac helicopter shuttling the wounded from battlefield to field hospital. Civilians got a taste of this in MASH, both the film and the famous TV series. But this was no comedy. Darrell had been shot down twice, wounded both times.

When he loosened up enough to talk about it, and that was rare, he recounted the tactics they used to fly into combat zones to pick up wounded and fly out again in the middle of a firefight.

"We were to fly in at very low altitudes, just above the trees, to give the VC less time to fire at us due to the low angle coming in. Going out was even more dangerous. I took a bullet in the leg on one mission; cut up on a crash landing another time; neither enough to get me sent home. I served two tours; 1967-68, and 1970-71. The first tour everyone was gung-ho, high morale, committed to the fight. The second tour was completely different; people were just trying to survive to get out; they were demoralized; there was a complete distrust for the brass and the Government that sent us there. It was like two different wars."

The scars from the war were not only physical. Darrell worked well with Andy and the two were good friends. But there were times that the slightest thing could set Darrell off and he would get verbally out of control. He would be ready to quit, which he tried to do a couple of times.

But Darrell was also a Landsman, from Miami, married to a Cuban immigrant, father of two (one son, one daughter). And Andy tolerated some of the temper problems, wrote them off to the stress of the job. Years later, Darrell called Andy, when they no longer worked together – Darrell had retired – and Darrell asked Andy to be a witness to his incapacity on the job.

"You want me to criticize your job performance? Why?" Andy asked.

"I'm fighting the V.A. for benefits. I was diagnosed last year with a form of PTSD. You know what that is?"

"Post-Traumatic Stress Disorder," Andy recited, slowly.

"Exactly. They owe me benefits from the shit I went through in Nam. But I need verification of the disease from those I worked with."

"This PTSD is tough to prove… It's so…mental."

"Yeah, right. That's why I need you as a witness."

"I feel funny about this, man. I never felt you couldn't do the job."

"Andy, I never told you much about what happened over there. And you never asked. Quite frankly, I didn't want to 'screw the pooch' by tipping you off that I might not be emotionally capable of the work. And I valued your friendship too much to let this all get in the way."

"Dude, I valued your friendship as well. We had a good run at Lambert. I'm sorry it didn't work out at AFG."

"Not your fault. The only thing that was your fault was that you valued our friendship too much to see that I probably shouldn't be doing regional work at that point. You never seemed to catch on to my situation. Hell, I didn't really catch on to what was happening to me."

"Don't worry. I'll have your back on this one." And Andy wrote a letter specifying Darrell's mood swings and temper on the job, sent into the V.A. per Darrell's instructions. Darrell did win his claim and was able to retire on a cash flow that included disability benefits in addition to therapy from the Veterans Administration.

Under Oliver Winters, Andy had a difficult time. The two had personality clashes from time to time. Oliver tried to call Andy on his insistence that "we're all line here," by challenging Andy to take on a much more visible role, accountable for sales results more directly. He offered Andy the chance to reorganize the Marketing Services Department into something called Sales Development. "You can stay as staff resource to the distribution channels if you want, or you can take a more visible role, with a 300-watt light bulb on you, accountable like Ian and me for sales results, as Sales Development."

The offer was a red herring, because Andy was already just as responsible for sales as Oliver and Ian, and it showed in his annual bonus formula, just not as generous a payout percentage. Andy went back to his management team – Marie, Barb, and Roger – and asked them what they thought. "Let's take the chance," said Marie.

"Let's be the Sales Development Force," chimed in Barb. And the SDF was born. Same staff, same roles, just a different name.

Also during this time, a question came to Oliver about his knowledge of Andy's "deal" with Tab and Billy about the Ph.D. and its funding. Human Resources, run by Paula Banks, was auditing these tuition funding deals. Paula felt that these one-off agreements would get the company in trouble. She sought on her own the counsel of "Snake" Samuelson and his people in Legal. It was determined that unless the tuition funding was necessary to the employee's current job, it had to fit within the qualified plan guidelines of a tuition reimbursement plan, specified in the employee benefits handbook and available equally to all in the company. Andy had informed Oliver of the deal he had with Billy, and believed that this agreement was in fact necessary to Andy's current job. "Otherwise," Andy argued, "I would not have agreed that my dissertation had to bring specific value back to the company in the form of life insurance research and analysis."

But when Paula Banks approached Oliver with the situation, Oliver – seeing a chance to cut the brash Andy Greene down a peg – professed to know nothing of this agreement and that the funding was not essential to Andy's current job. Andy furnished a copy of the confirmatory email from Tab, although Tab could not recall any specifics. "Billy handled all of that," was all he could say about the matter.

The email was ignored. Andy was allowed to finish out 2002 with the agreement. After that, it would be limited to $5,500 a year, the IRS limitation on tuition reimbursement. The Ph.D. program at GWU at that time was a 10-installment tuition of $5,000 per semester, or $10,000 a year. Andy would now be out of pocket for a portion of the cost, if he wished to continue.

Paula was not without her own ax to grind concerning what she saw as an "arrogant" attitude from Andy toward the home office execs. Paula Banks was the constant source of ridicule, behind her back. Short, with makeup deep enough to rival Queen Elizabeth I, she was referred to as "Portabello" by Jamie Keane, due to her mushroom-like platinum hair-do. Andy referred to her as "the Major," after the Margaret Hoolihan character in MASH, for her penchant for top-down management and all-too-obvious kiss-up to the Executive Office.

What she was really pissed over was the fact that one of Andy's staff had called her on a lie she had told in a company employee meeting involving benefits. What was so awful, in Paula's eyes was that the allegation of misinformation was leveled in public, in an employee meeting, where she was embarrassed by the charge; that Andy Greene had not stepped in to prevent the staffer from calling her on the lie was unforgivable in the eyes of "the Major." Paula felt that Andy's staff reflected Andy's brash attitude and held him personally responsible for the embarrassment, as if he had put the staffer up to it, wanting to humiliate her. Nothing about the content of the lie itself; Paula cared nothing for misrepresenting employee benefits. It was the image she was projecting that was the most important thing to her, not the accuracy of what she put out in front of the employees.

Oliver Winters' tenure as Andy's boss did not last long. There continued to be some friction between them. Oliver more than once threatened to fire Andy for insubordination. Andy never went over Oliver's head to complain about what Andy saw as a heavy-handed, imperial attitude displayed by this new Senior VP of Marketing. He didn't have to. The same behavior that was Oliver's trademark and alienated himself from Andy and from Ian for that matter was the way he irritated the folks in Omaha, especially Lou Pershing, who was now the COO over the entire company's marketing effort, including being Oliver's boss.

Lou had had enough of dealing with Oliver all the time. He sought a buffer for part of his working relationship with the prickly former GA. At the beginning of 2003, Lou decided that he wanted the inside marketing functions reporting directly to him. He already had Tom Wells among his direct reports. Now, he pulled Andy Greene out from under Oliver and put him directly under him as well.

Then, Lou Pershing went back in and pulled Ian Evans out from under Oliver as well. The result: Oliver had gotten the promotion to Senior Vice President, but had no more dominion and control in the company than he had before.

The Advanced Sales Forum continued to be a hallmark project for the new SDF; except the name of the meeting had become the Institute for Advanced Marketing (IAM), and it now involved A2I in the planning of the agenda. The lead Marketing Counsel was supposed to host the meeting; that had always been Andy's plan. But Andy began to notice some limitations on the part of Roger Carter. In company meetings, and in musical rehearsals, Roger would show a tendency to try and think in several different directions at the same time, confusing anyone he was trying to communicate with. In music, Roger would sit for hours at his Motif 8 electric keyboard and compose some beautiful melodies and chord progressions. In collaboration, Andy would concentrate on lyrics. But it became frustrating when it seemed Roger could never end a song. He wasn't much better at starting a song either. He was great at the middle, but could not keep organized enough to see a composition through from beginning to end.

Andy used to borrow from some of the great songwriters the rule, "It's most important how a song begins and how it ends." And this was the first sign of some friction between the two.

Andy got Roger to attend one of the National Guitar Workshop sessions in Connecticut in the summer of 2003, and the same erratic nature was noticed there as well.

In company meetings, Roger would stray away from the topic at hand, sometimes almost mumbling to himself. He earned the nickname, "Beautiful Mind," after the Russell Crowe character in the movie by the same name. Roger was a genius academically, had earned an LL.M. in tax law. But he seemed to think in 16 directions at the same time, and it affected his ability to stay on message.

Roger learned to master PowerPoint, the Microsoft Office application that was being used by business presenters everywhere by this time. But his slide shows dwelled on animations and all sorts of visual diversions that, while entertaining, detracted from the value of his message.

So, Andy decided that putting Roger out there on his own as host of the IAM was not a good move, and he took the host role for himself, much as he had done with Susan Blanque before.

The 2001 IAM was held in New Orleans, September 10-12. On Tuesday morning, the 11th, a general session speaker – an expert in estate planning – was speaking to the entire set of 110 attendees. Andy and some of the rest of the home office were sitting in the back. At around 9am, Barb Harmon came into the room and whispered in Andy's ears, "I just heard from my husband back in Virginia. He says a plane has crashed into the World Trade Center."

Andy looked up at Barb, in disbelief. "This had to be a scam, or an accident," he thought, but said nothing. Instead, he got up and left the ballroom to go up to his room and put on the television, tuned to ***The Today Show*** on NBC, just in time to see the second plane go into the other tower of World Trade.

Suddenly, he realized that in moments, everyone would be confronted with what was happening. He went back down to the ballroom and slowly made his way to the front, apologizing for interrupting the speaker. "I have some news for everyone here. It appears that two planes have crashed in each of the Twin Towers in New York. They think it may be a terrorist attack. All air travel is being grounded for now. I tell you this before you find out on your own." Then, looking at the speaker, "I think that continuing on with this presentation is the only thing we can do until we know more." And surrealistically, the presentation went on.

Andy exited the ballroom at that point, asking others not to, to go on with the session. Many of the attendees needed to earn continuing education credits for their licenses, and being in attendance at the sessions was required for credit. Andy saw in the lobby that monitors were being set up so people could follow events while they worked or went about business. Andy stopped to check on updates, just in time to hear reports of a plane crashing into the Pentagon.

Many who remember September 11, 2001, go immediately to recounting what happened in New York. Only a Washingtonian would immediately have the recollection of what happened in D.C. that day. Andy's son, Bob, a high schooler at this point at Langley H.S., was in full lock down, due to its grounds being adjacent to CIA headquarters. No one could communicate with their children at the school. Clearly, Sallie was in full panic mode. But when Andy tried calling home, he could not get a connection – land line or cell.

Then, news of a fourth plane crashing in Pennsylvania came through. Speculation immediately set in that this plane was headed for D.C., the Capitol or White House probably. So everyone Andy spoke to were still waiting to see if any more planes were out there, ready to strike another target in D.C. or Virginia. Meanwhile, after the general session ended, Andy had monitors brought into the ballroom so folks could follow events, and they all watched the two buildings come down.

As panic changed to depression and anger, later in the day, and Andy watched as Building 7 WTC also fell late that afternoon, he was reminded by Marie Frame that two people from Alger Funds were due to participate in the IAM. Alger was one of the fund families in the variable products at AAFG. David Alger was due to put on a general session talk by webcast from his home the next morning. Mike Boccardi was the wholesaler working with the company and was supposed to fly down to join the meeting that day. But David, although semi-retired at the time and rarely going into the office on the 92nd floor of the north tower of WTC, decided to go in to pick up some paperwork that morning and was a casualty of the first plane. Mike Bocchardi was also there, as he stopped off on the way to the airport to pick up some sales literature for the meeting. Neither one was ordinarily due to be in the office; both were, unfortunately.

The meeting, it was decided, would continue nonetheless. After all, the attendees needed their CE credits and had paid to be there. It was no use trying to go home as there were no flights anywhere, the airport was closed. Rental cars had all but disappeared from people all over New Orleans trying to get home. That evening, the IAM hosted a dinner speaker who had a comical look at the investments business as his after-dinner presentation. It seemed senseless to put him on, but Andy decided to go ahead anyway, and the comedy actually brought some temporary relief and diversion to the audience, who showed its appreciation with a standing ovation for the speaker.

By Wednesday, all attempts to continue the meeting collapsed. The IAM had lost its general session webcast speaker in David Alger the day before. And the meeting was due to end mid-day. Now, people could not make arrangements to get home. Everyone was stranded at the hotel. The hotel made a gracious offer to allow people to stay on for extra days at cost - $69 a night, until they could make arrangements to get home. All pretense at making a profit from this disaster went out the window. The organization hired to handle CE credits at the meeting put in for full credit for the attendees even without the last presentation.

By Thursday, people were becoming desperate to get home and be with family. Here, Roger Carter swung into action. As he was a veteran, he pulled some strings and got hold of two cars to rent for the ride back to D.C. Another vehicle, a mini-bus, was hired to take the Omaha home office back to Nebraska. Andy drove one vehicle, with Barb Harmon and a couple of people from the broker-dealer; Roger was in the other car, with people from the Society of Financial Planning Professionals (SFSP), the monitors for CE for the meeting. And they drove all day and all night back to Virginia to meet up with family. All at home were O.K., but it was a few more days before everything began to return to normal…

Well, nothing actually ever really returned to normal after that day. The first thing anyone who travelled by plane noticed was that the days of easy-on, easy-off travel by air were over. Security at airports became so onerous that one had to plan to arrive at the airport at least two hours before departure time or making the flight would be jeopardized. What you could carry onto a plane was also limited; Andy lost at least one Swiss Army knife that used to be on his key chain. And forget about that travel size Listerine that he used to have in his carry-on bag. This also meant that baggage claim was now the order of the day. Whereas the savvy traveler used to manage to go with carry-on only, this was made less possible now. And the wait at baggage claim after arrival could be hours at times. So, the pace of marketing in the field slowed considerably while everyone learned to adapt.

The years between the departure of Billy Carl in 2001 and AAFG's next corporate reorganization some years later went by without much fanfare. Lou Pershing took a step back from hands-on supervision of marketing and in 2004 Ed Daniels, who had been head of the company's group division, took over that spot and the fourth spot in the Executive Office that Billy had vacated. Andy reported to Ed, and the two had a cordial but not especially close working relationship.

The Sales Development Force built a reputation for working well with the field, diligently helping on any live case an agent brought its way. Andy continued to travel the country, wholesaling the company's strategic vision to the field.

In late 2004, a major revision of the computer illustration system was due. Being able to create sales proposals illustrating hypothetical performance of insurance policies had long become a mainstay of the sales process by producers to their clients. With a new wave of UL products, one new VUL to replace Investor 2000, and applications of the products to sales concepts, all coming out at the same time, it was important to release a new illustration system to the field promptly.

Andy came up with an idea, and worked it through Barb Harmon to speed up the release. Andy felt that the programmers responsible for the release moved too slowly. He wanted it speeded up. Andy wanted to prove that the SDF could deliver a quick-to-market illustration system. So, he went to Eric Wang and his people and offered a performance bonus if they could deliver a system ready to release to the field by January 2005. This was the first time this unit had been offered such a project bonus. A fund of $5,000 was set up in Barb's Sales Support budget to pay out to this group if they met deadlines. And members of SDF, including Barb, would test the system to make sure it was usable in the field. Andy even enlisted one person from actuarial to make sure the numbers calculated correctly.

Eric's group worked nights and weekends to make the deadline and qualify for the bonuses. The system was delivered just after Christmas 2004, and testing began.

There is a difference between Alpha testing and Beta testing. Alpha testing a system like this is to have home office employees replicate a "model office," and test as they think the system will be used in the field. Beta testing is more complicated, more expensive, and takes longer. With Beta testing, you find a few field offices you can trust and give them an advance copy of the software to test and see if they can find any "bugs" in the system. Beta testing is more comprehensive and reality based than Alpha testing. But because it takes longer, there was no time for that. They Alpha tested. The system was released just after the Martin Luther King Holiday weekend.

It doesn't take much to imagine that there were bugs in the release found in the ensuing two months, after it was given to the entire field force. The Alpha testing did not reveal the bugs. Meanwhile, the bonuses had been paid at the end of January, Andy feeling that payment should happen as close in time to completion of the work – Management Principle 101. Since the field had dealt with faulty releases in the past, most of the incident passed with little notice. But any quick-to-market result was lost in the redo that had to occur to fix the bugs.

As the years went by, the annual Club meetings for top producers began to get less and less exotic. In 2001, Marie had put together another Carribean cruise. In 2002, it was Bermuda. In 2003, Hawaii. Then, the meetings seemed closer to home. The 2004 meeting was in Orlando, Florida. Then, in May 2005, Club was held in a resort in Tucson, Arizona, where astonishingly, it rained almost every day during the meeting.

The rationale the home office gave for the domestic locations varied from tax regulations on international destinations to the higher expense of more exotic places. As to the tax regulations, this was at least partly valid. When a field producer was invited to Club, so was the spouse. The spouse would have to be taxed on the value of his/her attendance at the conference as compensation. And if an international destination, the qualifier him/herself would be taxed as the regulations about educational meetings became ever so tighter.

But as to exotic meeting locations costing more money, the Executive Office was confounded by the fact that, after finding lesser exotic locations, the meetings were still costing the same, all-in. What Perry Brooks and the others did not realize is the basic principle of these meetings: *You're going to spend what you're going to spend to make the meeting special to the qualifier and spouse. The less you spend on the destination, the more you'll spend on the add-ons, the activities, that the company subsidizes for the attendees.*

As Andy would often comment, "If you hold a meeting in Monte Carlo, it is such an exotic location that attendees will be attracted to working to qualify for the meeting such that you can transfer some of the add-ons, like meals, golf outings, sightseeing, onto the attendee, and he/she will willingly take that cost on. When you're taking him/her to Tucson, AZ, you'd better be paying for all the activities or the qualifier will not be impressed and not be incented to go for next year's Club meeting. What you save in travel and accommodations you'll spend while you're there. Pick your poison!"

But the real reason the locations got less ambitious is that the contingent from Omaha, especially Perry Brooks, did not like travelling, with all its restrictions. To the field, however, it got interpreted as the company was not doing well. Marie Frame would comment that "Club qualifiers measure how well the company is doing by how many shrimp are on the buffet at the first night reception."

One night at the Club meeting in Tucson, a dinner was put on at a "roadhouse" outside of town. It was essentially a converted barn turned into a party hall. Here, the company hosted a theme buffet and party – a biker theme, complete with replica Harleys and other vintage motorcycles. Attendees were encouraged to "fancy dress" in their best biker costumes. The home office, anxious to get everyone in the mood of the theme, of course, also dressed for the occasion. Leading the "pack" was Andy Greene, in leather vest, dusty jeans, the riding boots he'd bought years before, and bandana. Along with sunglasses to boot, with a beard he could have been in ZZ Top. He was "Bad, Nationwide."

At the party of almost 200, a relatively new qualifier, one of the few women qualifiers, was in attendance. Eleanor "Ellie" Wehring, was a self-described "Nice Jewish girl from Jersey." She had only the year before joined the company's field force, through A2I. She was a fee-plus-commission financial planner, not an insurance agent. But she knew what products paid the rent, and she had latched onto the Investor 2000 product big time, catapulting her to third highest rep at A2I and on the Leader's Club list, which by that time had an insurance sales minimum to qualify for Club, regardless of securities production.

Ellie was reasonably attractive for a middle-aged woman, slightly overweight, but not too much. Her looks were suitable for her profession and background. But her personality was huge. She had a gregarious approach, sort of New York style (so the Nebraska crowd thought), and she spoke her mind. Like her feminist politics, she minced no words; you knew exactly where you stood with Ellie.

Her target market was working with young families trying to fund for a child's college education. She knew all the angles to funding for college, all the programs available. And she knew how a well-placed VUL policy, if funded right, could play a critical role as a self-completing instrument to amass a large amount of capital, if one had 12-18 years to plan.

But when Ellie came to Leaders Club in Tucson, "against my better judgment" she would say, she felt enormously out of place. The attendees and the home office seemed very "Midwestern," culturally "white bread and mayonnaise." She appreciated Melanie White's position with the broker-dealer, and tried to "pal-up" to her, but to Ellie, it looked a little like Melanie had been positioned as the "token."

One has to appreciate the Jewish upbringing in New York, post-Holocaust. Ellie, Andy, and other New Yorkers among the Jewish community had been educated that they were not "white." When asked for ethnic or racial identification on applications or census information, it was common to answer "Other," rather than Caucasian. More than any other ethnic group in America, other than Blacks, Jews understood discrimination and persecution. The whites who came down from New York and other northern cities to be "Freedom Riders," helping newly enfranchised Blacks to register and vote, a disproportionate number of them were Jewish. The alliance in Civil Rights between Blacks and Jews came off the track after 1968, but historically both groups treated the mainstream "real Americans" with a degree of suspicion. Having lived all her life in the New York area, Ellie Wehring bristled at the "Leave It to Beaver" mentality she observed in many of the execs at AAFG.

So she latched onto the few minorities she found among the home office. And that included Andy Greene. Ellie was single, and so she attended the conference alone. Andy almost always went stag. At times, when he needed a companion, Marie Frame filled the bill. Andy lived culturally in that void between New York and the South, having worked so hard to be accepted by Virginia as one of their own.

During the party, Ellie looked a little lost. She had been talking with a few people, but felt out of place. At one point, a party activity included being photographed on a Harley-Davidson motorbike, as if one were truly a biker. Andy saw Ellie standing on line for one of these photographs; there was simply nothing much else to do. He went over to her and invited her to be photographed with him on the bike, as a lark. She had dressed for the occasion, and the photo taken with her behind him on the bike, as if she were his "biker chick," complete with her arms wrapped around Andy's waste, came out well. The picture, Andy got her one print and kept the other, wound up on Andy's credenza behind his desk at the office, a reminder to Oliver and anyone else who might question Andy's *bona fides* among the field force.

This was just a gesture of a home office exec trying to make a first-time qualifier feel at home. And Ellie appreciated the attention. For years afterwards, she would seek out Andy's advice on live cases. Andy visited her office in New Jersey a couple of times when coming through the area. All of this was part of the "service" a home office person was supposed to offer.

The fact that the field force was not only becoming more ethnically diverse, but gender neutral, meant that these situations would arise more often in the later years Andy was in the business than in the early years. The makeup of the field force was changing, and the attitudes of people in it had to change as well. And no one, including the "Gang of Four," thought anything of the gesture than an innocent attempt to pay attention to a valued field producer. In fact, the Midwesterners found dealing with the likes of Ellie Wehring to be a little out of their comfort zone as well. They were more than happy to allow Andy to focus attention on the "minorities" in the room.

At the IAM in D.C. that Fall, Ellie attended. This being local for the Greene's, Sallie got to attend the Tuesday night dinner that was always a part of the agenda for the Conference. On this occasion, Ellie made sure she got to sit with her Jewish "boychick" from New York, which meant sitting with Sallie as well. At one point, it was Andy's turn to "work the room," moving among the tables to make sure he said "hello" to everyone and checking to see that everyone was having a good time. Then, it was time for Andy and Roger to "*mach show*," play a little for the audience, and they had a blues tune called "Marketing Man," a parody of Muddy Waters' *Hoochie Coochie Man*.

During this period of absence, Ellie struck up a conversation with Sallie. "Your husband has been a great help to me in my practice."

"That's good to hear. He wants everyone to have success with the company."

"Yeah." Then Ellie paused, before commenting, "You'd better hold onto that man, or I might try and steal him away from you."

Sallie was taken aback by this comment, not knowing how to respond. So, she tried to put it out of her head.

Then, some months later, she came to Andy's office to meet him for lunch. And she saw the biker picture on his credenza. While saying nothing at the time, she unloaded on Andy later that evening at home, accusing him of having an affair with Ellie Wehring. This was the kind of thing that was beginning to afflict many marketing people who work with distributors: the increasing number of women in sales and marketing meant greater numbers of situations for on-the-job romance. And even if it were not so, the appearance of impropriety in the eyes of the spouse made it feel to Andy as if "I might as well have slept with the woman," for all the credit he was getting for "keeping it zipped up."

Sure, the attention of an attractive woman, whether it was Ellie Wehring or Karen Bruckner years before, was like catnip to Andy. Fact was, he was both too afraid of the consequences and too loyal to his children to let these flirtations ever develop into something more. But in his darkest and most private moments, he could not deny that the attention was gratifying, middle-class morality notwithstanding.

Chapter 13: Merger, Part II

In September 2005, word came down that American Atlantic was in negotiations with Valley Union Mutual Life of Columbus, Ohio, for a merger at the end of the year. In 2004, American Atlantic had performed a legal fiction by creating a "mutual holding company," in which technically the majority of the company was still owned by the policyholders through an umbrella holding company, but the life and other subsidiaries would have the freedom of going into the capital markets like a stock company. By keeping the company technically mutual, there would be no need to distribute policyholder equity (policy cash values) as part of an outright "demutualization."

The process of demutualization and the subsequent reformation as a stock company was, by this time, seen as a common precursor to an acquisition by another stock company. Sometimes, the "suitor," looking to acquire such a company would actually "sponsor" the demutualization – put up some of the capital to effect the change.

Those companies looking to stay mutual – they believed in the mutual form of business – suffered two-fold:

1. First, in the 1990s, Congress had legislated out of existence a rather esoteric tax advantage that mutuals historically had over their stock competitors; and
2. Mutual companies had no way of raising equity capital in the open market because their very nature meant they could not become publicly traded.

So, the mutual holding company was a hybrid corporate form that would become popular as the industry went into the new millennium.

In this merger deal, a new mutual holding company, known as Universal American (UA) Mutual would be formed, to hold the assets of three individual life carriers – Banker's American, Atlantic, and now Valley Union – and all their subsidiaries (broker-dealer, mutual fund family, and bank).

Valley Union had been a fierce competitor to both Banker's and Atlantic throughout the 1980s and 1990s. Its claim to fame was price competitive universal life and disability products, individually underwritten. Valley Union had a strong general agency (GA) distribution channel, with over 500 career GAs around the country, each operating their own P&Ls, and almost half of them successful enough to achieve the company's Leader's Club in 2005. Many of the GAs were multiple partner shops, with anywhere from 2-12 associate agent-advisors under each. The GAs considered themselves to be in the financial planning business, and called themselves financial advisors. But few of them charged fees for financial advice. Instead, revenue was derived from portfolio management fees and trail commissions on variable insurance and mutual fund sales, called 12b-1 fees (named after the SEC regulation that authorized them). The distribution channel had been headed by Wade Herrity for over 10 years and he had earned a lot of loyalty from the top GAs in the Valley Union system.

Many of Valley Union's producers avoided the trap of getting too deep into the investments side of the house, always making sure the insurance sale was part of every portfolio. Many also were deeply committed to the advanced markets – estate planning and business insurance. And the advanced underwriting unit at Valley Union was headed by well-known expert Peter Burns, JD, CLU, a member of AALU (Association for Advanced Life Underwriting) and LIMRAs Advanced Sales Committee.

The next level up from Peter was Mark Avalon, more a chief administrative officer than a marketing person. Avalon inherited the "inside" marketing position as an afterthought by COO Jacob "Jake" Rothman and CEO Gary Spencer. Avalon also headed up the underwriting and customer service areas. Jake and Gary were both ex-agents; Jake had been a GA at a large Eastern Mutual and was recruited away for the promise of eventually running an entire company. Gary had been a pension sales expert in the field in a former life.

Valley Union was an aggressive marketer, long on pulling sales into the company, at least individually underwritten insurance. Its broker-dealer was weak compared to A2I; it had no bank or mutual funds of its own, as AAFG did. But most of all, Valley Union had run into profitability problems. In its aggressive approach to product development and new sales, it had losses on the investment of the new revenue. The losses had been attributed mainly to some aggressive investments and to expenses in field distribution well in excess of budget and product pricing. Acquisition costs of new business were running at $1.45 against a margin in its life insurance products that assumed $1.10. And only because it had a large enough field force could Valley Union mask the losses by spreading them across a large flow of revenues.

Clearly, Valley Union, a mutual holding company itself, needed a merger partner, and AAFG – with its very solid portfolio at Banker's American – seemed a good fit. In fact, it would be fair to say that the Valley Union management saw AAFG as little more than a bank, a place to access a large portfolio of assets to fuel its future growth. It is also fair to say that Valley Union would have tried to acquire AAFG if the legalities of the mutual holding company form of doing business weren't in the way.

On the AAFG side of the equation was a management team that saw a way back into large amounts of individual life insurance sales, with access to the disability income (DI) insurance market to boot. Rather than try and grow its distribution organically, through developing and recruiting field relationships over the long term, this was a quick fix to a hole in AAFG's business plan. AAFG saw a Valley Union that was good at the top line of the income statement but needing the expense discipline that only the folks in Omaha could offer.

But first, a few obstacles had to be eliminated. At the beginning of 2006, Tab Davenport was paid in excess of $5 million cash plus other incentives to retire early. A similar arrangement was given to Lou Pershing. There wasn't much convincing needed for these two to take the deal; the future of their respective positions was somewhat murky post-merger and the chance to walk away with a huge bag of money was appealing. Ed Daniels, who had taken over the CMO slot at AAFG was also given an "offer he could not refuse," and retired early.

Perry Brooks was diagnosed with lung cancer in the Spring of 2006 and had planned in any event to retire at the end of June that year. Perry made it to retirement, just barely. Three weeks after leaving, he succumbed to the cancer, having given up tobacco kicking and screaming only in the last few months of life.

Before Tab Davenport retired, he offered to the Board Janeesh Rau as candidate to become President of Atlantic, one of the three constituent insurers in the new company. While there was an umbrella organization through which all three companies operated, each one still needed a "President" for state insurance regulation purposes. The position was largely ceremonial, involving signing off on legal paperwork and financial statements. This made the position a perfect fit for Rau. The way Tab announced the move was to call Oliver Winters, Ian Evans, and Andy Greene into his office to tell them.

"I want you all to know that Janeesh is taking over as President of Atlantic. Of course, he will have no direct authority over any of you. You will be reporting to the new head of the Individual Insurance Division. But I wanted to make sure you were not surprised with this announcement."

Oliver went white. "Well, Tab, I can't say as I'm happy with this move." Oliver had thought that he, not an empty suit like Rau, should be named President of Atlantic.

Ian and Andy looked at each other in disbelief. Tab saw the looks on all three faces. "Look guys," he defended, "Rau has got relationships on the Board that make him the perfect candidate. That's why he's being installed in this position. And I want you to promise me you'll give him your full cooperation, since the four of you are all that is left of the management team here in D.C."

"Of course, Tab," was all Andy could say, weakly at that. He never seriously thought he would have been considered for the job. And he didn't really want it had it been offered.

The last comment Tab made to Andy as they all left Tab's office, pulling Andy aside, whispering, was, "I'm glad to know that you'll have a 'box' in the new company." A "box" meant there was a space for the employee in the new org chart; as opposed to a "package," which meant you were being given a bag of money, your position terminated.

Ian felt pretty much the same way as Andy about the Presidency of Atlantic. He wanted to be on the front lines, doing the mission critical jobs that would grow the company. A ceremonial post – like President of one of those European countries that used to have a king but now is Parliamentary, a Prime Minister having the real power – would have made Ian or Andy a joke in the eyes of the field guys who depended upon them for support.

The real problem with Rau as President was watching someone who they felt had contributed nothing to the cause rise to a position that would guarantee him a wealthy retirement down the road; someone whose entire contribution to the company had been failure to supervise his own actuarial staff; spending his time as a "kiss-up" to the Board.

A month later, it was announced that Oliver Winters' position with the new company was being eliminated and Oliver was offered an enhanced retirement, one that was being given to anyone at the Senior Vice President level: two years salary guaranteed, plus a one year extra employer contribution to the terminated executive's 401(k) and a Social Security "float" (monthly benefit) to cover the executive until he reached normal retirement age. Oliver didn't need the last piece; he was about to turn 66 that spring. But it did help Howard Crowe, whose position as head of marketing operations was also eliminated

This again irked Andy and Ian. As regular VPs, elimination of their jobs would generate only a 6-month severance, no extras. And their jobs were not being eliminated anyway. They would be needed in the new organization. For those being asked to stay on, a merger bonus was being offered, to be paid after the end of 2006, to reward those who saw the merger through to complete integration of the three constituent companies. This would be in addition to the short and long term bonus formulas that applied to managers at their level. It was conceivable that they would participate in three bonus pools, if all went well that year. But none of it was guaranteed; it all depended upon merger integration goals over which each had only tangential control.

The new Universal American (UA) was organized officially as the integration of three separate insurance companies and would continue to carry their own product lines and their own in-force blocks of business. However, they would be run by a separate matrix of responsibilities on a day-to-day basis, without regard to company brand on the product. A group division was set up using the Banker's American brand. A2I absorbed the weaker broker-dealer at Valley Union and continued as its own brand. Chesapeake continued its mutual funds, and continued to be based in suburban Bethesda, MD, outside D.C. The Bank continued on for awhile but was eventually sold. Retirement plan products were organized as its own division, based in Omaha. This left the Individual Division – the place for individually underwritten life insurance, annuities, and disability insurance products – offered to the marketplace through a new GA distribution system that eliminated the PPGA and career managerial systems that had been at AAFG.

This Individual Division would be headed by COO Jake Rothman and its CMO and chief administrative officer would be Mark Avalon. Thus, the Individual Division would be based primarily in Columbus, although no one was being forced to relocate from D.C. or Omaha. The D.C. office building that had been the home of Atlantic Mutual was sold, however, in a deal that gave the Atlantic policyholders a one-time enhancement to their respective policy dividends, and thus gave Jeneesh Rau a reason to take credit for having engineered the real estate sale. What was left of the D.C. operation was moved to Bethesda to share space with Chesapeake. What was left was half of A2I, some of the Law Department headed by Snake Samuelson, the HR Department headed by Paula Banks, and about half of the Sales Development Force under Andy Greene.

Andy would inherit some of the other home office's marketing support people in a move that would double the size of the SDF and bring in people like Peter Burns in advanced underwriting. Andy would also get a marketing communications area that was far larger than what Marie Frame and Terry Cochrane were saying "grace" over prior to the merger. In Columbus, there was a mirror image marketing communications department headed by Sheila Grant, a long-time Valley Union employee.

Andy now had the problem of two leaders in Advanced Underwriting and three in Marketing Communications. In Advanced Underwriting, his choice between Burns and his friend and musical collaborator Roger Carter would be difficult. Andy did not warm to Peter Burns from the start – Peter came off pompous and distant to Andy and the staffs in Omaha and Bethesda. Peter had been doing advanced underwriting in the insurance business for longer than anyone could remember, always at Valley Union. He had the loyalty of a cadre of advanced producers in their field force. Peter Burns, at age 62, was going nowhere, and he considered himself a "finished product," not needing any mentoring or coaching from the likes of Andy Greene from Atlantic Mutual, a company which, Burns would be quoted as saying, "Was so close to bankruptcy that they needed us to bail them out in this merger." The home office execs, including Andy's new boss – Mark Avalon – left the decision of who to put in charge with Andy. But Mark made it clear, "You'll have a hard time convincing me and the field that Peter Burns should not by 'the guy.'"

The AAFG part of the field force, maybe a third of the combined distributors with the new company, were fine with Roger Carter as their Marketing Counsel. But the "Beautiful Mind" nickname attached permanently to Roger. Roger had a hard time staying organized enough to be effective as a spokesperson for the advanced sales effort at UA. In April 2006, Andy called Roger into his office in Bethesda to advise him of what was going to happen.

"Roger, I've had a hard time coming to this decision, but we're making Peter Burns the new head of advanced sales. You will be reporting to Peter going forward."

"I really think I should have had more consideration for the job than this."

"I have been watching you, my friend. You know we work well together. But you know I've had concerns with your follow through on assignments sometimes and your ability to communicate with the field effectively."

"I am really going to have a hard time with this." What Andy would come to learn months later was that Roger had already seen the handwriting on the wall. He had been working on leaving for a position at another company, and his notice came to Andy by email toward the end of 2006.

In Marketing Communications, Marie Frame was given the opportunity to stay with the new firm or take an enhanced severance benefit. Marie was 60 by this time. She had been with Atlantic since 1982. She was tired, and had recently come into an inheritance from her family. She didn't need to work anymore. The idea of "cashing out" for an enhanced benefit sounded good. Andy was very loyal to Marie, and she to him. But Marie made it plain. "Andy, please don't put me in the leadership position. I would like my position eliminated so I can take the enhanced severance and do something else with my life at this point."

"I hate the idea of you leaving. I have always been able to count on you."

"I'm still your friend. But I've had enough. I want out. This is my chance."

And Andy obliged her. This left him with Terry Cochrane or Sheila Grant. While Andy had a good relationship with Terry, a fellow musician, Andy calculated that the larger marketing communications apparatus was and would be in Columbus. Andy calculated that the decision between the two would be a "push," but that he would win points with the new executive team – Mark and Jake – if he chose a Valley Union alum. Terry would not leave Omaha – he had a wife and three kids there; he had lived there his whole life; there were no other substantial competitors anymore in the area. Andy felt sure that Terry would stay with the new firm, even if he were not tapped for the top slot. Even his former boss, Tom Wells, felt sure Terry would stay on and Andy could have both talents on the roster. So, he went with Sheila, to her delight and to Terry's subsequent resignation for a position with another company in Florida. Sometimes playing the odds does not work…

Barb Harmon inherited some "wholesalers" who ministered to the field by phone and live meeting. This raised her responsibilities beyond anything anyone imagined she would ever come to manage, given her lack of credentials and sales experience. Andy saw fit to have Barb promoted to an elected officer position, commensurate with her new responsibilities, and so she became "Second VP of Sales Support" in UAs new Individual Division.

Outside of the SDF, the elimination of PPGA left Ian Evans reporting to Wade Herrity as a regional VP in the GA system. They never got along. Wade sometimes treated Ian as little more than an administrative assistant. By the middle of 2006, Ian had resigned and moved onto another company. Ironically, his new company then merged and abandoned PPGA within a year of his arrival and he was again out of a job. At this point, Ian simply semi-retired, and went into independent distribution consulting, euphemism for unemployed.

Product development was another matter. At AFG and at AAFG, product development had always been a collaborative function, by committee, with marketing (Andy) and actuarial (now Roman Clay) the focal points.

Jake Rothman had come from one of the big "Eastern Mutuals," and he envisioned a product development infrastructure similar to what he experienced there. In the largest companies, product lines were managed by separate product managers, reporting directly to the COO. These product managers vied with each other for a piece of the finite resources available for new product development.

But Jake Rothman was not going to force the issue alone. In the merger integration plan, a series of cross-company committees were set up to deal tactically with the specifics of merger implementation, including the configuration of the new Individual Division. Senior management promised a hands-off approach, not wanting to poison the process or predetermine the best outcomes.

Jake sought at least a modicum of buy-in by consensus by having these committees slowly come to agree on the plan Jake had in mind all along. Seven such committees were constructed, covering all manner of merger integration. Three of them touched specifically on the Individual Division, the largest division of them all, by personnel and sales.

One committee dealt with all distribution channel issues, such as elimination of PPGA and the career financial centers inherited from Atlantic.

One committee dealt with marketing support, Andy's area, and paved the way for the decisions Andy would subsequently make as to personnel. Andy got his way on everything in that committee, save for the Law Department refusing to accept the title "Marketing Counsel" for advanced underwriting attorneys. Since Peter Burns didn't want the title anyway, Andy relented on this issue.

Another committee was the Product Development Committee, and its responsibility was to develop an organization in the division for this function. The Committee had five members on it, representing five people most intimately involved in product development in the former pre-merger companies. There was Roman Clay, the actuary from Omaha, and Tom Wells, the strategic marketing guy, also from Omaha. Andy represented Bethesda. Representing Columbus were Crystal Porcher, an actuary, and David Houser, a marketing manager with expertise in disability income (DI) insurance products both at Valley Union and prior competitors.

Crystal was a self-styled protégé of Jake Rothman, and hoped to follow in his footsteps as he advanced in his career. David managed a unit doing sales support for the DI product line at Valley Union.

As this Product Development Committee began to meet, with Crystal as Chairperson, it became clear that there was a division among the members as to whether the function should be centralized, as it was at AAFG or go into product manager silos, *a la* the big Eastern Mutuals. The split was largely but not entirely along company lines. Andy and Tom favored the centralized approached. They argued that the new UA was not large enough to de-centralize and compete for resources. To gain efficiencies, unless and until UA became large enough to be one of the "Eastern Mutuals," better it consolidate resources. "Act like a big company when you **are** one, not before," was the argument Tom gave at one early meeting.

Crystal and Roman favored the product manager approach. Crystal, outgoing and forceful for an actuary – who saw her abilities as including marketing knowledge – also saw herself as being able to develop product more independently of marketing oversight in this product manager model, as she would be the odds on choice to head up the life product line. Roman was more interested in annuity products. He had experience from prior companies there. And he also saw himself able to act more independently as the product manager for the annuity line; no one else could claim anything near his knowledge of that product.

This left David Houser, who watched the debate go on without much opinion one way or the other. He had come to distrust "Crystal the pistol," as he privately nicknamed her.

Andy and Tom saw some simpatico with David, a fellow marketing guy. Andy in particular found out early on that David was an amateur drummer, had played in rock bands when he was younger. David, now 52, kept a full drum kit in his finished basement at home. When Andy learned of this, he offered to bring his guitar and some of his gear out to Columbus next time there and they could jam. David went further than that. He knew a fellow guitarist, a retirement plans wholesaler in the Columbus home office, Luis Dominguez, and arranged to invite Andy and Luis to a cookout dinner and jam session at David's home outside Columbus. Then, Andy went even further. He got Roger Carter (still with the company) to come out with him to Columbus and join the group jam on keyboards. Andy went so far as to rent an SUV, pack his own Yamaha P-60 stage piano with his guitar gear, and he and Roger drove all the way from Virginia to Columbus, 8 hours, so that the group would have everything they needed. By day, the Bethesda group simply did their work in the Columbus office. Then they jammed the night away. Andy could tell that the evening was a success just by how late everyone stayed.

Not that it was on Andy's agenda to specifically influence David, but during the dinner, David commented, "You know, I like your thinking on the product development program. We're too small to be pitting product managers against each other for limited resources." Andy smiled, but said nothing, convinced that David was about to side with he and Tom.

To Andy, this was all just part of managing the cultural integration of this merger, just as he and Tom had done between Atlantic and Banker's years before.

But the fix was already in. Crystal, afraid that the Committee was deadlocked on the product manager model she was proposing, went separately to Jake Rothman to seek something to offer David Hauser to tip the balance she (and Jake's) way. In legal parlance, this was an *ex parte* communication, perfectly unethical when the new head of the Individual Division had promised no interference in the committee process. Jake assured Crystal that she could offer David the DI manager position if he went their way.

And Crystal communicated the offer to David, causing him to "reluctantly" decide that the product manager format was best, and threw in with Crystal and Roman. To make matters worse, David did not communicate his reversal of opinion to either Tom or Andy privately, but made his decision known to the Committee in formal meeting. Andy and Tom were totally shocked. Roman was surprised but pleased. Crystal looked like the "cat that ate the canary."

"I'm really surprised David," Andy started. "But if that's what you feel; well, my position stands."

Crystal answered, "Understood, but we're now in majority on this. We're going to propose the product manager model to senior management."

Andy had a personal stake in the decision as well. He knew that the product manager model would mean he would have less influence in product development decisions in the future. And as David had been a wholesaler of the DI line in the past, it was assumed he would take the wholesaling function with him into the product manager slot and away from Barb Harmon's Sales Support Unit, where she was overseeing wholesaling on life and annuity products (mainly because actuaries wanted nothing to do with wholesaling in the field).

"Look, man," Roman chimed in, "You have enough on your plate without continuing to try and drive product development." He was referring to Andy's new expanded Sales Development Force.

"Yeah," Crystal added, "You've got – what – 40+ positions in your department now? What did you have before…12? And you've got triple the marketing budget you had in your old company. That's plenty to keep you busy."

"I appreciate your concern for me, folks. But this is not about me."

Then, Tom chipped in, "I'd like to propose that Andy and I be allowed to post a 'minority' opinion to the recommendation, so Jake has the benefit of what the other side's argument was."

"Agreed." And Crystal quickly concluded the meeting.

And Tom drafted, with Andy's editing, their best counter-arguments, a 3-page tome designed to document what their point of view was. They both believed that Jake would soon come to regret this new inefficient model. The piece was delivered by email attachment to Crystal, so that she could attach it in turn to her "majority report."

In a later meeting with Jake, Andy learned that no such "minority report" was ever attached to the Committee's recommendation; that it was implied that all members agreed to this product manager approach. Indeed, Andy was upset. Meanwhile, the product managers – Crystal on life; Roman on annuities; David on DI – were introduced to the home office and Sheila put an announcement out to the field on the new structure. The deal was done. Andy never confronted Crystal about it, but he never forgot. And Crystal never stopped looking over her shoulder to see if Andy would do something to get even; or, more than even.

The Sales Development Force (SDF) continued moving forward, 40 positions strong, 19 of them in marketing communications; 7 in advanced sales; 12 in sales support; and Andy (with an assistant in Bethesda) leading the charge. Field Training, long reduced to "Little T" training in product and sales ideas, became part of the sales support unit. David Hauser did in fact take the wholesaling of DI with him into his product manager role.

Peter Burns was charged with taking over the IAM (Institute for Advanced Marketing), and a meeting site for the January 2007 conference was chosen by Andy at The Sanctuary on Kiawah Island,

SC. Andy drove the site selection himself, put on to the beauty of Kiawah by his long-time friend and colleague, Marie Frame, who owned property there. Always showing his acquired southern roots, Andy liked the idea of negotiating an off-season rate for a meeting in a mild winter climate. The Sanctuary had just gone through an ownership change and major renovation; restored to its antebellum resort glory. The owners were hungry to draw corporate meeting traffic there, and sacrificed price to fill space in the off season. Off season on an Atlantic island south of Charleston is not off season up north. Andy knew the weather there in late January would be in the 50s during the day. With any luck and no rain, golf after the CE sessions would be possible. And his luck held out; so good in fact that the sunshine and 65 degree temperature at the end of the sessions on the second day resulted in many of the attendees taking a walk on the beach, as if it were summer.

It was the very location that the Midwesterners in Columbus and Omaha knew nothing about. And it embarrassed the travel department in Columbus that had assumed it would drive all site locations for company meetings post-merger. The travel department, led by Sasha Buckley, had done all the meetings for Valley Union. Buckley was a favorite of senior management there. The merger had not specified her role, but Rothman and Spencer continued to use her to plan all company meetings, and Herrity had her plan out the annual Leader's Club incentive meeting.

Embarrassment became humiliation when the bills came in from the IAM, showing that the entire meeting spent less than $50,000 all-in, mostly for the CE filings in the states done by the SFSP – the outside industry consultant used by Andy for years. The field producers were more than willing to absorb the hotel room rate of $179, well below "rack rate," to receive 18 CE credits toward license renewal, and have a three day holiday in a 5-star resort to boot. Over the years of watching Marie negotiate, Andy learned a few tricks of the trade.

Then, late in the year Andy began to look at sites for the 2008 meeting. At this point Sasha stepped in, claimed that Jake had declared all corporate meetings go through her, and threatened, "If you want to do this on your own, I'll have to take this up with Jake and Gary."

Andy did not challenge her, not wanting to make this a bellweather territorial issue for top management. He knew that Wade Herrity as well was not pleased with what he saw as Andy upstaging the Leader's Club meeting by choosing top flight locations, albeit domestic, for the IAM.

Wade and the others were comparing apples to oranges. The Leader's Club was an incentive meeting in which the full bill for everything was borne by the home office. Between what the producer paid and the financing by "exhibitors" wanting access to the field producers, Andy was able to bring the IAM in at a small fraction of the cost of any incentive meeting.

Wade, Sasha, Jake, and everyone else who wanted a say in the IAM met privately to scope out what they considered to be acceptable locations for an IAM from which Andy could choose a location. The cities chosen would exclude any that were under consideration for a Leader's Club meeting. Sasha provided intelligence as to which cities would be more expensive, which less, and they excluded all the most expensive cities: New York, D.C., Boston, San Francisco, L.A., etc.

One that was left: Memphis, TN.

No one wanted to do an incentive meeting in Memphis, especially in late spring, when the Leader's Club was usually scheduled. The IAM was always in January, on the theory that producers would pick up new sales ideas to use in the new year. And Memphis had a major airport hub, easily accessible to all GA-attendees. Andy knew that Memphis could work, and set out with Sasha to test that market. Again, the southern markets, outside of south Florida, consider the winter to be off season.

Sasha helped Andy make a deal with the renowned Peabody Hotel, famous for its ducks that go in a pack up the elevator in the morning to the rooftop garden; then back down in the evening. The Peabody was right in the middle of downtown Memphis, which was considered run down in parts; but not Beale Street, one block away, famous for its Blues clubs; not for the old Sun Records studios, down the street, the recording birthplace of rock and roll; and not for Graceland, Elvis Presley's home.

Andy staged a takeover of a local Beale Street blues club complete with live music one night, accomplished simply by coming into the bar without a reservation with about 60 IAM attendees early enough when it was nearly empty and paying a little extra for the band to start up a little early.

The next night was a tour of Graceland, sponsored by one of the mutual fund families represented in the company's VUL and VA products.

During one of the lunch breaks, several of the attendees went with Andy to Lansky's, a men's clothing shop in the Peabody Hotel lobby. The old man, Bernie Lansky, long retired from day-to-day management of the place, was nevertheless in that day and showed the UA crew from the IAM some custom made silk shirts, a picture of him fitting Elvis for his first tuxedo, and claimed – though not proven – that he was the nephew of the infamous Jewish gangster, Meyer Lansky. That evening at the blues club, Andy was seen sporting one of Lansky's famous silk shirts, "Cruising with the

King," complete with an embroidered image of a pink Cadillac on the back.

Again, the meeting was a relationship as well as an educational success. Jake was in attendance for part of the evening festivities each night and he got rousing kudos from the field guys present. Basking in the glow, he could hardly complain that, once again, for pennies on the Leader's Club dollar, the meeting was a highlight (if not THE highlight) of the year.

Andy still continued to input into the product development process. It turns out that getting the job and doing the job are two different things, and Crystal and Roman found that DOING the marketing end of research into what products to develop was a little more complicated than they thought.

It was conventional wisdom to simply convene some leading field producers and use them as a sort of focus group to get field input. The problem was that the field people were only concerned that the commissions be high and the premiums low. When prototypes of products were put in front of them, they had nothing to input unless and until they could play with the product on the illustration system to see how competitive the pricing was and see the "target" premium schedule, the maximum premium contribution at which full commissions would be paid.

In addition, field producers are not necessarily the most forward thinking place to go for market intelligence, proven by a strategy committee convened by Tom Wells to look into developing new products to handle the problem of post-retirement income. The sense Tom was getting from his Strategic Marketing Unit was that the policyholder base – the target market of baby boomers that had comprised the majority of the company's life insurance sales over the past 30 years – was aging. Selling life insurance to 60 year olds would be difficult, especially with the end of the federal "death tax" that Congress had passed.

What these clients were mostly concerned with now was not dying too soon but living too long. Tom's charge was to come up with product ideas for Crystal and Roman that would appeal to this aging policyholder base. But when the field guys came in for input, many of them dismissed the whole process, simply saying, "My clients are not asking for these products now. I'll call you when my clients start asking."

Tom would later be heard to say, "Distribution is a lagging indicator of market trends." Tom knew that field guys live from sale to sale, never looking up to see what's coming "down the pike," so to speak.

Despite all the politics and fighting over territory, Universal American (UA) did well in its first two years as an integrated financial services firm, at least on the revenue side. For 11 consecutive quarters, running from merger at the beginning of 2006 through the summer of 2008, new sales grew at a double digit rate across an aggregate of all three product lines in the Individual Division; this, while the life insurance industry generally was running flat.

There is no doubt that credit for this performance had to be shared between product development, distribution and marketing support. In life insurance, UA developed a rider that could be added as an option to its universal life policy that provided for the insured's withdrawal of portions of the death benefit in the event of terminal or chronic illness. This truly changed the game in life insurance, because it now meant that the death benefit could be used to pay for long term care expenses. A stand-alone LTC policy would only cover long term care. If the client never needed the care – if, for example, death came suddenly without a long illness – the premiums for such a policy were wasted. With a long term care rider on a life insurance policy, premiums were covering either event. It reminded the agent and the client: *Life insurance is the only insurance that is guaranteed to pay off in a claim, eventually.*

Annuities began to sell themselves. Generically, an annuity is the opposite bet between a client and his insurer. Whereas in life insurance the client is betting on dying too soon – the insurer wins when the client outlives life expectancy. In annuities, the client wins by outliving life expectancy and the annuity continues to pay each month, even though the monthly benefit was a function of life expectancy at the time of purchase. Now, variable annuities at UA began offering a guaranteed minimum withdrawal benefit (GMWB), setting a minimum monthly benefit, reset periodically, regardless of subsequent volatility in the stock market. For the first time, a variable insurance product actually had contractual guarantees.

In DI, a rider extending coverage beyond age 65 was implemented. Understanding that clients were still working past age 65, protecting income past then was needed. So an age 67 rider, intended to take the client past his/her qualification for full Social Security retirement benefits, was added to the product.

None of this made UA a first entrant into new target markets. The strategy was for UA to be a "fast follower;" to let others make the initial mistakes in product development, watch what they did, and develop a better version without those design errors.

On the distribution front, the GA roster did grow, though slowly. The conversions of PPGAs and career AMs from AAFG to GA status at UA artificially made the roster look larger. The productivity of the GA in the field did grow, but mainly through A2I, the broker-dealer, which offered all sorts of securities-based products in a marketplace hungry to cash in on the boom economy of the mid-2000s.

On the whole, the company was doing well, and the three-pronged bonuses that were offered at merger time did in fact pay off. Andy's income in 2007 and 2008 were as high as he would ever earn in the business, even rivaling his short stint in charge of Commonwealth Financial Group.

Behind the scenes, as interest rates continued their long-term fall, insurers like UA became desperate to find ways to prop up their investment portfolios so they could continue to offer competitive rates to policyholders on permanent insurance products.

The investments people at UA, organized to report to the head of each Division, were very disciplined about not sacrificing "the spread" of approximately 200bps on life insurance. But with bond portfolios dipping below 6% and declining faster than years before from portfolio turnover, the contractual guarantees on the UL product at 4% caused a squeeze.

The solution was to allow more risk into the portfolio to earn higher returns. In the 2000s, this meant getting into more real estate mortgages, either directly or by derivative investments.

No, this was not the same as the AIG offer to insure against the default of derivative investments through collateral default swaps (CDS). This was a more mild, but still dangerous, practice of taking on risk beyond traditional prudent practice to stay competitive in the marketplace. For a company like UA, where "distribution is king," the pressure to find "whatever it takes" to make products sellable was irresistible.

Meanwhile, the work of running the Individual Division of Universal American was overwhelming for Jake Rothman. As a GA in the field, he could concern himself mainly with sales. Expenses were fairly straightforward. Now, as head of an entire division, with its own investment portfolio, actuarial pricing and asset valuation functions, underwriting, and strategic alliances with other divisions and outside vendors, this was truly like being a CEO.

Jake had not completely appreciated the complexities of the job. By 2007, he had decided, with advice and counsel from an outside consultant he knew from his former company, that he needed more talent directly beneath him. This included bringing on a CMO, a chief marketing officer, for the Individual Division.

By this time, Andy Greene had rationalized his way to being content where he was on the organizational chart. In 2006, he graduated with his Ph.D. from George Washington University, and was doing some adjunct teaching on the side. His dissertation, on universal life products, was his delivery on the promise to deliver research of value to the company and the industry.

He had also started a rock band, consisting of various and sundry baby boomer amateur musicians in the Northern Virginia area. It started as a collaboration with Roger Carter. As the relationship between Roger and Andy soured, Roger left the band. Andy continued the project with a variety of musicians he had recruited from open mic jams, Craigslist ads, and referrals from others.

The band, The Continentals, known for playing classic rock, blues, and 60's R&B (*a la **The Commitments***) were never meant for stardom, but they did see some success that most who listened to their demo recording and saw them at local bars and clubs thought exceeded their collective talents.

As a collection of musicians, marketing the band for gigs was Andy's job, as the only "salesperson" on the roster. Many such bands, with even better sound than The Continentals, languish with no work because no one actively goes out and asks for the gig. "Ask for the order," a basic principle of selling, was one of the first things Andy learned in the life insurance business, and it applied as well to marketing a rock band. So did the principle of 10:3:1, the ratio of people to see, to people who express interest, to people who buy. When most bands give up when rejected once or twice, or ignored by club owners many times over, Andy simply persisted.

The band got some work, low cut money that barely paid members' expenses, but they got on a stage. Andy was proud of the band's accomplishments, given no one in the band was under the age of 40; most with families.

The graduate research and the band both played toward keeping Andy off the road more than he had been since his beginnings in the financial services business. Fact was no one at UA's home office was encouraging Andy to go out on the road and wholesale the company message. And Andy had many people under him, including people whose formal role was wholesaling, who could do the job. By the end of 2007, Andy had begun to lose some of the relationships he thrived on in the field, the people who so valued his expertise that he felt he was untouchable by home office rivals who saw him as a threat to their own advancement.

Working against the complete dedication to marketing life insurance was Andy's belief, resting in some accurate assessment of fact, that he needed to find a way to advance in the company, if for no other reason than to be assured that should the job suddenly come to an end, he would be able to command a better severance benefit than he would get in his current position. The key for Andy was to get to the Senior VP level. All of Andy's former rivals for advancement – Jamie Keane, Oliver Winters, Ian Evans – were all gone by 2007.

The new rivals – David Hauser, Roman Clay, Crystal Porcher, Wade Herrity – had all been given roles that moved them out of the way.

When, at the beginning of 2008, Jake Rothman let it be known that he would be seeking a chief marketing officer (CMO), it was assumed by most in the home office that Andy would be a prime internal candidate. When it further became known that Jake had not put into the job description that it had to be based in Columbus, Andy's interest in the job increased.

Andy had been passed over for promotion in the past. It had always been to the effect of, "Andy, you know stuff. You're smart and the field loves you. We want you to be happy with what you are doing now. That is where your contribution to the cause is best applied." Andy would always be seen by many as an advanced underwriting attorney, and little more. And Andy had reconciled himself to the role he had, which at least was one step up from that advanced underwriter role.

But now, Andy's desire for economic security for his family, as much as advancement for its own sake or the desire to leverage all of his talents fully, led him to throw his "hat into the ring" and apply for the CMO position. Crystal and David also applied as internal candidates. Strangely, Tom Wells had no desire for the job, preferring to stay right where he was. Wade Herrity considered it for a moment, but decided against it.

Crystal was an actuary who felt she knew marketing as well. Like other non-marketing people, she felt marketing was a "soft" science that "anyone with half a brain could master." To her discredit, this attitude showed itself in her public persona and was a turn off to anyone who had actually performed a sales or marketing function.

David Hauser had begun to earn a reputation for taking credit for others' work. It created a friction with his product management staff in DI. He still had good relationships with some field producers and his DI wholesalers. But even Jake Rothman and Mark Avalon caught on that David had a leadership disconnect.

Wade Herrity had suffered a strange illness shortly after the merger that created a partial disability on one side of his body. He missed several months of work from it. And while legally and morally no one would question his ability to continue in his current job, any advancement of this 61-year-old veteran of field relationships was out of the question at this point.

Andy went through a rigorous interview process, not only with Jake, but with the outside consultant as well. Meanwhile, Crystal and David, realizing that they would probably not be seriously considered for the CMO job at this point, went together to see Jake one day in March 2008.

"We both came to see you, Jake, because we're concerned about the CMO position and who you might put in the job."

"What's bothering you about it? Is it the process?"

"Not exactly," Crystal did most of the talking. "We understand that the product managers will be reporting to this new position?"

"Yes, that's true. Well then, what's the problem?"

"It's the people you're considering for the job," David suddenly blurted out.

Crystal stepped in. "We both believe that we are fine with whoever you choose, but we need to tell you we won't work with Andy Greene."

The implied threat surprised Jake. But he did not directly respond to the comment. So, Crystal continued, "We feel Andy is too full of himself, somewhat arrogant, and it makes it difficult for us to work alongside him. But we'll persevere there. But working under him would be impossible."

Jake's only reply, "This is going to be a long process, very thorough. I appreciate your input. I'll take your comments under advisement."

What Crystal and David did not reveal was their fear; the fear that Andy would take revenge on them for the shenanigans they put on during the Product Development Committee process in the merger integration project; how the Committee came to its decision to endorse the product manager model; how the "minority" report never got into the recommendation. They were further afraid that Andy would find a way to end the product manager model and they would be relegated once again to pricing products and wholesaling DI, respectively.

Even over the recommendation of Mark Avalon, who had developed a positive relationship with Andy, even over the abstention of Roman Clay, the die was cast.

In early April 2008, Jake called Andy into his office. "I wanted to let you know before it was announced that I've decided to bring in someone from outside the company to take the CMO role here. His name is Alan Franks. He has done some annuity product development at his current company. He also has some product experience in other industries. I feel he is going to bring a fresh perspective to the job. Now you should know that I seriously considered you for this position; you were the only inside candidate I seriously considered. But I feel we need a new perspective right now." Jake could see the look of disappointment on Andy's face. "You have done great work in SDF. This is what you were meant to do. Be happy with where you're at."

All Andy could think of was to assure Jake, "You have my full support for the decision. I will make it work with this new CMO."

"I appreciate that."

Andy rose from his seat and began to make his exit from Jake's office, but then turned around to face Jake, a few steps from the door. "Jake, with the new guy coming in, I may be getting in the way here. If you choose to retire me early or offer me the enhanced severance that was given to those who left at the time of the merger, I won't oppose it."

Jake did not respond directly to that comment, but only rose and moved toward the door to shake Andy's hand. And with that, Andy's chance at moving into a CMO role was over.

In the Spring of 2008, HR in Columbus contacted Andy in his Bethesda office. "We have a problem with one of your reports – Peter Burns. We need you to come to Columbus for a full briefing; it's not something we should talk about over the phone."

And Andy flew out the next day to Columbus. In the briefing it came to light that one of the staffers in advanced sales, a non-lawyer – Harold Friesen – who packaged up advanced sales presentations on live cases for GAs, had filed a charge of abuse and harassment against Peter. This wasn't sexual harassment. This was more abusive language, overly harsh criticism and demands made on the staffer by his boss, Peter, which had been going on for months.

Andy was somewhat aware of some erratic behavior that Peter had shown over the past two years. First, before Roger Carter had left the company, he told Andy of some weird phone calls he'd been getting from Peter, some late at night, which detailed a crumbling personal life for Peter. Apparently, Peter was going through a nasty divorce and child custody of his 10-year-old daughter, and he was looking for a sympathetic ear. Roger could not swear to it, but he said the calls often featured Peter in slurred speech, perhaps brought on by alcohol or drugs. When Roger recounted these incidents, Andy remembered what had happened at Atlantic to the then head of advanced underwriting years before.

Then Andy remembered seeing Peter in various states of disorientation at times, such as at the 2008 IAM, when he was late for a general session presentation one morning and Andy had to get up and fill for a few minutes while others tried to find him.

Then, one of the sales support wholesalers, a friend of Harold's, got involved, and encouraged Harold to file a complaint with human resources; hence, the current situation. This meant that all of the SDF were probably in the know about what had happened with Peter and Harold. After the briefing, Andy sat down with Peter to go over the complaint.

"This is preposterous," Peter defended. "No such thing ever happened. I've always been very solicitous and respectful to everyone reporting to me."

"I'm just relaying to you what I've been told."

"Look. I have nothing to answer for. And anyway, nothing is going to happen here. The field supports my leadership in advanced sales, and that's all that matters. I don't give a rat's ass what some HR person in the home office says about me. I'll let my work with the GAs speak for itself."

"Peter, this is serious. This is not about your work in the field." At this point, Andy realized that Peter had made a tacit admission by falling back on something irrelevant to the charge.

Then, there was a further meeting: Peter, Andy, and HR. The complaint was specified and Peter's reply was recorded. For the first time, Peter realized this was serious. Apparently, HR had informally been advised in the past of some rather abusive language being leveled by Peter at various home office employees, staffers who Peter felt were beneath his standing in the organization and should have been more responsive to his needs (demands). As the HR rep was leaving the meeting, Andy asked if she would close the door behind her. "I want a minute with Peter myself."

And Andy looked Peter in the eye. Peter stared straight back at Andy in disgust for having even to defend himself to this loser from Bethesda whose company could not have survived without a "bailout" from the great Valley Union.

"Peter, we have to take this matter seriously. Whether the charges are true or not, you are an ambassador for the SDF, and that means me as well. I can't be defending you when we're both busy enough trying to do our jobs. I have to rely on you to take a softer tone with people, especially your own reports."

Peter would not be moved. "I have a responsibility to the field and my unit. I don't recognize this SDF of yours, it's a fiction."

"I'm sorry to hear you say that, Peter. But if you can't work with me as part of the team, you always have the right of opting out."

"Don't threaten me, Andy Greene. I have friends in high places that can make trouble for you. You would never be able to fire me. I have been too big a player for this company for too many years."

Then, Andy started to lose the plot, so to speak. "That may have been the case years ago, my friend, but lately, you've been slipping. And I don't think it's in your best interests to continue down this path with me."

And Andy and Peter got into a staring contest that went at least a minute, after which Andy got up and left the room.

Andy began a file on Peter Burns, to document what might eventually be cause for termination, something that rarely happened at UA. It was more often the case to sweep such controversy under the rug and instead get rid of the problem employee with a position elimination, a reorganization of the org chart that eliminates the position for economic or organizational reasons, not for cause, but still gets the employee out (hopefully without a lawsuit for wrongful termination).

About a week later, HR reported to Andy that Harold had inexplicably retracted his complaint against Peter. He had recanted all of the charges he'd leveled and asked for the complaint to be trashed. He claimed that he'd been put up to the complaint by others in the SDF (unspecified) and that the situation had been blown way out of proportion. Had Peter gotten to Harold, perhaps intimidated him? No one knew. The matter was dropped.

In June 2008, Alan Franks entered the Columbus home office to assume his role as CMO of the Individual Division. He was given an office in the executive suite, reserved for just Gary, Jake, and one or two other division heads. Even Mark Avalon didn't have an office there. Alan met with each of his reports, individually, over the ensuing two weeks, including Andy, Crystal, Roman, and David. Very little in specifics were discussed. Andy assured Alan of full cooperation. Alan was heard often to refer to "Six Sigma" as a verb to describe what, in goods manufacturing, refers to managing to zero defects. Andy hated that reference, feeling that Six Sigma had little relationship to a services business like financial services; it revealed Alan's lack of depth in insurance product. He seemed to need an "Insurance 101" course whenever he met with his staff.

In early August, Andy took a long planned one week vacation, on his own, to the National Guitar Workshop, to relax and play his guitar, away from the pressures at work and home. Months before, Andy had disbanded The Continentals, anticipating problems at work.

Andy had been doing most of the fronting of money for the band, taking a double share of the gig money in reimbursement. Andy did not want membership in the band to depend upon a member's ability to chip-in. Once Andy learned he was not going to be the CMO at UA, he started pulling in his outside investments to get ready for what might come.

On August 8, 2008, Andy got a cell phone call from Barb Harmon while Andy was between sessions at the Workshop. "Hey, Andy, I'm sorry to bother you on your vacation."

"That's O.K., we're on break. What's up?"

"I thought you'd like to know, before you come back on Monday, that Jake Rothman has resigned from UA, effective immediately."

Andy was shocked. "What? What happened?"

"No one is saying. But I heard through the grapevine that the Board was pissed at him. The Individual Division lost $85 million in one quarter, after losses the previous two quarters."

"How can that be? That's a huge number."

"Investment losses mainly, I heard. Seems Jake wasn't watching what investments were being placed."

"So, Jake saw the trouble in front of him and bailed out?"

"Exactly! He's going to be the COO at Kentucky Life in Louisville… And guess what?"

"There's more?"

"Yeah. He's taking 'Crystal the Pistol' with him as his lead actuary. We're finally rid of her, right?"

"Yes. I guess." But all Andy could think of was that the person responsible for putting a novice like Alan Franks in the position he should have had was now bailing out and leaving the rest of the Division to clean up the mess.

That next Monday, Andy came into the office. Moments after his arrival, Paula Banks knocked on the door. "Andy, there's a call you need to take from Alan in Columbus."

"And you know this?"

"Yes. And I need to be part of the call as well." Andy went to pick up his conference phone to call Alan's extension. But before he could, his own extension rang. It was Alan Franks. "Please put the call on speaker," Paula said. And Andy did as asked.

"Andy, this is Alan…"

"Good morning, Alan."

"I trust you had a good vacation?"

"Yes." But before Andy could go any further, Alan broke in.

"Andy, I wish I was calling you under better circumstances." Andy realized what was coming. He'd been there before. "We've made a decision in the Individual Division to make a change. Your position as VP of Sales Development is no longer available. We're eliminating the position, effective the end of September. You'll remain in the position until then. Paula, are you there?"

"Yes, Alan, I'm here."

"Paula will go over with you all of the details of your severance package. I wish you luck."

And that was that… Andy was out, all the way out.

Andy's only question to Paula, "Why not just offer me what the people who left in 2006 were getting or offer an early retirement for me." Both were better than the 6-months severance offered here.

"I spoke with Jake before he left about that. He said neither was applicable in your case. At 55, you're not old enough for early retirement and you got the merger integration bonus in 2007. So you can't now double dip and take an enhanced severance as if you hadn't stayed with the company."

"Flawlessly logical," Andy thought to himself. And while a terrible hurt to his ego at being fired, Andy had all the confidence in the world that he would land on his feet, as he always did before. Surely, with more than 20 years experience marketing and distributing financial products, he might yet end up ahead of the game.

Andy had toyed with fighting the termination. At 55, did he have an age discrimination case against UA? The severance was contingent on his signing a covenant not to sue. So, before signing, Andy took the time to consult a lawyer specializing in employment cases. But her advice was that the case was marginal and she would not take it on contingent fee, but would charge her $350/hr. rate.

Andy did the math and decided it was not worth the fight. On the Tuesday after Labor Day, he signed the covenant not to sue, qualifying him for half the severance up front, half paid as salary continuation after 90 days, provided he was still unemployed. Andy wanted to take the 3-month cash out and pocket it. He would have a new job within days and get to keep that money for his troubles – he'd never had a problem finding a new job in the industry before.

Chapter 14: The Wheels Come Off

In later years – in the classrooms at ERU – the story of Professor Greene's exit from UA would be told in a way that implied it as a direct result of 9-15, the collapse of the financial services industry on September 15, 2008.

On August 11, however, few people could see the collapse coming, least of all a middle manager who'd spent his entire 26-year career marketing financial products, not concentrating on what happened to the revenue once it came in the door. Even the $85 million loss the UA Individual Division suffered did not tip Andy to what was coming, although he had suspicions about his own future. Nor did Andy's age come into his thinking; looking for a job at 55 is not the same as looking for one at 35, no matter what the Age Discrimination in Employment Act (ADEA) says.

And at the start of Andy's job search, he was confident of finding something even better than what he was leaving. Over the years, Andy's career had had its ups and downs – never beaten but never to the "promised land." Andy used to paraphrase a line from a classic Star Trek episode, where the Klingon commander, fighting the Enterprise crew, would say in his best "Shakesperian" voice, "What is this force that feeds my fight but starves my victory?" This was Andy's best one-liner to describe his career.

UA had been gracious enough to grant him a 7-week pause between the termination meeting and his last day on the job, meaning he had time to use his office as a staging point to look for work. This was important; one is more likely to look attractive to an employer if still employed than if officially unemployed. Until the end of September, Andy was still UA's VP of Sales Development. Freed of any real management responsibility, however, Andy's entire day could be used for the job search.

There no longer being any significant life insurance company presence in the D.C. area, the next likely stop was to go north to Baltimore or south to Richmond. Andy did both, still looking at a map of the Middle Atlantic as if he were a regional rep.

While Baltimore offered an interview or two but no job offers, Richmond was another story. The city was home to a large stock insurer, General Southern Life (GSL), the consolidation of several smaller regional insurers through acquisition over the previous 10 years. GSL was hiring a product manager – yes, that's right, a product manager – for its annuity line of business. It felt that since the pricing of annuities was an actuarially simpler thing than pricing permanent life insurance, the real key to success in that product line was product development ideas and marketing knowhow. Andy went through three interview stages; the first just before Labor Day Weekend. He was invited back for a second round of interviews the Thursday and Friday after Labor Day. In this second round, it included interviews with other product managers and sales support leaders, who also convened a group lunch with Andy – to get acquainted (euphemism for, "check the new guy out and tell the boss if there's something you don't like about him"). At this point, Andy knew that if they were putting him in front of the colleagues he would have in the job that it was "my job to lose."

At the end of the second round of interviews, there was a scheduled phone call with a retiring executive. It was Elliott Kelleher, his old boss from the 80s at Atlantic Mutual. Elliott had gone from AFG in 1994 to take the place of Brandon Kessler at Royal Life in Alexandria. But that in turn was closed by the Toronto crowd in 2003, tired of investing in that "cowboy" culture in "the States." Elliott then went on to be CMO of what would become General Southern. By 2008, Elliott had opted for early retirement himself.

His last official act before leaving was to give his blessing to the new annuity product manager. The GSL crowd knew of Andy's history with Elliott, and so arranged for this to be the last item on Andy's agenda that day.

"Andy, how are you, my old friend?"

"I'm good, Elliott. Glad to hear that you landed well with General Southern."

"I've had a great run with this company, Andy. They have been wonderful to work with… The last I heard you were in the field running your own financial planning practice."

"Northern Virginia Financial Group. It's O.K. if you haven't heard of it. No one in Northern Virginia ever heard of it either." And the two of them had a laugh over the comment.

"Well, so you're up for the annuity manager position here. That's outstanding. I know you'll like it here. I'm sorry I won't be around once you're on board. My last day is September 30. I'm actually working from home today."

At this point, Andy could see that the conversation assumed Andy had the job. "So, Elliott, I have your endorsement for the position?"

"Not that you need it; not that my opinion means that much at this point; but of course you have my full support."

"Thank you, Elliott. That means a lot to me." And the two said goodbye. Andy felt like the goodbye to Kelleher was permanent. But he felt confident that the job was his.

Not that Andy didn't hedge his bets. He saw that Alan Franks had posted a new position in his charge that looked a lot like the VP of

Sales Development. It was labeled VP of Marketing Support, but it had all the same reporting lines – above and below – that his position had. It had all of the same responsibilities his position had. It was clear to Andy that the termination of his position was purely personal; a power play by Alan to get rid of his "rival."

Thinking that this entire manipulation was a blatant attempt at "wrongful termination," Andy went to see Paula Banks. Andy did not want to do anything to compromise the severance he was going to receive at the end of the month. But Andy wanted it to be clear that he knew what was happening. Perhaps, this could be leverage to "up-the-ante" and pad the severance a little more. Andy still wanted the deal that Oliver Winters had gotten; a Senior Vice President's package. He wanted that one big payday that he could pocket when he got the official offer from GSL.

"Hi Paula," Andy said, entering her office on a pre-scheduled meeting in mid-September. "I'm concerned about this new job description I see for the VP of Marketing Support. It seems like my old position."

Officiously, Paula answered, "Well, it's not. It's not the same."

"Fine. I won't fight the point. However, you are aware that I officially applied for the position? I do have that right while I'm still here to apply for other openings within the firm, correct?"

"I saw your application, and you are right. I'm glad you came by today because I've been meaning to talk to you about that. You must realize that Alan will in all likelihood be looking for someone outside of the company."

"I realize no such thing. What I remember is your oft-stated belief that hiring from within is always preferable, all other things being equal."

"Andy, all things are not equal. I want to say in confidence that I'd like you to spare Alan and the company any embarrassment at having to go through a formal interview process with you for a position you already know you are not getting."

"If I am the best qualified candidate for the job, and I am internal, I know of no reason why I should not apply."

"Andy, I have tried to counsel you in the past about this. You come off to others in management as a bit arrogant. You push the envelope a little too far to the edge. You have not fit in with senior management the way someone in your position should."

"And that's why I'm out? Better watch what you're saying, Paula."

"You see. That's exactly what I mean… Even now, you can't resist the confrontation, the arrogance. But I'm not speaking for Alan. His decision is his alone. I'm trying to give you some friendly advice. You are wasting your time applying for this job."

"And you are wasting your time trying to counsel me, Major."

"What's this 'Major' stuff?"

"Believe me, Paula, it's more gracious than what others here call you."

"Andy, I think we're finished here. Thank you."

"No, I don't think so. I **am** applying for this position. Your own file on me tells you I am more than qualified, so you **will** have Alan put me through the formal interview process with all other candidates. If you think I'm arrogant now, you've seen nothing yet." And with that dramatic coda, Andy made his exit – in true Clark Gable "Frankly my dear…" style – without looking back at Paula to see her reaction.

But Andy had already signed off on the covenant paperwork, so embarrassing the empty suits in the company once more was his only option, legal recourse having been settled. He did force himself into the process; the "suits" did not want to do anything that would give Andy a lawsuit. Alan very clumsily held an interview with Andy, as if he were a real candidate for the position. But of course no offer came.

On September 15, Wall Street collapsed. Ordinarily, this event in Andy's world simply meant his 401(k) had become a 201(k) overnight; not a good day but not a disaster. After all, the market always came back. Andy remembered Black Monday in 1987, and was confident the same thing would happen now.

There was one thing Andy hadn't counted on: the stock price of GSL on the NYSE, which stood at $42 per share the Friday before, had now fallen to $2 per share by the end of trading on September 15. Andy had been waiting for his formal offer, either by letter or by invitation to a third and final interview round, where the offer would be negotiated in person.

No call came on the 15th; not on the 16th, nor the 17th. On the 18th, Andy decided to call the recruiter at GSL who had originally brought Andy into the mix for the position. The extension went unanswered. An operator at reception picked up the forwarded call. She then transferred the call to a manager in recruiting, who curtly said, "I'm sorry, but that position was taken off the list of postings. Management has decided to indefinitely table the hiring of anyone. Even in my department, all of the recruiters have been laid off. I'm the only one left and I'm simply cleaning up some details before I leave at the end of the month." The job had simply disappeared.

"What a shitty day," Andy thought.

Andy, still confident that something would work out, did have a few additional interviews. These jobs were far from Northern Virginia and would have required relocation, something Sallie did not want to do. In every situation it seemed Andy got to be one of the finalists for the job, only to come in second. He wasn't sure but it appeared that companies were shy about hiring someone who had a limited time until retirement and would only add to the group insurance costs of the company – in other words, age was a factor.

He called in whatever "chits" he still had with Dan Zimmerman from DAZ. "You know how tough it is out there with the financial turmoil in the market," Zim explained. Dan offered to help, got Andy's updated resume, but nothing came of the effort.

He also responded to an online ad for an "executive placement firm," P.J. Merkerson & Associates." Andy immediately surmised that this firm "marketed" executives, for a fee, paid by the job seeker, not the employer. He'd always believed what he'd been told many times, "the employer always pays the fee, not the employee." But in desperation he went to an initial consultation with Peter Merkerson himself. When Peter emerged in the lobby to greet Andy and shake his hand, he motioned for Andy to follow him down a hallway, and asked, "Have you been through our website yet?"

"Not yet, I'm afraid."

"Well, that's not a good start for you," Peter commented, as if he were interviewing Andy, not the other way around.

Peter entered his office, with Andy in tow, and motioned for Andy to be seated at the other side of Peter's desk, which Andy judged as a typical power play to put him at a subservient role to Peter. Andy then took out a business card from his pocket and set it out on

Peter's desk. He then reached into another pocket for a copy of his resume.

"We don't do resumes here," Peter explained. "Well, what have you to offer in your own words to an employer?" Peter was still in interviewer mode.

But Andy was also in interviewer mode. "I was going to ask you the same thing."

At this point, Peter became offended and answered, "This is not an interview of me or my firm. We want to know if YOU have the making of someone we can market for the big job, the one you can't get on your own."

"And before I even consider hiring you to represent me, I want to know what you offer."

"If you'd been through our website, you'd have that answer." Peter's voice began to rise in anger. "This is about YOU, not about us. If you want a shot at the jobs that don't get advertised, you need us – we don't need you."

At this point Andy simply responded, "Oh, I see," and reached over to grab back the business card on Peter's desk, and rose, saying "Have a nice day."

And as he exited Peter's office, never looking back, Peter shouted, "That's right, loser, go away and hide. You'll never succeed with that attitude. No wonder you're unemployed, fool." The shouted insults were loud enough that all hands in the office could hear, almost as if Peter were using Andy as an example of a "loser," for the benefit of employee training.

This was the low point of Andy's job search, almost. All he could think on the way home was, "What another shitty day."

Andy still held out some fantasy that, like his father years before, the staff in the home office and the agents in the field, who had known him for up to 17 years, would rise up in revolt and force management's hand to keep Andy in the firm. He fantasized that, like his grandfather, his staff still in the firm would come to his aid in his time of dire need. But no one said a word.

A goodbye lunch was hastily put together on Andy's last Friday on the job. And it was well attended. Even Snake Samuelson stopped by to wish Andy well. Janeesh Rau was also celebrating his early retirement as President of Atlantic Mutual, and joined the celebration. There was good cheer and well wishes all around. But no one raised a word to anyone in support of keeping Andy with UA.

Those that could have had some say in saving him stayed silent. Even his first ally in the field, Art Presser, now in his 70s and giving most of the day-to-day running of his practice to his son, Ari, sent him only a "best wishes" email. Art had been concerned about turning over the business to Ari, who seemed more interested in fast cars and faster women than running a business. And Art had asked Andy years before to watch over Ari and try and keep him focused as the father backed away from the practice. And Andy did befriend the son.

But when the time came, nothing was said or done in defense of Andy Greene. It seemed everyone was more concerned with their own future with the company to stick their necks out for an old friend and colleague.

As a further hedge, Andy had been talking to a UA GA who had been originally recruited and trained by Andy back in the AFG days. Patrick "Pat" Earle had come into the business through the old

Northern Virginia agency under Frank Meaney, FX, who had mentored a lot of people in his time with Atlantic. Andy had helped Pat develop his practice, which included cultivating some small business clients in the Northern Virginia area. Pat could always count on Andy – both before and after the mergers – to cut a path through red tape and get something done in the home office that Pat needed. In a way, Pat had two mentors – FX and Andy. So, when word got out that Andy was leaving UA, Pat emailed a half-joking message that he had an office waiting for Andy and Andy could come in with him and go back into selling in the field.

Now, Andy responded for the first time seriously, "Keep my office seat warm. I'm coming to join you." And the two worked out a formula for paying Andy that gave Andy what amounted to an advance on commissions. Andy was to work Pat's clientele for any insurance sales opportunities. And as Pat was the sole Virginia GA left at UA that had come from the Atlantic side of the house, the home office made his agency the servicing agent for thousands of orphan policyholders in Northern Virginia (policyholders with no agent still with the company) going back decades. Pat had long since stopped being an insurance agent; like many others, he had developed the practice into a money management firm and preferred to manage client portfolios for an asset management fee. Andy made the perfect addition to Pat's practice; Andy would work the insurance side of the business freeing Pat to concentrate on securities.

Andy became expert at contacting these orphan policyholders and he did so through the remainder of 2008 and all of 2009. Many of these policyholders had universal life insurance with Atlantic and the policies were in danger of lapse for lack of premium contribution. This was the back side of the universal life scandal, the consequence of 25 years of declining interest rates coupled with a lack of communication between agent and policyholder that was now Andy's job to clean up, at least in Virginia.

Despite the bad news Andy often had to convey, he had what turned out to be his best year of selling he ever had in the field, given this was now his third try at it. And his work paid off for Pat Earle, who qualified for Top Ten honors at UA's Leader's Club in 2009 on the force of the life insurance production Andy provided the agency. And Andy at least validated any advances Pat had made to him. It tried Andy's patience, however, as Pat was a very hierarchical boss and Andy had to get used to working for his former protégé.

Back in the field, Andy maintained his NAIFA membership. Now, as a Past President of the Northern Virginia Chapter, he went to the monthly luncheon for the membership in January 2009. There, he saw and learned from Effie Eckhart that she had cancer, and that it had spread. She had been keeping the information from all of her industry colleagues as long as she could. Her husband had passed away a few years before, also from cancer. Speculation was that they both were exposed to something harmful. When the doctors finally told her that there was little they could do – "it's time to get your affairs in order" – Effie got up her courage and lots of makeup to make one final appearance at the Chapter luncheon. She was a hero to most, loved and respected by all, including Andy.

As usual, she did the kissy-kissy, huggy-huggy thing with everyone. And when she got to Andy it seemed they both held onto each other just a little longer than standard business practice. Little of any substance was said between them; just a look and a smile.

Andy had planned to visit Effie a few weeks later, but a fellow Chapter member warned him away, saying she had asked not to have visitors at this point. "Effie doesn't want people seeing her like this, and she's really too weak." So, Andy stayed away. Felicia Eckhart died two weeks after that. The funeral was mostly family; the wake was packed with friends; and a post-funeral memorial to celebrate her life looked like a national NAIFA convention.

If there is a Hall of Fame for financial planning professionals in Virginia, Effie Eckhart would be a charter member.

Throughout this period, Andy worked multiple jobs to make ends meet. He began giving group guitar lessons through a county recreation and education program. He did this also to cultivate a following for private lessons he would offer to those completing the group course.

Andy also began teaching again, as an adjunct at multiple schools. He even got a plum assignment in the spring of 2009 at Georgetown University, teaching their MBA level marketing course. George Washington used him for some adjunct teaching for awhile, but they would not hire him to a full time, tenure track position there, when such a position in the marketing department opened up. It seems the school had a policy of not hiring their own alums. Go figure. And when the spring semester at Georgetown ended, so did Andy's chance of getting additional work there – enrollment was down; so was the demand for adjunct professors.

Andy had also picked up some work as an advanced underwriting consultant in a local agency for one of the big Eastern Mutuals. The agency was called Platinum Financial Group (PFG) and the GA was a first generation Chinese immigrant, Jeffrey Chow. Andy was paid a small monthly stipend to come in every Monday and do a training class featuring an advanced planning tip the agents could use in their sales applications. Then, having demonstrated his expertise, Andy would be available to prepare case solutions and go on joint sales calls with agents that had live cases needing a technical expert.

Jeffrey asked Andy how he wanted the split of commissions to be handled. "I use the MDRT method of splitting a case into five distinct tasks; one of them being case preparation and another going to the final presentation and close. Each task is worth 20% of the case. If the agent uses me for case prep, it's 20%. If I go out on the close, another 20%."

Chow was impressed by Andy's knowledge of the "MDRT split method." It proved Andy knew something about field sales. And Chow and Andy came to agreement. Andy was even given an office in the agency, shared with the compliance officer (the "24") for the agency.

And Andy went back and forth from Pat Earle's office to PFG – the two offices were but ten minutes from each other, in Fairfax.

In February 2009, Jeffrey Chow held his annual kickoff meeting for the agency. It included a full day of education, inspiration, and morale building activities intended to rally the agents to have a great year of selling. Andy was put on the agenda as well, to dispense one of his famous advanced sales ideas. But knowing that Andy was a musician and bandleader, Chow asked Andy to participate in a little mini-talent show after lunch that day, to fill out the program.

Never one to pass up a "gig," even a non-paying one, Andy prepared both a technical presentation on the logistics of setting up an irrevocable life insurance trust (ILIT) and two songs to perform. The lecture was pretty standard. The performance was something no one in the agency had ever seen from their advanced sales consultant – having never gone to any of the seedy bars and clubs that The Continentals played for $40 a player and some free food and drinks; tips when the gig money itself wouldn't cover the expense of hauling all the PA gear in Andy's car.

And Andy worked the room like a pro. The ILIT lecture was like holding court in the classroom at Georgetown, complete with funny anecdotes and comical slides interspersed with technical information. Later, Andy reappeared in full gig costume, replete with his "Cruising with the King" silk shirt, black bandana (*a la* Steven Van Zant), and those riding boots he'd bought years before at Cavender's in Houston. He used only an acoustic guitar to avoid the need for amplification. But he had his percussion with him – tambourine, claves, and egg shakers – and he went into the audience and asked for help on **Willie and the Hand Jive**. One agent took the egg shakers; another, the claves. A staff assistant grabbed the tambourine, and the show was on. Andy then launched into his version of the Classics IV hit, **Spooky**. The show was memorable mainly because the crowd saw some old fart attorney pretending to be a rock star.

Afterward, one of the sales managers, Debbie Clarke, approached Andy. She had just been hired the previous month and was recruiting and building her own sales unit. She had inherited some throw-away agents in the meantime; producers that the other two sales managers in the agency, both men, had given up on.

Debbie was 41 going on 25 – dressed to the "9s" with a bold attitude and an outgoing style, the kind needed by a woman in this still-male-dominated business. She stood at only 5'2", so she always wore heels to bring her profile higher. Her apparel and makeup were professionally flawless. She was slightly overweight but still extremely attractive for middle age. Her favorite color to dress in was black, believing it best hid her own "balcony of affluence." She had two daughters, 12 and 9, and lived out in horse country, Loudon County, making a hobby of her equestrian pursuits for her and her children and her commute somewhat trying on the highways of Northern Virginia. She immediately reminded Andy of Effie Eckhart; her beauty sometimes worked to her advantage and sometimes to her disadvantage, as some of the men took her gregarious personality the wrong way.

"Hello there, Mr. Greene," Debbie said wryly as she ambled up to him at the end of the sales meeting. "I don't think we've met, yet. I'm Deborah Clarke. Everyone calls me Debbie, even though I don't like the informality."

"Then, I shall call you Deborah," Andy retorted in mock formality.

Debbie smiled at the remark. "Oh, don't do that. It will make everyone think you're in some kind of different league with me than they are. Pay no attention to my complaining about my name. I'm just a little nervous meeting new people."

"Really? I would have thought just coming over here to say hello meant you had no fear."

"I usually don't. But you put on quite a show out there. I will say about your singing, 'Don't give up your day job.' But the advanced sales stuff was really informative."

"Thank you, I think." And they both had a laugh over it. She had an infectious laugh.

"Are you a member of the Bar?" Debbie asked.

"Unfortunately, though I try not to admit it."

"Why? It puts you on a higher level than the rest of management here." And she motioned a high-handed wave across the room.

And Andy began to tell the story of how he tried using his Bar membership years ago as entre into the membership for the purpose of selling financial services, and that the membership did not take kindly to the marketing approach.

"Their loss, I say," Debbie cut him off from going too far into the self-deprecation. "You know, I have been thinking about going to law school, part time, and eventually becoming a lawyer myself."

"Oh, I hope not. I usually try and talk people out of the idea. We have enough lawyers as it is, especially in this town."

"Just the same, I've been wanting to do this for some time."

"Well, if you're serious, then I have a suggestion. Before you make a final decision, I want you to observe court cases live. I've done this with other people. I take them to the courthouse to watch live cases. I should take you to the courthouse here in Fairfax and you can see for yourself what you're in for."

"I'll take you up on that. I'm going to hold you to that."

And sure enough, a week later, in the PFG office, Debbie sat in on one of Andy's Monday morning advanced sales sessions with the agents. Afterward, without any other comment, she pulled Andy off to the side of the room and whispered, "So when are you taking me to court," and gave that wry smile again.

"O.K., let's find a day we can get away from here. It can't be a Friday, that's 'Motions Day' in Fairfax. But perhaps a Thursday?"

"You tell me and I'll make it happen."

And on a hot and humid Thursday in June, the pair played hooky from work and went over to the Fairfax County Courthouse, to watch trials.

The first one was a criminal case. But when Andy saw the defense attorney from behind, he panicked. It was a friend of long standing and colleague of Sallie, and suddenly the idea of Andy with a voluptuous colleague in the back of the courtroom evoked a vision he would rather not have get back to Sallie.

So he whispered, "We need to get out of here," took Debbie by the hand and led her quietly out of the courtroom before the attorney spotted them.

In another courtroom, they watched a very depressing child custody case. Debbie was glued to her seat at the back of the room. They were momentarily mistaken for witnesses by the judge and Andy had to explain that they were observing the hearing.

Later, over lunch across the street, Debbie and Andy discussed what they had seen. "That custody case hits close to home," Debbie commented.

"Really?" Andy saw what was coming – an unloading of some intimate details of her own life.

"I'm going through a divorce myself, and I worry about the effects on my daughters." And she went on with the details, including some scandal about her husband and an embezzlement of funds from a country club in which they were both members and he was treasurer. She said that she had been drawn into the scandal by association and didn't know what her husband had done until it was brought to light by the executive board. "It's all over the local papers out in Loudoun. If you don't believe me, you can read about it. Just Google us and you'll see, but don't believe all of what you read." She said the husband was staying in their guest house but she would be able to force him to move once the divorce was final, which she expected to happen any time now.

And at this moment, Andy started to feel drawn in; he remembered Karen Bruckner. "I don't need to Google you. I believe you."

And Debbie then asked, "Explain to me that bit about leaving the first trial we were sitting in on. Why did you take me out of there?"

"The defense attorney was a friend of my wife's. Not a good idea to be seen at the back of the courtroom with you."

"Mr. Greene," Debbie joked in a fake southern accent, "Why whatever are you implying?" And the two had a laugh over the comment. Debbie did not take the matter any further.

And the friendship that seemed to be there also became a sometimes flirtation, though neither person made any move to push it further, at least for the time being. Andy had experience on how this all ends, still feeling the guilt of leaving Karen hanging.

Meanwhile, panic began to set in at home. Sallie was allergic to the idea of going back to work. Even though their sons were now grown, she refused to work at anything other than as an attorney. Hanging out her own "shingle" again would take a long road, just like starting a new business. And after two decades out of practice, she felt it was a long shot to sign on with a firm.

The couple had managed to hold onto portions of the severance from UA, as they tried to live off of the cash flow coming from Pat Earle's operation. But by summer of 2009, the savings began to drift down.

It is true what they say about couples fighting over money. The money problems caused a rift in the marriage; they already had enough problems without this added burden. By the summer of 2009, there really was no marriage anymore in Andy's mind. In fact, the marriage had effectively ended some years before that. It was just that neither one of them wanted to admit it. They were both so tied to their children that the idea of breaking up while Bob or Jack were still living at home seemed out of the question.

Then Andy saw a posting for a full time position in New York, teaching in a business school at a college Andy had never heard of. And in November he got a chance to go up to East River University and interview.

The interview included being in front of a panel of faculty. This did not unnerve Andy, whose sales skills kicked in and he carried a conversation with three faculty members that went into and through a lunch. After that, it was time to give a trial lecture in front of a live student audience in a "gateway" marketing class of undergraduates. Andy was told to present for 30 minutes on a marketing topic of his choice. To Andy, this was just like wholesaling, "Have PowerPoint, Will Travel," and Andy held court for half an hour on the 4 Ps of marketing and how they relate to a services business (like financial services).

Andy was made an offer, for about one half the salary that had been his base at UA. In this kind of job there were no bonus plans to augment compensation either. It was a hit to household income, but with Sallie working it would be enough.

Sallie was not about to take any old job. And she was not about to move to New York. She was Virginian, emotionally and legally – she was a member of the Virginia State Bar, which would not qualify her to practice in New York. It was an excuse for a final showdown with Andy.

"You can't expect me to just pick up and follow you anywhere," Sallie argued, from their family room at home.

"Well, actually, I can. There are no real job opportunities for me here. You are not yet employed. Under the circumstances, there is no real choice."

"After 20 years raising your kids, this is not fair… Not at all fair. You treated me like household help all these years while you went off doing whatever you wanted with whomever you wanted. And we have little in savings; you spent left, right, and center on yourself whenever you wanted, leaving me with little."

Then, Sallie went downstairs to the basement, where Andy had all of his musical equipment. He had used the basement as the rehearsal studio for The Continentals. After the band broke up, Jack, who fancied himself a guitarist, started using the same gear, jamming with his friends. "Follow me," she commanded, "Let me how you something."

And Andy reluctantly followed her downstairs.

Sallie didn't even wait for him to get off the stairs before she let out. "You see all this stuff you bought; with our money? For what? So you could pretend to be a rock musician with a bunch of other misfits with a stale dream?"

"A lot of this 'stuff,' as you call it, was paid for by gifts from my mother. She wanted me to pursue something that gave me joy. The rest of it was paid for by the double share of the gig money we got for the few jobs we played, and by the lessons I gave for the County and private. I didn't make a profit, but I broke even, at least."

"Maybe. But my point is: it was all about YOU. Even now, you refer to this whole project as if you were the only one affected. You never gave any concern for the family."

"Do you mean Bob and Jack? Both learned to play guitar on my watch. Both went with me to musical retreats and camps as teenagers? What is this "family" you speak of?"

And Sallie repeated, "After I raised your children, this is what we have to show for it? We're broke, you're unemployed… O.K., underemployed. We're running out of money, and your only solution is to move so you can start a new career. What about me?"

"That's what this is about then... It's about you! You didn't raise our children alone. I was there too. I did my part. We live in the richest town in the richest county in America. How do you think that happened?"

"So, you think you can do whatever you want with whomever you want? I made it possible for you to pursue this career you've now lost. I took care of the home and the kids while you were off doing whatever."

"Whatever? What are you talking about?"

"You know I know about your women."

"Really? I have told you over and over, whatever you think was going on out there did not involve sex, or affairs."

"But I'll bet you wanted to. I'll bet you were having emotional affairs."

"Did I ever 'lust in my heart'? Sure. Did I ever do anything about it? Absolutely not."

And for the final time, there they were; two attorneys arguing their case with no judge in the room to decide who was right and who was wrong. And Andy would move to New York in January 2010, without Sallie and without a marriage.

In the prior December, Andy planned a trip to Manhattan at his own expense to look for an apartment. Having traveled extensively for years on business, Andy built up a huge reserve of frequent traveler points with Marriott, and so the hotel stay cost him nothing out of pocket. As a Platinum Rewards member, Marriott had all of Andy's preferences in its system – he preferred a high floor, extra towels, king bed, non-smoking room, a mini-fridge for his bottled water to keep cold. And Andy simply made the reservation using those default specifications.

When Andy ran into Debbie a day later in the PFG office, he told her of his plans to leave Northern Virginia and teach in New York City.

"That's great news for you," she commented. "I know this is what will make you happy. A professor, wow! And in New York City, double wow!"

"Thank you," Andy responded. "I'm going up next week to look into apartments there. I always said that if I'm going to work in Manhattan, I need to live in Manhattan."

Then Debbie got serious. "You know, I have not been especially happy here at PFG. I feel like I'm a second class citizen among all the testosterone here."

"What are you thinking of doing?" Andy knew something was up with her.

"You know I came here from a company whose home office is in New York City. I was thinking of renewing my contacts there and see if they can get me into a sales management position in one of their agencies here."

"Well," Andy slowly said in hushed tones so others would not overhear, "I have a reservation at the Marrriott in Lower Manhattan for next Tuesday through Thursday, if you're OK with sharing, you can save the hotel expense. I promise no hanky-panky…O.K.?"

Andy looked for some clue on Debbie's face for a reaction. She was separated, after all, and Andy, having taken to the family room futon to sleep, was in the process of separation, after all. "Is there a problem here?" He was thinking.

Debbie's only answer, "We can make that work."

And so, the next week, Andy took an Amtrak to Penn Station in NYC from Union Station in D.C. The day before, Andy had developed an awful cold, at least that's what Andy thought it was. As the day wore on, the cold seemed to get worse. By the time Andy arrived at the hotel on Tuesday afternoon, he was weak, feeling a bit feverish and achy, but he had only an hour before going back to the train station to meet Debbie, who was coming in on a later train. Andy didn't even think about the room accommodations. When Debbie arrived with Andy by cab from Penn Station, and she saw the one king bed, she said nothing, but thought, "Is this what he means by no 'hanky-panky'?"

Andy admitted to his not feeling well, apologizing for the possibility of spreading his germs to her. Debbie, once a nurse by training, didn't think twice. She found some Nyquil for Andy to take, got him some hot soup for dinner and kept him company in that king bed as if they were an old married couple, watching a rerun of ***The Good Wife*** on TV.

The next day, Debbie went to see some of her colleagues in her former home office. Andy went apartment hunting, and they met up at dinner time at an Irish-style pub in Tribeca. Debbie immediately ordered red wine; Andy decided to drown his illness in a shot of Bushmill's, followed by a pint of Harp. They shared the details of their day and their plans for returning to D.C. the next day. Debbie seemed sure she had restarted her network in her old company and something good from it would soon be coming; they had told her the GA in Leesburg was looking for an agency recruiter for the entire agency. This would put her much closer to home. Andy had found a reasonably priced one-bedroom rental, walking distance from ERU, if you could ever talk about an apartment in Manhattan as "reasonably priced."

Then Debbie, on her third glass of wine, decided to get to something that had been bothering her since the two arrived in New York. "It really caught me off-guard when I got to the hotel room and saw there was only one bed."

"Yeah. I'm sorry about that. It's in my profile and I didn't think to change it."

"Andy. You don't have to play coy with me. You could have changed it, even after we got to the hotel. I didn't say anything, but you didn't either. I just trusted you to know the boundaries."

"Do we have boundaries, Deborah? To tell the truth, I'm not sure what we are together. We seem to be playing at the possibilities of something more than colleagues and friends."

And Debbie did not respond. She simply took another sip of her wine, as the waitress came to take their dinner order. Andy did not pursue the matter further.

After leaving the Pub, the two walked back to the hotel. On the way, the examination of Andy's motives continued. At one point, Debbie bluntly asked, "Is your marriage really over?"

"I would say so, given I'm in the family room now and making a list of what in the house I can take with me, alone, to Manhattan."

"Before you moved into the family room, though, you were a couple?"

"That depends on what you mean, 'a couple.'"

"I don't want to find out that **I'm** the reason you two are separating. Were you guys still having sex?"

"That's rather personal, Debbie. But since I sense concern about my situation and your part in it, let me assure you – there had been no sex going on for some time."

"For how long?"

"I think it's been 8 years now."

"Eight years? EIGHT YEARS?? How could you stand that – 8 years???" Andy became a little embarrassed at her response and being overheard by others. "How do you share a bed with someone for 8 years like that?"

"You do some strange things when you're preoccupied with raising children, I guess."

Back at the hotel, Debbie began to argue with Andy. "You really assume a lot, the way you set this whole trip up."

"Look," Andy defended, "Even if I wanted something to happen, I'm in no condition to make love right now. I've been feeling like crap all day."

"Making love? Is that the euphemism you choose to use, huh?"

"It's the term I choose to use when it would have been more than just physical. I'm not interested in having 'sex' for its own sake. I'm as horny as the next middle class, uptight, straight, white boy from Northern Virginia. But I prefer it have a little more meaning, if you get my drift."

And Debbie realized that whatever she felt for this man in front of her, he apparently felt something, too. It was all a matter of whether they wanted to do anything about it.

At this point, Andy went into the bathroom to change – t-Shirt and boxers to sleep in. Debbie, seeing him get into bed, face up, pulled down the comforter he had pulled over himself. She then took off her own shirt, revealing a black lace bra, clasp in front, and climbed over Andy, straddling him, sitting directly on his crotch. And she just sat there, tipsy but motionless.

Andy had a quick decision to make: Was this the moment that he actually indulged his passion. "She's divorced; I'm separated. "What's the problem here?" he thought. The feeling of her on top of him was quite arousing; the smell of her perfume added to the moment. And he reached up to unclasp Debbie's bra.

But she backed away, refusing his advance. "What's the problem?" he asked.

She didn't answer. She just looked straight at him. So, he tried again for the bra. Again, she leaned back, away from his grasp.

They then just froze in place, not saying a word. After a minute or so, Debbie climbed off of her bedmate. Taking off her skirt, leaving her panties on, she pulled the covers back over both of them, turned out the light, and went to sleep. Andy did not move, not wanting to be refused a third time.

The two would not talk of the incident again. But the next morning, sure enough, Debbie had begun to show signs of the symptoms Andy had. She had caught his "cold."

The next week after they returned to Northern Virginia, Andy held his normal morning advanced sales presentation to some of the agents. He noticed Debbie was not in attendance at the meeting. Andy went in to give his notice to Jeffrey Chow, as he had with Pat Earle the previous Friday. But Chow looked a bit distracted.

"Jeff, I hope I didn't disappoint you that much with this news," Andy sympathized.

"It's not you… I had to fire someone in the office this morning, and it really pissed me off what happened."

"Well, are you going to tell me what happened?"

"Well… It seems Debbie Clarke's been recruiting agents to a competitor while she was still a sales manager here. She was two-timing us!"

"Really?" Andy did not let on anything about his relationship with Debbie, about New York, about the hotel room. Andy had no idea Debbie was already recruiting for the Leesburg office. She had only told him they were looking for a recruiter.

"I've really lost a lot of respect for her. She was building 'portfolio' to take with her to her new job, before she told us she was leaving."

"That sucks, Jeff. Sorry to hear that."

"I know you and she had done some work together…"

"I knew nothing about this, boss. I'd have told you if I had." But Andy wasn't so sure he would have. He was relieved that Debbie had kept him in the dark about her activities.

"I got the information from one of the agents in her unit; ratted her out when she tried to recruit him away."

When Andy exited Chow's office, he went up the hall to Debbie's office, but it was empty and dark. One of the agents saw him looking into Debbie's former office.

"We really lost a lot of respect for her today," the agent repeated almost word-for-word Chow's feelings.

As he went back down the hall to his own office, another agent in Debbie's unit stopped him. "I know this sort of thing happens. She wanted to build a cadre of producers to take with her – to prove she could recruit. I know the GA in Leesburg probably asked her to do this, to prove she could 'bring portfolio.' But it still sucks, and I'm personally hurt. I looked up to her. I did everything she asked me to do, and now she leaves me holding the bag."

Was this the "rat?" Andy thought.

Afterwards, in his last act in the PFG office, Andy sat down at his computer and started Googling Deborah Clarke, her husband, and the whole embezzlement situation. And it became clear to Andy that she was up to her ears in the scandal. Then, he looked up what she had said was her divorce case pending in Loudoun. It had been dismissed. They were still married. The case apparently had been dismissed by her attorney due to fees owed the attorney by Debbie which remained unpaid. The dismissal was dated in July, 2009. There been no active divorce case for months.

And Andy thought to himself, "Sometimes it's better to be lucky than good."

But Andy would not be so lucky. In January, Andy was served with a set of divorce papers himself, while in Manhattan. In the complaint, Sallie alleged an affair between Andy and Debbie. Upon discovery that spring, Andy would find out that Sallie had spent over $10,000 of their joint funds in 2009 to track Andy in Fairfax and Manhattan to find out what was going on with him. The private detective had found the hotel room the two were staying in and was able to observe the king bed while the maid was cleaning the room. His report did not specify hearing anything other than a TV going when he listened at the door, and there was no observation or photos of the two. There was also nothing about their work together at PFG.

This being an allegation of something that occurred after their separation began, Andy tried not to take it seriously. But this did mean that the end of his marriage had become official. Divorcing a divorce lawyer is a dangerous undertaking, and it took most of what Andy had in savings and a lot of debt trying to pay lawyers to finally get to a settlement. The settlement gave Sallie most everything they had together, lump sum in exchange for no spousal support going forward. Sallie got her bag of money; Andy got his freedom.

Chapter 15: So Now What?

An email came in to adg@eru.edu one day in 2011. A reporter from a financial journal had been referred to Andy for comment on the Wall Street Meltdown of 2008 and its aftermath. As an academician and former marketing executive in the financial services industry, Andy made a good candidate for commentary. The reporter, a woman 35 years Andy's junior and just out of journalism school at Ithaca College, was too young when the Great Recession first hit to fully comprehend its true impact on the economy and society.

Andy answered that they could arrange for a phone interview and he would be happy to supply what commentary he could.

When she phoned Andy a few days later, it was to get an inside angle, hopefully an angry angle, at the unjust and unequal impact the Recession had on those in the industry.

Reporter: Mr. Greene.

Andy: Excuse me, but I prefer Dr. Greene, if you please. My mother always wanted a doctor in the family and she finally got one so I don't want to lose the title, for her sake [a chuckle].

Reporter: Got it. Dr. Greene, do you feel as though we're finally out of this Great Recession?

Andy: Technically, we have been out of the Recession since July two years ago. The definition of a recession is two consecutive quarters of negative economic growth. That ended with the second quarter of 2009.

Reporter: I didn't mean that, exactly.

Andy: I think I get it. You mean, emotionally?

Reporter: Yes.

Andy: People continue to think we're still in recession because they still feel the pain. People are either still out of work or they are working multiple jobs to try and make ends meet... And sometimes even that isn't enough.

Reporter: Who do you think is most to blame for causing the Recession?

Andy: Everyone. A corporate world that manages to quarterly earnings instead of long term strategy; a government in the pocket of that corporate world; a political system that rewards fundraising over common sense solutions; an electorate too ignorant to understand that they are voting against their own self-interests; trading partners around the world that pretend to be our allies while they stab us when our backs are turned. Shall I go on?

Reporter: Do you feel that Dodd-Frank is a law that will cure the ills that caused the Great Recession?

Andy: I prefer to call it by its real name – the Financial Services Reform Act; and no, I don't think it will cure all ills. But it is all we have to work with right now and it is at least better than nothing.

Reporter: Does this mean you see another "too-big-to-fail" happening again?

Andy: It's inevitable. Absolute power corrupts absolutely. And the investment banks were left with all the financial power.

Reporter: You blame both the government and the corporations, but if we get government out of regulating, if we shrink the government, reel back the spending, won't that be a partial cure? After all, the national debt, growing all the time, is sapping our ability to do anything, right?

Andy: The national debt is a function of people unwilling to pay for the government they want. We don't have a spending problem in the government; we have a revenue problem.

Reporter: So you think taxes should be raised? Won't that kill the recovery?

Andy: Did it kill the recovery in the 90s? Politicians – I won't say who – like to point to the "waste, fraud, and abuse" in government as an excuse to starve the government of the resources necessary to care for its people. Well, I have to tell you – after living in the Nation's Capital for 30 years and also being in the corporate world for that long as well – when I compare – the waste, fraud and abuse that goes on in government would pale in comparison to the waste, fraud and abuse in corporate America.

Reporter: So all corporations are evil, is that it?

Andy: That's not what I'm saying. Please don't put words in my mouth. Small business does not have the luxury of waste, fraud and abuse. But the large corporations carry a lot of unnecessary overhead – not the least of which is employing people who look good in a suit but contribute nothing to the business.

Reporter: And you think the Government is competent to run the financial health of the country, after racking up trillions in debt?

Andy: Leading question, counselor… But let me at least give the Government – the Feds, that is – credit for managing the immediate crisis. The economy was saved, and the bailout money was paid back. The taxpayer actually got a little profit in the end from having doled out the almost $1 trillion dollars in funds to save the investment banks, the car companies, and AIG.

Reporter: It's true that the investment banks and the others seemed very quick to pay back what they borrowed.

Andy: Not just borrowed. The Feds took equity positions in some of these firms. Shhh... Don't tell the voters that this is the definition of socialism, but that's exactly what the Feds did. And having taken over these companies, they were able to make senior management very uncomfortable with politicians watching every move they made. It gave a great incentive to prepay the loans and buy back the stock – to get the Government out of their business.

Reporter: And you think the Government consciously knew that this would be the result? That the companies wanted to get the Government out of their boardrooms?

Andy: If it wasn't intentional, the Government got lucky. That means the taxpayers got lucky, and I'd rather –

Reporter: You'd rather be lucky than good... I get it! So everything is fine now, right?

Andy: There are some people who will never return to their careers after this and I have questions about whether that was fair.

Reporter: What do you mean?

Andy: The senior management of these firms all had obscene exit packages worked out years in advance with their boards, so they cried all the way to the bank, so to speak. The people at the bottom of the org chart; well, some lost their jobs, but for most their wages were so pitifully low that they fit within the budgets of any company acquiring the troubled firm. It's the people in the middle – the middle managers – the ones just below senior management, whose jobs will likely not return, ever.

And after a few more questions, it became clear to the reporter that Dr. Andrew Derrick Greene – Masters in Financial Services and Ph.D. in Marketing – was giving forth more on a topic of business management and corporate ethics than he was on matters of financial management and the marketing of brands.

This was not the only time Andy would be interviewed for comment by the press. Earlier that year, he was asked to comment to a higher education journal about the recent allegations about admissions and financial aid abuses at some "for-profit" colleges. Although the article when published would not name ERU as a culprit, the emerging scandal cited admissions of students who were not prepared properly for college but who were admitted anyway so the school could collect the financial aid offered through the Government's FAFSA program. When the student ultimately flunked out or failed to complete his/her degree, the student would invariably not have enough income to service the accumulated loans. The student would default. The loans were not collateralized. The school had pocketed the loan money. The taxpayer got stuck with the bill.

There was also the feeling that these "for-profit" schools were not real colleges, in that they lacked the reputation that traditional universities carried.

But Andy had come to value the model that ERU was following, and said so in the phone interview.

"A traditional university, with tenured faculty, it is all about research and publications. 'Publish or perish' is the order of the day. The faculty do not even do most of the teaching; they have TAs (teaching assistants) – grad students – that do most of the work, especially grading exams and papers. And with tenure, the professor has little incentive to concentrate on teaching skills.

"Here, there is no tenure. But I don't consider it a drawback… I never had tenure in the private sector anyway. And here, we are a 'teaching centric' institution. The education experience of the student is job one. Yes, scholarly publications are valued, but not as much as teaching excellence.

"And what do you think the student values more, the reputation of the school because its faculty publishes frequently? Or the interaction and mentoring from faculty who treat the student as the priority, rather than their ongoing research study?"

Andy had "drunk the Kool-Aid" for his brand of higher education. He had internalized his satisfaction with the job he now had, seeking nothing more than the privilege of offering students who otherwise could not access a college degree the opportunity to do just that. And it is this internalization that gave him satisfaction; in the classroom, in one-on-one student meetings, at graduation commencement exercises.

Andy had been forced to live with less – less money, less living space, less accoutrements of title – but had come to terms with the losses. At least with this profession now he had little responsibility for anyone other than his students, his "clients," as he sometimes liked to call them.

In the financial services business, he had always taught that money freedom is also time freedom. But now he realized that no longer chasing the "short" dollar actually freed him up for other pursuits.

Caught between the longing for love and the struggle for the legal tender. Jackson Browne, *The Pretender*. This was one of Andy's favorite rock lyrics.

He now pursued music once again. He met up with a couple of cohorts from his days in Oneonta, from WONY, who lived in the area. He added an ERU colleague who played drums and who brought a childhood friend who supplied a female vocal track to their classic rock and blues repertoire. The new band, called "Old Farts," had no members under the age of 40. They played no music that was released before Carl Perkins' **Blue Suede Shoes** was stolen by Elvis Presley, or after The Clash broke up.

And once again, a band gave Andy an outlet to play those songs that kept ringing in his head all the time, as if were the songs to stop, he would stop too. And Andy would write a few songs himself. Though mostly love ballads, a sort of "You broke my heart, now get out of my face" genre of what Andy called "Alternative Country," one song of a different stripe was called "Empty Suit." In a jazzy blues progression and three distinct verses, the song told first of one empty suit, a man; then, a female empty suit; after which the singer him/herself is revealed to be an empty suit as well.

And once again, Andy, as bandleader, applied what marketing and sales skills he had acquired over 30 years of peddling life insurance to getting the band into some gigs.

Most of the band's work delivered barely enough to cover each member's expenses plus maintenance of their instruments. Andy's goal was that each member go home with at least $100 in their pockets. But regardless of the gig money amount, he applied the philosophy of an insurance agency manager to the band's business. When paying each band member his/her cut of the gig money, Andy would arrange payment immediately after the gig, in cash, and place each person's cut in a #12 envelope with the member's first name hand printed on the front. The band would usually arrange to meet up at a nearby all-night diner for an omelet and coffee. Andy would walk in after the others had already arrived at the diner, armed with the envelopes, and carefully call out each person by name at the table and hand out each envelope in turn. Even though there may be only a couple of $20s in each envelope, they were all "professional musicians," Andy would remind them. "If you play for pay, be it

$20 or $2000 or anything in between, you are a professional, never forget that."

Andy was always most popular with the band members at these moments.

When marketing, Andy would apply the prospecting skills he'd learned selling insurance and mutual funds. He would walk into the bar or club, usually open for lunch, sit at the bar, order a small meal, then ask the bartender "Who books the bands here?"

Being a paying customer, the bartender dared not refuse to answer the question. One thing about tavern owners: They usually work days, not evenings. Andy would ask to say hello to the owner or whoever books the talent. They could not very well say "no" to a paying customer, so the owner would eventually come out to be introduced to Andy; whereupon Andy would put the media kit, complete with demo CD, in front of the owner. Though the booking would not happen then and there, Andy collected contact information to follow up, and 10:3:1 operated here as well. It took walking into 10 establishments to get three owners to say they were interested to get one booking. But he got them. This again proved that selling is 90% perspiration and 10% inspiration; most bandleaders would have given up too soon.

One booking was at a small restaurant that offered live music Thursdays – Sundays, in the evenings, after the dinner traffic started clearing out, around 9pm. Called *The Masquerade*, a New Orleans style motif and creole cuisine, this would be the band's first chance to play in Manhattan, as opposed to out in the suburbs. *Old Farts* had just recently recorded a new demo, and the demo had become more of a full length album. The band saw this as a CD release opportunity. That the venue was in Midtown meant that Andy could try and draw a crowd from amongst his students. They would love to see their "Professor" making a fool of himself on stage, right?

When the night came to play their set, very few of those students showed up. The audience was about a dozen, mostly family and significant others of the band members. They played their set in any event, including all of the tracks on the album. This included **Empty Suit**, and a new song Andy had written, **In My Head**, with a chorus that ended with the line,

I'll surely know that I am dead, when the music stops playing in my head.

After the set was over, Andy went over to the bar to settle up with the owner, who was none too pleased at the meager turnout. Andy had agreed to variable compensation for this event; the band would share 50/50 with the house whatever the bar took in that evening. It wasn't much. Andy, having not told the band specifically what they would be paid, augmented the envelopes with an extra $40 for each member, out of his own pocket.

He went off to a darkened corner of the restaurant to fill each envelope. As he did so, he began to feel faint, with a pain on the left side of his chest. As the pain worsened, he lost control of his body but managed to grab onto a sofa in that corner and settle onto it, lying down, before losing consciousness.

In a silent, misty haze, Andy could see figures in the distance. He rose slowly from the sofa. The first face he recognized was his mentor, Frank Meaney, old FX.

"Frank," Andy called out, "What are you doing here? I thought you died a few years ago."

But FX did not answer. He just looked at Andy and, after a few seconds, began to smile. Then he walked on past Andy.

Andy turned to look back, but FX seemed to vanish slowly in the mist.

Turning back, Andy recognized Theo Pulliam, his one-time client. Theo did not look up, as if he was embarrassed to see Andy. Andy called out, "Theo, how are you, man? I heard of your ailment, I'm sorry for your trouble, but you seem to have come through it."

But Pulliam continued his avoidance of Andy and walked on by, vanishing just as FX had.

Effie Eckhart then appeared in the distance. She looked straight at Andy with that winning smile of hers. Andy reached out for the inevitable hug and kiss, which never came. Effie just seemed slightly out of reach for Andy and then disappeared just as easily as she had appeared.

Tim Wheaton was the next person Andy saw... He seemed to have blood on his face, hands, and shirt, the same clothes he wore in that fatal elevator ride. Andy was unsure of how to handle the situation; the possible confrontation brought up bad memories. But Andy needn't worry very long; within a few seconds, Tim had glided past Andy and went back into the mist as if he'd never seen his one-time object of revenge.

Off in the distance Andy could then see Shel, Andy's father. With him was someone he could not quite make out but Andy assumed it was his mother, Stel. Odd that his mother's face seemed not quite visible. Odd that she was there at all. Sheldon Greene had died suddenly in 1998 of a stroke, leaving Stel a widow. Andy moved toward the two of them. "Dad, what are you doing here? I haven't seen you in over a decade. And Mom, I can't see you very well. How are you?"

Sheldon Greene was never one for a hug, but always shook hands as the only man-to-man physical gesture he could manage. Andy held out his hand for the shake, but Shel did not respond, only looked at

Andy with a faint smile. "Andy," he said, "I'm surprised to see you here. I really didn't think this would happen so soon."

"What do you mean, 'so soon,' Dad?"

"Take a look around, my boy... Where in G-d's name do you think you are?"

And Andy did look around, and it started to make some sense. "But Dad, what is Mom doing here?"

"This is not your mother. She is just a placeholder, for later."

As the mist began to fade, so did the image of Andy's parents. And a new image began to appear.

"Mr. Greene, can you hear me," came the voice of what appeared to be a medic of some kind. After a few seconds, Andy realized that a paramedic was trying to talk to him.

As it was explained to him, Andy had had a small heart attack. Although having lost 25 pounds since his separation from Sallie, Andy still had at least another 25 to go, and the years of hard living and bad food indulgences had taken its toll. But Andy would survive, and with medication and a stent to open a blocked artery, Andy would in time recover.

At the end of 2011, Andy's divorce became final, just in time so he could file taxes as a single person. Although filing jointly with Sallie, with no income of her own to speak of, would have generated for that year a lower tax bill, Andy simply did not want the burden of fighting over the taxes with his ex-spouse any longer than was necessary.

Andy left behind most of what the couple had accumulated over 28 years of marriage, the price for his freedom from any further responsibilities to her. Bob and Jack were grown, out of college and self-sufficient, and so they were not an issue. Bob knew that things had not been right between his parents for some time before the split, but Jack was surprised and saddened – it took some time before he was able to deal with the divorce.

In early 2012, Stel, Andy's mother, was diagnosed with an advanced cancer of the bladder. After months of radiation and chemotherapy, the doctors had decided that there was little they could do to stop the advance of the cancer. Stel, on her own, decided to enter Hospice care. She would pass away that summer, joining the love of her life wherever that place was where Shel was waiting.

Before she did, however, Stel decided to unburden herself of some family secrets that had been kept from her children.

"I want to tell you of something about your Grandpa-Mikey," Stel began. "This is something your father never told you about because he did not want to ruin your image of your grandfather."

Mikey had been Andy's closest and favorite relative, all the way until Mikey's passing 20 years before. Stel continued, "Dad wanted you to continue to hold your grandfather in the high esteem he knew you always had for him. This is about things that happened long before you were born; starting when Dad was a kid."

"The only thing I knew about Grandpa-Mikey was that he was a foreman on the shoe assembly line when he was living in Boston," Andy responded.

"Yes. And that he was good to his employees."

"Yeah, right."

"Well, there's more to it than that." And Stel took a breath. "You see, Grandpa-Mikey was quite the ladies man in his time, a real charmer…And it got him into trouble." Another pause for a breath. "During the War" (WWII) "he sold war bonds, as lots of folks did at the time. But he pocketed some of the money he collected and used it to support a mistress that he had."

"I find that hard to believe," Andy responded with amazement.

"Well, it's true. And if that weren't scandalous enough, he was caught and did some time in jail for embezzlement." Another pause, then, "Dad, just a kid then, was very close to his father. But this incident made him lose a lot of respect for him; respect that never would fully return."

"But Dad did everything for him, even got him out of Mattapan and put into new housing…I was there."

"I know you were. Dad was the dutiful son, and he never wanted you to think any less of your grandfather."

"But how does any of this relate…"

Shel cut in, "That's not the whole story…Just the background…There's more."

At this point, Stel pointed to the water glass on the nightstand by her bed. Andy brought the glass to her and she took a sip. Handing it back to Andy to put back on the stand, she continued. "Through the years after this, there were further incidents of Grandpa's fooling around with women, all the time while married to your grandmother. You know that she died many years ago from cancer, right?"

Andy nodded.

"Grandpa used to play up her illness for sympathy from people, implying that no real marital relations were going on. It was his excuse for playing around. One of these affairs went on with one of his employees on the assembly line. You know her as Angie, his second wife, the one he married after moving out of Mattapan."

"You mean there was a relationship there from before?"

"Yeah. And there's more…Angie bore him a son, a little older than you."

"I always thought Dad was an only child."

"And that's the way everyone played it. When Grandpa died, Angie came to Dad and asked if, after all these years, he would like to meet his half-brother. Dad said no, and the secret was kept."

"Did Dad only know of the brother then? Or before?"

"He knew pretty much all along. It was no mistake that Grandpa drove to Angie's house the night he was beaten in Mattapan. He had just come from there, to see her. The deal was, her family would pull strings to get him put at the top of the list for subsidized senior housing, and Angie would move in with him to look after him, but only if Grandpa married her – make it official. That's how she came to be part of our family."

Andy could not speak for a moment, then, "A lot to digest, but I don't think it changes my view of Grandpa, really."

"I hope you always feel that way."

And with that, the dutiful son hugged his mother for what he did not know would be the last time he would see her conscious.

After the heart attack scare, Andy began to take on a different attitude toward life. And after the divorce was final, Andy kept his mind on rebuilding some degree of financial security. He taught simultaneously at other colleges, as an adjunct instructor – a "hired gun professor" – Andy would call it, in order to earn the money it took to live in Manhattan.

Andy did get to Northern Virginia on occasion, as Bob lived there as a staffer for a "Beltway Bandit" defense contractor. On one trip, shortly after his mother died, Andy let Marie Frame know he was coming to town, and she arranged an Atlantic Mutual reunion of sorts. Marie got Andy to cash in some of those Marriott points he'd accumulated through years of travelling the country wholesaling insurance and investment products, and a party in the smaller of two ballrooms at the Tyson's Corner Marriott was arranged for just after Labor Day. Marie had retired, Andy learned; really retired, in that she was now a lady of leisure. But she was still relatively young, played soccer in a 50+ women's league, owned a polo pony stabled in Warrenton, the capital of horse country in Northern Virginia.

Barb Harmon came to the reunion. She had recently been laid off from UA, part of the slow dismantling of anything left of the Bethesda presence in the company. And she had stories to tell of the exit of others from the office. Paula Banks had been found to be carrying on an affair with one of her married staffers and the two resigned after they were found out – to stop the obvious embarrassment. Barb herself had decided that it was time to get some of that field sales experience she had been lacking, and was a TAP agent with the local Productive agency in Reston, just west of Tyson's.

Soris Maximus – Nellie – made a brief showing as well. He had gone into partnership with two other financial advisors and took over an investment advisory firm in Leesburg with a very affluent client base. The three partners had bought the firm from a retiring colleague Nellie had known and had tried to recruit at one point to AFG.

Surprisingly, Billy Carl showed up at the reunion. The last Andy knew Billy had become the South Asia president for AIG. But when the financial crisis hit the company especially hard, all bets were off. Billy had enough of a generous exit package lined up, however. He would continue to do occasional consulting work for companies, always looking for that one-more big payday. But the payday never came. Billy was 65, and had not kept up as well as younger competitors in social media and other outlets for marketing service products.

Also in attendance was Q, who had managed to raise three daughters over the time since he left Atlantic. However, one of them suddenly died of a rare cancer before she was 18, and it left Q forever changed.

Marie managed to get some of the members of The Continentals to participate. Some of them had gone onto other bands; most stopped playing entirely once Andy had disbanded the group. But they did get up to play a few of the old tunes, such as **Mustang Sally**, **Not Fade Away**, **Mr. Jones**, and **Knocking on Heaven's Door**, with Roger Carter on keyboards. Roger had moved out to Ohio a few years before, but his daughter was in her last year at UVA (University of Virginia), so he got to the area from time to time. The opportunity to jam together again seemed to make whatever hard feelings remained between Roger and Andy disappear.

Back in Manhattan, Andy kept a low profile socially, except for the occasional "date" that would usually go nowhere, maybe to bed, but not to anything more permanent. In New York City, like many other cities, a 58-year-old divorced man was outnumbered by women his age by a huge margin, making it possible for him to have female companionship whenever he wanted. But this all eventually became boring; every encounter resulted in a cul-de-sac; nothing that appealed to him for anything more than sex. And without "a little help from his friends" – a little white pill – even that was a non-starter.

By late summer that year, Andy had bored of the lack of any true connection. He considered online dating but turned away from it on philosophical grounds, saying, "Men like me don't look for women online. That's for desperate people." Old school, but that was Andy's position and he was sticking to it.

Instead, he went online for some sort of support group whose members were going through a similar change of life as he. And he found a divorce support group (DSG) right in Manhattan. For a while, Andy sat on the sidelines, keeping an online conversation going with some of the leadership of the group. From time to time, he would RSVP an invitation from the DSG to some event they were hosting, only to back away in fright over the social pressure.

In early October, he saw a DSG event inviting all members to its annual Picnic in Central Park. Andy was somewhat intimidated about meeting so many new people all at once, but what else was he going to do with an open Sunday in the fall? So he made a commitment to the event and literally forced himself to go, walking all the way to the park, backpack on his back with bottled water and his food contribution – some cut fruit and yogurt dip.

What Andy did not bring with him was his guitar, a prop Andy would use as a teenager and college student that assured him – he thought – of acceptance at parties and other social situations. This was the first time since then that he was attending a purely social event alone. But he left the prop home. Andy Greene had at last stopped looking for ways to hide himself from others. He had finally earned some of what Shel used to called "WTF" (What the Fuck) attitude.

And as he made his way onto a grassy knoll opposite a walkway from the "Strawberry Fields" memorial to the late John Lennon, the area the Group had set aside for the picnic, he was greeted by veteran members who seemed instantly to welcome him.

"They must have seen the look of terror on my face," Andy thought. And the veteran members, an odd lot of New Yorkers scarred by divorce and the difficult and expensive life in the "Big Apple," would simply not leave him to himself. One of the organizers of the Group was especially careful to make sure Andy knew this was a nurturing and low-key group.

"This is not a meet-up to hook-up," he made clear. There was the obligatory, "So tell us your story," as if it was an initiation to membership for a new member to share their grief and anger at the loss of their marriage.

"I've been divorced just since the end of last year," Andy began.

"Does it still hurt?" one of them asked, assuming that he'd been the "leftee" in the relationship – the one left behind. About 75% of the DSG membership were "leftees" in the relationship. "Leftors," members of the Group explained, "have already processed their grief and moved on. We're left to try and catch up."

"Actually, I was the one to initiate the breakup," Andy specified, "but truth be told, we both wanted the divorce. I was just the one left to call it quits."

"How do you know she wanted the divorce as much as you?" asked one of the women listening to Andy's story. The women were usually the ones more interested in sharing and listening to grief.

"She was the one who eventually filed for divorce," Andy answered. "I'm not really sorry it all happened, other than the financial burden of walking away practically broke." And he let out a laugh to show he had no hard feelings.

The Group in attendance made sure to help Andy feel at home, so much so that before long that day Andy was greeting late arrivals of new members to the picnic as if he were a veteran member himself.

"What do you do for a living, Andy?" One of the male organizers asked.

"I'm a college professor here in Manhattan."

"How long have you been doing that?"

"Only about two years or so."

"Really," chimed in one of the women who were listening in on the conversation. "What did you do before that?"

"I was in the financial services business. I marketed insurance and investment products, both as retailer with clients and as wholesaler with advisors."

"Why did you leave that business?" She pursued.

"September 15, 2008." And the woman looked somewhat confused by the answer of only a date in history. "You don't know what happened on that date?" Still no recognition of the significance. "That was the date"-

"When Wall Street melted down," chipped in the organizer who was continuing to listen to Andy's tale.

"That's right," Andy confirmed.

"Do you like teaching?" Came the next question from the woman.

"Yes, I do."

"Do you miss the financial services business?"

"Sometimes. Mostly, I miss the feeling that I could walk into a meeting and people actually listened to what I had to say. They thought I 'knew stuff.' I would walk into a room and people would know I was there. They would turn around to catch whatever wisdom I could dispense to the meeting."

"Sounds powerful! Is the power what you miss?"

"What I miss is the feeling that I was impacting the future of the firm. But then I remember: I am still impacting... I'm impacting the future of students, now. Other than it doesn't pay as well, I'm content with it. I didn't get to be the first Jewish President of the United States, but I guess I had my fun."

And the group laughed at the reference. For the first time since college, Andy was not socializing mainly for pecuniary or career gain. He was just hanging out, and it felt good.

From time to time Andy would visit Len's Bagels, a coffee shop on 1st Avenue, near Andy's apartment. Andy taught mainly on a two-day-a-week schedule. The rest of the time he could work mostly from home. He had time freedom, if he didn't have money freedom.

And on these occasions at Len's, he would meet up with Leo Finkel, his colleague in the Business School at ERU. Leo frequented the Shop regularly, in the mornings, occupying his same seat in the "dining" room adjacent to the counter where orders for bagels, lox, challah loaves, babka, knishes, and assorted delicatessen items were handled and paid for.

Len's Bagels was an institution in the Turtle Bay neighborhood, Midtown East, near the United Nations. And Len's was a study in the multi-cultural nature that had become modern day New York

City. Where once upon a time, New York was a checkerboard of neighborhoods, each segmented by a distinct ethnicity, by the turn of the Millennium everyone was everywhere. When Andy was growing up, you knew someone's national heritage by simply knowing the neighborhood in which they lived: Harlem was Black; Williamsburg was Jewish; Hell's Kitchen was Irish; Bensonhurst was Italian, as was the old section of Howard Beach.

Now, everyone mixed much more, and "this is a good thing," Andy thought. "Better not to carry the burdens and scars of the 60s around."

Len's was still owned by a Jewish family in what had been a largely Jewish enclave of the East Side of Manhattan. But the workers in the shop were almost all Muslim, some Palestinian, or Hindu – the very fact that Muslims and Hindus were working side-by-side was unique to New York in any event. But Palestinian immigrants working in a Kosher bagel shop? Only in New York! And the customers were also a multi-cultural crowd. The old-timers who came in for breakfast were still mostly Jewish. But the last two decades had seen a migration of immigrants from Ireland, after the Celtic Tiger of the 1990s melted away and jobs in the old country became hard to come by.

Leo had turned Andy onto the Shop, and the two of them would often meet up there on weekday mornings. On a typical morning in early November, Andy entered to see Leo already sitting with his coffee and bagel. The bagel itself had been decimated; Leo would take the inner parts of the bagel out, leaving just the shell of each side of the cut bread, and he would dunk the shell into a small cup of olive oil. Andy would come by with a large Hazelnut coffee, 2% milk and two Splenda packets, and a banana nut muffin. Andy wondered why Leo ate so little; he was already quite thin. Leo wondered how Andy could eat so much, even though this was half of what he used to have in the mornings before the heart attack.

Leo was sitting, back to the wall, holding court, with some of the old timers he'd known there for years. Andy would sit opposite Leo, facing the wall – even though this was somewhat uncustomary for this one-time lawyer (lawyers typically like to sit with backs to the wall, always in defensive posture).

Around Leo was gathering a small crowd. Andy knew them only by first names. There was Danny, the Irish tenor who'd retired as a "super" for one of the rental buildings in the neighborhood. There was an 80-year-old Jewish man everyone simply called "Doc," as he was once a surgeon. Myra was the only woman with the "balls" to sit with the old men; she was a political activist and widow who'd inherited millions from her late husband, a successful entrepreneur. And there was Sol, a retired financial analyst with one of the big investment banks.

Everyone had lived a full life of affluence and career success, although they came from such different backgrounds. They all considered Leo the *de facto* leader of the group. Leo had made it big in the "rag" trade, the garment business, wholesaling and retailing for several different well known brands over a 40-year career. But Leo lost most of what he earned; first in a nasty divorce; then helping family members out. Leo had little left of his former wealth. Many of the group had similar stories to tell, though none were unable to get by.

"Good morning, Andrew," came the greeting from Leo when he saw his protégé approach, coffee and muffin in hand.

"Hi Leo," and the group turned to smile at Andy, the most junior member of the group. A murmur of acknowledgement of Andy's presence was heard from the crowd, but it was as if everyone was more interested in telling their own stories. As in the faculty room at ERU, Andy was more listener than talker here.

"So I have this idea of how to market a software program," declared Sol. "Hey, Andy, you're a professor. Listen to this. You write up some content for a course in business to offer to high school students and their parents, and we'll put it on disk and make it available for download or streaming. It's to prepare the kid for what he can expect if he pursues a business degree. It's great! We can sell it through one of the banks I know who want some value-added piece to attract customers looking to fund college education for their kids."

"Yeah," Leo added, "You could use your contacts to get a meeting where we could present the idea. Andy, would you put together a proposal that we could use in the presentation?"

"Sure, Leo." But Andy knew this idea would go nowhere; just like all the other ideas the old men would come up with at Len's Bagels. The old men were looking to regain some measure of dignity and self-respect lost when they retired.

"I'll put together what we used to call in my business an Opportunity Assessment, or OA. It just outlines the opportunity, 3-5 pages, no more. What I don't want to do is to write whole chapters of content on spec. I'm past the point of my life where I want to create on spec. If your contact likes the opportunity, he cuts a check for $50,000 to pay me to build one prototype. If he likes the prototype, he cuts another check for $500,000 and buys me out." Andy knew that naming prices would end the discussion.

"But Andy," Sol argued, "No one is going to start cutting checks before seeing the prototype."

"Sure. Then you'll need to get someone else to write the content. Leo, you can do this, right?"

Leo got a little shy at this point. "Well, I don't have the credentials you have, Andy. We need you in this project."

"Fine, my friend, when I start seeing checks being cut, I'm in."

"That's not how it works," said Sol.

"I think I agree with Andy," Doc chimed in.

"All my life, in music, in business, everyone wants a piece without paying for it. When I would recruit musicians for my bands, it was always 'Well, I don't need to rehearse. I'll just show up at the gig and play.' And I'd answer, 'The gig money compensates you for the time you rehearsed with us. You don't rehearse, you don't get paid.' I'm sick and tired of people wanting something from me without earning it."

Danny now contributed. "Man, you really got some attitude today, yeah? What happened to you, you get laid last night?"

"Why do you *shlubs* of men always think it has to be about sex," bellowed Myra. "If my late husband, may he rest in peace, were to hear what I have to listen to here, he'd die all over again."

And the group all let out a collective laugh, although Myra seemed to be only half-joking.

And the conversation went on for another hour at least, each person pretending to be someone they used to be but were not anymore. Every one of them was a *macher* in his day, someone to be listened to, to be respected, maybe even feared. And for Myra, she loved a *macher*, although it didn't hurt to love someone with a lot of money.

As Andy watched Myra argue with the men, he remembered something that his father, Shel, used to say his own mother used to admonish him with: "It's just as easy to love a rich woman as it is a poor one."

After the hour went by Andy, listening but saying little, began to mentally step back, as if he were watching the scene from a distance.

This might have been one of those times he "zoned out." But in watching all the brave talk but no action, he became somewhat depressed. "Is this going to be me in a few years? Is this what I have to look forward to?"

And Leo, sensing Andy had "checked out" mentally from the conversation, asked, "So, what's your story," as a way to get him back into the conversation.

"I'm happy just doing what I'm doing. After what I've been through, I just enjoy any day when I can get out of bed. As the song goes, '*Undertakers bow their heads as [I] go walking by'*." The others did not get the reference to an English folk song recorded in the 60s by Fairport Convention.

Doc seemed disturbed by the comment. "Oh, stop with that crap. You look so self-satisfied, it's disgusting."

"Well, gentlemen," Andy boasted, "I have to say that I think I have met someone."

"Oh shit," Leo muttered, shaking his head. "You don't fall in love anymore at our age."

"Well, I'm still a bit behind you in years, my dear friend, and maybe, just maybe, I want to take one more shot at it – just like you guys want to have one more shot at greatness in business, yeah?"

"Well," Myra interrupted, "At least tell me she's Jewish."

"Sorry, I stopped dating 'in' after age 17." And Andy rose to take what remained of his breakfast to the trash container in the front room.

"Wait a minute, you can't leave it there," called Danny.

"Yeah, Danny, once you go Irish, you can never go back, right? But I think I'll keep this to myself for now. All I'll say is that I met someone at a picnic for a divorce support group and she has potential... **real potential**."

"Hey," Leo, called out to Andy, still standing by the trash container, "I have some interesting news for you."

And Andy made his way back to his seat next to Leo. "What's up?"

"Did you hear about Lester?" Polander, that is. "Got fired last week."

"What? Didn't hear about THAT!"

"Yeah. Got him on sexual harassment." This was getting juicier and juicier. "Seems he was emailing a female student of his some pretty racy stuff. He had a crush on this girl, was pursuing her, and sending her emails...But using his ERU email address."

"Whoa! Everyone knows the school monitors that stuff."

"But it didn't catch this email trail until the girl reported it to the administration."

"Pretty stupid of him," Andy surmised.

"Pretty desperate act of an old man trying to vicariously hold onto his youth by chasing 20-somethings. I'll bet he wouldn't know what to do with her if he caught her, like the dog that chases the car? What happens if the dog ever catches the car?" And the whole group laughed.

And Andy then rose to bid the group a good day, and onto 1st Avenue. He was heading back to his apartment for a day of grading exams and papers and preparing for the next round of lectures. He would have a podcast lecture that evening, broadcast from his laptop computer, for an online school based in the Midwest. He took out his iPhone from his right inside blazer pocket to check for any texts or emails. He then pressed on the view screen of the phone to open the ESPN app he had and navigated to the NBA scoreboard to see how the Boston Celtics had done against the Washington Wizards the night before.

"How the world has changed," he thought, using all this technology. "And how the world really hadn't changed that much," as he thought of the personalities he'd spent the morning with and the issues that came up.

And Andy Greene stopped at a corner newsstand, a *bodega,* and bought a hard copy of the *New York Times.* He could have read the online version on his phone, but it just didn't seem to be the same without getting his fingers full of newsprint. And instead of using his debit card to pay for the paper, he pulled out a $5 bill from his right pants pocket – cash might have become an anachronism in 2012 Manhattan, but some habits die hard.

ABOUT THE AUTHOR:

David A. Glazer currently serves as Professor and Chair of the Marketing Department at Berkeley College's Larry L. Luing School of Business, a 9-campus institution in New York City and suburban New Jersey. He has also done lecturing, both on site and online, at several other colleges.

Previously, he was a marketing executive in the financial services industry with several national firms, managing the marketing support and product development functions in each. During his tenure in the industry, he served as a FINRA broker-dealer principal and registered representative and was also a licensed life and health insurance agent in several states.

Dr. Glazer has earned four different graduate degrees in four different disciplines; a law degree from American University, a Masters in Financial Services from The American College, and both an MBA in Management and a Ph.D. in Marketing from George Washington University.

His dissertation - *The Effect of Commission versus Non-Commission Benefits on Customer Value: The Case of Life Insurance Policy Performance*, was published in article form in **Financial Services Review** (2007) v.16, p.135-153.

Dr. Glazer has also served as a Board member of the D.C. Chapter of the Better Business Bureau and is a Certified Financial Planner (CFP) as well as a Certified Life Underwriter (CLU) and Chartered Financial Consultant (ChFC). He is as well a LIMRA Leadership Institute Fellow (LLIF), a designation identifying future senior executive talent in the financial services industry. And he has been a member of the Virginia State Bar for the past 40 years.

Made in the USA
Coppell, TX
03 December 2020